# DUKKHA
## REVERB

"*As much as I scramble through the ruins of my memories, I find that time, that other time, fresh and untouched by forgetfulness...*"

— Ida Fink

*Also by Loren W. Christensen…*

**Fiction**
 *Dukkha—The Suffering*

**Non-Fiction**
 *Warriors*
 *On Combat*
 *Fighter's Fact Book*
 *Solo Training*
 *Deadly Force Encounters*
 *Speed Training*
 *Fighting the Pain Resistant Attacker*

 *and many others…*

LOREN W. CHRISTENSEN

# DUKKHA
# REVERB

*A SAM REEVES
MARTIAL ARTS THRILLER*

YMAA Publication Center, Inc.
Wolfeboro NH USA

**YMAA Publication Center, Inc.**
Main Office
PO Box 480
Wolfeboro, NH 03894
800-669-8892 • www.ymaa.com • info@ymaa.com

| ISBN Paperback edition | ISBN Ebook |
|---|---|
| 9781594392634 | 9781594392665 |

Editor: Leslie Takao
Cover Design: Axie Breen

20250203

### Publisher's Cataloging in Publication

Christensen, Loren W.

Dukkha: reverb / Loren W. Christensen. -- Wolfeboro, NH : YMAA Publication Center, c2013.

p. ; cm.

ISBN: 978-1-59439-263-4 (pbk.) ; 978-1-59439-266-5 (ebk.)

"A Sam Reeves martial arts thriller."
Summary: After six weeks of being intensely investigated for the accidental killing of a young boy, Portland police detective and martial arts instructor Sam Reeves travels to Saigon, Vietnam to visit his newly found family. Although he hopes to find peace and refuge, Sam, along with his family and a bizarre set of new friends, suddenly find themselves thrust into a nightmarish world of sex trafficking, a deadly warehouse of Buddha statutes, and a dirt tunnel that leads to a suffocating death.--Publisher.

1. Reeves, Sam (Fictitious character)--Fiction. 2. Families--Fiction. 3. Ho Chi Minh City (Vietnam)--Fiction. 4. Human trafficking--Fiction. 5. Tunnels--Vietnam--Fiction. 6. Martial arts fiction. 7. Mystery fiction. I. Title.

PS3603.H73 D857 2013          2013935650
813/.6--dc23                  1308

This is a work of fiction. Names, characters, places, and incidents either are the product of the author's imagination or are used fictitiously, and any resemblance to actual persons, living or dead, businesses, companies, events, or locales is entirely coincidental.

**Editorial Note:** *Dukkha:* a Pali term that corresponds to such English words as pain, discontent, unhappiness, sorrow, affliction, anxiety, discomfort, anguish, stress, misery, and frustration.

# PROLOGUE

Thang's tooth was killing him, the pain a steady thump as if keeping time to that terrible American rap music that Toan made him listen to whenever they pulled duty together in the warehouse. Thang had only one tooth left in his top row, but it hurt so intensely that it felt like forty, no, fifty rotting teeth, all rhythmically pounding in his mouth. Adding misery to his rotting tooth was a night so humid that it made his body feel like it was covered with glue. The steady rain that came late in the afternoon cooled only a little of what had to have been one of the hottest days in months in Bien Hoa, but the dark brought with it a sticky and thick mugginess.

It was nearly midnight now and he slumped drunkenly on the gnarled wooden chair. The maddening cries from the garden had finally quieted, and Thang was just about to thank Buddha for his compassion when a scream ripped through his brain and once again triggered the piercing agony in his mouth.

"Quiet!" he shouted toward the door, which set off a machine gun volley of awful throbs in his tooth.

The thunder passing overhead was so close to the earth that the flimsy guard shack in which he had the misfortune of being assigned this horrid night shuddered from each deafening, tooth-jarring concussion of air masses. With the electricity knocked out, the only illumination came from sporadic lightning flashes that found their way through the cracked and dusty window to bathe briefly the sad interior in harsh whiteness. No matter. He did not need a dim light bulb to know that the shack contained only empty bottles on the dirt floor, and an unopened one atop a decrepit table.

It was about eleven p.m. when Thang decided to open the scorpion wine. He usually drank cheap Chinese wine when the boss made him watch the garden all night, but he ran dry about eight tonight, long before it had dulled the pain in his mouth. The expensive delicacy, one that would cost a year of his wages, he acquired when a wealthy and foolish woman set down her bag on a Saigon sidewalk to answer her cell phone. He out ran the old hag even with his crippled leg.

He had hoped to sell the wine but his mouth needed it now, desperately. He had heard that scorpion rice wine is as delicious as it is strong, and it is good medicine to treat back pain and other ailments. He hoped it worked on a rotting mouth too.

Just as Thang lifted the bottle from the table, lightning washed through the room, illuminating a large scorpion floating in the amber liquid, and a cobra coiling lethally from the bottom of the bottle to the top where its evil mouth clamped tightly on the midsection of the scorpion. The serpent's eyes pierced into Thang's. Mother fuck!

Another scream emanated from the garden, making Thang scrunch his face against the pain. Then another, even louder than the last.

With hands trembling from the wine drunk earlier, and from what felt like nails stabbing into the roots of his lone tooth, Thang ripped off the yellow wrapper from the neck of the bottle and stabbed his knife into the cork. His face dripped as he twisted the blade left and right until it began to lift. When he twisted it too hard and unevenly, the cork broke off, with nearly half of it still jammed in the bottle.

Cursing, he stabbed the blade at the cork again, missed, and rammed the knife blade deeply into his thigh, the very same leg that bad karma had twisted and deformed at his birth sixty-seven years ago. "Oooiii!" he cried loudly, and immediately as if an echo, several voices cried out from outside the flimsy wooden door.

"Shut up, you fucks!" he screamed, clutching his thigh and watching as blood oozed over his boney fingers. "Ooiii!"

Moaning, he stripped off his filthy T-shirt and wrapped it around his thin leg, tying a knot tightly over the wound. "Ooiii!" he cried again.

Another scream burrowed its way into his rotten tooth.

He angrily twisted about in his chair and punched the door with his fist, nearly dropping the bottle. He started to punch it again but instead waved his hand at the door with disgust, and turned back to dig out the last of the cork. The knife slipped again, miraculously missing his leg this time. Finally, he speared out the last chunk, tossed it and the blade onto the table, and upturned the bottle into his mouth. He wasted no time swallowing, but with eyes closed, he poured the burning liquid straight down his throat and into his stomach. He drank for a long glorious moment, and when he opened them, just as lightning flashed, he looked straight into the cobra's eyes. And the snake looked into his.

Emitting a guttural cry, he snapped the bottle away, slopping some of it onto his legs and onto the floor.

"Shit," he wheezed, his breath on fire from the powerful liquid. He tilted the bottle again to his wet, trembling lips just as another flash from the heavens lit the small room long enough for him to see that he had drank nearly half and that the scorpion was—gone.

He slammed the bottle onto the table and beat frantically at his chest. "Where…?"

The wine had acted fast on his brain, blurring his vision and making his head feel like mashed rice. "The shcorp… scorpion," he slurred, continuing to swat at himself. "Where is the shor-pion?"

A gush of wind slammed rain against the side of the shack and the little window. The lightning flash was briefer this time, but it lasted long enough to see that the scorpion was still in the bottle. He giggled to himself for a moment. Of course it was still in the bottle, but still he drew his feet up under his stool.

Gripping the sides of his chair to keep from falling off as the room rocked and spun, he realized the pain in his mouth was now no more than a dull ache. When an especially loud scream came from the garden, he started to grimace, but realized he felt no pain. Even his leg no longer hurt. He giggled again. It is said that the power of the cobra and scorpion can heal.

"Me agree," he said aloud. "Did I say 'me agree'?" he asked the darkness. That made him laugh too.

He had not checked the garden since early evening. Maybe the cabbages had grown. That thought made him giggle again.

He used the table to pull himself to his feet only to fall back into his chair with a hard thump. "Oooii," he said, then laughed like a fool because he did not feel anything.

This time he got up and stayed up, but swayed dangerously. When he tried to pull open the door, it struck his foot and bounced closed. Cursing, he lumbered to the side so he could open it all the way.

Ah, the rain felt good splattering against his hot face and bare chest. It had eased a little and the lightning flashes were not as intense as earlier. Still, they were bright enough to illuminate the metal walls that encased the small, open garden, and the mud puddles and murky, little streams that wound around the cabbage heads.

"How are…" he swayed for a moment, grabbing the doorframe to keep from falling. He shielded his eyes with a bloodstained hand against another lightning flash. "My cab-chages," he called, squinting to see. "How are my cab-chages?"

An explosion of near thunder startled Thang. Another flash of lightning lit the garden long enough for him to see the cabbages, all twelve of them, three rows of four.

He stumbled about to go back inside the shack, when another hysterical scream pierced his tooth.

"Ooiii," he groaned, one hand on his mouth and the other over his ear. Damn, the wine must be wearing off already.

Another scream. This time he saw the one that did it. The one in the second row near the ever-widening pool of muddy water.

"I will be right back, you loud cabbage," he said, straining to see the noisy little bitch. "Let me see how much you scream with a big, fat cobra wrapped around your pretty little neck."

# CHAPTER ONE

*I'm sitting at a table with Samuel and Mai. We're all slurping noodles from our bowls of phở. I somehow know we're in a restaurant although everything beyond us is in complete darkness. Mai smiles at me with those heart-stopping, almond-shaped eyes, then giggles at my clumsiness with the chopsticks.*

*"You know, Son," Samuel says, around a chunk of meat, "use that spoon with your chopsticks and you won't drop so many noodles on the table."*

*I start to snicker at his tease, but a burst of laughter from the next table over stops me. The next table? We were the only table a second ago…*

*Oh no. No!*

*"Surprise!" the acne-faced tweaker says. Blood is leaking from a bullet hole just below his nose. "Bet you didn't expect to see us here and eating this shit, did you, detective?"*

*"Vieeeeet-nameeeese fooood," the skinny naked man says in a syrupy voice. He stirs his fingers in his broth. He's got a bleeding hole in his face. "Do Vieeet-nameeeese people call it Vieeeet-nameeeese food?" His laugh is wet, ugly.*

*Next to him, little Jimmy slams down his chopsticks in frustration. Blood oozes from a hole in his chest. "Can we go get a Happy Meal, pleeeease?"*

*Mai and Samuel continue to eat. Can't they hear or see the graveyard customers?*

*No, they can't. Only I can see them. Well, I'm not going to look at the dead ones again, no way. I try to look away, but they are always there, and they're looking back at me.*

*Their eyes… my God, the eyes in each pale face are gone, and they stare at me from empty hollows.*

*Accusing me.*

"*Of ruining our daaaay,*" *says the naked man.*

"*What?*"

"*We're accuuuuusing you of ruuuining our day, Deeeetective.*"

"Happy     meal!"     *the     little     boy     blurts     impatiently.* "*I—want—a—happy—meal.*"

*The tweaker laughs at the boy.*

"*Pain in the asssss,*" *the naked man hisses, nodding his head at the boy.* "*I was going to kill the little shit, youuuu know. But you beeeeat me to it.*"

"*It was an accident,*" *I shout.* "*You know that.*" *I look at Mai and Samuel for help, but they just keep shoveling long noodles into their mouths. Samuel looks up, smiles, and jabs his chopsticks at my spoon.*

"*You beeeeat*"—*the naked man's awful voice forces me to look at him*—"*me to iiiit.*"

"*No!*" *I shout, looking from face to pale face.*

"*You beeeeat me to iiiit.*"

"*No!*" *I look at Samuel.* "*Father, help me.*" *He looks up, a long noodle dangling from his closed mouth. He bobs his eyebrows and sucks it up until it disappears.*

"*You beeeeat me to iiiit.*" *I jerk my head back to the naked man.*

"*Sir?*" *I look over at Mai. Her eyes look into mine, but not the way she did the last time I held her.* "*Sir?*"

*Why is she calling me that?*

"*Sir?*"

"Sir?"

Hand on my arm. Shaking me. "Wha… What?" I open my eyes and look into a pair of incredibly blue ones. It's the blond flight attendant who greeted me as I boarded the plane. She's kneeling beside me.

"I'm sorry to wake you, sir, but you were having a bad dream. You were shouting something. About noodles, I think." She smiles at that.

I blink into reality and scoot up in my seat. "Sorry. Pizza gives me nightmares." I haven't eaten pizza, and it doesn't give me nightmares, but I have to tell her something. "Maybe I should have had noodles." She smiles again. "Are we up yet?" I ask, still disoriented.

"Not yet." She pats my arm and stands. "There will be a short wait so passengers from a late Orange County flight can join us. It shouldn't be too long. You going to Vietnam or Seattle?"

"Vietnam."

"Enjoy your trip. It's a long one." She smiles again and moves up the aisle.

A middle-aged Asian woman across the aisle is looking at me through thick glasses, the corners of her mouth turned down. Must not have liked my yelling about noodles. "Sorry," I say with a shrug. She looks back at her magazine and, for just a heart-stopping moment, the way she turned her head… she looked like Jimmy's mother.

I wish now I hadn't been in such a rush to get on board. The moment the flight attendant announced rows twenty-five through fifteen, I ran like an escaping felon toward the door, my airplane ticket gripped tightly in my extended hand as if it were the key to my freedom, which in a way it is. After I settled into my seat and the last few stragglers had found theirs, there were still two empties next to me. The last thing I remember thinking was that if they remained empty for the entire flight,

I could sprawl my six-foot, two hundred-pound self across the three seats and maybe get the sleep that has eluded me for so long. As the tension of the last few weeks began to ooze out of my body, I zonked off into dreamland—it turned into nightmare land—that same one.

I look at the seats again. If my not-so-good luck continues, the late-arriving Californians are going to sit right here, gypsies with a screaming baby, one trained to pick pockets.

Damn, it's hot in here. Tarzan jungle hot. I vote we leave without the Californians. We need some air in the plane.

I slip out of my light jacket and stuff it under the seat in front of me. Why does a plane have to be flying for the air conditioner to work? I close my eyes and lean my head against the window. Tired. So anxious about this trip that I haven't slept much in the last couple of weeks, and not at all in the last two nights. Hope it's because I'm anxious about the journey and not because of what Doc Kari talked about in our last session. She said that my poor sleep is likely part of my PTSD: fear of the dark. Not the dark in the room; the dark behind my eyes.

For a few weeks after… after it happened, I didn't sleep at all; I just ran around on frayed nerves and Starbucks. Then I had a period where I'd sleep like I'd been knocked out, like the time I got cold cocked by that muay Thai fighter in LA. I'd wake up after a dozen hours and feel worse than before I went to sleep. Sweaty too. Sweaty and cold. That lasted a couple of weeks and then my sleep pattern was hit and miss, mostly miss.

I cross my arms and adjust my head a little against the window. Two orange-vested guys down on the tarmac are leaning against a white pickup and sipping from coffee mugs. They're laughing about something, probably the fact that we're all baking in here. Baking like biscuits. The plane's vibration on the side of my head is soothing, like the sounds inside of a mother's womb, a mom weighing about eight hundred thousand pounds, or how ever much it is.

I take a deep breath and slowly let it out. Contrary to what Doc Kari said, at the moment I'm enjoying the darkness behind my eyes, the sense of being alone, no one judging me, no one persecuting me, no one wishing me dead.

"Be in the moment," Samuel said the two times we meditated together when he was in Portland. "Just follow your breath."

I squirm a little deeper into the seat. Breathe in, hold it, breathe out, hold it… breathe in, hold it… breathe out… Getting sleepy in this… heat. I'm really liking the hum against my head. Better… than a sleeping pill. Just… got to… figure out how to get a… seven-forty-seven into my… bedroom. In… out… in…

"Hi."

I jerk toward the voice. A boy, sitting next to me, Asian— Vietnamese, I think. Maybe fourteen or fifteen.

"Sorry," he says, looking like he means it. "Your eyes were open. I thought you saw me sit down."

"Oh, uh, yeah. No problem," I say, shaking my head to awaken for the second time since I've been on board. Weird. I was following my breath and I must have dozed again. With my eyes open? Okay, could I get any more strange? At least this time I didn't dream. That's a plus.

I start to think about the dream. I've been having it, or variations there of, almost every night for the last two weeks. Even worse, sometimes I dream it when I'm awake. I quickly push it out of mind, most of it. I can still hear the naked man's slimy voice. *You beeeeat me to iiiit. You beeeeat me to iiiit.* I squeeze my eyes shut for a moment and think of a lake near Mt Hood, Trillium Lake. Fifty some miles out of Portland, Oregon. Gorgeous blue, reflecting the snow-capped mountain on a windless day.

There, that's better. My mind's good now, good to go.

"No problem," I say turning to the boy. Did I already say that? "Oh, we're finally taxiing. You must be the guy who kept us waiting. The California guy. Just one of you?"

"Yes. My plane was a little late," he says seriously. "I'm embarrassed to have held up this flight."

He's not a gypsy. Ooorah! Nice looking kid. Polite. A little somber, though. "Well, there were passengers chanting 'Kill the California guy.'"

"Reeeeally?" His eyes widen.

"No. Not really." I give him a blank face.

He bunches his eyebrows and looks at me for a moment, then sputters a laugh. "Oh, okay, so that's how it's going to be."

"Sorry," I say, smiling.

We're silent for a few minutes while the plane noisily takes off. The kid has a mop of raven black hair falling down his forehead, dressed in a red T-shirt with "Westminster, California" in black bubble letters across the front, and gray cargo shorts. On his lap, black ear plugs, the cord running into a big pocket on his thigh. After spending an intense week a while back with several Vietnamese who spoke broken English, it's a tad strange to hear the boy speak without an accent. No doubt he's second or third generation, so of course he wouldn't have one. It's still strange.

Once we're airborne, the kid continues where we left off. "People say I'm too gullible. Guess I am." He extends his hand. "Bobby Phan. You are?"

I resist smiling as we shake. Kid's got the demeanor of a confident twenty-five-year-old, though he can't be much over twelve, fourteen at the most. He's Vietnamese for sure. I had a Vietnamese student named Phan, a lawyer. Made it to brown belt before he took a job with a higher paying firm in Seattle.

"Sam Reeves. Nice to meet you, Bobby. May I ask how old you are?"

"Yes," he says.

When he doesn't say anything I lift my eyebrows.

"You didn't ask me." His mouth struggles against a smile.

I laugh. "Oh, okay, so that's the way it's going to be."

"Yup," he giggles, pointing at me. "I'm almost seventeen. You thought older, right?" When I nod, he says, "I get that a lot. I'm only five feet three but I'm told I'm mature for my age. My aunt says I'm an old soul. Not sure what that means, but it sounds better than 'butthead,' you know? Hey, you got some serious guns, man."

Guns? I'm not packing…

"Your arms," he says, pointing. "Huge. I pump iron too."

I'm wearing a short-sleeved blue polo shirt and blue jeans. "Oh. Yes. Thanks. I can tell that you lift." Actually, I can't tell, but what's the harm in giving a kid a boost?

"Thanks." He studies my face for a moment. "Wait a minute. Reeves? You said *Sam* Reeves, right?"

Oh, please. I know the shooting was on the newswire, but who would have thought a sixteen-year-old in California would read the newspaper.

"You're into the martial arts, right?" The kid's brain is going a hundred miles an hour while I'm still trying to wake up. "I thought I recognized you from somewhere when I first sat down, but I wasn't sure because your eyes were half shut and you were twitching and stuff." He continues to study my face and look me up and down. "Yeah, that was you all right. In *Black Belt* magazine last winter, like the November or December issue, right?"

I nod. "They did a little story on me, a retro piece about my competition years."

"Yes! That was it. Oh man, how weird is it that I'm sitting here next to you on a plane?"

Yes, it is. In fact, maybe too coincidental. The plane is full except for a couple seats next to me. Then a guy sits down and "recognizes" me from a magazine. Says he's seventeen, looks younger, but maybe he's older than seventeen. Can't always tell with Asians. Maybe he's working with Lai Van Tan, the big man in Saigon who sent goons after Samuel, Mai, and me.

Geeze. Maybe I'm too suspicious for my own good. For sure, that horrific week in Portland took its toll on my paranoia. Of course nearly everyone really did want a piece of my hide, or at least it seemed like everyone.

"I practice martial arts, too," the boy says. "Taekwondo. Got my black belt in February."

"Very good," I say. "That's a wonderful accomplishment."

"Thank you. I love it," he gushes, lifting his fists to each side of his face as if guarding his head. He does a quick bob and weave. "I'm a good kicker but I need more training on my hands. My teacher is great but we mostly train our legs."

Okay, he's not a secret agent for the big boss. And I'm wrong about him being somber. If the kid gets any more excited, he'll explode. I'd love to have had him in a class. Some students I have to continuously encourage to practice. Enthusiastic guys like Bobby, though, I have to rein in so that they don't over train.

"That's the thing about the United States," I say. "We're a melting pot of martial arts schools. Maybe you can talk to your teacher about helping you with your hands or you can look for another school that emphasizes hand techniques. There's got to be a lot of them in Orange County."

"There is. There's a Japanese school that's close, shotokan, I think. There's a kung fu school too, and a muay Thai gym. There's a Vietnamese school too. *Vovinam*."

"All good, although I don't know anything about *Vovinam*. Visit each one a few times and see which one fits your needs and personality. Talk to the students to see what they say about their teacher and the instruction."

"Thank you. How long have you trained?"

"Almost twenty-nine years. Started when I was around six. My grandfather and mother would drive me to my classes."

"Whoa, twenty-nine years!" he says too loudly. "Almost twice as long as I've been alive."

The same flight attendant who woke me from my dream appears next to Bobby. "Good morning, gents. May I interest you in something to drink?" Her eyes flirt with mine. She smiles.

"Milk," I tell her. "And could I also have some water?"

"You certainly may." She does the eye contact thing for a long moment before turning to Bobby.

"Coke… no wait." He looks at me, at my arms. "I'll have milk too, and water, please."

"Coming right up."

"Dude, she was so hittin' on you," Bobby teases, after we get our drinks and the attendant moves on. "She was eating you like a sandwich."

"Hey, some guys got it," I say, shrugging with feigned nonchalance. "Sadly, some don't."

LOREN W. CHRISTENSEN

So it takes a smile from a pretty flight attendant and a little idol worship from a kid to pull me out of my nightmare funk. Usually I'm a whole lot depressed after I have one of my dreams, which I get about twice a week now, down from nearly every night. They increased after Samuel and Mai left six weeks ago and increased even more during the grand jury hearing. About three weeks ago, the dreams slowed to every other night; this week I've had only two: One on Thursday and the other a few moments ago, another daytime one. Doc Kari would probably say that it was brought on by the stress of this trip, especially the stress of the last few days. Ah, stress, food of champions.

Bobby takes a chug from his milk carton and sets it down on the tray. "There were lots of pictures of you in the article, one of you wearing a tank top. You're ripped man. How much training would it take to get me into that kinda shape?"

"Thank you," I chuckle. "Just keep at it and you will be there faster than you can imagine."

He frowns. "Can I ask you a weird question?"

"I'm not sure."

He chuckles. "What's the difference between being a bully and just being strong enough not to be afraid of anyone."

The kid continues to impress. He might be sixteen, but he's sharp and savvy beyond his years. His aunt is right: He's an old soul.

"It's all about intention, about why you train. The whales are some of the biggest mammals on earth. There are few creatures that prey on them so they're "allowed" a gentle nature. But if you threaten a mama whale's baby, mama's a formidable foe."

"I get it. So is that why you train so hard?"

"There are a lot of reasons. Physical fitness is part of it. Self-defense. A fascination of the art and science of it."

"How hard was it for you to go through the ranks?"

"I worked hard, but in many ways I was lucky."

"How so?"

"Nature helped me, to begin with. The way the genes fell into place determined that I took to the martial arts somewhat naturally. When I began weight training, at about your age, I discovered that my muscles responded quickly, even when I was doing some of the exercises incorrectly. So because of the genes my mother and father gave me, the weights and martial arts were somewhat easier for me than for people who aren't so blessed."

"Never thought of it that way," Bobby says thoughtfully. "I guess I was a fast learner too. I went through the belts quicker than everyone I started taekwondo with."

"Let me ask you, how did you get to your classes and who paid for them?"

"My parents," he says, then ponders that for a moment. "Okay, I hear what you're saying."

"That's the second half. First, your parents gave you their genes and then they gave you their time and their support. My mother and grandfather drove me three and four times a week to my classes. I couldn't have achieved any of my belt ranks and early competition wins without their help, their time, and without the support they gave to me."

"I get it," Bobby says softly, looking at the seat back in front of him. I must have hit a nerve because his face sucked into that solemn look again.

"In my mind," I continue, "it's hard to think that I'm all that when I'm responsible for only part of what I've achieved. Maybe the smallest part." When he doesn't comment, I continue. "Think about this. In Tibet when someone thinks he's better than other people, it's said that he's like someone sitting on a mountaintop: it's cold, it's hard, and nothing will grow. But if a person is humble and puts himself in a lower place, then he is like a fertile field at the base of the mountain."

"Where things grow," Bobby says. "Where he learns, right?"

"Yes, sir."

"Cool."

We sit in silence. I don't know what Bobby is thinking, but I try to think about nothing and thumb through a flight magazine. I reach the last page without a clue of its contents, replace it into the chair-back pocket, and press my forehead against the cool Plexiglas. Nice view. It's as if I'm floating among the clouds in the lower stratosphere.

Two months ago, Vietnam was a war movie: *Platoon* and *Full Metal Jacket.* A place where my father died. I never thought of it as someplace I would want to visit. Then I meet my "dead" father and his stepdaughter Mai and, well, here I am, on a plane.

According to Google, Ho Chi Minh City, or Saigon, as many people still call it, is a growing economy in which the United States has an ever-increasing number of business interests. People vacation there and hike around the country. Who knew? I wonder how many non-Vietnamese people like me go there to visit their supposedly dead father and to spend time with his gorgeous stepdaughter, who, thankfully, isn't related to them?

"I read more about you online," Bobby says, cutting into my thoughts. "In a blog or something. Said you're really fast."

"Speed is relative," I say, thinking of Samuel and what he calls his teacup trick, how his hands were virtually invisible when he switched our cups. Just when I thought that that was the fastest thing I'd ever seen, a few days later he showed me what he called The Third Level. He was so fast that it was frightening. It was as if I had witnessed something paranormal. Mai said there was a Fourth Level, one so extraordinary that it was beyond comprehension, even for Samuel. He said that he had achieved it only a few times, but because he was afraid he couldn't control it, he wouldn't do it again without more guidance from his teacher.

That was the day he reduced me to a beginner, one who knew so little that I didn't know what questions to ask.

"How did you get so fast?" Bobby asks, pulling me back. I'm guessing that he doesn't know what 'speed is relative' means. "I'm pretty quick," he says, snapping out a backfist that looks good and makes the elderly woman across the aisle look over at us. She frowns at me and looks away. Probably thinks I'm a bad influence on teenagers. "But I want to be faster."

His dark cloud has left and the sun is out again. Reminds me of me at that age. I could train every day, twice a day sometimes, sleep like a log at night, and then do it all over again when I woke up. I really miss the high-octane zeal and innocence of those years.

"You got a girlfriend, Bobby?"

His face flushes. "A couple, why?"

I shake my head as if he's a lost cause. "Because if you want to be fast, I mean really fast, you can't hang around girls."

"Oh," he says, his face disappointed. He shakes his head. "Shoot." He looks past me and out the window for a long, thoughtful moment. Then, with a sigh from having just made a profound decision, he says, "I guess I'm fast enough."

I nod, chewing the inside of my cheek. "You are indeed fast, young grasshopper."

"Thanks," he says, studying my face for a couple of seconds before a flash of enlightenment crosses his. "Okay. Okay! You were bullshittin' me, right?"

"Indeed, my son." I punch his shoulder. "I certainly was." He leans away and laughs.

Damn.

Jimmy!

Damn-it!

When he leaned away… he looked like… Jimmy… when he slumped over… on the bed.

Bobby snorts, oblivious to what's going on in my head. Feels like I've got a two-by-four caught in my throat. I turn toward the window and take a slow, deep breath. That's what Kari said to do whenever I have one of these… intrusive thoughts; I think that's what she called them. Sometimes when I see someone make a gesture or say something, my mind sort of superimposes on the person an image from that terrible day. It startles the living hell out of me every time it happens.

I exhale a long breath to try to get all the crud out before I turn back to Bobby, who is too preoccupied with his tangled earplugs cord to have noticed my departure from reality. "Sorry, man. Didn't mean to tease. You seem like a good kid."

"And you seem like a good old man."

"Touché. Your parents onboard?"

"No," he says, too quickly considering the simple question. "They're in Vietnam, in Saigon. I'm going to meet up with them. My grandfather is sick. My father says he is dying."

Hmm, that sounded too smooth, too rehearsed. What's going on? Could he be working with Lai Van Tan? No, no way. He's a kid and he couldn't be that good of an actor.

"Sorry," I say, watching his eyes. "That's rough. I lost mine a few years ago. You close to him?"

"Never met him. I've been to Saigon two other times but he was always away. He had a business; can't remember what it was."

That didn't sound as practiced. Still, why wouldn't the grandfather have made himself available those other times? That's a spendy trip and a long ways for the family to have flown and… Maybe I'm making too much of it. I ask, "What do you think about going to see him?"

He doesn't say anything for a moment as he fiddles with his cord. "My family is into ancestor worship," he says, not answering my question.

"Really? I'd like to hear about that?"

He looks at me. "You think it's crazy, right? Worshipping dead people?"

"Right now I don't have any feeling one way or the other because I don't know anything about it."

"Lots of people think it's crazy," he says, still fiddling with the cord. "I'm not sure what I think. Maybe if I was born in Vietnam and grew up there I might be cool with it, but I'm a kid from Westminster, California. Ancestor worship seems pretty out there, know what I mean?"

"I do."

"All my parents' friends and my aunts and uncles are into it. They believe they must worship family members who have died, especially on the anniversary of their birthdays. They believe the spirit lives after they die, and stuff. They worship them and ask for help in their business, or help with a sick kid or something. So I respect that and go along with it." Bobby is quiet for a moment, then shrugs. "I might get more into it when I'm older. I don't know."

"I think that's a very mature and intelligent way to handle it."

"Thank you. Where you going? You getting off in Seattle or Tokyo, or are you going all the way?"

"All the way to Vietnam."

"Business, huh? What kind of business?"

"Not business. Personal."

"Personal," Bobby says, reading me for a second. "Okay, no prob."

What sounds like the blond flight attendant's voice on the PA announces that we have begun our descent into Seattle, and that we need to put our seat backs up and store our things. That was a fast forty-five minutes.

"Hey, I got row 12B in the new plane," Bobby says, looking at his ticket. "What do you got?"

I retrieve mine from my pocket. "Let's see… 12C."

"Sweet. We could talk some more."

What's the chance of us sitting together twice? Could someone have arranged it that way?

"That okay?"

"What?"

"That we talk some more on the next flight."

"Oh. Sure. But I'll need to sleep. I'm really trashed. Been through some rough times recently."

"Not a problem. You old people need your beauty rest."

"On second thought, maybe it's not too late to get a seat change."

\*

The plane change was non-eventful. We had enough time to grab a Whopper, walk off our meals, and buy some treats and magazines at a concession. We boarded the new plane, found our seats, and now we're ascending to the heavens. Next stop: Tokyo in just over thirteen hours. Oh, my cramping back and knees.

We chat for a couple hours, mostly on ways he can build speed in his kicks and punches. He has a quick mind, quick wit, and asks questions that are ten years more mature than his age. A good listener too, a stark contrast from many young teens I've had in class over the years. If he keeps training, and I'm guessing he will, he's going to be a fine martial artist and a good teacher. I do wonder about the weight he's carrying on his shoulders.

We ride silently for a while, Bobby listening to his music, and me reading a *Newsweek* and doing the groggy head-nodding thing.

I touch his arm to get his attention. "I have got to get some sleep. I'm going to conk for a while."

"I'm cool with that," he says. "Got my cell. You can borrow it later if you'd like. Got like twelve hundred tunes on it. There might be a couple things from the olden days." He shoots me a smirk.

"I got your old days right here, homey. Now let me catch some Zs." I fold my arms, lean my head against the window again, and close my eyes.

It's twenty minutes later now and I can tell that I'm not going to sleep. The earlier nap took the edge off, but the thought of another day-nightmare adds a dash of trepidation about sleeping, at least during the day.

For a couple weeks after the incident, I had lots of middle-of-the-night nightmares, terrible ones where I woke up shouting and sweating like a pig. Those fun times are sporadic now, at least the nighttime dreams. Recently, I started having them during the day when I take the occasional nap and sometimes even when I'm awake.

I hear the flight attendant ask Bobby if he wants anything to drink. He orders a water for himself and one for me too. Thoughtful kid, polite, has a zest for life, a passion for the martial arts, and he's funny. I like to think I had some of those things when I was sixteen. Actually, I think I still do, though I did have a brief struggle with the zest for life thing recently. Meeting my father and Mai helped get it back.

My passion for the martial arts has always been there through the ol' thick and thin. It was there when my mom got killed in a traffic accident, and when I got divorced. The divorce I didn't take hard because the marriage shouldn't have happened anyway. It lasted only a few months. I was young and stupid and so was she.

Mom's death was hard. The police chaplain and my dear friend Mark, who is also my lieutenant, came to my house and broke the news to me. When they left, I went out into my garage and began hitting the heavy bag, harder and harder until I was pummeling it like a man insane, which I was right then. After I don't know how long, I went into the house and slept all afternoon.

When I got up, I went out onto my patio and began throwing combinations, doubles, triples, sometimes throwing ten shots in one all-out burst. I punched the regret that I felt for not telling my mother that I loved her the last time we spoke. I punched the lonely life she must have had without a partner. I punched my father for abandoning her. And I punched God for giving her such a violent, painful death. My rage was irrational, most of it, but it made sense to my insane mind at the time.

All I did for two days was sleep, train, and eat a little. After forty-eight hours, give or take, I had lost seven pounds, sprained my wrist, and my neck and back were so tight that I walked around like Robo Cop for three days. Inside, though, I felt better. The anger was gone, the blaming was gone, and the guilt was mostly gone. Thanks to the martial arts, I was able to begin mourning and dealing with the funeral.

My martial arts were there after my shootings. Training like a madman helped to burn away my crazy thoughts, to cool the adrenaline that boiled for days, to ease my fear, to push back the questions, such as what if I was forced to kill again? What if my hesitation caused the death of another innocent? Was my soul forever blackened? My near heart-stopping workouts did as much for me as my visits to Doc Kari, the department-mandated police psychologist.

I was already at my limit when out of nowhere my, as it turns out, not-so-dead father appears in my life. Coincidence of coincidences, or maybe not, he's a martial artist. Actually, comparing Samuel's martial arts skill to mine is like comparing Luciano Pavarotti's pristine voice to mine when I do an *Oh solo mio* in the shower. Samuel's ability is… what? Beyond comprehension? For sure. Mind bending? Oh yeah, definitely. On top of that, he says that compared to his teacher, Shen Lang Rui, he's just a beginner. While I can't begin to imagine how that's even possible, I guess I'll find out when Samuel introduces me to his venerable master.

Samuel. Dad? No, calling him dad is just too awkward. He *is* my father, I'm convinced of that, but calling him pops, dad, or whatever is, well, my mouth stops working when I try. It's just too hard for me to go from thinking my father was killed before I was born to suddenly saying, "Hey, Dad, wanna toss the pigskin around?"

What an entry he made. I got sucker punched to the sidewalk in front of a coffee joint and like a white knight wearing red sneakers, Samuel kicked the guy's ass. And, somehow, he hauled my unconscious self across the street to a park bench, waited patiently for me to wake up, and bought me a coffee.

Then there's Mai, incredible, outrageously gorgeous, and without peer, Mai. For a couple of awkward days, I thought she was my half sister. After all, Samuel referred to her as his daughter, and since he said I was his son… Well, it caused me all kinds of confusion, since I was overwhelmingly attracted to her. Gratefully discovering that we were not related by blood, I got the breath knocked out of me when I found out that she was experiencing the same attraction to me. And then the world went really crazy and "kapow," I'm part of some high-octane kung-fu movie fighting off attackers from every direction.

The plane bumps hard a couple of times.

*"Ladies and gentlemen, we're passing through some turbulence. The captain has turned on the seatbelt signs. Please return to your seats and remain there with your seatbelt fastened until the captain turns off the seatbelt sign. Thank you."*

I'm still belted in so I can keep faking sleep. I'm not a white-knuckle flier, but the thought of problems twenty miles above a shark-infested ocean, or however far it is, doesn't do much for my already shredded nervous system.

My body and mind had been running on fight or flight fuel for six weeks, and my *dukkha* was not finished with me yet. Four nights ago, I was preparing for bed when the sound of the doorbell ignited my fight or flight. Any other time, I would have answered the door with gun in hand, but my service weapon was lying in the bottom drawer of an old dresser, and

I wasn't about to get it—ever. Since my survival skills were still mostly intact, I peeked through a side window before opening the door.

It was Mark, standing on my porch with his overcoat collar up against the steady rain, his face glaring at me. My friend and boss has an incredible pair of thick eyebrows that crowd together just above his nose when he is angry, which isn't often. That's where they were that night, though his face looked more disappointed and hurt. This was not good.

I thought about not opening the door and pretending that I wasn't home. The old hide-under-the-blanket-from-the-monster sounded like an excellent plan.

"Mark, come on in," I said, opening the door. He brushed by me without speaking, without looking at me. I shivered, but not from the cold air rushing in. He knows, I thought. God help me, he knows. But he didn't know all of it.

I closed the door, but not before I had a fleeting thought of charging out into the night and running as fast as I could down the dark street, and off the edge of the earth.

When I turned, Mark was standing with his back to me, his head moving from one side of the room to the other, as if it were his first time in my home, not the two hundredth, or so.

"Mark?" I whispered, not wanting him to respond, not wanting him to turn around to show me his disappointed face.

His shoulders seemed to sag in his long, gray overcoat as if carrying them hunched too long. He slipped out of it and draped it over his arm. He still hadn't turned to face me when I heard him inhale deeply and exhale a long, pained breath.

"Damn you, Sam."

I stared at the back of his graying head and thought again about bolting out the door.

He turned around. The lines in his fifty-six-year-old face seemed deeper than when I saw him four days ago, his eyes glistening. "*Damn you*, Sam," he said, just louder than a whisper. My heart was beating so hard it hurt. "I figured it out." He honed in on me, his eyes accusing, tearing. "I got eighteen months to retirement and you do this."

His next whispered words stabbed into my chest. "I know, Sam... I know you were involved in those deaths."

I stepped back reflexively, as if to avoid his punch, though his arms were hanging limply along his sides as if too weak to rise. His eyes were at once, sad, disappointed, and angry. I lowered myself onto my sofa and looked up at him.

"It took me a while to see it, to figure it out," he said. "I don't have any proof right now but..." He waved the air with his hand as if trying to wipe away his disgust. He plopped down on the other end of the sofa, his overcoat in his lap, and looked at the far wall. He turned and looked at me, shaking his head. "What's going on with you, Sam? What's—" He slammed his fist on the sofa arm, which made me jump. "Goddamn-it!"

I was half expecting for the last several weeks for someone from the PD to confront me, but I wasn't expecting it to be my best friend and boss. I raised my hands to indicate I didn't know what to say.

"Tell me," he said softly.

I remember shaking my head and taking a deep breath before I spoke. "Mark... I'm asking you as a friend to trust me on this. I... I didn't have a choice in what I did and what I didn't do. I wasn't trying to hide it from you. Okay, maybe I was a little. Mostly I wanted to protect you and protect my family. I wouldn't do anything to harm you, your career, and especially our friendship. You're my best friend, my boss. Sometimes you've been like a father to me. I know asking you to trust me on this is huge, but that's what I'm doing. I'm going to Vietnam in three days and try to sort out my life. I just need some time. A couple weeks."

For a long moment Mark didn't say anything. He wouldn't even look at me. Finally, he stood and picked up his overcoat. "You're lucky you planned the trip," he said. "And you're lucky that I'm the only one who figured it out." He slipped on his overcoat and said, "I need time to think too. We'll talk when you get back. We clear?"

*

The airplane bumps hard, bringing forth a chorus of grunts and gasps from passengers in front and behind me, and forcing me to twist toward the boy.

"Whoa!" Bobby says. "Good one."

"You do know this isn't a rollercoaster, right? You do know that there is nothing but five miles of sky between us and a school of man-crushing squid."

"Oh, right," he says, his eyes widening. "Forgot." He looks around the cabin. "You think we're okay?"

I shrug.

He scrunches his face. "You're supposed to comfort me. I'm just a kid."

"Oh. Okay, we're fine then."

"You really believe that?"

I shrug.

The plane lurches again. I hear the crash of what sounds like dishes from the galley and gasps throughout the cabin. A few feet down the aisle, an overhead storage door pops open, sending a blue backpack to the floor, drawing another gasp from passengers.

Bobby white knuckles the arms of his seat, looking at me.

"Air turbulence, Son," I say, seeing that the bumps are truly frightening him. "That's all. Lots of goofy air currents and such over the sea."

"Nothing like this the last two times I flew over," he says, his eyes impossibly large.

I wave my hand to affect nonchalance. "Air patterns change all the time, every day."

"Okay," he says, gulping audibly.

My convincing tone seems to calm the lad. Thing is, I haven't a clue about air currents. One trip to Hawaii was my only time over the ocean.

A sudden cant of the plane to the left sends the empty cups sliding off our trays and down onto the floor. The aircraft levels for a moment before jerking hard to the right. A female voice from somewhere behind us shouts something in what sounds like Vietnamese.

Okay, now *I'm* getting spooked. Fortunately, Bobby has his eyes squeezed closed so he doesn't see the color leave my face.

I slowly inhale to a count of four, hold it for four, and release it for a count of four. A tad calmer now, I ask, "What did that woman cry out, do you know?" I'm still assuming that Bobby is Vietnamese.

He opens his eyes, nods. "She said, "'Jesus Christ.' Then 'Buddha, please save us.'"

"Covering all the bases, huh."

"What do you mean, Sam?"

"Nothing. How you feeling?"

"I'm okay, I guess." His entire body is shaking likes he's got palsy. "You think there will be any more of those things?"

"Maybe," I answer, like it's no big deal. "Just air currents. They're unpredictable and invisible." A tear is about to erupt from the boy's right eye. "Tell me more about your training, Bobby. You like forms?"

He looks away from me and wipes his eyes. When he looks back, I pretend not to notice that they're wet. "I love them," he says, the quiver in his voice less apparent. "I know two extreme forms. I've entered them in tournaments."

"Great. Were you nervous? Any kind of competition is a good way to face your fear and to learn something about yourself."

"Ooooh yeah. Seriously nervous."

"And you survived." I pause, hoping he sees the connection to what is happening now. "How'd you do?"

"Aced it," he says, with a grin that is both shy and proud. His "palsy" appears to be gone. "I got a third place the first time I competed as a black belt and then got two firsts after that. I've only entered three tournies since I got promoted."

"Excellent! You like it, I take it?"

He nods vigorously. "Yes! I like everything I've done so far in my five years of training. Most of the people are nice. I don't like haters, people who criticize everything. You see that a lot on blogs and on YouTube and stuff."

"Sadly, the martial arts have haters and bullies, too, but I like to think not as many as in football and basketball." My mind flashes on Tiger Woman, her hands braced on the sky-walk railing behind her, her right leg straight up, the sole of her black boot flush with the sky in preparation of delivering an axe kick. Her face, reflecting insane hate, unaware that she has only seconds to live.

My entire body flushes hot for a moment.

Bobby is looking at me like a question mark. Before he can ask, I close the ugliness in my brain, and hit him with some questions. "What are your goals? What do you want to do with your life and with your martial arts?" The aircraft rocks from side to side a little, though not as intensely as before. Bobby doesn't seem to notice.

He shrugs. "I'm almost seventeen so no big plans yet. I would like to teach martial arts no matter what I do for my career. I teach a little now, the kids' class mostly. I really like seeing younger kids get it. Know what I mean?"

Bobby is himself again. The ol' distraction technique never fails to work.

"I do. Teaching is wonderfully rewarding but it also can be frustrating. Mostly it's rewarding."

"Who is your teacher, Sam?"

How to answer that? It would open up a can of worms if I tell him that my most recent teacher is my father who showed me a couple of things about the martial arts that I didn't know were even humanly possible, things that defy science.

"I haven't had one for a while," I say.

"You probably don't need one, right?"

"Wrong. You, me, all of us will always need teachers, mentors."

"But you don't have one."

I thought teenagers didn't listen. He looks at me, waiting. "Well, I don't have a teacher in the way you're probably thinking, but I have mentors, mostly friends in the martial arts who I learn from. We chat via email and send each other video clips of things we're working on."

"Everything okay, gents?" The flight attendant, a young man, asks.

"Yes, thank you," Bobby says. "Are we safe? With the plane going crazy, I mean?"

The attendant smiles reassuringly. "The captain thinks we're out of the worst of it. This patch can be rough at times.

I think we're in for smooth sailing now. We'll offer some more drinks in a bit."

"We got a dude this time," Bobby teases when the attendant moves up the aisle. "Too bad. That blond attendant in the last plane was ripe for the picking."

I laugh, surprised that he knows that expression. "Well, I think this dude is into you."

That cracks up the kid.

"I'd be interested to hear about your parents," I ask. "What do they do?"

His smile disappears, just like that. "What do you mean?" He reacts as if I just told him that I think the air currents are going to get worse. My question wasn't complicated and didn't warrant his abrupt change of demeanor. Unless there's something else going on.

"What does your father do?" I ask, turning up my detective sensors. "For work?"

Bobby looks down the aisle for a moment, reminding me of every perp who has ever contemplated fleeing. I should apologize for getting too personal, but I think I'll wait to see where he takes this.

He looks down at his cell and fiddles with his music selection for a moment. "My father owns… a store," he says, straining to squeeze each word out.

"I see. Does your mother work there?"

"Not really." He pulls the plug out of the cell and puts it right back in again. "Do you want to borrow this," he asks, without looking at me.

"I'm good, thanks." I study him for a moment. Why would a simple question about his parents bring on this one-eighty? Maybe he's just worried about his grandfather and about how his visit will play out. Maybe there is something to my earlier suspicion.

"I think about my grandfather all the time," I say. "He taught me a lot about being a young man, about keeping my head straight when I started winning tournaments, and about respect, especially respecting my mother. She raised me by herself. My grandfather helped a lot, but the day-to-day stuff was all her."

Bobby looks at me for a long moment until his eyes start to glisten. He looks away as he did earlier and wipes away the tears.

"Bobby? What's—?"

"What happened to your father?" he asks turning back to me. "Did they get… divorced?"

So that's it. Trouble on the home front.

"Did they?"

For a second I think about lying and telling him yes and that everything turned out fine. I'm not good at lying, though; I'd just screw up my story. "No. Until a few weeks ago, I thought he was dead. Killed in a North Vietnamese prison during the war, before I was born. Then out of the blue he shows up."

"Wow! That had to like mind freak you or something."

I smile. "It did exactly that."

"Bet your mother was shocked, huh?"

I shake my head. "She died two years ago. Car accident."

"Whoa. Sorry, Sam," he says, with real compassion.

"Thank you."

"Sometimes life sucks," Bobby says softly.

"Life is like a bowl of cherries," I say sagely.

"What do you mean?"

"How the hell do I know? I'm not a philosopher."

Bobby looks at me for a moment, then laughs.

Good. My work here is done. I unfasten my seatbelt. "Gotta wiz, my fellow warrior. Then I got to catch more Zs. I'm about a month behind on sleep so I'm trying to catch up."

"Gotcha," Bobby says, stepping out into the aisle to let me out.

There are a few non-Asian folks sprinkled here and there but everyone else is Vietnamese or Japanese. A woman points at my arms as I pass and says something to the man sitting next to her. He looks at me, smiles, and shoots me a thumbs up while nodding several times.

When I worked uniform patrol, I was used to being a minority and looked at, but this is different. Now it's about race. Feels strange not being in the majority skin-wise. According to some of the online tourist blogs I read, foreigners are stared at a lot in Vietnam. Mai said that I'd get extra looks since I'm so much larger than the average person there.

A seventy-something, white-haired Asian man opening the restroom door sees me approach, smiles and gestures for me to enter. Having worked the park restrooms a few times when assigned to Vice, my first thought is that he wants me to join him in the can. I force that sick thought out of my head and gesture for him to go on in. He gives me a short bow and hurries inside.

Grateful that there is no one else in the back, I step behind the partition and circle my arms a little to loosen my shoulders, and do a few forward bends to pop my back and stretch my legs. Feels good, but what I wouldn't give to do my regular stretching routine.

The man steps out of the restroom. Vietnamese, I think. His face is deeply lined, no doubt reflecting a hard life that I couldn't begin to imagine. His smile softens it.

"Thank you, sir," he says, his English accented. "Are you enjoying your flight?" He's wearing a wooden bead bracelet, Buddha beads, I think.

"Yes. It's a long one, isn't it?"

He sighs. "Ah, yes. But I do not like to complain. I make the trip many times to see my brother in Hanoi. You go Vietnam or Japan?"

"I'm going to see my family in Saigon." Wow, that came out before I could censor it. It's true but it still sounds strange.

He frowns. Guess he thinks so too.

A heavyset Caucasian woman wearing all black excuses herself as she sidesteps behind my new friend and me. She struggles with the folding door for a moment before squeezing herself in, pulling it shut behind her.

"Oh, so sorry," the man says, covering his hand with his palm. "Did you have to piss very, very bad?"

I chuckle. "I can wait, thanks."

"Okay, good. Maybe she won't sit too long."

I shrug without saying anything since the woman can probably hear through the door.

The man half nods, half bows. "Maybe I see you in Vietnam."

"Yes, I hope so. Enjoy the long flight."

He shoots me a salute and heads up the aisle.

A moment later, the woman pushes open the door, glares at me, and slides her ample frame through the opening. I give her a big smile, happy that she didn't sit there too long.

# CHAPTER TWO

After a seven-hour nap, a Disney movie, and few more chats with Bobby, we landed in Tokyo for an hour, just long enough for us to grab a bento box for—I don't know if it was for breakfast, lunch, or dinner—and wash up a little in the restroom. Our last plane is Cathay Pacific Airways, my favorite so far of the three. Bobby was seated a couple rows forward, but he managed to charm the guy next to me into switching seats. It was the boy's turn to sleep this time, which he's been doing for the past few hours.

Although I'm enjoying the break from all his questions, the cabin is anything but quiet; the closer we get to Vietnam the louder and more excited the chatter throughout the plane.

Most of the Japanese got off in Tokyo and were replaced by Vietnamese, who now make up about ninety-nine percent of the passengers. Some are probably returning home from abroad and others, like my restroom pal, are likely American citizens making a routine trip to the motherland. I wonder if there might be some on board who haven't been home since fleeing the invasion by the North in the seventies. If so, I can't imagine their emotions.

What's Bobby's story? I like to think that I can read people but the boy is a challenge. At first, he came across as a charming kid with an abundance of enthusiasm for the martial arts. Then a couple of times I thought he might be working in some capacity for Lai Van Tan and trying to uncover something useful about me and my family. Curiously, he became subdued and evasive when I asked about his parents, and he remained so during the last leg of the flight into Tokyo, and throughout the hour-long layover.

Once we were airborne, flight attendants handed out Arrival/Departure Cards and Baggage Declaration forms to everyone. The boy helped me with mine and said that I shouldn't lie about anything because the customs police could be pretty hard. He said they are harder on Vietnamese Americans than on Caucasian Americans, but it's still important to be honest so as not to give them any reason to harass. Once we completed them, he twisted in his seat and rested the side of his head on the seatback, his face toward me. I had a fleeting thought that he wanted to keep me in his company as he went to sleep. He conked out in a minute and has yet to awaken six hours later. Cute kid, but what's going on behind that cherubic face?

In the last few minutes, the rising sun has splashed the ocean of clouds with orange, blue, red, and some other colors that only a poet could describe.

I look for a hint of Vietnam in the distance but there are only more clouds and blue. When I was a rookie in uniform, one of my first training coaches was a Vietnam vet. Elmer didn't talk about it much, and whenever the topic did come up his entire body, especially his face, became so tight that he looked as if his skin might rip open. He did open up a little once and told me about his initial arrival into the country.

Elmer and I were on a stakeout in the middle of the night, sitting in our car and watching the front door of a house half a block down the street. We sat mostly in silence for a couple of hours when out of the blue he just started talking about it.

"We were on our way to Nam. It was nighttime," he said. "About two in the morning, like now. After the captain announced over the PA that we were entering Vietnam airspace, he shut all the lights off in the cabin, except along the floor. You know, so the VC down below couldn't see us. It was real spooky in there, and there wasn't a peep out of any of the troops. Down below we could see an occasional flash outline the mountains. Artillery. I remember how my hands trembled… no, not trembled, they were shaking like crazy, so were my legs, and my head. As we got lower and lower, I could see tracer rounds down below on the ground. Not coming up at us. Moving parallel with us. A firefight.

"I wasn't the only shaky kid. At one point, someone way in the back of the plane screamed, 'I ain't getting fuckin' off. No way in hell am I getting fuckin' off the plane.' Someone yelled at him to shut up and he did. Then the guy next to me started throwing up. He had been all about killing VC all the way over, but when we started descending he threw up. Not in a bag. Down on his chest and lap. He just puked and sat there looking across me toward the window, like he didn't know he was doing it.

"When the plane was descending, there was a sudden, metallic clattering throughout the aircraft. When all of us fresh-faced, wide-eyed, and scared-shitless boys looked around, we could see a long line of inch-wide holes along the aisle floor next to the small lights. The plane was still too high to hear the weapon that did it, and we didn't see tracer rounds coming up from the ground, but there was no doubt that all those quarter-sized holes were from big rounds that had punched through the bottom of the plane, passed through all the luggage and structural members in the belly of the plane, and ripped through the floor. Once we landed and the lights were turned on we could see holes in the ceiling where the rounds exited."

Then Elmer let out a bark of laughter, "It would have been a real pain in the butt if those metal-piercing rounds had punched up through the floor a couple of feet to the right or left of the aisle and had gone through the occupied seats."

*"Ladies and gentleman, please make sure your tables are up and your seats are in the upright…"*

The announcement brings me out of my reverie. I can see the ground now, flat, large squares and rectangles of green. Rice paddies? Surreal. Two months ago, I had been planning another trip to Maui. Man, my life would make a great amusement park ride, except some of those hills and curves haven't been all that amusing.

"Hey, Sleeping Beauty," I say, giving Bobby's shoulder a nudge. He's still facing me, not having moved an inch in hours—ahh, to sleep like that again… "Time to wake up and meet the Land of the Rising Dragon."

He stirs and opens his eyes. "We're landing?"

"Either that or we're crashing veeeery slowly."

He sits up. "Wow, I slept the whole time." He leans over me and peers out the little window at the panorama of green earth, the brown snaking rivers, and a sprawling city that grows larger as we near the runway.

"Amazing," I say. "I saw something on the *History Channel* about a Viet Cong attack on *Tan Son Nhat* Airport in the late sixties. The footage showed lots of explosions, sputtering small arms fire, and spirals of black smoke. Look. There's *Tan Son Nhat's* runway, and beyond it, some buildings. No explosions. That's a positive."

"You nervous?" Bobby asks, perceptibly.

"Nervous? Nah." Actually, it feels like there is a herd of butterflies having a shit- kickin' barn dance in my gut. It's the unknown that's bothering me. I haven't a clue what to expect in Saigon: the culture, people, Samuel, Mai, Kim. The ongoing problem with Lai Van Tan.

Mai. I think it was love at first sight with us, though neither of us has said it in so many words. I can feel it, though, in our phone conversations, emails, and webcam chats. Man, the way she looks at me through the screen. The big question is will it continue now that things are more normal than they were in Portland? Sometimes distance can end a relationship and sometimes it can distort feelings, making one think that there is more to it than there is. When we actually see each other in the flesh again, might it dawn on us that there is nothing more between us than that initial crush we had in Portland?

The plane touches down with a bump and a jolt and a screech of rubber. Is that long beige building at the end of the runway the terminal? Samuel won't be meeting me because he had an emergency to take care of. Mai told me that yesterday on the phone—or maybe it was two days ago. Time is upside right now. It's either noon or early evening today, or it's some unknown time tomorrow.

The laughter and chattering in the cabin is quite loud now, the energy palpable. The thrill of coming home, I guess. That butterfly hoedown in my gut is now a bare-knuckle brawl. I can't tell if it's excitement, fear, happiness, anxiety, or dread. Dread?

Bobby and I stuff our things into our backpacks as the plane taxis to the gate and a female attendant's voice gives us the welcome message, first in Vietnamese and then in English. English last. Toto, I've a feeling we're not in Kansas anymore. It's three-thirty in the afternoon, she says.

"Here," I say, handing Bobby a slip of paper. "My cell phone number and the cell number of Mai Nguyen, the friend I will be visiting here. Maybe we can have a Coke or something one day."

"Okay," he says distractedly, looking through the window at the working ground crew. A moment later, he looks at me as if he just realized what I said. "Oh. Cool." He takes my number, stuffs it into his pants pocket, and looks back out the window. "Thanks."

The aisle is jammed with people pulling things from the overheads. "Let me ask you the same question, Bobby. You nervous?"

"Nervous?" He's still looking out the window at the ground crew.

"You seem nervous. Just wondering."

"No." He looks at me and back out the window. "Yeah, maybe a little."

Don't know where his head is so I'll leave him alone.

I'm told that we go to Immigration first, Baggage Claims, and then to Customs. Mai and Samuel both said it's a fairly smooth hour-long process, sometimes less. That's going to be one long hour knowing that Mai is waiting for me on the other side of it.

We're jostling down the aisle now, Bobby in front. He's carrying a large backpack, so big that I'm surprised they let him carry it on board.

"No hassle about your pack, huh?"

"Almost, just barely made the size limit," he says over his shoulder. "They really hassle American Vietnamese in Customs, especially if you got a lot of luggage. They want you to pay them something. So all I have is this."

No luggage. Hmm.

Five minutes later, we're out of the plane and walking through a jetway to the terminal. My God! The heat is overwhelming in this thing and the breathable air is negligible. My clothes are already sticking to me and my face is dripping. A half dozen people rush by, bumping and jostling us without apology and without slowing. Those crowding in front and those pressing in on us from behind are raising the heat and humidity into the death zone. Plus I'm starting to feel a whole lot claustrophobic. Just when I start to think that there is no end to this hellish tube, and that I just might freak out and start swimming over the top of everyone, I see people bunching up at what must be the exit point.

A minute later we're regurgitated out into a modern-looking terminal, where the heat is happily a few degrees lower than in that tube. Didn't expect shiny tile floors, massive cement pillars, chrome and steel all about, and everything as clean as a whistle. This isn't the same *Tan Son Nhat* Airport I saw in the documentary.

"We need to go over there," Bobby says, pointing toward a series of counters. "Immigration."

Glad I'm with him. The heat, the rush of people, and all the instructional signs in Vietnamese is a bit much.

"There aren't many people right now," he says, "so we should get through without a problem." He leads the way, jerking his head right and left like my cat does on a windy day. Looking for what?

After about thirty minutes of working our way to the front of the line, two stern-faced officials light upon Bobby. The one wearing impossibly thick Coke-bottle glasses looks over his passport as if searching for microscopic flaws in the paper. Satisfied, but looking unhappy about it, he hands it to the younger man who examines it even more closely. I'm assuming the scrutiny is because the boy is young and traveling alone. After responding to several sharply worded questions, Bobby retrieves a folded sheet of typing paper and hands it to Coke-Bottle Glasses. The man looks under the top fold, then wads whatever is underneath—I'm guessing money—into his palm and quickly stuffs it into his trouser pocket. Both men speak sharply to the boy, all the while he responds with several quick head bows. The younger officer slaps the passport onto the counter top, dismissing him with a jerk of his head.

"I'll wait for you over there," Bobby says tightly. "It shouldn't take *you* long."

I start to ask him if everything is okay but Coke-Bottle Glasses asks me in English to step up to the counter. He thumbs through my passport, checks my ID, asks why I'm in Saigon, and how long I will be. I tell him that I'm visiting friends, skipping the part that one is my father and the other is kind of a girlfriend—I think, I hope. He nods, stamps the pages and hands the passport back to me. "Go get bags now and go Customs."

"It's easier when you're white," Bobby says bitterly as I walk over.

"Hey, look around, dude. I'm the minority here. It's probably because you're a kid traveling alone."

He shrugs and flips his backpack over his shoulder. "Come on. I'll show you where you get your luggage. You're getting picked up, right?"

I shoulder my pack. "Yes." Did I tell him that? "Your parents picking you up?"

He nods distractedly as he leads me into a throng of people, past a food court with a myriad of smells, and finally to a carousel where I spot my two burgundy bags on the floor. He picks up one to carry for me.

"Please call me," I say, as we jostle our way through another crowd of sweating people. "I'll buy you a bubble tea."

He makes a face. "I hate that stuff. Don't worry, I will call. But for *phở*."

I look around waiting for the Boogey Man to jump out from behind one of these giant pillars. Maybe I shouldn't have watched those war documentaries before I came over. Or maybe Bobby is making me paranoid: sitting next to me on the plane, no luggage, odd behavior. And the way he's been looking around since we debarked, like he, too, is expecting the Boogey Man to leap out. Or Lai Van Tan.

"*Phở* it is," I say.

It takes a couple of minutes for us to snake through the throng before the boy points at a sign ahead of us. "Okay, there's Customs. Hopefully, it will be easy for me this time."

We wait in line for another thirty minutes in which I drop four, maybe five pounds from sweating. It's so damn hot and humid it's funny. Actually, it's not funny; it's miserable. Bobby goes first again, and this time he breezes through. My trip through is uneventful as well, though it was a little embarrassing when the pretty girl smiled at my underwear, new stuff I purchased before I left.

Bobby and I walk a few feet away from the crowd to say our goodbyes. "Good meeting you," I say, shaking his hand. "You're a nice young man. I'd be proud to have you as a student."

"Thank you," he beams. "I'll take you up on that. My ride is at the far end."

I don't know if it's my imagination, but suddenly the invisible weight Bobby was carrying earlier is gone. Just like that.

We walk silently side by side out onto the sidewalk where a mob of people look anxiously at us to see if we're their loved ones. I start to scan the crowd looking for—

"Sam."

I freeze. I know that voice.

"Over here, Sam. To your right."

At nearly six feet, Mai towers over everyone, many of whom are staring at her unabashedly. She's behind several people so all I can see is her cascading raven-black hair framing a face that would make a monk question his life choices. What sends my heart rate so high that I'm in danger of needing a defibrillation are those exquisite brown eyes, their hint of elongation. Even from fifteen feet away they electrify each and every nerve up and down my spine.

Bobby's voice comes from somewhere off to my side. "Dude! Is that tall chick the one you're coming to see? Daaaamn!"

Mai snakes her way to the front of the crowd only to have another group move in between us. She laughs as she slips around them and resumes heading toward me.

"Excellent choice," I barely hear the boy say. "Her legs in those jeans go on and on."

"Mai," I half whisper as she nears.

"I'm out of here, Sam," Bobby says. "I'll call you in a couple days." He sings, "Have fuuuun."

"Sure," I say, without moving my eyes from Mai's.

Mai and I lightly grip each others arms. She warned me on the phone that we can't kiss or hug because it's still considered taboo by most.

"Hi," I whisper.

You know, people joke about those romance novels, but man-oh-man, it's just as those writers described. The room really does spin and sounds really do muffle.

"Sam. I am so happy you have come," she says with a slight nod, acting properly for those watching us. "Did you have a good trip?" I can see the green specks in her eyes now.

"Yes, thank you." I so want to maul her. "It's an incredibly long trip." That's all, just maul and maul and maul. "I hope you didn't have to wait long." And maul. "Time is a bit confusing to me right now. I'm not sure if we were on time or not." Maul.

She smiles. "Yes, you were on time. It is five-ten in the afternoon."

We had emailed each other dozens of pictures and did the face-time thing on the computer, but seeing her again in person just about sucks the breath out of my throat. Every doubt I had is sucked out with it.

"Mai," I say, it sounding almost like a sob. "I am so happy to see you. I cannot express how much…" Am I tearing up?

Her eyes penetrate mine and tickle the inside of my skull. She nods almost imperceptibly, whispering, "I know. I thought this day would never come. My…" she looks down for a second, and then lifts her eyes to meet mine. "My heart has hurt for all these weeks. But now… it sings."

My face muscles spasm into what can only be a goofy-looking smile. "Mine too."

Oh man, if the guys on the Detectives floor could see me now, their teasing would be relentless. *Hey Sam, is that your heart I hear singing?*

I don't bother wiping away my tears. "I can't believe that I'm actually here—"

Shouts. Movement from my left.

"Something is happening," Mai says, gripping my arm.

A woman's scream. Another. The mass of people that had been waiting for arrivals press back from the disturbance. From where I'm standing it looks like… a fight?

When the crowd begins backing in our direction, I pull Mai protectively behind me. In an instant, my inner cop kicks in and I'm back on my beat working my way through a crowd that has surrounded a street fight.

"Sam, no," Mai says in my ear, her hands on my shoulders. "Do not interfere here."

I stop. "Whoops. I was on autopilot there for a second."

"I do not know that word but it is very important that you not interfere. The police here are not the same—"

"Bobby?" I say, spotting him through an opening in the crowd. The boy is struggling with two men, both dressed in dark slacks and white overshirts. "What the…"

"You know him?"

"Yes, Bobby Phan." They each have one of his arms, gripping hard as the boy writhes to get free. "We rode together all the way over. Who are those men?"

"I saw them when I was waiting. I noticed because they looked so serious and everyone else so happy. And they looked at every young face."

"Lai Van Tan's men?" But why would they attack him? Was he supposed to lead me to them?

"I do not—"

"Bobby!" Female voice coming a few feet from my left. "Bobby!" There, pushing through the crowd. A teenage girl, orange blouse, black satin pants.

The men are pulling Bobby in opposite directions. If they were stronger they would pull his arms out of their sockets. I take a step in that direction.

"Mai, I just can't stand here and let them—"

Bobby launches a beautifully executed roundhouse kick into the face of the man on his left and, without returning his foot to the sidewalk, hook kicks his heel into the side of the other man's neck.

"Oh, man!" I blare, shocked at the sight of the men stumbling back, one clutching his blood-spurting nose, the other swaying drunkenly as he reaches feebly toward his neck. "Bobby!" I shout, but he doesn't hear me. He grabs his backpack and dashes for the girl's extended hand. She leads him quickly through the crowd, and they're gone.

The nosed-kicked man shouts something that I wouldn't understand even if it wasn't muffled by his hand that's holding his nose in place.

"What should we do, Mai? I'm out of my element here. I don't—"

The man shouts something again at the crowd and begins pushing his way through the people who have closed the path that Bobby and the girl took.

"Wait, Sam" Mai says urgently. "Do not do anything."

I start to say that we have to find Bobby, but Mai's raised palm hushes me as she strains to hear what the man who ate the neck kick is telling those holding him up.

"Okay," she says. "These men are not Lai Van Tan. They are *canh sát*, policemen. He says the boy is… what is the English word? He leave parents. He run…"

"Bobby is a runaway? A *runaway*?"

"Yes, that is the word, runaway. Policeman say he leave his home without permission. *Canh sát* were trying to, uh, catch him for his father in California."

So that's why his demeanor changed when I asked about his parents. That's why he was acting so suspiciously after the plane landed and while we were processing out. He was watching for the police.

"Can we go look for him, Mai? I want to see that he's okay."

"Yes, we are going that way anyway." She picks up one of my bags.

She leads me around the crowd and over to the curb where there are lines of parked taxis of every make and color, and a mad horde of drivers calling to us and reaching for our arms as we pass. He could be in any one of these cars and—

"Sam!" Bobby's voice penetrates the street noise.

Mai points toward a moving car. "There."

Bobby is pushing his face out the back side window of a blue taxi that's jockeying to get into the flow of passing vehicles. He waves at me, and puts his thumb to his ear and his little finger to his mouth.

# CHAPTER THREE

"Never a dull moment with you," Mai says, watching her side mirror as she jockeys her Volvo out into the chaos that appears to be the traffic pattern here. She does some kind of wave out the window, which is either a "thank you" or a "cram it up where the sun don't shine" gesture. Either way, it sets off a cacophony of honking. A motorbike roars around her driver's side, its accelerating engine deafening through the open window. A second one passes so closely that Mai nearly loses her side mirror. Another cuts around us and comes within four hairs-width of clipping her front fender.

"My God, Mai. This is nuts. Has there been a *coup d'état*? Is everyone fleeing the city? Is China attacking?"

She laughs, a sound that's big, like it's coming from a 300-pound opera singer, a trait I really like. "No, everything is fine," she says, closing the window. "If any of those things were happening, traffic would be really—" She brakes hard when a white truck cuts into our lane, just inches from our hood. "Really bad," she finishes. A motor scooter shoots from the right lane between the truck and our front end, swoops into the left lane, and disappears around the truck.

"Mother of Buddha!" I cry.

She laughs again. "We will be out of this airport traffic in a minute and then it will be even more crowded, but there will be some organization to it." She looks over at me and croons. "Oooh, don't be scared."

"Watch the road, will you?" I relax my clenched fists and try to retrieve my machismo. "I guess I'm just not used to it—" Two motorbikes pull up along side us, one by my window and one by Mai's, the riders are young, both wearing pale blue shirts and wrap-around sunglasses. "These guys want to get inside our car?"

Mai smiles. "Personal space, even in traffic, is different here than in Portland. After a year in your city, it took me three weeks to get used to this again. Same thing when I returned from my year in Paris. I see now how crazy our streets might seem to foreigners, but as you say in America, 'It is what it is.'"

The motorbikes are still close enough for their drivers to tap on our respective windows.

"I can't believe I'm here. It's surreal."

"I am so very happy now. I hope you will like it here."

I make a big motion with my head as I look her up and down. "I like the scenery so far."

She giggles and punches me in the thigh.

"Ow!" I blurt, not faking. She hit me in the nerve just above my kneecap.

"Sorry," she says with phony concern. "Was that too hard?"

"Uh, yeah. I guess I shouldn't undress you with my eyes, huh?"

She laughs. "I am not sure what that means but it sound very, very good."

"Well," I say rubbing my leg. "When someone looks at…"

The motorbike rider on Mai's side turns toward her and for a second I can see her profile in his mirrored sunglasses. When he lifts his head ever so slightly, I see my face in them. He smiles and lifts his left hand from the handlebar, his pointing index finger and upright thumb shaped like a gun, and shoots at me.

"Hey!" I shout, and he "fires" at me again. "Mai, that guy on the motorbike—"

"What?" she looks toward me.

The motorbike driver banks hard to the left.

She jerks her head toward her side window. "Guy?"

I look out the rear side window and see him merge into a mass of traffic moving down a side street.

The one outside my window is gone too.

"The rider next to your window looked at us and then did this with his hand. You know, like he was firing a gun at me."

"Are you sure? Oh, I'm sorry, Sam. Of course you're sure."

The white truck hangs a right, revealing hundreds of motor-bikes, bicycles, cars, and pedicabs, randomly cutting right and left.

"Could it have been Lai Van Tan's people?" I ask. "Were you followed, maybe?"

Listen to me. I'm a hysterical teenage girl. Get control of yourself. Try to impress the woman a little.

"I do not know, but I don't think so."

"Then who was the guy? Is that how you welcome newcomers here—make bang bang gestures?" So much for impressing her.

Mai looks at me, eyebrows bunched. "Sam? Are you okay?"

I take a deep breath. "I don't know. Just tense I guess. It's been a crazy few weeks. Meeting you, meeting my father, my school burns down—and everybody was kung-fu fighting and dealing with all the legal stuff, and then Mark coming to me telling me he knows what happened. The whole time I was at the airport in Portland, I kept waiting for the detectives to show up and put me into handcuffs. I'm finally here, and I'm exhausted and jet lagged, and the young man I flew with turns out to be a runaway who kicks cops. Now motorbike guys are pretending to shoot at me."

She shrugs. "It could be… just a moment." She maneuvers the car to the far left lane, slows, then tapping her horn, begins to inch across the oncoming lane. Actually, it's more like an oncoming, thunderous tsunami wave of about a billion cars, motorbikes, scooters, and odd-shaped large and small vehicles that I've never seen before. They stream around the front and back of us as if they were a surging river and we were a rock, except we're moving too. Incredibly, we make it across in one piece. The new street is a tad less congested.

"The man could have been just teasing," Mai says.

"Teasing?"

"Not the best word? Being a… jerk?"

"You don't think he knew us?"

"No. Maybe he does not like white people, especially a white man with a Vietnamese woman."

My cop instinct is telling me otherwise but then what do I know? I'm a white guy in Saigon who's been here less than two hours. "Will there be much of that? People not accepting me with you?"

"You are going to be with me?" she asks, struggling against a smile. She leans on the horn and swerves around a Toyota.

"Thinking about it," I say, faking a lack of enthusiasm.

"I see." Her smile begins to win the struggle.

"Where are you taking me?" I ask, then blurt, "Holy!" as half a dozen motorbikes from a side street to my right accelerate directly across our lane.

Mai leans on her horn and swerves just enough not to kill them, still wearing that faint smile. "I am taking you… here," she says, turning onto what appears to be a dirt, potholed alley between two buildings. She guides the car a short distance and pulls into a small parking lot next to one of the structures. Scaffolding on its front extends all the way to the roof, one, two… eight floors. Tape crisscrosses some of the windows on the ground floor.

"You live here?" I ask, not having to shout this time since the buildings and trees substantially reduce the traffic roar.

"I wish. No, this is a new building, called Vinh Tower One, owned by a friend of my father and me, mostly Father's friend. It is still a few months away from being finished. He has a… what do you call..? A business on his side?"

"A side business?"

"Yes, a side business. He is a building contractor but he enjoys buying and selling jewelry on his side. The side. My father sometimes buys from him for our stores."

"So can I kiss you now? No one is around."

Was that too abrupt? For a hair of a second, the intensity of Mai's smile reminds me of the movie *Christmas Vacation* when Chevy Chase plugs in the cord that lights up all twenty-five thousand Christmas lights that envelop his house.

"No kissing, sorry," she says, reaching for the door handle. "Come, I want to show you something inside."

My face is either hot from embarrassment or from the wet blanket of heat that greets me outside of the air conditioned car. I start to say something when a lone motorbike enters the alley from the steady mass of traffic passing by the opening. It's not a man wearing a blue shirt, dark sunglasses, and armed with a pointy finger, but a young woman, her black hair blowing behind her. She smiles at me as she passes and continues down the alley.

"Many pretty girls in Saigon," Mai says. "They think you pretty handsome."

"Not one of them is as pretty as you," I say.

"Good answer, soldier." She points with her chin toward a small door under the scaffolding. "We enter over there." She slips a card into the door's card lock and it clicks open. "Follow me," she says, leading me down a hallway illuminated only by outside light coming in through a high window. "I think you might enjoy what I will show you." We stop at what looks like a service elevator.

"An elevator! Awesome!"

"Funny. I am laughing on my insides." She slips her card into a slot. "I think I understand what you are feeling right now. Like I said, it was hard for me to readjust to Vietnam after Paris and Portland. I think life is more intense here: so many people, the noise. I think it might be hard for you to make the transition."

We step onto the elevator and she inserts her card into another slot. She pokes the eighth floor button and turns toward me. She drops her chin a little and looks up at me. "I will help you."

"Nah, I'm good."

She smiles. "Same Sam as before. Always joke." She looks at the digital numbers on the panel. "Our friend loan me this key card so I can show you something. I hope you will like it."

"What is it?" The elevator stops.

She makes a dramatic, sweeping gesture with both hands as the doors swoosh open. "It is... Saigon. Ho Chi Minh City."

The open and empty floor is at least a hundred feet wide by a hundred fifty feet long, with the smell of freshly laid carpet. Beige. There are four-foot thick cement pillars here and there, and floor-to-ceiling windows on all the outer walls, creating a sense that we're floating in the sky.

"Wow! And wow again! What a magnificent view, Mai," I say, as we cross the floor to the windows. Large rolls of beige carpet lay off to the side. "Saigon is huge! It goes on and on in all directions."

"Yes," she says, her voice pleased at my reaction. "Nine million of us. That cluster of tall buildings way over there is the center of the city. That is the Ho Chi Minh River beyond that. To the right, way over there by that small river, that is Cholon where many Chinese people live. There to the left, maybe five miles away, you can see the top part of the Reunification Palace. That used to be Presidential Palace during the war. Maybe you have seen the famous film of the North Vietnamese tanks smashing through the gates."

"I have. In fact, the only image I've ever had of Vietnam is the Vietnam at war. You know that I thought my father had died here. I compulsively watched all the movies that came out, and lots and lots of documentaries, *The History Channel* and *The Learning Channel*. The only image I had was of exploding rockets, rolling tanks, and street battles. But this… this is just incredible. Magnificent."

Mai nods. "Yes. If this building were here during that time, this would be a different view. My mother said that every night, beginning when the sun went down until it came up again, there were flashes in the distance and the rumble of artillery. Most people who live here now were born after the war. So they do not know. They do not even think about it much."

"It's just magnificent," I say, scanning the panoramic view.

"The sun will be setting in a few minutes and it is even more beautiful then with all the lights. But we cannot watch it tonight because we must go to see Father. We can come another evening." She is looking out the widow but I can tell she is watching me in her peripheral. "Maybe we will bring a bottle of wine and glasses."

That doubled the ol' heart rate, and I barely manage to wheeze, "That sounds fantastic."

"Good," she says, watching a plane descend in the far distance. "Since our friend gave me the key card I have come up here many times. I sit on those rolls of carpet or on this window ledge and just look out at the view. I like watching the sunset. It makes me feel special, but at the same time it makes me feel... humble, I think."

"I look forward to watching it with you."

"Yes," she says softly, turning toward me. "I imagined you up here looking out the window with me." She looks into my eyes and I get that wheezy feeling again. "We can kiss now, if you still want to."

I do, for a profoundly long time.

"Hi," she breathes, when we finally separate.

"Back at yuh," I manage. "You got to change your no kissing and hugging rule at the airport."

"I knooow, right? Some things are much better in America." We're embracing, our lips whispering against one another's ears. "Like sushi. USA has good sushi. Vietnam, no sushi."

"Technically, sushi really isn't American," I say, nipping her earlobe, making her inhale sharply. "It's Japanese. In Portland, most sushi is made by Hispanics. My favorite sushi place is owned by a Korean guy who hires Hispanics to make the Japanese sushi."

Mai chuckles. "Well, I will take you to a good *phở* street cart that is owned by a German man."

"Sounds delicious. Will there be sauerkraut and *mmrthmm—*"

Mai's lips smother my words. Seconds pass and I no longer remember what I was babbling about. Somewhere the Star Spangled Banner plays.

"Whoops," Mai says against my lips. "That might be Father."

Not again, I think, turning quickly toward the elevator. He was constantly walking in on us in Portland.

"The phone, silly," she says, launching that dragon-slaying smile at me as she pries her cell out of her pants pocket. "It is. Hello, Father. Did I pick up Sam? Sam who?" She winks at me. She laughs at something he says. "Yes, I have him. He has put on about fifty pounds. He is very fat now." She listens, laughs, and says, "I am sure you will. You want to talk to him? Okay. We will be there in a short while. I am showing him the view from Mister Troung's building. Yes. Okay. Good bye." She flips her phone shut. "He will talk to you at our house. He will explain to you why he could not come."

"Sounds good. So I have gotten fat, eh?" I say with a chuckle.

"He says not to worry. He will work it off you. He is excited about training with you and introducing you to his teacher, Sifu Shen Lang Rui."

"I am excited to see Samuel. And a little nervous."

She smiles. "He can make people nervous. But you are his son. You should not be." Mai takes my hand and we sit next to each other on the window ledge, our legs touching. "Have you thought much about him?"

"Not as much as I would have liked. I had to put important parts of my life into compartments so that I could deal with the grand jury for my... shooting. I wasn't worried about shooting the abductor... but the..."

Mai takes my hand in both of hers. "You are *not* at fault. The ju... judgment says that it is not your fault. I know that does not make you feel better. But I think... what is the expression? Time... in time, yes. I think in time your mind will be fine. Healed."

I called Mai the moment the grand jury came back with a No True Bill, meaning they didn't hold me at fault for the accidental killing. My emotions were all over the place and I didn't know if I wanted to stand, sit, lay down, or scream from the roof. I did know that I needed to hear her voice. I was blubbering so much that she couldn't understand me, but she was kind enough and savvy enough to let me come down from my rush before asking me questions. I tried to explain that I was happy I was spared a trial, and all the horrific emotions and public persecution that would have come down on me. At the same time, I had this immense guilt because I was feeling good about the No True Bill. I had killed, and a nine-person jury decided that it was okay.

It wasn't though. I thought I should be punished for it, punished severely. But I was happy that I wasn't going to be. My head was on the verge of exploding and all I could think of was that I needed to hear Mai's voice. I knew there wasn't anything she could say from the other side of the globe to make it all go away or make me feel better, but I just wanted to hear her say hello.

As soon as she picked up, I began blubbering like a child. When I finally came up for air—I don't know how long I'd been wailing in her ear—I could hear her sobbing. When I asked if she was crying with me, she said, "Who else? I'm sitting in a room by myself talking with you." That made me laugh for some reason and then she started laughing. Then we cried again.

When I finally calmed, Mai asked if I remembered the meditation sessions that Samuel taught me. I said I had been doing it every other day. She suggested an increase to two or three times a day, to sit quietly and just follow my breath, in and out, in and out. Every time a stray thought came into my mind, I was to look at it for a second, then just let it float away and go back to following my breath. She added, "And kick the shit out of the heavy bag once a day. Then meditate again after the shit kicking."

Like an obedient child, I did what she said, and it helped, like a Band-Aid sometimes makes a cut feel better. The extra meditating helped me get some control over my thoughts, and the extra hard bag work made me too tired to think at all, at least until morning came around again.

"You okay, Sam?" Mai asks looking into my eyes.

"I am now."

She smiles. "I am happy for you to meet my mother and I want to show you so much about my life, but I am scared that you might not like it here. You might be bored."

"Impossible. Like I said before, you and Samuel caught me during a bad week." A shadow passes across Mai's face before she looks away. "Sorry," I say caressing her arm. "Bad joke. You know, we have yet to talk about Portland State, those deaths. I wanted to many times but I wasn't sure how to bring it up."

"I want to talk to you about it too, but not now. Now I want to just be happy to be near you," she says, looking at me and then out the window.

I gently turn her head toward me and kiss her.

"I wish we had more time to spend here, but we need to go to see Father. Maybe in a few days when you are rested, we can talk then."

"Just say the word."

Mai nods. "Okay, I will say the word." She scoots off the ledge, steps in front of me and slips between my parted legs. She takes both of my hands in hers, squeezes them and without an ounce of shyness, moves those gorgeous eyes to my shoulders, down my arms, across my chest, and all the way down to my shoes. Then slowly, caressingly, she moves them back up to my eyes. She exhales slowly with a little shake of her head. "Come on, Sam." She steps aside so I can scoot off the ledge. "We better go, *now*. Before I… we just better go."

I've gotten a couple of compliments in my day, but that one, without uttering a word, ranks at the top. I can even hear the electricity crackle between us as we walk hand in hand to the elevator.

"Sam, who was the boy at the airport, the one who made such a quiet entrance into Saigon?"

Good idea. Talk about something else since there is no cold shower available. She pokes the elevator button.

"Bobby Phan, or so he said. He told me that he was coming here to meet his parents and spend time with his dying grandfather. Appears that wasn't true since his father filed a runaway report on him in California. He also said he had a black belt in taekwondo." The elevator doors open and we step in. We begin descending "At least the black belt story was true. Did you see his kicks? Hit two guys in the head without putting his foot down."

"Not just guys, Sam. Policemen. They will be hunting for him now harder than before."

"I wonder then if he will call me… wait. I didn't tell him that I'm a policeman and I don't remember if the magazine article he read about me mentions it. So maybe he will call. You know, for a while on the plane, I thought he might be connected with Lai Van Tan."

She shakes her head. "Oh, I don't think so. Just a… running away, no, runaway. Lots of people come here when they run away."

"I was just being paranoid."

"What does that mean?"

"It means I'm on suspicion overdrive, I guess."

"I understand," she says, squeezing my hand.

"When I'm not suspecting Bobby of being a Russian secret agent, I see him as a great kid. Apparently one with some big problems. I'd like to help him. He's got my cell number, and yours."

Mai moves into me. "Always wanting to fix things, right, Sam?" she kisses me before I can answer.

# CHAPTER FOUR

Mai is laughing as she leans on the horn and brakes to avoid a young girl on a motorbike who streaked out from a side street and passed by our hood just inches from earning a grave. The sky is in twilight mode and the streets and sidewalks are beginning to light up like a carnival.

"That's considered funny here?" I ask.

Mai laughs again. "The girl? No, not funny." She shrugs. "Of course it is dangerous but it is also like I said: It's just the way it is." She gestures at the vehicle riot outside our windows. "I was laughing because for a moment I was seeing all this through your eyes. How mad it must seem compared to Portland."

"It's un-freaking-believable," I say. "I heard about it, but nothing prepares you for the enormity of the mass confusion of thousands upon thousands of vehicles going every which way. And the roar!"

She nods. "I said 'how mad it must seem,' but you must understand that it is not mad at all, it is not as you say, 'mass confusion.' There are about a thousand traffic deaths a year in Saigon, but that is not many when you consider that there are millions of motorbikes and other kinds of vehicles on the streets. It is not mad because all, well, most drivers pay attention to where they are and where they are going. We all cooperate. This is most important when you have to cross the street. Okay, look over there. See that little girl at that far corner?"

We're parked at a red light, actually hundreds and hundreds of us are parked at a red light at the entrance of what appears to be a traffic circle of some kind with about five streets feeding into it, each of them jammed with thousands of vehicles. Traffic on a couple of the feeder streets appears to have stopped for a light, while motorbikes on streets that have the green light move in mass into the circle, then regurgitate haphazardly onto feeder streets where they battle with oncoming traffic trying to get into the circle.

"No," I say. "How can you see one little girl in all this."

"Over there, to the right," she says, pointing. "Black pants, blue top. She looks about six years old."

I see her, a tiny thing on the corner of one of the feeder streets. "Yes, cute. What about—" She steps off the curb. "Mai! She's walking out into traffic. My God, she'll be killed."

Mai laughs. "She is fine. Watch how every driver is paying attention and how the little girl crosses through the traffic very smooth."

My heart is pounding as hundred of motorbikes swarm around her, some passing in front, some behind. One slows just enough for her to finish a stride and then accelerates through where her leg had just been. It's almost as if they've practiced it.

"See," Mai says. "Her mother taught her well. Because she is walking very smooth, without hesitating or speeding up, the traffic can, uh, estimate where they have to go so they do not run her down."

"But she's a little girl!" I half shout.

"Yes, one who has to cross the street. See how everyone works together? If she stopped suddenly, it would cause much confusion to the traffic. Some would swerve into others and some would be forced to stop, which would make others hit them from behind. Do you see how some motorbikes are carrying large loads, like that one with many baskets piled high into the air? Or that one there with three riders on the back? See the one with two women on in it, one holding a baby? They do not want to crash. So it is important that everyone cooperates."

The little girl steps up onto the curb and begins skipping to wherever she is going.

"Unbelievable. Have you ever been in an accident?"

"Yes. I have not crashed in a car but I have three times on my motorbike. Not for a while, thank Buddha, God, and my ancestors."

The light changes and a thousand of us move into the circle, the roar of engines all consuming. About half way around, Mai works the car to the right, her hand steadily tapping the horn. She finishes the merge successfully and now we're on a street with much lighter traffic.

As has been the case with all the streets I've seen, the sidewalks are cluttered with what appears to be food carts, card tables, and spread blankets where people sell everything from toilet paper to tires to perfume to boiling pots of whatever. The buildings on both sides of the street are three of four stories high, the top floors appearing to be apartments, while most of the ground level spaces look to be shops and eateries—the aroma is making me salivate.

"I'm liking this," I say. "The traffic? I'm not so sure about yet, but the rest of it—the architecture, the extraordinary variety of smells, the crowds—yeah, I really like the feel here. And it's getting dark already."

"It gets dark here earlier this time of the year compared to Portland," Mai says, accelerating around a motorbike piled high with—eggs. "We are close to the equator." The stacked egg crates extend at least three feet over his head. "I am very happy to hear that you like this. I think my stays in Paris and in Portland helped me see Saigon as a… unique?… yes, a unique place. I love it because it is my home but I also love it because it is so unique. Unique is the right word, yes?"

"Definitely. I certainly can't argue with that assessment because… Hey! That man!" I twist hard to look out the back window.

"What is the matter, Sam?"

"That man sitting on his motorbike back there. I'm sure of it."

"What?"

"That's the same guy who was riding so close to your window. The one who made the shooting gestures."

Mai giggles and says in a funny voice, "You know all us Oreo-entals look alike."

For some reason that irritates me. "I know what I saw. I've been around Asians all my martial arts career. And for the last fifteen years my job has been to watch people, to read them."

Her smile disappears.

"Sorry Mai. Jet lag's making me grumpy."

"What was the man doing?"

"Looking at me. His bike was on the kickstand and he was sitting on it with one foot on the ground and the other resting across the seat. He was smoking. Made eye contact and deliberately blew his smoke toward me."

"I do not know what to say. What do you call it… oh, yes, worse case scenario. The worse case scenario is that Lai Van Tan knew you were coming. Or, okay, do not get mad again, that man just *looks* like the shooter man. Look around, many men wear white shirts, blue shirts and gray slacks. Everyone has sunglasses."

"If they know I'm coming, why are they in the open? Harassment? Terrorism? A promise of things to come?"

"Yes, yes. Father say that they are not like the *Viet Cong*. They don't live underground, pop out, do something terrible, and then go back underground again. They like to be seen. And feared. Terrorism. You are right."

I know Lai Van Tan is still a threat, but I was hoping like a child hopes that it was over. I still haven't gotten everything that happened in Portland sorted out in my head.

"Sam?"

As awful as it was in Portland, at least I was on my own turf, in my city, my state, my country. Here, in a Communist country, or whatever it is, where Americans are… What? I don't know how I'll be perceived yet, but I got a feeling it won't be as peachy as the travel brochures claim.

"Sam?"

I look over at her.

"I can see you worrying. Do not do that, okay? Right now, we really do not know anything about that man. I know you are an expert on how to look at people, but I would bet that he was not the same one as before. Even if he was, maybe it was a coincidence. He is on the street and we are on the street in a car that stands out from all the bikes and other cars. Maybe right now he is afraid because he thinks we are following him."

I chuckle. "Okay, I'll stop with the paranoia. Not a good way to start out as a guest in your country. But if I see him again…"

Mai laughs as she makes a right onto another street. "Then we would truly be in the shit bucket."

"Nicely put."

"Thank you, sir. Oh, how is Chien?"

"Your kitty is fine, sort of. I was actually planning on bringing her with me to surprise you but she got sick about a week ago. So one of my students is taking care of her."

"Oh no. Very sick?"

"Something with its lungs. The vet gave her a couple of shots and he gave me some pills to give daily. Said Chien would be fine in a week or so but that she shouldn't travel."

"Very sad. I miss Chien a lot."

"And Chien misses you. This area is nice, do you live around here?"

"We are almost there. I live upstairs in a space that is about as big as the apartment I had in Portland. Father and Mother live downstairs, and Ly, Mother's nurse, lives in a room in the back of the house. Since I'm a modern woman," she says, overacting an air of sophistication, "I would have my own apartment somewhere else." She abruptly frowns. "But Mother is sick, so I like to be there to help Ly and help when Ly takes time off to see her family."

"I'm so sorry about Kim."

"Yes, I am very sad. Mother is not doing very well. TB is a difficult disease. She suffers from fever sometimes and she coughs very hard."

"She going to be okay?"

Mai goes inward for a moment, then softly, "I do not know."

We turn into a short cobblestone driveway and stop before an ornate, black double gate that's lit by lamps on each corner post. She lowers her window and exposes her face. The gate swings open.

"Video surveillance?"

Mai smiles. "Father will explain everything," she says, guiding the car into a brick-covered parking area big enough for a half dozen limos. The two-story house is gorgeous: dark brown tile roofing, light beige siding, lots of glass, bricks, stones, potted trees, and well-placed lighting to show it at its best. This would be considered upscale even in the Hollywood Hills; I didn't expect to see it here.

"Wow!" I say. "The jewelry business has been very good."

"Father *is* a good businessman, a rare one because he is honest. But this house— Oh, there. He is coming."

Samuel waves from the top of about a dozen steps, his face beaming. He is dressed the same as he did in Portland: white overshirt, gray slacks, and red Converse shoes.

I wave back. "I am so happy to see him," I say, reaching for the door handle. "He looks really good. Less stressed than when… What—the—hell?"

Mai covers her mouth and giggles. "I just thought something. I do not think you know about best friend of Father. He did not tell you?"

"That would have to be a no," I say, gawking at a middle-aged Vietnamese man following Samuel down the steps, hand over hand, his legless torso swinging back and forth between arms that look disproportionately too long and too big for what remains of his body. He's wearing a black tank top and blue Nike shorts; the empty pant legs drag on the cobblestone. If he does have legs, they don't extend more than a couple inches from his pelvis.

"Son," Samuel says, as I climb out of the car. He presses his palms together against his chest as if in prayer, his face beaming. "I am so happy to see you, so very happy you are here."

Should we hug? I decide to err on the side of caution and extend my hand. "I'm happy to see you too, Samuel," I say. He takes my hand into both of his, squeezes it gently, nodding his head several times. He's either affirming his happiness or doing a series of short bows. Maybe both. He might be Caucasian, but he has spent the majority of his life here in Vietnam. Mai once said that he is more Vietnamese than American and what little I saw of him in Portland, I'd have to agree. His slight build, clothing choice, sun-browned skin, stilted speech, and demeanor all add to the confusion.

"Son, this is my very good friend, Tex Nguyen," Samuel says, stepping aside so I can see the legless man whose head is no higher than my pant's zipper and who seems to be resting—balancing?—on his torso. Should I offer my hand? Wouldn't one less support limb make him fall over? Did he say *Tex* Nguyen?

The man leans on his left hand and extends his right, which is about as big as a dinner plate. Tattoos cover his thickly muscled arms from his fingers to his thick shoulders. "Okay to meet son of best friend mine," he says, his voice soft, gentle, the accent thick but understandable. "Many things hear about you."

"Nice to meet you, sir." He appears to be in his sixties, with a gray buzz cut and a wispy, gray Fu Manchu moustache that extends down the sides of his mouth to dangle in tight, three-inch braids of ornate knots below his chin. Some cops have a way of looking at people, sizing them up in an instant. Tex's eyes do that. I've been told mine do. "Father and Tex have been friends since the war," Mai says. "He is Father's assistant at the…" she says something in Vietnamese to Samuel.

"Rest home," he says.

"Rest home," Mai repeats. "I do not remember if we told you that Father owns a rest home for old soldiers."

Samuel smiles. "I do not think we talked about it. We were busy that week in Portland."

I nod, feeling a little like I just walked into the middle of a movie.

He laughs, hooks his arm into mine, and guides me toward the steps. Tex hand-walks along behind us. "I think maybe all of this is a little overwhelming to you, Son, and you must be tired. It is much cooler inside. And my Kim is anxious to meet you." He looks around me toward Mai. "Did you mention that Mother speaks freely? Bluntly?"

"Oh, I forgot," Mai says, smiling. "Mother says what is on her mind."

He chuckles. "It is at once refreshing and disarming. Be warned."

We climb the brick steps to an open red door. He points at a spot by the entrance where there are sets of shoes and sandals laid out. "Please remove your shoes here."

We pass through a foyer lined with large, gray stone pots of black bamboo that form a canopy of delicate green leaves, and walk into the living area. The floor is gray slate, softened with a large red, blue, and black Oriental rug, its main design focus a blue dragon, its mouth open, talons reaching. The room's atmosphere is modern expensive, complete with a long, black leather sofa, a matching black love seat, glass tables, and a black entertainment center. Three large ceiling fans stir the air.

My eyes are drawn to a large painting over a flat screen TV of an achingly beautiful Vietnamese woman. She is standing in a grove of sun-filtered bamboo, the shifting shades of green around her a stark contrast to the radiant red of her high-necked and long-sleeved fitted tunic. There are slits along each side revealing wide-legged white trousers, the fabric painted to fall caressingly over her form. I can see Mai in the woman's beautiful face, especially those eyes that even from twenty feet away, reveal intelligence, warmth, and a not-so-subtle sensuality.

"That is Mother," Mai says, walking over to the painting. "Father hired a friend to paint her two years ago. The dress is called *áo dài*. You have seen it already on the sidewalks."

"Kim is still angry that I insisted it be displayed up there," Samuel says with a mischievous grin. "She is shy, you see. Very humble."

Mai smiles. "But I think she is also pleased that Father likes it so much that he wanted it in this room."

"It's an amazing painting," I say. "I can see where you get your…" My face flushes.

"Mai's good looks?" Samuel teases.

"Father!"

Tex giggles as he cartwheels himself up onto the leather love seat. He leans into its corner and rests his muscled arm on the rest. "Mai be a fish out of ocean missing you," he says, looking at Mai for a reaction, his fondness for her obvious.

"Tex!"

Samuel places his hand over his heart and sighs dramatically. "It reminds me of a poem. 'If I had a single flower for every time I think about you, I could walk forever in my garden.'" He sighs again.

"Okay, *boys*. I am going to go check on Mother. You stay here and have a giggle party." She looks at me as she passes, winks, and disappears through a doorway.

Samuel snorts a laugh and points toward the sofa. "Please sit down, Sam." He remains standing. "Let me say first off that Tex is privy to everything that happened in Portland. Everything. He has been my friend for over forty years. We met in hell. Somehow he pulled me away from certain death and did so just minutes after losing his legs." My mouth drops open. "You heard that right, Son. He pulled me to safety right after his legs had been blown into a fine, red mist."

I look at Tex, who looks embarrassed by the story. He shrugs and smiles, his eyes not so much. "Tea? I go talk to Ly to make." He launches himself off the sofa and scoots hand over hand across the floor, faster than I walk, and disappears through an arched doorway that must lead into the kitchen.

"He's amazing," I say.

"I sometimes forget how much so," Samuel says with admiration as he looks at the doorway. He looks back at me and smiles as if I caught him at something. "He is a good friend, and a good fighter."

"Fighter. Really?"

"He has a great teacher—me."

I laugh, remembering how Samuel has a way of blending humility with singing his own praises. In this case, the humility is real and the boasts are based on fact. Like my grandfather used to say, if you can brag without lying, then brag. That's Samuel.

"I have seen legless martial artists before," I say. "I know of two who lost theirs in Iraq. They were amazing and made me appreciate what I have. For sure they made me stop complaining about my old knee injury and weak ankles. How long has Tex trained with you?"

Samuel thinks for a moment. "Over thirty years. His skill is quite unique."

I chuckle. "Coming from you that means a lot."

"Did you get in much training after we left?"

"Not as much as I would have liked. There was the grand jury to contend with, three long days on the stand. After each session, I would go home and sleep from six at night until seven the next morning. I had to talk about the shooting everyday, relive it everyday, and I'd dream about it every night. I knew that if I could train a little, even just stretch, it would be helpful, but I had no energy for it. None."

Samuel sits silently, looking at me for a moment, his hands folded on his lap. "The fourteenth Dali Lama said, 'Through violence, you may solve one problem, but you sow the seeds for another.' In your case, you did solve the problem of the evil person, but other problems were created by that action." He raises his palm. "Do not take that as a condemnation of what you did. Your intention was right action, which is one of the aspects of Buddha's Eight Fold Path. But even with right action—well—sometimes shit happens.

"Remember in Portland when I told you that when I was with the Green Berets, I got fourteen confirmed kills? There were more but that is the number confirmed. Each one was in the heat of battle; each enemy soldier was trying to kill me or my brothers. I was using right action, but each one caused me great problems; each one haunted me for a long time… sometimes they still do."

Samuel pauses and looks at Kim's painting for a moment. "Each man had a family, you see, who suffered when he did not come home to them. But with the death of each enemy, one or many of my men lived. But someone who loved those I killed suffered pain of the heart. But with each life saved, another wife, another child, another mother did not suffer." He shrugs, glances toward the foyer and back to me. "But but but, eh? This is the terrible burden the warrior must carry."

"Jesus," I whisper, as the full impact of his words hit me.

"And Buddha," Samuel says. "Both great men." He leans forward as if to emphasize his next words. "Son, there are no magic words that will make the pain go away. What I just offered is nothing more than another way to think about it."

We sit silently for a few moments. Sitting together without speaking is something we did a couple of times in Portland. It was never awkward or uncomfortable. In fact, it felt… right. I know he is letting me digest what he said, though it will take a lot longer than a few quiet moments. A lifetime?

"Or longer," he says.

"Dang! I keep forgetting that you can do that."

"Samuel bobs his eyebrows. "He-he. Not all the time and with only a few people. Like I told you before, it is easier with you because we are blood." He thinks for a moment. "Do you know who Pema Chodron is?"

I shake my head.

"She is an American woman, in her eighties now, I think. She is an ordained nun in Tibetan Buddhism. She wrote, 'It isn't what happens to us that causes us to suffer; it is what we say to ourselves about what happened.'"

"Hmm, I like that." I chuckle, thinking about my shrink. Samuel knows about her. "Doc Kari would agree."

"Did she help you?"

I nod. "She's a tough gal who takes no prisoners and suffers no b.s. from her patients, which is good since she has to deal with pig-headed cops all the time. Seriously, she's good, and she always seems to find the right thing to say to make me feel better."

"It sounds like she is a good sensei, a good guide. You probably know this, but one of the definitions of sensei is one who points the way."

"I do. Sort of like a wise father."

Wow, I just referred to him for the first time as my father. His eyes flicker with surprise, while mine, I'm sure, are less subtle. To be accurate, I didn't actually say, you're my father, but it was pretty darn close. Straight from the subconscious, I'm guessing.

"Tea come," Tex says, slapping quickly across the floor toward the love seat.

"More on this later, Son," he says, his eyes blinking rapidly.

"Before you sit back down, Tex," Samuel says. "I told Sam about your martial arts and he doesn't believe me."

"What?" I say loudly. "Tex, I never—"

Samuel laughs. "I am kidding, Tex. But would you mind a short demonstration?"

The legless man plops his lower torso on the floor, leans on one hand, and makes little chopping motions with his other hand. "Heee-yah! Your father teach me that."

"Everyone is a comedian," Samuel says. "How about you throw a roundhouse kick at Tex?"

"Uh…"

"Well said, Son. But give him a kick and do not go easy."

Tex nods, "Fast better," he says. "Easier for me." He centers himself on me, his torso planted on the floor, arms raised, palms forward. When he smiles, it's with his mouth, not his eyes.

I'm not a stranger to Samuel's somewhat freaky fighting style, so I'm a tad reluctant to do this. But I'm the son so I have to. I stand and shake my legs a little to rid some of the stiffness from twenty-some hours of flying. Tex is motionless, still doing that stony-eyed smile thing.

I skip up with my back leg and snap out a lead-leg roundhouse to the man's head. He ducks it easily and steps hand over hand behind my kick.

He nods a couple of times. "Pretty kick. Pretty slow. More fun time for me when kick fast. You can do fast, right?"

"Yes," I say, my machismo tweaked a little. "I wasn't sure how fast you wanted."

"Fast, Son," Samuel says. "Do not insult Tex. You will not like it if he gets insulted. That is a variation from what David Banner says in *The Incredible Hulk*."

I was just thinking that I've yet to hear a movie quote from him.

"I was going to wait a while," he says, unnerving me. "Now kick him!"

I shuffle step to confuse him as to which leg is kicking, then fire a fast lead-leg round at his waiting, smiling face, which is no more than three feet off the floor. He ducks again, but this time snaps up an arm and hooks my leg in the crook of his elbow as it passes over him. The weight of his hanging half body pulls my kick to the floor, but not before he swings on it like a monkey on a vine and loops around it to slam his torso stump into my chest. The impact feels like I've been hit by a battering ram and I'm the Middle Ages' castle door he's trying to break down. It sends me sprawling onto my back. Fortunately, I tuck my chin to keep the back of my head from colliding with the stone floor.

Tex is standing now, or whatever he calls what he does, on my abdomen. He's actually heavier than he looks making it hard for me to get a complete breath. Just as I think that he is going to jump up and down and screech in triumph, he reaches out and tweaks my nose with his thumb and forefinger.

"That is what Mr. Miyagi did in *Karate Kid*," Samuel says excitedly. "You saw that one, right, Son?"

I choose to ignore the question. Tex scoots off me and pulls my arm to help me sit up. "That was amazing," I wheeze. "Very creative. You might have mentioned that it involved a take-down on a stone floor."

"Sorry," he says, dusting off my back.

"That is a good point, Tex," Samuel reprimands. Then to me, "Usually when he does that defense, he climbs up the kicker like a spider and makes like Buddy Rich."

"Who?"

"Old time band drummer. He was known in music for having the world's fastest hands."

Tex apologizes again, and says, "Kick very fast. Surprised me. I did not expect you to kick a man with no legs so fast."

Samuel laughs at that and helps me to my feet. "He is a real card, no?"

"Samuel," Tex says. "You please tell panther story."

Samuel chuckles. "Okay." He looks at me and winks. "He identifies with this. It is a story about a wise old dog and a hungry panther. One day an old German shepherd dog was in a forest chasing rabbits when he discovered that he was lost. As he tried to find his way back, he spotted a panther moving quickly in his direction with a look in its eyes like he just found his lunch.

"The old dog thought, 'Oh, oh. I'm in deep poo-poo.'"

Tex laughs uproariously. "'Poo-poo.' That funny."

Samuel smiles patiently at his friend. "Anyway, about then, the old dog found some bones on the ground. He quickly laid down with his back toward the approaching panther and began chewing on them. Just as the panther was about to leap, the old German shepherd smacked his lips, and exclaimed, 'Boy, that was one delicious panther. I need to find another to eat.'

"Hearing this, the young panther, with a look of terror on its face, stopped in mid-attack and slinked quickly away into the trees.

"As he was trying to calm himself after such a close call, a squirrel who had witnessed what had happened, saw a way to put his new found knowledge to use and trade it for protection.

"So the squirrel went to the young panther, told him what the dog did, and made a deal with him.

"The panther was embarrassed and angry that he was made a fool of, and said, 'Get on my back, squirrel, and watch what I do to that old dog.'

"The old German shepherd once again spotted the panther creeping toward him, this time with a squirrel on his back. So the dog quickly devised a plan. Instead of running, the wise dog sat down with his back to the panther and the squirrel, and acted as if he hadn't seen them.

"Just as they were close enough to hear, the old German shepherd said, 'Where's that squirrel? I sent him away an hour ago to bring me another panther to eat.'"

Tex laughs hard, a sort of high-pitched cackle. "Understand, Sam? It means... I do not know how to say. Tell him what means, Samuel."

"Okay," Samuel says, smiling at his friend. "The moral of the story is you should not mess with old dogs because the years have given them much smarts, much b.s. ability."

I laugh and Tex extends his hand for a fist bump.

A middle-aged woman dressed in a white *áo dài* and white pants enters the room carrying a tray of cups, a teapot, and what looks like white face masks, the kind that fit over the mouth and nose.

"Thank you, Ly," Samuel says, picking up the masks. He hands one to Tex and one to me. "Mother is coming to meet you so we need to put these on. TB is very communicable."

I wear these when I mow my lawn because of my allergies, but I didn't expect to wear one here. Mai enters a moment later, pushing a woman in a wheelchair, both are wearing masks. The woman's eyes find mine.

\*

"Please sit down, Sam," Kim says, with just a touch of an accent. She's wearing a rich burgundy *áo dài* over white satin pants. She's more frail than in the painting, but the TB hasn't dimmed her beauty. Actually, her mask underscores her incredible eyes. I sit on the long sofa and she gestures for Mai to push her up until we're nearly knee to knee. Sam has joined Tex on the love seat and Ly is nearby preparing the tea. "Mai did not exaggerate. You are quite handsome and your body is well developed."

About to sit, Mai quickly straightens, her face suddenly crimson. "Mother!"

"Sit down, Mai," Kim says with merriment in her voice. "I love to tease my girls."

Mai sighs and does as she's told.

"I am glad to meet you, Sam. Your father has been very excited since he found you." She gestures with her chin. "So has my daughter."

Mai sighs again, plops herself down and folds her arms across her chest.

The delicate white cups filled, Ly carries the tray over, stopping in front of me. I'm not sure of the protocol. Shouldn't Kim take one first?

"Please," Kim says, apparently seeing my awkwardness. "Take a cup. It is a very special green tea. Mai said that you would like it. It is most good for you."

"Thank you. I love green tea."

When everyone has a cup, Kim lifts hers. "*Một, hai, ba, yo!*" she says loudly. Everyone takes a drink from their cups. I follow.

"That means one, two, three, down the throat," Mai says. "It is said when drinking alcohol but Mother says it to welcome you."

"It is more fun with alcohol," Kim says with a wink. "It is sad, but my doctor says that I cannot drink because of all the medicine I take."

I'm liking this woman. Bet she was a feisty one when she was younger, a trait I can see Samuel liking, and one I like in Mai. He seems to have relinquished the floor to his wife.

"You will be staying with us, of course," she says.

"Oh I don't want to be a bother. I have a reservation at the Majestic Hotel that—"

"No, no," Kim says, waving me off. "Your father has fixed a room in the small building in the back of the house. It is very comfortable. This will allow more time for you to visit and for us to know each other." She looks over to Ly who has been standing dutifully by the tea tray. "So sorry. This wonderful lady is Ly. She lives with us. She makes things run smoothly around here and she…" She says something to Samuel.

"Doubles," he says.

"Sorry," Kim says to me. "I did not know that word. She doubles as my nurse."

Ly's eyes crinkle into a smile. She nods.

"Ly," I say.

"She helps me and so do my wonderful daughters. And of course my Samuel." She smiles at him. "Tex is responsible for everything outside the house, the parking area, the back garden, the fish pond, and he helps Samuel with the old soldiers. We consider Ly and Tex important members of our family. Loved members of our family. Now we also have you, and I welcome you."

I bow slightly. "Thank you so much. I am excited to be here and honored to stay with you. I have been looking forward to it for weeks."

Kim returns my nod, her eyes studying me. Clearly, this woman is the hub of the wheel around here. The power of her presence when she first came into the room camouflaged for a moment just how pale she is, and how deep the lines are around her eyes. But there is no hiding the clarity in them, the intelligence, and the watchfulness.

"Mai is my oldest daughter, Sam, and she is everything to me." Kim's tone is just short of driving home a point. "She is much more than a beautiful woman. She is attracted to you—"

"Mother, please," Mai says, without raising her downcast eyes.

"Aaaand," Kim continues, hushing her daughter with a raised palm, "because she is attracted to you I have concerns. I can tell you that a mixed-race relationship is not easy. There are many, uh, obstacles. Problems. Your father and I have experienced them all, and still do occasionally. I want to protect my child, all of my children, but I also recognize that she is a thirty-three-year-old woman, one who is highly intelligent, educated, and experienced. I trust her judgment. Still, I am a mother and mothers worry."

"Thank you for explaining your feelings, Kim. I'm not a mother but I understand as much as is possible. My mother worried about me all the time, especially when I joined the police department." Kim's eyes don't just look at me; they watch me, like a mother lioness. "I promise you that my intentions are honorable." Okay, that sounded stupid. "What I mean is that I'm very fond of Mai, and I will treat her with respect and kindness." That was lame too, but it's all I got on such short notice.

"What year were you born?" she asks.

Curious question, and abrupt. "Uh, nineteen seventy-four."

She nods, looking intently at me. "In the Vietnamese zodiac, you are a tiger. Quick to anger, indecisive, but you can easily, uh…" She looks at Samuel but figures it out before having to ask. "Accommodate. You can easily accommodate your personality to fit the situation. Is that you?"

I chuckle, but cut it off when she remains serious. "I think that is about right. I do see the negative things in myself and I'm trying to fix them."

"I see," Kim says, not giving away if she thought that answer was a little too good, which it kind of was. "Mai is a dragon. Interesting that you are a policeman, because it is dragons that are the protectors and usually a symbol of the male. Dragons are short-tempered and stubborn."

"Uh oh," I say, glancing at Mai. She smiles then raises her eyebrows threateningly.

Kim watches me as she sips from her cup. "Tigers, dragons, pigs. I think the zodiac is a lot of bullshit, but it is interesting, is it not?"

I start to smile, but stop myself when she doesn't. "Yes, very. I don't believe in it much either."

"I see," she says, eyeing me. "That answer was very tiger. What if I had said that I believed in it? What would you have said?"

I swallow hard. "I uh… I would have probably agreed with that too."

She nods. "I like your honesty, Sam. It is rare these days, is it not? I like you, so understand that you do not have to, what is that phrase? Kiss up?" Samuel nods. "Do not kiss up to me. Be honest and we will be fine, you and I."

"Yes, ma'am."

Kim nods once and watches me a moment longer before turning to Ly. "I am tired and would like to go back to my room now." She looks back to me. "Your father will inform you of the, uh, situation with Lai Van Tan. I am afraid you have come at a dangerous time." When Ly starts to back up her chair, Kim raises her hand to stop. "I am happy to meet you, Sam. I am happy that Samuel has his son."

I stand quickly, bow. "I am very pleased to meet you. Thank you for welcoming me to your home. I look forward to talking with you again."

She nods regally and wiggles her fingers at Ly.

"Subtle, is she not?" Samuel says, after Ly has rolled Kim through the archway. "But do not worry. She likes you. If she did not, she would have eaten your face down to your skull." He stands. "Mai, Tex, I am going to take Sam to the garden."

Tex scoots off the sofa and, incredibly, lands softly on his hands. He extends his right one. "Nice for you to meet me," he says. I try not to smile and I say the same thing in return. He hand-slaps out the front door.

"Sam, you must be exhausted," Mai says.

"More than exhausted. I got a thick fog in my head, and my stomach feels like I've eaten a bushel of green apples. I could go to sleep right now but I'm too excited to see both of you, and to see Vietnam."

Samuel and Mai both nod. "It is seven thirty now," Samuel says. "I want to show you the layout in the back, then we will move your things into your room and you can crash if you want. Do they still say 'crash' for sleep?"

I smile. "It's a little dated but I think most would understand."

"Mai, please finish the books for the Cholon store. I need to take them to Lin in the morning. Then join us in the dining room in thirty minutes. Sam, would you like a bowl of *phở* before you crash?"

"Yes, that would be wonderful."

"See you in thirty minutes, Sam," Mai says with a smile that makes my heart rev up like one of those motorbikes.

*

I follow Samuel through the archway.

"This is the dining room," he says, moving around a gorgeous, black lacquered dining room table that must be ten feet long. One entire wall has been painted an abstract of what looks to be Saigon at night. The artist has used reds, yellows, and blacks to depict a chaotic scene of excitement, movement, and happy faces jammed in a congestion of pedestrians, cars, and motorbikes.

"I think I was in that a little while ago," I say.

"No doubt," Samuel says. "You will eventually get used to it as well as to the noise. Come this way."

I look out a sliding glass door at the darkness beyond. "It would still be light in Portland."

Samuel laughs as he slides open the door. "Many differences here."

I follow him out onto a small cobblestone porch that overlooks a walled yard that is at least twice the size of my backyard. Artfully laid ground lighting follow stone paths that wind around groves of bamboo, illuminate large stone lanterns, show off towering palm trees, and encircle a large pond. On the left side of the yard, sparser lighting reveals a one-story building, beige, I think, separate from the main house and partially concealed by a long hedge. The structure extends to the rear of the yard. That must be where I'll be bedding down.

"Beautiful, Samuel, absolutely incredible. It reminds me of Hawaii. Are there *koi* in the pond?"

"Yes, come look." He points at a cluster of sandals at the side of the porch. "Please choose a pair. The bigger ones are mine. I think they will work for you." They're too small but I don't say anything. We move down the half dozen steps and follow the lit stone pathway to the pond. "I know how much you like to play in *koi* ponds" he says.

I nod, remembering the desperate "playtime," slip-sliding around while trying not to get clobbered by a drug-crazed behemoth.

"Here," he says, gesturing to a single stone bench. "Let us sit. There are nine *koi*. Three of them are over fifty years old; one is my age, sixty-five, that one there, the mostly white one with the black spots on its head."

"They're magnificent," I say, looking at the color-splashed fish twist and turn.

"Yes, they are. In Japanese folklore, the *koi* represents a symbol of strength and bravery. It is said that it first shows its courage by battling its way up a waterfall. When it is caught, it shows its bravery again as it lies still on the cutting board, awaiting the knife like a samurai facing a sword. In ancient China, legend tells of how any *koi* that succeeded in climbing the water falls, a point called Dragon Gate on the Yellow River, would be transformed into a dragon. The *koi* represents the will, you see, the will to go against hardship to reach its destiny. And the dragon, of course, represents power and ferocity."

"Interesting," I say, watching the white one swim circles around the others. When Samuel doesn't say anything for a moment, I look up at him. He's watching the white *koi* too.

"Their journey is like ours, no?" he asks. "Yours and mine?"

My eyes mist over. Hope he doesn't notice.

"My sifu, Shen Lang Rui, has taught me many things over the years. I was a mess after I was released from prison. My head case… is that still the expression?"

I nod. "Dated. Very nineteen sixties, but I understand."

"Thank you. My head case was not because of the four years I spent in prison. My experience there was hard but not impossibly so. In fact, it led me to my teacher, and for that I am grateful. No, it was the haunting of the men I killed. Sifu's training me in the martial arts and teaching me meditation techniques helped me through the pain. After about three years, I think it was, when my head was on straight again, he told me to get a tattoo of a *koi*, to celebrate my progress."

"For overcoming obstacles."

"Yes. Sifu is a Buddhist… actually, he's Christian too… but speaking from the Buddhist part, he said that the *koi* represented my struggle against suffering. So I did as he told me."

"You did?"

"Yes, and about ten years after that, which was about twenty years ago, he told me to add a dragon tattoo to it."

"To represent your power and fierceness."

"No, I am a pussy cat. It was to represent my journey with him in the martial arts, my training in the way of the Temple of Ten Thousand Fists style."

"Like a belt promotion."

"It was. And the tattoo had to be specific."

"Where is it?" It's not on his arms or his upper body. I know because I saw him with his shirt off. I shudder slightly remembering the old bullet hole scars all over his chest and the long-healed whip marks on his back.

"On my leg," he says, standing. He moves over next to a ground light and, without a moment's hesitation or an ounce of modesty, drops trou. With his slacks bunched up around his ankles—thankfully he's wearing boxers, white ones with little red hearts—he pivots his right leg, revealing muscles that aren't large but are quite defined. The tat has faded some but the myriad colors are still breathtaking. The fat, red- and black-scaled *koi*, its body curved in mid-zig, covers Samuel's entire calf, its tail overlaps his Achilles tendon, its open-mouthed head just below the bend of his knee. Circling the *koi* is a ghostly serpentine body of a lightly tinted red- and green-scaled dragon. "The dragon is emerging, you see?"

"Beautiful. Makes the black belt seem rather drab."

"No, no," he says pulling up his pants. "By the way, Kim bought these boxers for me."

"Suuure."

He sits back down next to me. "The black belt and my tattoo are both about struggle and conquering it. Facing weaknesses and overcoming them. Learning about ourselves and fixing what needs to be fixed."

What a pleasure it is to listen to him. The week we spent together in Portland was insane and didn't allow for much time to get to know each other. Fate dropped us back into each other's lives and then all hell broke loose. Before we had a chance for a sit-down, he and Mai had to fly home. When I thought about him here, I imagined something like we are doing right now:

talking, listening, being together. It's also how I imagined that he lived, not the opulence of this house, although Mai told me that they owned a number of jewelry stores, but rather him surrounded by family and enjoying his life.

"Do you like this?" Samuel asks, gesturing at the yard.

"It's such a peaceful place," I say. "I can barely hear the traffic. You no doubt meditate out here?"

"At least once a day, usually two times. I sometimes work out over there behind that far grove of bamboo."

"That a heavy bag?" I say squinting toward a part of the yard where there are fewer ground lights. "It's huge."

"Yes, three hundred pounds. We will play on it when you are rested. When I train with Sifu, we often go to a nearby cemetery. We have trained in many of them over the years. He likes cemeteries because they are usually shaded and quiet. He also says that they are convenient because if he kills me by mistake, he doesn't have to carry me anywhere. That is his idea of humor."

I laugh. "Fun guy."

"Well, sometimes not so much." Samuel stands. "Let us walk a little."

He clasps his hands behind his back and looks around the yard, his face relaxed, at peace. I start to mimic his posture, but stuff my hands into my pants pockets instead. He moves along the side of the pond and hesitates when he reaches the end. He looks at the swirling creatures, frowns, and studies them for a moment.

"Peace starts within, does it not? Even when it is hard to find externally, in the world I mean, there is always one quiet place to seek refuge." He taps his chest. "That place is inside of us." He smiles. "I am touching my fingers to my heart, but in reality, the peaceful place is here." He taps his head. "Sometimes we need help to reach that quiet place. I have found that this small backyard helps me get there. I have also found it sitting on a river bank, resting under a tree and, a few times, I have found it sitting in the middle of a traffic jam."

"I don't know if I'm ready to seek it in one of your traffic jams, but I can see how it would work in this garden. Palm trees, even. I never thought of them in Vietnam."

"Oh yes," Samuel says looking up at the closest one. "And these are particularly interesting, they grow video cameras."

He points toward the top of a lofty palm that reigns over the yard a few paces in front of us. "Look between the two lowest limbs there on the right. It is hard to see in the dark."

"I see it. Video security?"

"It is one of twelve cameras. Come." He leads me around the hedge, and onto a cobblestone pathway, toward the beige building. Each of the three doors is illuminated by a yellow bug light. "The structure is somewhat like a triplex, you see. You will stay in the center one. We will move your luggage in there shortly. Tex stays in the first one. It is the last cottage I want to show you right now."

"*Chào* Samuel," a short, stout man says opening the door before Samuel knocks. He looks to be older than Samuel, wearing tan shorts, sandals, and a white tank top. The skin on his left forearm is lighter colored and smooth in some places, darker and heavily wrinkled in others—scars of a severe burn. Tucked into his waistband, a Glock 9.

"*Chào* Lam," Samuel says returning a bow. "This is my son Sam. Sam, this is Lam. He works the day shift but he is working a few extra hours tonight. He's an old soldier."

Bet that's where he got the burn. Lam extends his hand.

"Please meet you," he says with a nod. I say the same.

"Lam is my main security man." Samuel jerks his head toward the room. "He set this up for us."

"*Beaucoup* monitor, number one," Lam says, with a smile that reveals only a couple of teeth. He steps aside and gestures toward all the screens. "Plenty monitor. No muther fuck get inside."

"Fuck-*er*," Samuel corrects.

Lam nods, embarrassed. "Fuck-er. Sorry, English bad."

I fight a smile. "No, no. Your English is very good. My Vietnamese is nonexistent."

Lam frowns and looks at Samuel who says something in Vietnamese, probably translating. Lam smiles and shakes my hand again. "No sweat. I help you."

"Okay," I say. "*Cám ơn.*"

"Yes, yes," Lam says, nodding. "You say 'thank you.' Very good." He turns to the large flat screen monitors, six of them evenly spaced around a long semicircular desk. He gestures for me to follow him to the other side to see the screens. "See everything," he says, pointing at them. He sits and centers himself on the six screens.

"Each screen is split vertically to show two locations," Samuel says. "For example, the one on the right shows the outside gate where you came in. When one of us walks or drives up, we just show our face and the man in here opens the gate. The next one shows the outside doors to the living room. Each of these other screens show various locations around the backyard, and the other three show different angles on the outside wall. We have cameras mounted on four outside buildings, you see." The screen changes to another view. "We get a new angle every fifteen seconds, and we can freeze a shot for as long as we want. There, that is the gate you and Mai came through earlier. Watch." He clicks the mouse and the camera zooms in so tight that I can see the bumps in the black paint.

"Very impressive," I say. "What happens if Lam sees someone trying to get in somewhere? Do you call the police?"

"It depends. I'll explain more about that later. I do have people on the outside of the walls."

"Will your people confront intruders?"

Samuel smiles. "You are always the policeman." He steps over next to Lam and touches his shoulder with affection. "We are all getting old, but we are still soldiers. Lam served in the same unit as Tex. Both worked with my Green Berets near Cambodia." Samuel turns toward me, his face chiseled, eyes like those in a stuffed deer. "If someone comes onto this property to hurt my family or my friends, that person's heart will cease to beat where we find him."

I saw that look on his face in Portland. He isn't blowing smoke.

"So all this is to defend against Lai Van Tan?"

"Mostly, yes," he says, his face softening. "If it were just me, I would live in a small village somewhere by the sea. I do not need a house like this, or this kind of high tech security. But I have a family—a wife, children, friends who stay or live here, part time and full time. I must protect them from Lai Van Tan and, of course, from others who want what is in the house.

"Sometimes in life we have to make concessions, do we not?" he says, leaning against the desk and folding his arms. "My family is everything to me, Sam. I will do anything to make them happy and safe. Buddha said, 'If you light a lamp for someone else it will also brighten your path.' Very true. It makes me happy to make my family happy."

A blink ago, his eyes were those of a predator, now they are filled with love. I wonder what it would have been like to have been raised by him. I bet I wouldn't have been the obnoxious teen that gave my mother such a hard time. On the other hand, to quote Popeye, "I am what I am."

Lam says something in Vietnamese and Samuel turns to look at an exterior screen. It shows two men, both wearing dark pants and white overshirts, standing side by side, their backs to the wall. The one on the left is smoking a cigarette and the other is drinking from a can. The exterior lighting bathes them in tungsten orange.

"Maybe just two men taking a break from whatever they are doing," Samuel says, his eyes watching the screen intently. The one smoking says something and the other laughs and pats the smoker's shoulder. They hang out for a few minutes, talking, laughing, before shaking hands and walking off in opposite directions.

Samuel turns to me. "It appears to be nothing. We have only been in this house for a few weeks so we are still new to it and maybe a little hypervigilant. Much of our tension is because we are unclear about what is happening with Lai Van Tan. Kim's brother, Lu, has an inside source who says that the man is hungry for revenge. It doesn't matter to Lai that the death of his son resulted from the orders he gave, or that his son and his partner were the cause of their own demise. His twisted reasoning makes him even more dangerous."

"You said in our last email exchange that he hasn't done anything since you've been back from Portland. Why do you think that is?"

Samuel shrugs. "Maybe he is just stewing on it, maybe he is making plans to do something and he doesn't want to bungle it as his people did in Portland. Maybe maybe maybe. I do not know. That said, I do not believe that he will make a big attempt, such as storming our walls, because it would get too much attention from the government, the police, and the media. I think he will try to pick us off when he thinks we do not expect it, and he will do it low key. That is another maybe. Desperate people are capable of desperate things, like storming walls."

I watch Lam zoom in on a woman walking by the front gate. She stops, looks through the bars, and moves on. Lam restores the screen to normal view and moves his gaze to another monitor.

"Just wondering," I say, looking back to Samuel. "Mai picked me up at the airport by herself. No worries about that? I mean, you have all this video security but then she is driving around town."

"Good concern. As we saw in Portland, these people are terrorists, but we choose not to be terrorized. We go about our daily business, but always in high alert. I trust Mai's abilities. She has been well trained."

"I remember," I say. She caught me off guard two or three times in my school with her extraordinary speed. Her techniques were a bit fancy-smancy for my taste, but she did them flawlessly and made them work. And when she had to use her techniques in a real fight for our lives, her skill and viciousness were disturbing. When the timing is right, I want to ask her about that. Or maybe I'll ask Samuel.

"Mai has great skills," Samuel says proudly. "I know my daughter was alert to everything around her on her journey to the airport, at the airport, and on her way back. But I wonder, Sam," he says with a slight smile, his head tilted a little. "I wonder how observant *you* were."

"What do you mean?"

"Did you notice anything about Mai when she picked you up?"

Oh man, did I, but I'm guessing that's not what he's talking about. "Not sure what you mean."

"Good," Samuel says. "She even fooled the veteran police officer, a trained observer. She was carrying a Glock 26, nine millimeter handgun in an ankle holster."

He laughs at the surprise on my face. "You were in good hands, Son."

I chuckle and shake my head. "She never fails to amaze me."

"I would have gone with her, but one of the old soldiers in the home died two days ago. I was attending his funeral. He had been a member of the *Thủy Quân Lục Chiến,* the Republic of Vietnam Marine Corps. He served in the two hundred fifty-eighth Marine Brigade, fifth Battalion. The 'Black Dragons' they called themselves. Poor man had never got over the horrors he had seen. That is, until the last five years of his life when Alzheimer's removed his terrible memories. The disease was a blessing of sorts, I think."

"I am anxious to hear more about the soldiers' home, and see it."

"Tomorrow. You look like you could sleep a week."

"Two weeks, actually. About Lai Van Tan, do you think he knows that I'm here now?"

"I think he knows the color of your underwear."

"Oh man."

"About those 'maybes' I mentioned earlier?"

"Yes?"

"There is one more. Maybe he will act now, be more

motivated now that you are here." I must have a pained expression on my face because Samuel adds, "I am sorry. I know you came here to help clear your head."

"Yes, and get to know you and Mai better, and meet Kim and my sisters. But I don't want to add to the risk. I don't want anyone to be hurt because I'm here."

Samuel smiles. "We will deal with it, Sam. That is what warriors do, no? And we will deal with it as a family, and you have a big family here. Besides, even if you had not come, he would have done something eventually. Your presence might hurry him up. Or maybe not. Maybe, maybe."

I get what he's saying about the inevitable, but it still bothers me that my presence might be the cause of someone getting hurt, or worse. I don't need any more of that.

"You hungry? I think the *phở* is ready for us. Lam, Ly will bring you some shortly."

"*Cám ơn*," Lam says with a salute. "Oh, Sifu come tonight?"

"No," Samuel says, opening the door. "We will let Sam rest. I think tomorrow my teacher will come."

"*Trời ơi!*" Lam says shaking his head. "Sifu same like wind."

Samuel smiles. "He is indeed, sir. He is indeed."

Samuel closes the door behind us and once again we're out in the wet heat. Alex, a Vietnam veteran-cop-partner, used to say that it would get so hot here that the water buffalo would evaporate. I believe it.

Samuel is chuckling. "Lam gets frustrated because Sifu has shown up three times without being seen on the monitors."

I shake my head, not understanding.

Samuel shrugs. "I do not know how he does it. I come out into the backyard and there he is, feeding the *koi*. I think he does it because he can and to annoy Lam. Sifu likes jokes."

*

Mai enters the dining room and kills in her black satin pants and white blouse. I saw lots of women wearing the same thing on our way here this morning but none looked so breathtaking.

"Mother is sleeping," she says, sitting down. "Ly will take her something when she awakens."

"I hope my presence has not tired her," I say.

"On the contrary… that is the right word?" I nod. "On the contrary. She looked forward to meeting you very much. And she insisted on doing so dressed and out in the living room." She smiles shyly. "Mother liked you very much."

I smile at that and Mai's smile fills the dining room.

Samuel shakes his head with mock disgust.

Ly sets steaming bowls of *phở* in front of us and a plate heaped with spring rolls in the center of the table.

Mai points at my bowl. "This *phở* contains vermicelli noodles, sliced beef, bean sprouts, chopped peanuts, and mint leaves." She picks up a small bowl of red sauce and places it in front of me. "Please add bean and chili sauce to your taste, and squeeze in the fresh lime wedge juice to your taste. Oh, and please have the spring rolls. They are called *gỏi cuốn* in Vietnamese. The outside is rice paper and inside is sliced cold shrimp, mint leaves, and cold vermicelli noodles." She sets a small bowl of nearly clear, orange liquid next to my bowl. "Please dip the rolls in this sauce called *nước mắm*."

"Oh, man," I say around a mouthful of spring roll. "I could get used to eating this way."

"You will have to," Mai and Samuel say simultaneously.

Twenty minutes later, as Ly removes the dishes and Mai fills our cups with green tea, I ask Samuel how long he has lived in this house.

"Only since we've been back from Portland," he says. "It is not my house; it belongs to a friend."

When Mai and I had pulled into the driveway, she said that her father got it from a friend but I assumed that he had bought it.

"He is quite wealthy. This is just one of four he owns, the other three houses are much larger than this one. He is kindly letting us stay here until the problem with Lai Van Tan is settled." He gestures toward the ornate backyard. "I prefer a small condo to all of this. A small place better suits my personality and is less conspicuous. And inconspicuous is a wise choice when you are a Caucasian living in Vietnam, married to a local woman, and running a successful business."

Mai says, "Father and Mother will retire someday to Châu Đốc, a small town on the water at the edge of the Mekong delta near the Cambodian border."

"We have visited there many times over the years," Samuel says smiling. "We love its quiet, at least quiet compared to the frantic insanity of Saigon. It's a picturesque place known for its fish sauces and catfish export business. Kim and I..." Something passes across his eyes. He looks out into the blackness beyond the sliding glass doors then back to his tea. His voice is softer now, pensive. "We want to spend our remaining years in a peaceful place surrounded by beauty, friendly people, and wonderful food."

Samuel seems so much more in his element here than he was in Portland. For sure, thirty-five years in one place will do that to a person, but in his case it seems like the connection is more... spiritual? Yes, I think that's it. His connection here is more than him being used to the traffic, noise, and crush of humanity. There's something else.

"I love Vietnam," he says, sipping from his cup. "I love the country, the people, the heat, and the intensity of how we live here. I have spent over half my time on earth in this country, and I hope to remain for the rest of my days. In my mind, I am Vietnamese." He looks at me for a long moment, his eyes dancing with remembrance. He looks down at his soup and back to me. "It's ironic," he says softly. "This country that enveloped me in such incredible violence, is the place where I have found an inner peace."

"I'm pleased to hear that, Samuel," I say. Mai lovingly pats his hand. "But why? Why here in Vietnam?"

"A good question, Son. To be clear, I did not need to be *here* to find peace. It was within me all the time, you see, and it is within you." He is thoughtful and doesn't rush his words. "But Vietnam is where I was when I found it, and I think being here helped me find it sooner. I do not know for sure because I have only here to compare it to." He smiles at me. "Am I confusing you?"

"I think I understand," I say, meaning it.

"Then maybe you can explain it to me," he says with a chuckle. "What I do understand for certain is that now I must be mindful of doing good, doing it every day. I cannot change what happened in the past, but I can do what is right today."

We slurp our tea, comfortable without words. I know that there will never be a sudden "aha" moment that makes everything all right for me, but I've learned over the years that words are powerful, that they can heal, or at least start the healing process. Samuel has been there, done that, and come to terms with it. I hope to learn from him and come to terms with what I've done.

"Have I showed you my teacup trick?" he says nonchalantly,

munching on a spring roll.

"*Yes* you have, Father," Mai says, pretending exasperation, "And you know very well you have."

"I did?" he says, holding back a grin. "Must be getting old. No memory and I am getting slow."

I snort. "I don't recall you being slow when you switched those teacups... I've never seen such extraordinary speed in my life."

"Really? How about my coin trick? Did I show you that one?"

"Father, I think Sam probably wants to get some rest. Maybe show it to him tomorrow."

"Mai thinks she is clever. She is trying to distract me because she knows that tomorrow I will forget."

I laugh at Mai's feigned innocence, and say, "I am tired but I'd like to see it."

"Good good good," he says, enthusiastic as a child. "Do you have some change in your pocket? Oh, very good. Put all of it on the table here."

I set two nickels, a dime, and two quarters on the bamboo place mat.

"Pick up the dime," he says. "We should stand." We both get up and he moves directly in front of me. "Okay, place the dime in your palm, please. Then hold your open palm out toward me."

I do as he says.

"Mai will count to three. When she says 'three,' I will try to grab the dime before you close your hand into a fist. This is a demonstration of speed from Temple of Ten Thousand Fists style."

When he showed me the teacup trick in Portland, I didn't

see him move at all. I perceived something, a sense of air being displaced, I think, but I didn't actually see him move his hands toward the cup.

"Okay, Sam. When Mai says three, close your hand as fast as you can so I don't get the dime. Okay? Ready? I think I can beat you but I am not sure."

"Yeah, right," I say, looking at Mai who shoots me a you-won't-believe-this look.

"Mai, begin the count." I've seen people play the snatch the coin trick before, but they did it by hovering their hand over the coin. Samuel positions his right hand about eighteen inches away in front of mine, palm down, and his left palm on the table. "I used to do this demonstration with both of my hands on the table," he says with a shrug. "But Father Time is a cruel beast."

"One," she says.

His hands are too fast so it would be useless to watch them. So I'll watch his shoulders. No matter how a person moves, they give it away by moving their shoulders first.

"Two."

My muscles are at a relaxed ready. I talked with Bob Munden once, a guy who holds multiple world records in quick draw with a handgun. He said that he relaxes to about ninety percent before the buzzer sounds the signal for him to draw his gun and fire. He said that any less, like eighty percent, he would be too tense, and any more, like ninety-five percent, he would be too relaxed. He knows what he is talking about: He can draw, fire, and hit the target in less time than it takes to blink.

"Three!"

I snap my hand closed.

I don't see Samuel move, but similar to what happened during the teacup trick, I detect something, a change in the air, a disturbance in the space between our two hands, I'm not sure. Samuel's left hand is still resting on the table and his right is still floating palm down a foot and a half away. It remains open so it couldn't hold a coin, unless he's really good at pinching it somehow in his hand. Wait. Isn't his… yes, I'm sure of it. His right hand is a tad to the right of where it was a moment ago and I think his right shoulder is a little higher. So he did move, it's just that—

The coin. I can still feel the coin in my hand. He didn't get it. I beat him.

I lift my fist in the air and bob my eyebrows at him.

"You are indeed fast, Son," he says seriously, though I detect a twinkle in his eye. "Fast like lightning."

"Oh, Father," Mai says, shaking her head.

I frown. "Uh, okay?" I'm not understanding the demonstration.

"Look at your change on the table, Sam," Mai says.

"A nickel and two quarters. I'm still not understanding…"

Samuel turns over his palm. Empty.

"I know," I say. "I still have the—"

He lifts his left hand off the table, revealing a dime resting on the table. He bobs his eyebrows at me. I look back at the table. Wait. Didn't I set down two nickels?

I slowly uncurl my fingers…

Jefferson's profile mocks me. I'm holding a nickel.

"No—Damn—Way," I breathe.

"Father switched the coins before you closed your fist, Sam."

Wait, he would have had to have grabbed the dime with his right hand because it was closest. But how did he transfer it to his left that was resting on the table? And he would have had to pick up the nickel from the table with his left and transfer…

How is it possible that someone can move that fast?

She laughs. "Your mouth is hanging open."

I look back at Samuel.

"But I didn't see you move."

"Good," he says sitting back down. "My vitamins are working."

*

"Did you bring earplugs?" Mai asks, her lips tickling my ear.

"Yes," I manage, nuzzling the silkiness of her hair. "I did as you told me."

"That is good because the new noises might keep you from sleeping." Her nose is making little circles on the side of my neck. "And it is also good that you obeyed me."

"I must obey you, huh?" I ask, nibbling her earlobe.

"But of course." Her body leans into me. "You have a problem with that?"

"Not even a little bit," I squeak, just before our mouths meet and my head roars like one of the rocket attacks that slammed into Saigon forty years ago.

After we finished our tea, Samuel, Mai, and I sat at the table chatting about Vietnam's weather, politics, crime, customs, and food. When I started to bring up what happened at Portland State University, Samuel lifted his palm, and said, "Let's not talk about that your first day here." And that was fine by me. I just brought it up because it seemed like an elephant in the room.

I was starting to slur my words, and was grateful when Samuel suggested that we carry my luggage to my room and say goodnight. He said it was an hour past his bedtime. He grinned when I asked him if he moves more slowly when he's up late.

That "coin trick" was an amazing feat of speed. I refuse to

think that his hands were invisible, but the more I think about it, it's hard not to. I saw, or perceived, or felt, some kind of movement, plus there was evidence that he had moved. But the fact remains, he carried out a complex maneuver of picking up the nickel, snatching the dime out of my hand, replacing it with the nickel, handing off the dime to his other hand, and moving his grabbing hand back to where it started, hovering about eighteen inches from mine.

After we hauled my luggage to the triplex and Samuel showed me where things were, he shook my hand, and said, "Jet lag is demonic. Get up when you feel like it." As he headed away, he shot Mai a fatherly look that I interpreted as: Listen up, soldier girl. Have your goodnight kiss and then move out sharply to your own room.

For the past half hour, we have been standing outside my door under a bug light chatting, laughing, and laying some lip action. The hedge blocks the view from the house, but we're still under video surveillance by whoever is watching the monitors tonight.

Finally, we separate slowly and painfully as if we were Velcro. Not because we want to, but because we're losing our balance and about to fall onto the cobblestone walkway. It makes us giggle. Yes, euphoric from jet lag and from all that is Mai, I actually giggle.

"I better go in, Sam," Mai says.

I hold her upper arms and step back. "I agree, but I don't want you to. But I agree."

"English is such a hard language to understand."

"I need a cold shower."

"That I understand. And I agree."

Neither of us move.

"Are you going in?" I ask.

"Yes. Are you?"

"Yes."

Neither of us move.

Finally, Mai extends her hand. "I will be the stronger person. Good night, Sam. In Vietnamese good night is *chúc ngủ ngon.*"

"*Chúc ngủ ngon,*" I say, shaking her hand.

"Yes, very good." She pulls me into her for one final, all-too-quick kiss, and a whispered, "*Chúc ngủ ngon.*" Oh man. I've never heard anything so sensual.

She walks quickly to the end of the walkway, turns and shoots me that heart-stopping smile, and disappears beyond the hedge.

"Die-amn!" I say, and step into my room for an ice cold shower.

# CHAPTER FIVE

Usually, I can do full splits, but two days of sitting has tightened my hamstrings and groin muscles so that I'm about a foot short of going all the way down. No problem, my muscles will loosen in a couple of days. I get to my feet and throw a few easy front kicks, some muay Thai roundhouses, and a dozen jab and cross punch combos.

Slept like a baby for eleven hours. The earplugs shut out any strange sounds and the mattress was sent from heaven. A couple of lizards parked on the ceiling above the bed worried me for maybe a minute before I drifted off to la-la land. They could have laid on my lips all night and I wouldn't have known.

I drop down onto my back and rep out fifty jackknife sit-ups, fingers to toes as fast as I can do them. Okay, that's enough. My body doesn't feel quite right yet and my head feels as if it were full of oatmeal. Don't want to burn up what little I got before the day even begins.

My cell rings.

"Reeves," I say, my mind still in Portland.

"Reeves. Nguyen here."

"Smart ass," I laugh.

"I never understood that," Mai says, with feigned confusion. "How can the word smart and ass be in the same sentence?"

"Well, an example might be, Mai Nguyen is very smart and has a great—"

"Okay, Sam. You woke up… feisty. Is that the right word?"

"Frisky. You would say 'You woke up frisky.'"

"Thank you. You woke up frisky today. Do you want some croissant and fruit, and some coffee?"

"That sounds wonderful. I'll be right over after I clean up."

I take the fastest shower ever, get dressed, and I'm out the door six minutes later.

"Did you sleep well, Son?" Samuel asks. He and Mai are seated at the table. Ly sets down a plate of croissants and sliced papaya.

"I think he woke up frisky, Father," Mai says.

He frowns. "Frisky?"

"I slept wonderfully," I say, looking at Mai over the rim of my cup. "Gosh, this is really excellent coffee."

"I am happy you like it," she says, missing my not so subtle change of subject. "It is called *Trung Nguyên*. It is our, uh, domestic coffee."

"It's fantastic. Do you have Starbucks here?"

"No Starbucks," Samuel says, thankfully forgetting the frisky comment. "I like their French Roast but nothing compares to *Trung Nguyên*. Many critics say it is the best in the world. Besides, a cup of coffee here is fifty cents. In America, a Starbucks costs four dollars or more. No Vietnamese here is going to pay that much for coffee."

Mai refills my cup. "It is hot today already," I say, appreciating the ceiling fan.

"Always warm in Vietnam," Mai says. "This is the rainy season now. It will be hot and rainy and... muggy?"

Samuel nods. "Muggy, yes. You have not seen it rain until you see it rain here, Son. The streets flood for a couple of hours and then everything is dry and hot again."

I stuff a piece of croissant into my mouth. "I'm so thrilled to be in Saigon." I wave my hand at the table. "This is all really fantastic. The way you live. Everything. It's not what I expected."

Samuel's face sobers. "We are very fortunate. As you will see, there is great poverty in Vietnam, especially in the countryside. In Saigon, it is not always as obvious, except for street beggars in the core area, and in a few scattered parts of the city. That is because we are the third wealthiest city in all of South East Asia. Others in Vietnam are not the same."

"Father will not say much about it, but he and Mother give much to the poor and to organizations that help people. The old soldiers' home cost much money to operate and Father pays for it himself."

He waves her off. "That is fine, Mai. Everyone helps when they are able."

"That is so not true. You and Mother are extremely generous—"

"Have some more papaya, Sam," Samuel interrupts. "It is quite sweet this time of year. We have many types of fruit here…"

His predator eyes return.

Mai touches his arm. "Father? What…"

He turns toward the glass doors. Did he hear something?

The *Superman* overture tinkles from Samuel's cell.

"Intruder," he says, calmly looking at the screen. "In the yard." He scoots his chair back and stands before the full meaning of his words sink into my still jet-lagged brain. He stands to one side of the glass doors and quick-peeks around its frame.

The *Superman* overture continues.

"Remain here," he says, opening the glass doors.

Mai and I look at each other for a second before getting to our feet. We follow him like the disobedient children we are.

Samuel stops at the top of the landing and looks toward the *koi* pond, his head blocking my view of whatever he is seeing. From the left, Lam is sprinting toward the pond, shouting, his Glock held in a two-handed grip. He sounds pissed.

When I lean out to look around Samuel, I see the back of an elderly man sitting at the end of the cement bench where Samuel and I sat last evening. His posture is calm and relaxed. Incongruently, there is a groaning man lying on the ground next to him, kicking his bare feet and flailing his arms as if he were trying to swim on dry land. The old man is casually patting the back of the prone man's head as if consoling him.

Lam stops behind the bench looking confused as to how to proceed. He says something to the old man. If he got an answer, I didn't hear it.

Samuel moves quickly down the steps and over to his security man. Samuel says something to him and Lam lowers his weapon.

"What's going on?" I whisper.

"I am not sure," Mai says. "Lam asked Sifu if the man gave him trouble. I did not hear what he said."

"That's Shen Lang Rui?" I ask, though Mai just said it was. "Who's the guy on the ground?"

Samuel speaks with the old man, who continues to pat the moaning man's head. The downed guy is doing a great imitation of Olympic swimmer Michael Phelps—sans pool.

"An intruder, I think," Mai says. "I think Sifu caught him. *Slapslapslapslapslap*

Tex streaks hand over hand between Mai and me, bounds down the four steps, and slaps his way over to the others.

Lam jerks the dazed young man to his feet, and is about to smack him, but Samuel steps between them. When Lam lets go, the intruder's wobbly legs give out and he crumples back to the ground. The old man scoots off the bench, kneels on one knee, and touches the front of the man's neck. He rubs it in small, gentle circles. In no time, the man shakes his head and gathers his bearings. Sifu stands and nods to Samuel.

"Shen Lang Rui healed him," Mai whispers with admiration. "So he can stand."

Before I can ask what she means, Samuel and Lam pull the man to his feet, his legs no longer appearing wobbly. Lam wants a piece of the guy so badly that he can barely restrain his twitchy self. I'm guessing that he doesn't like his security breached. A touch on his shoulder from Samuel calms him a little.

Samuel leans in close to the intruder, their noses nearly touching. The young man listens, his face vibrating with fear, then he begins blabbering as if he has only seconds to get it out. Sifu has resumed sitting, his back to the action, once again watching the undulating movements of the *koi*.

I glance at Mai.

She smiles, shrugs. "All this must seem weird to you," she says.

"It doesn't to you?"

"The man is a thief, uh… what you call it… a burglar. Lam said that he came over the wall on the south side. There is a tree on the outside of it that Father is having removed because he thought that something like this could happen."

"He isn't one of Lai Van Tan's people?"

"I think that Father is believing he is just a thief. He is nineteen, he said. Just a stupid boy. He is poor and was looking for something to take to sell."

"Are you calling the police?"

Mai shakes her head. "I do not think Father will want that."

111

"Why not?"

"Father will explain."

"I don't understand about Sifu. Did he catch the intruder?"

"I think so. I think he was holding the thief on the ground waiting for Lam to come. Sifu knew that Lam would see him on the monitors. He always teases Lam by coming in… un… undetected."

I shake my head. "This is crazy. What was he doing to the kid's neck?"

"The patting? It was to hold him down. Sorry, I do not know that nerve technique. It is advanced."

This is all a bit much even if I weren't still jet lagged.

Lam heads back to the monitor room, his gun tucked in his waistband, while Mai and I remain on the porch. Samuel is speaking quietly to the thief, but the hapless kid is trembling like a bumped bowl of Jell-O.

"Father is scaring him," Mai says, "so that he tells other people never to come onto our property. Father says that the next time the old man won't tease him with his kung fu, but he will send him to his ancestors."

Samuel hands the sobbing would-be thief some paper money from his pocket, all the while the boy bows nonstop. Tex hands Samuel a rag from his pocket which Samuel secures over the boy's eyes. A moment later, the two men escort him up the steps, past us, and through the glass door.

"Father gave him money to buy food, and now he takes him through the house and out the front gate. He did not want the boy to see the inside. Father is quite compassionate, no?"

"Has this happened before?"

"First time since we have been here. It is too easy with the tree."

"Sam," Samuel says coming back through the door and moving down the steps, as if the thing with the burglar was no more than a neighbor borrowing a cup of *phở*. "Sorry about the disruption to our breakfast. Let me introduce you."

Sifu has remained seated on the cement bench, his back to us, elbows resting on his knees as he watches the *koi*. At least that's what he appears to be doing. Judging by what Samuel and Mai have told me about him, he might be having a nice chat with the fish.

Samuel stops a respectful distance from the old man and murmurs softly. Sifu stands and turns about. I start to gasp, but manage to stop myself.

His eyes.

I read somewhere about a painting of Jesus in St. Catherine's monastery in the middle of the Sinai Desert. The writer was startled by the painter's depiction of Christ's eyes, how they reflected two different expressions. The left eye conveyed Christ's anger at sin and the right eye depicted his compassion and forgiveness. A monk told the writer to gaze at each eye for a while and reflect on what he felt from each one. The man did and was so moved that he left the monastery forever changed.

It would be strange enough that a Chinese man would have blue eyes or green ones, instead of the usual brown. But Sifu has one of each, one blue and one green. If the mixed colors weren't peculiar enough, the *way* he looks at me is so… It's as if he's seeing into me, seeing into my… being. Like he already knows me, understands me. I want to break eye contact with him, but I can't.

"Son, this is my sifu, Master Shen Lang Rui, founder of Temple of Ten Thousand Fists."

Sifu brings his palms together below his chin in a praying hands gesture and bows his head. "Happy," he says softly.

I return the salutation, feeling oafish. "Nice to meet you."

The master is dressed in tan slacks, a pale blue overshirt and—blue Converse shoes. Samuel wears red ones. They shop together? He's slight, maybe one hundred and fifty pounds, with a mop of healthy salt-and-pepper hair befitting of a much younger man. In fact, his posture, bearing, and his eyes—those eyes!—are of a man in his thirties, twenties even. Mai said once that he is in his mid or late sixties.

Just as I was wondering if I should offer my hand, he extends his, a surprisingly small one, fragile looking, like a dry fall leaf. He covers mine with his left one and moves it up and down slightly. "Happy," he says again, just barely louder than a whisper.

I smile back and… I feel something—a surge of heat beginning at my hand and streaking up my arms, flushing my face, and flooding through my torso and legs. What the hell?

I relax my grip, but he holds onto my hand for a moment longer, his strange eyes interlocking with mine. Then he lets me go. I reflexively step back.

Samuel and his Sifu speak aside for a moment. Samuel nods respectfully.

"Sifu must leave now."

"Oh?" I say, disappointed.

"He just stopped by to meet you. He has to go now to a dentist appointment. He has a toothache."

Don't know why that strikes me funny. I fight to keep it inside. "That's terrible," I say.

"It is okay," Samuel assures me. "Sifu just needs a filling."

I bite the inside of my cheek.

"See you," Sifu says, running the two words together. Again he does the palm-to-palm thing.

He and Samuel head up the steps.

"He is amazing, is he not," Mai says, gesturing for us to sit on the bench.

"I almost laughed about the dentist. A toothache just doesn't fit a man like that."

"Father does not think it is a bad tooth. Sifu sees a regular doctor. The master has not said anything, but Father thinks he might have health problems. It is something that Father senses about his teacher, I think. Maybe Father is per... perceiving something, I do not know. Father is worried, but he has not asked Sifu because he does not want to embarrass him."

"I'm so sad to hear that," I say.

"Yes." Mai sits on the cement bench and gestures for me to do the same. We watch the *koi* for a moment, then, "Tell me, what did you feel when Sifu touched you?"

"I didn't imagine that?" I ask, sitting next to her. The sun is getting hotter and the stirring breeze doesn't help much.

"Did you feel warmness in your body?"

"It started in my hand and moved through me. What was it?"

"*Chi*. You know *chi*, right?"

"Of course. I understand the concept of *chi* as energy flow, life force, that sort of thing. Most demonstrations are fake, though."

Mai nods. "Yes, I have seen false ones on YouTube. When you awoke today, how did you feel?"

"Pretty good. I was still fuzzy brained, though, from the jet lag."

"Was?"

"Yes… Wait."

"No more jet lag?"

I rotate my head a little and look about. "You're right. My head is clear; I feel sharp." I look at her. "He did that? That's crazy."

"He helped you, right?" When I nod, Mai says, "Then maybe not crazy. Sifu does that with my family all the time. He feels something wrong and he tries to make it better. Most of the time you do not have to tell him that something bothers you. He will touch you and he will feel it."

"Amazing," I say, too dumfounded to say anything more intelligent.

Mai sobers. "But he has not been able to help my mother. TB is a very bad problem."

"I'm so sorry, Mai."

"Thank you." We watch the *koi* for a few moments without speaking.

"You might have warned me about his eyes," I say, smiling. "It took me back for a second or two."

"Took you where?"

"It surprised me."

"Oh," she says. "Sorry. I forgot because I see him all my life. Father tell me a long time ago that there is a village in China where people have either blue eyes or green eyes. Some people say that a lost army, a Roman army, maybe two thousand years ago, be in this village. So some people now have blue or green eyes. Sifu got one each." She laughs.

"Amazing. And the way he looked at me, into me."

Mai nods. "It is exciting to see Sifu brings his *chi* to his martial arts skills."

"I can't wait."

"You want to get some tea? We can walk down the street and get some at a sidewalk café. When we get back, I think Father wants to show you some more about our security. It will amaze you."

"So far everything has. Will Samuel join us for tea?"

"No. He has office work to do."

Mai and I go into the house to tell Ly that we're going out. In the parking area, Tex is leaning on one hand and watering a large potted tree with a hose. He nods several times and wishes us a good day.

Mai pushes a buzzer on a concrete column and the double gate opens. It closes behind us with a heavy metallic sound similar to a jail cell door. "This way," she says pointing to the left.

Samuel's house is on a quiet, tree-lined street, quiet compared to the traffic anarchy I saw yesterday. There are not many pedestrians and just a few motorbikes passing each way. About fifty yards ahead I can see where this one feeds into a cross street and, judging by the mass of motorbikes and cars rushing past the opening, it looks like those insanely busy ones I saw yesterday.

Looking at me, Mai says, "Do not be obvious, but do you see that green building to the right across the street?"

"Yes," I say, detecting it out of the corner of my eye.

"There is a man on the top floor. You cannot see him because he is back from the window, but he is one of our security people. We have another man who watches from a car in the alley behind the back wall. I think it was the man in the window who called Father when we were eating at the table."

"Impressive. How do you feel about it, the security I mean? Do you feel safe?"

"Not until all this ends." She points to a woman selling

fruit near the corner. "We buy our fruit from Qui." She smiles and nods at the old woman, who smiles back with bright red lips and teeth. The woman looks at me, laughs, and says something. Mai laughs heartily and waves goodbye.

"What was with her mouth," I ask, when we're a few feet away.

"Oh, you will see that many times. People, especially older women, chew betel nut. It is common here for hundreds of years. They get a little, uh, buzz?"

"Buzz? You mean like a drug high?"

"Yes, yes. Not too strong. But it stains the mouth."

"Interesting," I say, though I really mean weird.

"She say that you are a very handsome man and that you should be in *Playgirl* magazine."

I sputter a laugh. "*Playgirl?* How does she know about that?"

"Popular here," Mai giggles, bobbing her eyebrows.

What a day so far. I meet the most venerable Shen Lang Rui, who *chi*-zaps my jet lag away and now I'm walking with my Mai, talking about *Playgirl*, in Vietnam. It's excellent except for one thing. After another unabashedly staring person passes us, I say, "I feel a little self-conscious."

"It's your size. Everyone looks because you are so big and you have the muscles."

"Also because I'm so good looking?"

"Oh yes," she says, banging me with her shoulder. Small pleasures. I'd like to hold her hand, but I'm guessing that would be a no-no.

"Sifu is an amazing person," she says. "He is about the same age as Father, but our father sometimes thinks of him as his father. Also his brother and his best friend."

"That's wonderful. I still can't believe that Samuel is

sixty-five. If I didn't know, I would have guessed a very fit man of fifty. But he moves better than most people in their twenties."

"You will learn much from both of them. Okay, we turn left here. This street is much busier."

Oh man, this is the bedlam I remember from yesterday. I barely hear Mai laugh over the roar of a million motorbikes.

"Sorry to laugh," she shouts into my ear as we zig and zag around a mass of people on the sidewalk. "Every time I see this through your eyes it cracks me."

"Cracks you?" I shout. "Oh, you mean, 'cracks me up.' Well, I think it's sort of frightening."

"Oh, there is Hung," she says waving at a shirtless, elderly man squatting before a partly dissembled motorbike. He is smeared with grease from his bare feet to his concave chest to his matted hair. "He fixed my motorbike about two weeks ago. He is a very sweet man." She waves as we approach. "Chào Hung."

The old man looks up, his grease-covered face instantly brightening upon seeing Mai. "Mai!" he cries, as he struggles to stand. "*Chào, chào, chào.*"

Mai speaks warmly to him and gestures toward me. The old man nods several times as he presses his greasy palms together. When he smiles, I don't see a single tooth.

"He says he is sorry, but he will not shake hands with you because he is so dirty. But he is happy to meet you."

"Please tell him I am also happy to meet him."

She tells him, and the man responds, then laughs with a cackle.

"Hung say to tell you that he is going to marry me. I am actually thinking about it because he fixed my motorbike very, very good."

"Tell him that he is a wise man."

"Thank you, Sam," she says with phony sweetness. They converse for a moment longer before we nod our goodbyes.

"Sweet man," she says as we proceed bobbing and weaving our way along the busy sidewalk. "He tell me before, that place on the sidewalk has been his bike shop for thirty years. He is ninety-two years old. No retirement here."

"Incredible," I say. "We got it so good in America."

A motorbike jumps the curb five feet in front of us. We wait as the elderly woman driver jockeys her ride across the sidewalk and parks in front of a shop. She looks at me, smiles.

"Here is tea cafe," Mai shouts, pointing to a storefront bearing an overhead sign: Café Eighty-Nine. "In Vietnam, many names of businesses are the same as their address."

The sidewalk tables are occupied so we take one of two empty ones inside, ignoring all the blatant stares from other tea sippers. Happily, the traffic roar isn't as overwhelming in here, so we don't need to shout at one another.

Mai says something to a cute little girl who can't be more than ten or twelve. The girl turns to me for a moment, her expression serious, then it transforms into a huge, brilliant smile.

"I ordered for you," Mai says. "Green tea, of course."

"Thanks." The heat has flushed Mai's face a little. Looks great. "So, good lookin', is this our first date?"

She gives me that Las Vegas lights smile. "I think you are right." She tilts her head down slightly and looks at me from under her eyelashes. "Do you want to touch me as much as I want to touch you?"

I love her straight forwardness. "More." My face feels hot and this time it isn't from Vietnam's heat.

"Impossible," she says, still doing that flirtatious head tilt thing.

Oh man, I must have done something right in a past life.

The young waitress sets down two small cups and a teapot, looking at me the entire time. When I wink at her, her face erupts into that huge smile again. She's going to break a lot of young men's hearts in ten years. She turns and walks away a few steps before looking back at me over her shoulder. She's got the flirting down already.

"Thanks," I say when Mai scoots my full cup over. "You must get looked at a lot. I'm almost six feet and you're practically eye to eye with me."

She shrugs. "I do. But I am used to it. Being tall bothered me when I was in my teens, but I do not care now." She looks up at me from under her naturally long eyelashes. "Did I stare at you when we first met?"

"Oh man, you were shameless."

She giggles. "Well, you were... what do you call it? Oh, yes, eyeballing me first."

"No way."

"You were," she laughs. "I felt violated. That is the right word, right?"

"Yes, but you're soooo wrong. Remember, for a couple of days I thought you were my sister."

She shakes her head in mock disgust. "Then you were an eyeballing pervert."

"Okay," I bring my cup to sip, "maybe I'm guilty on both—"

I'm bumped from behind. My tea sloshes onto the table.

"So sorry," a male voice says, with more laughter in it than apology. I twist around to see two men, mid twenties, both in blue jeans and tank tops, one red and one blue. They pass behind me and sit at the next table over, heads bobbing and smirking contemptuously. Two card-carrying assholes, my cop instincts tell me.

Mai leans toward them and speaks rapidly. Their eyes widen with surprise. They snicker and say something back.

"What's going on?" I ask.

She turns away from them and says in a low voice, "I ask the one who bumped you if he did it on purpose. He said—"

"Ameri-*can*," one of the men says in a tone that's pure challenge. I pivot on my stool to look at them. "Ameri-*can*, right?" says the one in the blue tank top. He said it like, 'You're cow shit, right?' The one in the red tank sucks deeply on a cigarette, his eyes laughing at me.

"I am." I say to Blue Tank. I sip from my cup to show him how calm I am.

"I speak English," he says. He sits straight, his hands fisted on his thighs, his elbows pointing outward as if he's about to spring forward.

The young waitress approaches their table and Red Tank snaps at her, which sends her scurrying away looking as if she were about to cry. You can tell a lot about someone by how they treat servers, especially ten-year-old children.

"Your point?" I ask. He's got a wispy little moustache. Nice effort but it's not working for him.

Mai touches my hand. "Sam—"

Blue Tank says something to her, the words over enunciated, his eyes glaring.

"What's going on? What did he say?"

"Exactly, Ameri-*can*," Blue Tank says. "I live in Saigon and I speak Vietnamese *and* English. You come to Saigon and you don't understand anything. You must ask the bitch."

"Hey pal!" A surge of adrenaline washes through me.

Again, Mai leans forward in her chair toward the two punks, her beautiful face hard, her eyes flashing anger. She rips into them. When she finishes, the two men look at her, Blue Tank's mouth hanging open, Red Tank's cigarette frozen half way to his mouth. Blue Tank recovers first, points at her and sputters into laughter. He even holds his stomach. Red Tank's cigarette finally makes it to his mouth, his eyes studying me as he sucks on it.

"You think you big man, eh?" Red Tank says.

"That's it?" I ask. "That's all you got?" Okay, that's not exactly a diffusing technique, but these guys are starting to wear thin.

Mai rattles something off. She doesn't shout it, but it's clear that she's ripping them a new one, probably about what a lousy welcoming committee they are. Whatever she says quiets them.

Both tank tops look at her, at me, and back to her again. I'm suddenly aware that all the chattering has stopped at the tables. I turn just enough to see in my peripheral that the other inside tea drinkers are watching and that people sitting out on the sidewalk are standing to get a better view. I remember how all the folks in line at the coffee joint in Portland looked at me just before the fat guy punched my face. Maybe there's some cosmic rule that says I'm not supposed to visit coffee and tea joints.

"Sam, we should go," Mai says quietly, scooting back from the table.

Red Tank does that cackle laugh again. Then, "*Con lai!*"

Mai jerks her head toward him, her posture ready to spring.

"*Sam*," Blue Tank mimics in falsetto, though Mai's voice is deeper than his normal one. "*We should go*. Yes, go, Sam. Go with the bitch. Go with *con lai*."

"Hey!" I say, again not sure how I'm going to follow up. I'm out of my element here.

Blue Tank's eyes widen and he makes a wide gesture with his open palms. "Hey. That is all *you* got?"

"Sam?" Mai stands. "Come on. We must—"

"*Con chó*!" Red Tank says, getting up, his eyes trying to burn a hole through me. His buddy stands. Red Tank wiggles his fingers as if shooing me away. "You go *con chó*."

I don't know what that means but it can't be a good thing.

"Leave Vietnam, muther fuck," Blue Tanks says. "Muther fuck *con chó*."

"Hey, American," someone calls from the crowd behind me. "He say you same as dog," A couple of people laugh, others murmur disapproval.

Mai takes a step toward Blue Tank and says something just above a whisper. Her face has gone to that predator look I saw a couple times in Portland. How can such a beautiful face contort into something so frightening?

Blue Tank takes a step back, though his smile doesn't fade. If his goal is to get us riled, he failed. I'm not angry and I don't think Mai is either. Of course, I'd like to punch that wispy moustache off his upper lip and I'm guessing Mai wants to, too. But riled? No, not even close.

Red Tank's face turns hard as he steps forward and reaches toward our teapot. Mai responds with a pile driving front kick into his abdomen. Okay, guess she's a little bit riled.

Red Tank belches a loud "Ooomph!" as he simultaneously jackknifes forward and shoots backward as if yanked from behind by an invisible rope. He lands on the little table where he had just been sitting, riding it across the cement and into the wall. The table tips over, spilling him unceremoniously onto his rear, his legs sprawled out in front of him. He does a freeze frame for about five seconds in which he grimaces and holds his middle, then plops over onto his side, breathing all wheezy like.

I've been so focused on Red Tank's crash and burn that I'm surprised to see that Mai is now behind Blue Tank, her arms wrapped around his chest, her face braced against his upper back. It takes me a second to see that her fisted hands are squeezing his nipples through his thin tank top. Then, answering the question—What could be worse than having one's man nips squeezed?—she yanks them to the right and left as if trying to pull them under each corresponding armpit. Actually, she yanks so hard that she might be trying to pull them all the way behind him.

The crowd's laughter nearly drowns out the flailing man's screams as Mai drives with her legs and shoulder to push him through the onlookers. At the edge of the curb, she releases him with a hard knee to his butt, launching him off the sidewalk and into several parked motorbikes.

"We must go, Sam," she says, as I step up behind her and look down at Blue Tank tangled within the knocked-over motorbikes, his trembling hands reaching toward his damaged nipples.

The crowd parts for us as we scurry down the sidewalk, neither of us speaking until we round the corner onto the quieter street that leads to her house.

"I hate racists," she says, looking straight ahead, her stride hard and fast.

"Really? I hadn't noticed."

"I've put up with it my entire life. Because I am mixed, I have been a target many times. Father has been a target. Now you are a target of this ignorance. It makes me *very* angry."

I don't say anything, deciding it's probably best to let her vent.

"Why do you not say anything, Sam?" she says, her words clipped, angry. "Did I embarrass you?"

"Embarrass? No. Well, I did feel a little impotent standing there while you kicked ass. Actually, you kicked stomach and ripped nipples."

When Mai doesn't laugh, I say, "What did you say to him?"

"I said his actions embarrassed me. I said he was *ngu như heo*. He was as dumb as a pig. And some other things."

"Dumb as a pig, huh? Is that pretty serious here?"

She looks away, but not before I see her smile. "Yes. It is not in America?"

"I guess so. Technically, though, pigs are quite smart, and clean. It's humans that put them into dirty pig pens and say they aren't clean."

"I'm not going to laugh, Sam," she says, still looking away.

We walk in silence for a moment. As we pass the woman selling fruit who thinks I should be in *Playgirl*, I ask, "Will the police be involved?" The woman winks at me and flashes her red smile.

Mai looks at me. "*Cảnh sát*? No, I do not think so... Maybe." She looks behind us. I do too. No one is following. "Not good for you to get involved with police here."

She centers herself in front of the double gate and looks toward the house. It unlatches with a metallic click and we enter. Tex is standing, or whatever you call what he does, by the steps, holding a short broom.

"Trouble?" he asks.

I don't know what he's perceiving because Mai looks calm and collected now, and I'm trying to be.

"Problem at tea," she says in English.

"Yes, I think so," he says. "You kick ass, Sam?"

"Uh, no. Mai took care of it."

Tex shakes his head and chuckles. "She good, no?"

"Yes, good," I grunt, feeling like a girlyman.

Then, to pour salt on my wounded manhood, he says, "You plenty safe with Mai. She tough."

I was hoping we could go out and sit by the *koi* pond and collect ourselves, but Samuel and Kim are seated at the dining room table drinking tea. I take a quiet, deep breath to ensure that I look calm.

"Good day, Kim," I say. "I hope you are feeling well." She's in her wheelchair wearing a face mask, a high neck white blouse, and black pants. Both look silk. Her color looks better than yesterday. Her eyes study me.

"Trouble?" Samuel asks through his mask before Kim can say anything.

It's like I'm vacationing at the Psychic Network.

"Jerks at the tea cafe," Mai says, picking up two masks from the table. She hands me one. "Racists." She and I slip them on.

"Did you get to finish your tea?" he asks. He's probably thinking how Mai hates racists and it couldn't have ended well for them.

"I do not care for any, Father."

"I'm good," I say, sitting.

"Did you sleep well?" Kim asks.

"Yes, thank you," I say, thankful for the change of subject. "It's very comfortable quarters."

She sips her tea and looks at me over her cup, and I realize it's just a momentary respite. "Tell me, Sam, these racists, how did it, uh, bother you?"

I start to say that I wasn't bothered but those intense eyes would see through my lie. With her, it's better to be truthful.

"First, it took me by surprise and then it made me angry."

"Why did it make you angry," she asks, sounding a little like my shrink, Doc Kari. Like Kari, I think she already knows the answer but is interested in how I respond.

"It made me angry because all I wanted to do was enjoy a cup of tea with Mai. Then I was singled out because I'm Caucasian. It wasn't because I'm American; they didn't know that at first. They had to ask me if I was. So they initially singled me out because I'm white."

"I see." She looks at me intently. "Do you think that it might have also been because you were with Mai?"

"With Mai? You mean they might have been jealous?"

"Of course," Samuel says. He looks at Mai and says something in Vietnamese. I make out what sounds like Andre and Dimitri. Who are they?

"No," Mai says, looking at him sternly.

"Mai," Kim says sharply.

Mai does a short head bow to her mother and another to her father. She says something to Samuel that sounds like an apology.

"Sorry for speaking Vietnamese in front of you," Samuel says, turning back to me. "I do not know the things Mai has decided to share with you; I will let her decide that. For now, understand that you might have more problems, so you need to always be alert when you go out together."

"Okay," I say, wondering about Andre and Dimitri. Maybe she had problems with other boyfriends. Andre. Sounds like a skinny guy who'd wear tight pants and a black turtle neck, and probably a French beret. But then there was Andre the Giant, that behemoth wrestler.

"Sam," Kim begins but is stopped by a grimace of pain. Mai covers her mother's hand with hers. After a moment, Kim's face relaxes and she continues. "I am sure that you have noticed that Mai is much more beautiful than most and that she is much taller, as well."

"Oh my gosh, Mother," Mai says, looking down.

"No, I haven't noticed that," I say. Mai smirks, her head still down, but Kim frowns. Whoops. "Sorry. Yes, I have noticed."

Kim sips her tea, watching me over the rim of her cup. "Americans and Europeans are no longer the novelty they once were in Vietnam after the war ended, but people still look and because you are with Mai they will look even more. Do you understand what I am saying?"

"I understand that our height and such is of interest to people. Please know that being looked at isn't new to me. Twelve of my fifteen years as a police officer were spent in uniform. When a cop is around, everyone looks at the cop. Like us or hate us, everyone looks. I know the two situations are different, so I guess what I'm saying is that I'm used to being looked at, so I try to conduct myself accordingly all the time."

Kim smiles a little and nods. "Yes, conducting yourself accordingly is important. This is what I have taught Mai." She looks at her daughter. "She has not always had it easy. When she was a child, mean children would call her *bụi đời*. It literally means 'living dust.' It was used to refer to abandoned American Vietnamese children. She was not abandoned but they said it anyway. She also has been called *người lai*, which means almost the same except it means mixed-race person. She has even been called *tập chung*, which translates to a child who was born without her own will. They are most ugly terms. All mixed children have heard these, but I think Mai has heard them more because she stands out from the others."

My chest hurts knowing that Mai has had to endure this in her life. It makes me angry, and I want to strike out. But at whom?

"Racism is ugly and it is ignorant, is it not?" Kim says. When I nod she adds, "You felt a little of it today. Imagine growing up with it."

"Mother," Mai says without looking up. "Many people have hard times in their life."

"Can you understand her anger?" Kim says, ignoring her daughter's humility.

"I think I do," I say. "I felt anger myself and I have not experienced this to the extent that Mai has."

Kim nods. She strokes the back of her daughter's head. "It is a terrible ugliness, but we cannot beat up everyone who crosses our path with it."

Mai looks up. "Mother, it was self-defense."

Kim pats the side of her daughter's face lovingly. "Then I hope you kicked their ass. Asses. Asses means more than one, no?"

"Yes, asses," I say. I look away, fighting not to smile. When I look back her eyes are smiling at me. She looks at Samuel.

"What is the thing you always say about fighting, my darling?"

Samuel pretends to thinks for a moment. He lifts his finger. "Oh, I remember. 'No matter how much cats fight, there always seem to be plenty of kittens.' Abraham Lincoln. That one?"

I laugh out loud, but Samuel keeps a straight face. Mai cautiously peeks up at her mother.

"Buddha of mercy! What a man." Kim says with feigned disgust. "Now tell Sam the correct one."

"All right," he says smirking. "'Do not hit at all if it can be avoided, but never hit softly.' Theodore Roosevelt. That one, you mean, my bamboo blossom?"

"That is the one." Kim says. "And stop trying to make Sam laugh by calling me that."

Samuel tightens his lips, but his shaking shoulders give him away.

Kim waves him off with pretend annoyance. "I am glad you are here, Sam," she says. She touches Mai's arm. "I would like to go to my room now, child. I am tired."

I stand as Mai moves behind the wheelchair.

Kim looks at me. "I am sorry about what happened at tea. It probably will not be the last time."

"I promise I will be alert as Samuel suggests."

Kim nods again, smiles at her husband, and gestures to Mai.

"Let me emphasize something," Samuel says, after they leave the room, his voice lowered. "Many men are going to be jealous of you with Mai. Some will think you got her because they believe you are wealthy. They will disrespect her because they think she is after your money. It does not matter if you have money or not. This is what they believe."

"I was hoping for a peaceful visit."

"I hope it will be. But like anywhere, you must pay attention to your surroundings. He scoots his chair back and stands. "I want to show you one more part of our security."

We head out the sliding glass door and make our way over to the triplex. "May we go into your quarters, Sam?"

"Of course," I say, stepping inside. I haven't a clue what he wants to show me. I've seen everything in here: the bed, dresser, wicker table, chairs, and a small bathroom.

"You might find it hard to believe that you slept in one of

the safest places on the property last night."

I look around.

"To be precise, you slept *over* one of the safest places. Help me move the bed over a few feet. Grab the foot and I'll get the headboard." We slide the bed over next to the table. "Ta-dah! Surprised?"

A trapdoor on the floor, about three feet by three feet, right where my bed was.

"Help me lift out the door," Samuel says. "Insert your fingers into the cutout in the top there and I will get this side." We lift. It's about eight inches thick and heavy. "We can set it to the side here. Good. If you had to get down it in a hurry, you would just slide it over far enough so you could slip into the hole. Then you would wrestle the bed back over you and pull the trap door back into place."

"What on earth…" I say looking into the opening.

"*In* earth, would be more accurate."

"A hole?" I ask, noting the wooden ladder that descends six or seven feet down. "To hide in?"

Samuel smiles. "It is a little more than that."

# CHAPTER SIX

I'm sitting on a small bench next to a wooden table about as big as the one Mai and I sat around at tea. "This is unbelievable," I say, looking at the dirt ceiling, walls, and floor.

"The room is about twelve feet by fifteen feet," Samuel says, leaning against a wall.

"Do you come down here often? I mean, what is this for? Is it one of those Viet Cong tunnels they had during the war?"

A low-watt light bulb extends from a socket near the top of one of the walls, bathing us in a sick yellow hue. My hands, forearms, hair, and clothing are dirty from having to crawl on my belly through about twenty-five feet of narrow passageway that's barely wide enough to accommodate my shoulders. Actually, I didn't crawl, but rather inched my way through it by pulling with my hands and sort of bumping my butt up and down. In a couple places, I had to scrunch myself as small as I could to squeeze through. It was a whole lot creepy, to understate it.

"No, this one is freshly dug in the last couple of years, but it is similar to those dug by the North during the war. Some were about this size, and some were several miles long and several stories deep." He scrapes his nails down the wall, sending dirt flecks to the floor. "We were living here about two weeks before my friend, Thanh Van Le, the owner, called me and told me about it. Said he forgot to mention it because he had not worked on it for over a year. He wants to plaster the ceiling and walls, and add... what is the term? Lots of bells and whistles. That is the term, no?"

"Yes. But why did he build it? Or dig it?"

Samuel shrugs. "That was his job during the war. He has a degree in engineering from Hanoi University."

"Really?"

"He jokes that he got a degree so he could dig holes in the ground."

"So, he fought for the North? Against us?"

Samuel looks at me for a moment. "Is that strange to you? To be staying in a house owned by someone who was the enemy?"

"I don't know. A little, I guess. Isn't it to *you*?"

"Sometimes yes, but many years have passed since the war. The distinctions—North, South, Americans—are blurred to many people these days. Now we all walk down the same street, shop at the same markets. Some of the people I pass... well, I killed their fathers, sons, and husbands. Some of them killed my friends. Now I smile at them and they smile at me, and I work with them, buy goods from them, and sell to them. Strange world, is it not?"

Given the last three months, I would have to agree two hundred percent. "Why do you think your friend dug this?"

"Paranoia, maybe. Old habits take time to fade, if ever. Remember that Vietnam has a long history of being at war: Japan, France, America. The old timers are, of course, anxious that there will be another one. My friend Thanh Van Le is one. This is his, uh, security blanket."

"A dirt one."

Samuel chuckles. "Yes. A thick dirt one. We are six feet down, which means there is six feet of dirt and rocks above us. The walls end," he shrugs, "who knows where? Probably wherever there is a building with a basement."

I'm getting a serious case of the heebie-jeebies. "Has your friend ever said anything about his tunnels caving in."

Samuel shrugs. "No, but I saw it happen in the field. Too shallow of a tunnel, water seepage, and dropped B-52 bombs all contributed. But, this one will last. I do not see bombs and rockets in our future."

Okay, suddenly the walls seem to be pressing in, the ceiling too. How on earth did the Viet Cong live in the tunnels for months on end?

"I think you are ready to go topside," Samuel says, either reading my internal panic or noticing my sweaty brow and my hyper-tapping foot.

"Thank you," I say, standing quickly, my head just lightly grazing the ceiling. I drop onto my all fours and slip into the tunnel entrance on my belly. Samuel follows. I try not to kick him in the head in my rush to get out.

"This tunnel is actually larger than most of them were in the war," he says, his voice muffled by the close confines. "They were made to fit the smaller stature of the Vietnamese soldier, which made them difficult for the average American to crawl through. So we had to use very small GIs, called tunnel rats, to go into them and kill any VC they found. Thanh Van Le made this bigger because he has a fat wife."

The tunnel's ceiling scrapes my back and the side walls rub my shoulders. I swear it's getting more narrow and the air… thinner. Harder to breathe now. Goose bumps creep over my flesh. I want to butt bump and finger pull faster, but I'm at my max now.

"Maybe he *should* have made it smaller so she couldn't get in," Samuel says. "That way he could get himself a slimmer wife when the bombing ended."

I know he's trying to distract me. It's not working.

\*

I'm marveling at the spacious, bright room, and tasting the good air. Ahh, space. Space is good.

"I want to clean up," I say, as we push my bed back over the trap door.

"Of course," Samuel says. "But would you like to hit the bag a little before you shower?"

"Anything outside sounds fantastic," I say, wondering if my heart rate will return to normal soon.

Up close, the hanging bag is much larger than it looked from across the yard. In fact, I don't think I've ever seen a bigger one.

"It is big," Samuel says, leading the way across the yard. I wonder if he is even aware now of when he picks up my thoughts. "Most of the time," he says, without looking back at me. "I had a friend make it for me. It weighs about one hundred thirty-six kilograms, about three hundred pounds. How much did the heaviest one in your school weigh?"

"Hundred pounds. Most were sixty."

The bag hangs by a chain from a heavy metal arm that extends from the palm tree about fifteen feet up the trunk. The bag is at least four feet across and made of rough canvas.

"Try it, Son. I think you will get a kick out of it."

"Funny," I say, pushing it with both hands. It's like pushing a cow—I guess over here it would be a water buffalo, and it moves about as much, which is to say it barely moves at all.

"Does hitting a bag this hard and heavy hurt your joints?" I ask, spreading my legs and bending down to touch my head to each knee.

"No," he says simply, watching me loosen up.

"The hard ones I've worked on hurt my shoulders and knees." I rotate my hips a few times to loosen my lower back.

Samuel shrugs his shoulders up and down a few times and does a few head rotations. "Might be you are hitting with just your muscles. That will make you feel the shock of the bag's hardness."

I nod, though I don't understand what he means.

"Hit the bag, any hit, it doesn't matter. But don't hit it as hard as you can."

I lift my fists to each side of my jaw, sidestep around the bag a few steps, then slam it with a hard right cross.

*Whap.* The bag turns a little, as if blown by an ever-so-slight breeze. It returns to where it was.

"Your shoulder?" Samuel asks.

"Hurts a little," I say, rotating my arm a couple of times.

"You are quite strong, Son. You hit like one of those machines that hammer big poles into the earth. But that kind of power goes just so far into this type of bag. A lighter bag, one of your sixty or hundred pound ones, will fly away and come back. Not this one. Its weight and mass stops your blow so that the energy rushes back into your arm and shoulder."

"I'd have to agree," I say, feeling a tiny throb in the front of my shoulder.

"This bag is excellent for testing speed."

"Speed? But this monster doesn't move."

"No problem. Great speed penetrates, you see, like a laser beam. When a technique is fast enough, it sends energy through the bag, all the way through. Understand?"

"Yes," I lie. I know Samuel's style, Temple of Ten Thousand Fists, is based on speed, but how is it developed on this monster?

"I will demonstrate." He steps up to the bag and smoothes the wrinkles out of the canvas with his palm. "With a punch."

"O—"

A blur and a simultaneous *Whump!*

"—kay. Damn!"

Samuel turns around. "Yes, yes, it was quick—"

"Quick? Cats are quick. That was, I don't know what that was." I remember thinking in Portland after I'd seen him move fast that he just might be an alien from Jupiter or Saturn.

Samuel smiles. "Did you notice that the bag didn't move much?"

I run my fingers over the fist-sized indent where he had previously smoothed the canvas. "I don't think it moved at all."

"You are right," he giggles. "I was being humble. But do you understand my point about the difference in my blow's energy from how you hit it?"

I shake my head. "Sorry, I guess I don't." My hit made the bag turn a little while his hit was impossibly fast but didn't turn it at all. I get that part. But I'm not understanding the energy thing.

"Move around to the other side of the bag, Son, and stand so that your chest is against it."

I do as I'm told and stretch my arms about half way around it.

"Don't hold the bag. Just put your chest against it, arms at your side. Yes, like that. Okay, I will hit it again."

I must look like I'm getting a mammogram. With Samuel, you never know what he's going to—

"Oooof!" I stumble back, my hands reaching protectively toward the burning sensation in my upper chest. "What the… " I pull the collar of my T-shirt out and peer inside, expecting to see burnt flesh. My skin is intact, but there is a fist-sized red mark above my pecs.

"You okay, Son?" Samuel says moving around the motionless bag to my side. When I nod, he asks, giddy as a cheerleader, "Did you feel it?"

"I did," I say, tapping my chest with my fingertips. "Still am."

He pushes my hand away. "Best not to touch it for a few seconds. By the way, I deliberately aimed my punch so that you would feel it above your heart."

Oh man.

"Tell me, what does your chest feel like?"

"There's an intense burn, like I leaned my chest onto a hotplate. Just above my pecs." I look at his calloused knuckles, ensuring that he's not holding a police Taser or a stun gun, though none of those would penetrate the bag. "Now the burning sensation is spreading in both directions across my chest." I look at my fingertips, expecting to see blood. There isn't, but it feels like there ought to be. "It's spreading over my shoulders now and into my arms, but it seems to be… yes, it's subsiding at the same time."

"Good," he says. "I mean good that you felt it and good that it's going away. That, Son, is what I mean by hitting like a laser beam. It was not a big crashing blow, one that transfers energy back into your arm and shoulder, such as the way you did it using only your muscles. It is one that is so fast that the energy cannot splash back."

I walk around the bag and look at where he hit it. Just a slight indentation. "So, you're saying the energy of your blow went all the way through the bag?"

"Yes," he says excitedly. He points at my chest, smiling. "And into you."

I look at him, look at the bag, and then back at him.

"Amazing, no? But I am still learning, you see." He shakes his head as if annoyed with himself. "I need to practice harder."

"For what?" I practically shout.

He smiles. "You were leaning against it and felt the energy. I want to hit it so that someone standing behind the bag, say, one or two feet away from it, feels it."

"My God!"

"I need to practice harder to coordinate my mind with my body. I think maybe in a year I will be able to do it."

As usual when Samuel demonstrates something, I'm at a loss for words. I don't even know what to ask.

"You remember the Third Level I showed you in Portland?"

"Of course," I say. That night he threw a flurry of at least two dozen blows so fast that they were nearly imperceptible, all of which just barely touched me, yet sucked nearly every ounce of energy from my body. He and Mai said there is The Fourth Level too, one that is beyond imagination.

"Was that the Fourth Level?" I ask. "Just now?"

He shakes his head. "It is a step in that direction, but still Third Level. There is much more to it than this simple demonstration."

"Incredible. No, incredible is too feeble of a word to describe it. Does anyone else know how to do this?"

"No. Sifu developed it on his own, although he credits his many teachers in China, some who were Buddhist monks, masters of unique meditation disciplines, and a host of teachers from different fighting systems."

"Is this something you can teach?" Once again, I'm talking like a beginner.

"Yes, but you are maybe too young."

"I'm thirty-five."

He nods. "Oh, for sure then. Too young." He chuckles. "Sometimes I think I am too young to learn all this, especially Level Four."

\*

"Lu here," Tex announces from the top of the porch.

"Thank you, Tex," Samuel says. To me, "Lu is Kim's brother, the one who has an inside into Lai Van Tan's organization.

Tex walks hand over hand down the steps and heads in our direction. "You train, huh?" he says as he nears. "Samuel pretty good?"

"Yes, *pretty* good," I say, looking down at him and shaking my head in amazement. "Like Michelangelo's painting the ceiling of the Sistine Chapel was pretty good."

"I will explain later," Samuel laughs, when Tex looks at me with a blank face.

"Lu here," Tex says again. "Come taxi." Then in a confidential tone to me, "Lu pretty damn weird."

Falsetto voice from the stairs. "*Chào* Samuel! *Chào* Tex! *Chào* pretty man."

I'm seeing it but I'm not understanding it. "That's…?"

"I say already, Sam," Tex says out of the corner of his mouth. "Weird."

"I thought Lu was Kim's brother," I whisper as I watch a forty-something woman move carefully down the stairs in a tight, strikingly pink *áo dài* and white satin trousers.

"He is," Samuel says. "*Chào* Lu. Come meet my son Sam. Sam, this is Lu."

Lu's a transsexual, a ladyboy? Now *that's* funny.

"Hell-ooo," Lu says extending her hand, palm down as if I'm suppose to kiss her ring. I twist my hand to catch his—hers?—in mine, and shake it with less grip than I normally would a guy's. He's—she's—whatever—is actually quite attractive: nice figure, pretty face, shiny black hair past her shoulders. What am I saying?

"Checking me out, eh?" she says, flashing a pearly white smile. "Hong Kong. Got it all done in Hong Kong. Ten thousand Euros." She looks me up and down. "Such a dirty big man. I liiiike it."

At first I think he means how I just looked him up and down. Then I remember my dirty clothes. "Samuel and I were in the tun—"

"It is all good," he says with a dismissive wave. "I like."

I smile and nod, not trusting myself to say anything. It would have been nice if Mai or Samuel had told me.

"Let us go inside and have tea and hear what Lu has learned," Samuel says.

"How you like Vietnam?" Lu asks, taking my arm and peeking at me through a strand of hair that has fallen across one eye. We all move toward the steps.

"I like it very much," I say, feeling a whole lot uncomfortable but trying not to show it. Lu's English is heavily accented but quite good grammatically.

"I understand now why Mai likes you," he says touching my biceps. She tightens her grip on my arm as we move up the steps. "They make the steps too steep. Hard to walk in *áo dài.*"

"I bet," I say, thinking that the Portland liberals would be proud of me right now. Tex shoots me a wink.

Ly is waiting in the dining room. "Tea, please," Samuel says, "and some fruit. And please ask Mai to join us." He looks at me. "Mai has been on the phone talking to a jewelry broker in Hong Kong."

I nod, sit. Lu pulls out a chair next to me and poses her perky breasts for a moment as she lowers herself. Hong Kong must sell everything.

Tex and Samuel converse for a moment. Tex nods to me and heads back out the sliding glass door.

Samuel sits at the front of the table. "Tex needs to fix the air conditioning in the monitor room. I will fill him in later on what we discuss here."

"Hello, everyone," Mai says, coming into the room and instantly brightening it. *Chào* Lu. I see you have met Sam." She glances at me, winks. When I make a oh-you're-so-hilarious face, she fights back a smile and sits to Samuel's right.

"*Chào,* my beautiful niece," Lu says, pulling out a pink Hello Kitty notepad from his purse.

Mai alerts on it. "That is soooo cute, Lu. Where did you get it?"

"Thank you, sweetie. Ebay. A Japanese store in Tokyo. I just luuuuve it."

"To business," Samuel says breaking up the girl chat. "Lu, what do you have." I'm assuming he's not asking about more Hello Kitty stuff.

"There are two things I learned," Lu says, searching for the right page in the notepad. "Here it is." A long strand of hair falls on the page; he tucks it behind his ear. "I think you already know about this but maybe I have new details. First," he looks at me, "they know that you are here, Sam. I did not learn what they might do but they talk about you. And I know from before that they hate Samuel and because you are his son, they hate you and want to hurt you. Maybe they will follow you sometimes, I do not know."

Lu isn't much on softening bad news.

Samuel nods. "I knew that would happen, Sam. Nothing new. We just need to be very cautious. Mai, you must be alert when you two go out. Wear hats, sunglasses. Use the scooter instead of the Volvo. Sam, if you brought a coat, wear it. We will talk more about this later. What else, Lu?"

"I have been hearing rumors about prostitutes. No, not prostitutes. Kids that they kidnap and make into prostitutes to send to America and Europe and all over Asia."

"Sex trafficking," I say.

"Yes," Lu says. "I forget that word. My, uh, source say that the girls are taken to a..." He says something to Samuel in Vietnamese.

"Warehouse," Samuel translates.

Lu nods, and that tuft of hair falls back across one eye. He brushes it away with a flip of his hand, both gestures more feminine than Mai's. "To a warehouse in Bien Hoa."

"That is about twenty miles from here," Samuel says. "It is an industrial center and there are many factories and warehouses there. Some are owned or partially owned by the Japanese, Swiss, and Americans." His face hardens.

"Do the police know about it?" I ask.

"Probably," Mai says. "But some are paid to look the other way. When I was at the university in Portland, I wrote a paper on the problem for a sociology class. The more I learned the more angry I got because I know two families that have lost girls to it. One was the family of my best friend, Phuong. Her daughter's name is Qui, it means turtle..." Mai pauses for a moment, looking at her hands as she wraps her right one around the fingers of her left. She squeezes them until her knuckles turn white. Her eyes return to mine. "She was snatched off the street here in Saigon about three years ago. Qui was eleven years old then. The police, father, mother, my sisters, and me all tried to find her, but we did not. We did not know where to even look. The other girl was a daughter of one of our workers."

"Nhung," Samuel says sadly. Remembering.

When he doesn't say anything further, Mai continues. "Nhung's little girl's name is Tuyet. She was also eleven. She was the only children... er, child of Nhung. The father died in a traffic accident just outside of Saigon about a year earlier. Again, we looked and looked but we never found her."

"Nhung took her own life about six months later," Samuel says just above a whisper. "We tried hard to give her hope but in the end, she had none."

The dining room is quiet for a moment. Lu breaks it.

"In the countryside, older girls go with foreigners who promise them marriage and a life in another country. Country life is very hard, so many girls will do anything to leave."

"Marriage?" I ask.

"Yes," Lu says, turning to face me. "Men promise marriage but then they take the girls away and sell them into, uh, sex traffic."

"Cambodia has many Vietnamese girls for sex trade," Mai says. "One of the sources for my paper said that there were fifteen thousand in Phnom Penh, most of them from southern Vietnam."

"Fifteen thousand?" I half blurt. "Not fifteen hundred? Not that that's any better."

"Thousand," Mai says.

I shake my head in disbelief. "Incredible. I know that this is a problem, but I didn't realize how enormous a problem it is. I did see something on *Nightline* or one of those news shows a couple years ago."

Samuel shrugs. "You live in Vietnam long enough and you learn that many parts of the world do not know and do not care about what happens here. Not many people have concern for the children and farmers who are blown up from the old, but still live, explosives buried and left here during the war. Why is that problem not bigger news in the United States? *We* left the arsenal here." Samuel's eyes have narrowed and his words are coming out faster and faster. "The press always has an excuse why they do not tell the story. They say something like, 'Americans have Vietnam fatigue. They do not want to hear about anything that happens here.' Well, I am sorry that the US is tired. But over forty-two thousand people have been killed by unexploded mines and bombs since the war. One expert said it will take three hundred years to clear all of the explosives. America is tired, Vietnam is still dying."

"Father," Mai says softly.

"I used to write to the American media and tell them about the huge problem. Most ignored me. Some sent me a letter of thanks. I know there has been a few stories on it and one or two celebrities have lent their names to the cause, but other news stories always come along and the issue gets buried. So it is not just the media's fault, it is everyone's. How many Americans know about it? How many care?"

Mai lifts her finger tips a few inches off the table. "Father."

He blinks a couple of times at her, then, "Yes. Thank you."

We sit in silence again. Three minutes ago, I knew very little about sex trafficking here and nothing about unexploded ordinance left over from the war. I didn't have anything to do with these things, still I feel some kind of culpability, at least for my ignorance.

"I got sidetracked," Samuel says, calmer now. "I just love this country and the people so much."

"No problem," I say. "I feel bad that I'm so ignorant on these things. I promise you I will educate myself on them."

Samuel nods, smiles. Mai does too.

Samuel releases a big exhale. "Back to the issue at hand. Prostitution is already a big problem in this country. There are thousands of working girls."

I'm shaking my head again unable to fathom the numbers.

"Thousands and more thousands," Mai says. "Because there are more and more visitors and businessmen coming to Saigon and other parts of Vietnam to visit and do business, the demand for prostitutes is growing all the time."

"Lu," Samuel says, "can you tell us how long Lai Van Tan has been involved in sex trafficking? I heard something about it only a month ago."

"Same time," Lu says. "One month. I told he is still in a lot of pain about his son's death and that he has gotten… greedy?" Samuel nods that the word is correct. "Maybe the death make him greedy. Maybe he thinks money will make his pain go away. I do not know, but my friend say Lai getting much crazy."

"Whatever the reason," Samuel says, "he remains a dangerous man. Anything else, Lu?"

"I am sorry, no. But I will search for more."

"Thank you," Samuel says, getting up. "You did good work."

I start to stand but Mai gives me a subtle shake of her head.

Lu scoots back from the table. "Thank you, Samuel," he says. He turns to me and extends his hand palm down, but with a little less flamboyance than when we met a while ago. "Nice meet you, Sam. I hope you enjoy visit."

I take his hand and tell him I enjoyed meeting him as well. He smiles, turns, and does a wiggly finger wave to Mai. "Please tell my sister that I hope she is feeling well." Samuel follows him out.

"That seemed a little abrupt," I say.

"Father will explain in a moment." She studies me for a couple seconds. "It was dangerous in Portland, and now it looks like it might be crazy dangerous here."

"You mean because my seatmate flying over here kicked two policemen in the face minutes after landing, and you and I got into a fight at tea, make that, you got into a fight at tea, and now we learn that Lai Van Tan has gone nuts and is into sex trafficking, and who knows what he's going to do to us? That what you mean by crazy?"

Her eyes fill with apprehension. "You mad because you are here?"

"Not even a little bit. There isn't anywhere else I'd rather be than here."

She smiles.

"Okay," Samuel says heading to his chair. "Sam, let's all sit down at this end so we are cozy. Did Mai explain the situation with Lu?"

Mai and I look at each other as I sit. She turns to Samuel. "I told him that you would explain, Father."

Samuel fills our cups and picks up a piece of melon. "What did you think of Lu?"

"Well, no one told me that he was a transsexual. That caught me by surprise."

"Did you find him attractive?" Mai asks.

"Mai," Samuel says, his tone just short of a reprimand. "I mean, what is your feeling about him? Your police instinct?"

"May I be frank?"

"That is what I want."

"I have had several informants over the years, and I've never trusted one of them. They give you only enough so that you pay them. Then they give you a little more in a couple of days for seemingly new information. In other words, they get paid twice for information they acquired once. Sometimes they play the double agent game—they give you information about the bad guys and then give the bad guys information about you. They get paid by both parties."

"And Lu?" Samuel says, his eyes hard.

"My first thought with any informant is to wonder how are they getting the information. All that you have told me about Lai Van Tan, it makes me wonder how Lu gets his. Does he know someone inside? Is he paying someone? It would seem to be a big risk for him." I pause for a moment. "Sorry. I'm being rude. Lu is Kim's brother."

Samuel waves off my concern. "I ask you because your experience in these matters is important. He told me about three months ago that he has a lover, one of the lower echelon members of the organization, a man who does not have complete access to all that is going on, but he does hear things."

"May I ask if you trust Lu?"

He sips from his tea. "I have to… with caution."

"Would Lu ever do something that might harm the family?"

"Lu does not get along with Kim," Samuel says. "We have always known that he is a homosexual. That fact has been disturbing to Kim for years. Although she is a Buddhist, a discipline that is more tolerant of such things than others, Kim is not tolerant of that. She has put up with Lu for years because he is her brother and he did not flaunt his homosexuality in our faces. But about a year and a half ago, Lu went to Hong Kong on what he said was personal business. When he returned two months later, he showed up at our other house dressed, well, like he was dressed today. And apparently he had had breasts added to his body."

"Mother blew up," Mai says. "Like a bomb. She even hit my uncle with her fists. She said his karma was forever cursed and that she did not want to see him again."

"So sorry to hear all this," I say, not knowing what else to say when one's uncle suddenly sprouts boobies.

"We did not see him for several months, but when all this happened with Lai Van Tan before I came to Portland, he showed up at our door and wanted to help. And you remember how helpful he was when we were in Portland. He supplied me with a flow of information and helped Kim and the others relocate until Mai and I could get back and move into this house."

"But still you don't trust him?"

"I do not, and for the same reasons you mentioned why you never completely trusted your informants. Kim hurt Lu deeply, when she, as Mai calls it, blew up. I do not know the depth of his embarrassment and anger toward her. And I do not know if there are other issues going on in his life that might cause him to turn against us."

"So what's the plan?" I ask.

Samuel shrugs. "How would you deal with such an informant?"

"I wouldn't tell him anything that you're doing defensively or proactively. I would just listen to what he offers, questioning him to see if he knows more info that he's holding back or that he doesn't think has value. You should listen closely to him to determine if he might have another motive to tell you these things besides family obligation. Every snitch I've ever had informed so as to feather their own beds."

"What does that mean?" Mai asks.

"They informed for money, they informed to keep the cops off their backs since most were still involved in crime, and they informed to try to learn what the police were up to and what they knew. I don't know Lu, so I don't know his motivation. And, it sounds as if you're not sure either. So all the more reason to be careful. Oh, one other thing. Don't let him come here. I always met my snitches on street corners, at coffee shops and the like. I never let them see the inner offices of the PD."

Samuel scrunches his face. "How naïve of me. I never thought of that."

"Have you shown Lu your security system, the monitors, the tunnel?"

"No," Samuel says.

"Good. Don't mention them. The less he knows the better."

Samuel nods. "I will do all that you say, Son. You have been very helpful. Any questions, Mai?"

"Not a question, Father, but a comment. I think it is possible that Lu informs because he cares about us. Yes, he knows Mother is upset with him and yes, he was at one time angry with her. But he loves me and he loves you and I think he still loves her."

Samuel pats her hand and looks at me with that twinkle in his eyes whenever he is with his daughter. "She is very wise, Son. Be careful."

I nod with feigned seriousness. "Good advice, sir. Thank you."

Mai rolls her eyes.

"Are you going with Mai to District One?" Samuel asks.

"I have not had a chance to ask him yet?' Mai says. "Sam, I have to go to our store in *Phạm Ngũ Lão*. It is part of Saigon. Would you like to go with me? You can see lots of the city."

"Are there other guides I can choose from?"

Samuel chuckles.

I'm ninety-nine percent sure it's her foot under my pant leg tickling my ankle.

"No," she says. Her toes are stroking my calf now. Hello! Who knew the calf nerves were connected to—

"I have business to attend to, children," Samuel says scooting his chair back. "I am going to the *Hai Ba Trung* store briefly and then the soldiers' home. "I will see you this evening?"

"Yes, Father," Mai says to his back as he exits the room. She scoots her chair back and smiles innocently at me. "Maybe you should change out of those clothes. Shall we meet back here in twenty minutes? Is that enough time? You are quite a dirty boy."

\*

Mai called me just as I stepped out of the shower and said to give her twenty more minutes because she had to call a supplier about late deliveries or something. I was nearly dressed when my cell rang again. I was going to answer this time by commenting on how she played footsie with me under the table, but something stopped me. Good thing because it was Bobby, the kid from the plane.

He began by apologizing about lying to me. Said he was worried that I might tell someone. His voice sounded tired, scared, and out of breath. When I asked if he was okay he said he was, but that he didn't know what to do. Said he wanted to meet me somewhere tomorrow to talk about his problem. I said I would check with my hosts and call him in the morning. I asked him again if he was okay and if he needed to meet me now. He thanked me and said tomorrow would be fine.

Amazing kid. How many other sixteen-year-olds would apologize for their actions? But I'm worried for him. What I understand is that Vietnam is not a good place to be the target of the police.

Mai calls again to say she is ready and to remind me about the coat and sunglasses.

# CHAPTER SEVEN

The trip from the airport to the house in Mai's car is about the scariest thing I've ever done, that is, until now. My legs are hugging the sides of the little Honda motorbike so tightly that I might crush the engine, and I'm bear hugging Mai's waist like a drowning man. When we first took off, I was hugging her even more tightly until she shouted over her shoulder that I was interfering with her driving. Good point. I want her one hundred percent engaged as she zigzags through the tsunami of metal, rubber, and blaring horns. I don't know if I'm sweating from stress or from my jacket and baseball cap Samuel wanted me to wear. It's a light jacket but still hot. Mai is wearing a baseball cap, a jean jacket, and dark slacks.

I'm not a control freak per se, but I've never liked riding on the back of a motorbike at the mercy of someone else's ability to keep a two-wheeler upright. Mai seems to be at one with the bike, though, leaning us hard to the left at the last second to avoid a bus, braking to avoid tangling with a mass of motor-bikes that suddenly surge across our lane, goosing the throttle so that another truck passes behind us with just inches to spare, and swerving to avoid a large pothole.

"How are you doing, Sam?" she calls over her shoulder.

"I have to go pee-pee," I say into her ear.

That cracks her up just before she leans hard to the right to miss a stalled motorbike stacked high with lumpy gunny sacks.

"Never mind. I just went."

Mai's hearty laugh is interrupted when another motorbike's mirror clanks against her left one. She shouts something at the driver and he moves over, but not far because several other bikes are jamming his left side. A motorbike on our right has moved in so close that if he had a left mirror it would hit our right one. His knee brushes my thigh.

"Mai! The guy on the right just touched my leg," I say in her ear, struggling to restrain my panic.

Mai gooses the bike to zip us between two taxis and into a small clearing where other vehicles are about three feet away on either side of us. After another fifteen minutes or so of zigging and zagging and braking and goosing, Mai announces that we're almost there. I quietly thank God, Moses, Buddha, and my TV repairmen back home.

*Phạm Ngũ Lão* doesn't look much different than the streets around Samuel's place. Traffic is a little lighter, but the sidewalks are crowded with pedestrians, vendors selling anything and everything, and motorbikes parked every which way. There are lots of Caucasians walking around too, many with backpacks.

"This is a favorite place for travelers, American students, and European ones," Mai says, pulling to the curb. "We are here now."

She parks just inches from an elderly woman sitting on a low bench before three large pots of squirming eels. The woman laughs when I deliberately get off on the far side of the bike, and gestures for me to come closer to the pots. When I shake my head, she gives me one of those toothless, red-stained smiles. Mai says something and the woman laughs.

"This is our store," Mai says, pointing to an open-front shop with a painted sign overhead that reads Kim Le Jewelry

Four Seven Two in English and probably the same thing in Vietnamese. Mai muscles the Honda over to the curb and parks it at the side of the store. Two middle-aged women, both wearing red *áo dài*, call out a greeting to her from inside. Mai smiles and waves. "Come in, Sam," she says.

"I can't believe that a jewelry store would have no front wall like this," I ask, slipping off my sunglasses and coat.

"Oh, the front rolls down at night," she says, pointing at the overhead door. "And whenever the clerks have *ngủ trưa*, uh, sleep, like siesta." She pulls off her shades and cap. "It is like the garage door you have on your house. It is metal and very secure."

Inside looks like a typical jewelry store with glass cases full of gold and silver pieces, and what I would guess are medium-range necklaces displayed on the wall behind the two women. Small, strategically placed lamps set a nice mood and accentuate the sparkle and glitter.

"Please meet Da`o and Hoa, our two best jewelry experts," Mai says. "This is Sam, father's son."

The women nod several times. "Nice to meet you," I say, not sure if they understand.

"Nice to meet you," they both say in English, nearly in unison.

"It's a most beautiful store."

"Thank you," Mai says, pointing at the lighting. "Da`o has worked here for twelve years and is responsible for the look."

"Very nice"

"Thank you. I enjoy very much. Samuel, Kim, and Mai same my family."

"You are part of our family, Do`a," Mai says. She touches the other woman's arm affectionately. "Hoa has been here for about one year and is an excellent sales person."

"Very good," I say.

Hoa drops her head into a slight bow. "*Cám ơn.*"

"Sam. I have something I have to talk with Hoa about in the back. I will be ten minutes, okay? Maybe you would like to look around out front. But do not go too far, please."

"Sure, no problem. Nice to meet you ladies," I say, and turn to step toward the store's opening, nearly tripping over a squatting child, a girl, I think. "Sorry," I say, touching the mop of dirty hair. Do`a speaks sternly to the kid who glares defiantly at her before standing and walking haughtily away.

I move out onto the sidewalk and decide quickly that the best defense against getting swept away by the fast moving passersby is to stand next to a weathered tree by the curb. There is no way I'd ever get bored watching the steady roar of passing vehicle traffic and the mass of people moving in all directions, and hearing the confusion of Vietnamese and American music coming from… not sure where, and the loud chatter from vendors verbally advertising their wares. It's a mad circus and I wouldn't be the least surprised to see elephants and jugglers.

I was in New York City once in July, a time when the heat and humidity was awful. I was doing the tourist thing in Times Square and the sidewalks were as packed as they are here. The heat was miserable, as were the crowds, but there was some semblance of order to it all. Here, it's about the heat, the crowds, the traffic, the cacophony of sounds, the explosion of colors, the myriad smells, and the overall sense of confusion, madness even. Maybe if I were to live here for a while it would no longer be bedlam, but I'm not so sure.

"You!"

I look down. It's the same kid who just got eighty-sixed from Mai's shop. She's a girl for sure, no more than ten or twelve with stringy black hair, wearing dirty tan shorts, blue, new-looking Nike shoes, and a yellow T-shirt that reads "San Diego Zoo." She stands directly in front of me, hands on her hips, her expression serious.

"What about me?" I ask.

"You American, okay? Okay?"

"I am. How are you?" She has beautiful brown eyes.

"How long you be here now. Here. Ho Chi Minh City? How long?"

"Two days. How long you been here?"

"You funny, you. But I not laugh, you see?" Half a dozen backpackers, speaking what sounds like German, pass behind her, all the while her focus stays on me.

"I guess it wasn't that funny."

"No. Sorry." She shrugs as if I were a hopeless case. "Not funny too much you."

"Sam," I say, tapping my chest. I point at her. "You? Your name?"

"Baby Cakes," she says.

I tighten my lips to hold back a chuckle and extend my hand. "Baby Cakes is a very pretty name. Nice to meet you."

"Hello, Sam," she says, pumping my hand. Hers is as rough as a logger's and about as dirty. "Why you stand here?"

"I'm waiting for a friend."

Her dirt-smudged face smiles for the first time. "Okay, okay," she says nodding with the wisdom of an old sage. She takes my hand. "You want fuck, okay?"

"Wha-at!" I say, at once shocked and trying to swallow a laugh.

"I get girl for you. Very pretty. She not fuck too much today already."

"Uh, no Baby Cakes."

"Boy? You want fuck boy? Okay, no problem. I take you now. To bar we go you."

"No, thanks. But it's been real, real nice meeting you. I have to go inside. To see my friend."

"Okay, okay. Sometime you want girl, boy, you find me. I here all time. I fix you up good. No problem."

I head back into the store, shaking my head. That was disconcerting. Kid must be a pimp for a bar or something.

"How you like Vietnam?" Da`o asks pleasantly, as I walk back in. I don't think she heard the exchange outside.

"Uh, never a dull moment. I mean, I love it."

She laughs and claps her hands. "No, never dull for sure. Mai very beautiful, no?"

I shrug indifferently and grin.

She points at me and tilts her head. "I know Mai long time."

"I see." I know where this is going.

"She is same as granddaughter to me. I take care of her many, many times when she little."

I nod.

She taps her chest. "Big heart. Easy hurt. Sometime she care too much."

"Yes."

Da`o looks at me for a long moment, then, "You no hurt her, okay?" I lift my hands to indicate that that would never happen. "She tell me about you and I see how she be now. She like you." Her hand is resting on the top of a display case. I pat it a couple times, not knowing if that's out of line.

"Da`o, I promise you I will not hurt her. I am not that kind of person. She is very lucky to have someone like you watching out for her."

She looks deep into my eyes. "I tough old woman," she says. "Two bombs not kill me in American War." She makes an arc in the air with her hand. "Rockets. Attack my village. They no kill me." Her eyes mist over. "Mai, I love same-same daughter."

I take her hand in both of mine and look into her eyes. "I care for Mai very much too. No worries."

"You good man?"

"I like to think I am." I guess this isn't the time to mention that I've killed three people.

She studies my face. "I think so, yes."

"I see you two are chatting," Mai says warmly, emerging from the back room. "Sam, Da`o baby sit me many times when I was little. She is like my special auntie."

"She told me. We have been getting along nicely."

Mai puts her arm around the woman's waist and speaks Vietnamese to her. Da`o nods and pats Mai's face. Lots of affection going on there. Hoa comes out from the back.

"Father call when I was with Hoa," Mai says. "He wants to show you the soldiers' home. We will go there now."

"Great."

"Nice *talking* to you," Da`o says, her tone that of an engraver making one more chisel mark in the stone. I nod that I concur and that I got her not so subtle point.

When I step to the side a little, Da`o's eyes look at something below me. I turn to see Baby Cakes once again squatting by the entrance. Da`o and Mai both speak sharply to her, and the girl backs out the entrance, across the sidewalk, stopping next to the tree where I was standing.

"She and I were talking a while ago," I say. "She's a pretty tough kid."

"Tough kids steal from shops," Da`o says.

"That's too bad," I say, looking back over at Baby Cakes who is talking on a cell phone. She steps away from the tree, glances at me for a second, and joins the stream of passersby.

Mai and I bid farewell to the ladies, and five minutes later we're once again rolling in the battle zone, both of us wrapped up as if it were winter in Montana.

"Da`o, Kim, and Tex are sure worried about you liking me," I say into Mai's ear. "Guess I have to be nice to you."

"Yes you do. My family very much protects me."

"And you protect them."

"Yes. They protect my heart and I protect their bodies," she laughs at that, while swerving our motorbike to miss a truck.

"That little girl who was watching us came up to me on the sidewalk and asked if I wanted a date, of sorts. She couldn't have been older than twelve and didn't pull any punches."

"What does 'pull punches' mean?"

"She didn't mince words. She came right out and said what I could do to the girl. How does a child even know about such things?"

"Some children have to grow up quickly in Vietnam," she says. "It is very sad. The violence to young children—it makes me so angry."

Mai maneuvers us through a throng of motorbikes crossing in our path. I know the subject angers her because I can feel the tension in her back.

"Well, I didn't come over here to 'have a girl,'" I say into her ear.

She navigates traffic for another block, then with a smile back in her voice, she asks, "Not even to have me?"

"I will make an exception for you," I say softly in her ear. I pinch her butt.

"Hey!" she says with a giggle. "I know how to block that."

"But you didn't."

"Correct."

I push my chest tight against her back, put my lips against her ear again, and say, "I like you, Mai." I nibble on her ear.

She honks her horn at a truck that is within inches of touching our right legs. It moves over a little and accelerates away.

"Not a good idea to bite your driver's ear in this crazy Saigon traffic."

"Sorry."

She pushes back against me. "Later it is okay to do."

*

Mai banks the motorbike to the left onto a narrow alley that's just wide enough for one vehicle. She does an amazing job of maneuvering around large potholes for about a hundred yards before she slows and turns into a small cracked-cement courtyard. It fronts a one-story building, beige, old but kept up. The Volvo Mai drove when she picked me up is parked off to the side. Three motor scooters are parked next to it.

"Hi, Tex," Mai calls as he slaps out the door wearing a sleeveless and faded green Army fatigue shirt and the same blue Nike shorts. His muscular, tattooed arms ripple with his every "step," his torso rocking freely between them.

Out of the corner of her mouth, Mai says, "Tex always wears his old army shirt when he works here."

"Happy you come, Sam," he says, as I dismount. "Your father very happy show you house."

"I'm excited to see it. I'm not really sure what it's about."

"Sam. Mai," Samuel greets us at the door. "I am glad you are here. I was planning on showing you this tomorrow, but it turned out I did not have to go to the *Hai Ba Trung* store today after all. I hope I am not interfering with your plans."

"It is fine, Father," Mai says. "I was just going to show him some of the city and get something to eat. We will do that after."

"Very well." He takes my arm and gestures for us to go in. "Welcome, Son. I want you to meet some special men, some old warriors. As I told you, Ngo Bao Chau died a few days ago, so now there are only five. But a new man will move here in a week or so. Soon we plan to add a second floor so more can join us."

We step into what appears to be a living room with sofas, chairs, lamps, and a television. A thin man in his mid sixties wearing black shorts, sandals, and a white tank top sits on one end of a sofa. Both of his arms end about an inch below his elbow joints.

"This is the sitting room, where the men can come anytime they want to talk, play games—"

"Play games means gamble," Mai says, smiling.

Samuel nods. "Gamble, read, smoke, or watch television. Please meet Phouc." Samuel speaks to the man in Vietnamese. I hear my name in the mix.

"Hell-o, son of friend me," Phouc says, saluting with his stump. I smile, nod.

"He is a good man," Samuel says. "I teach him kicking and how to fight with his stumps. He is pretty good. Stump-fu."

"Stump-fu," Phouc says, waving his stumps about. "Pow pow pow."

"That is Dung across the room," Samuel says, gesturing toward an immense man with thinning gray hair sitting at an empty table, his back to us as he gazes out a window. "Big, no? He is about your height and weighs over two hundred fifty pounds. He was mentally slow before the war and now he suffers from PTSD. One nurse said that he has a mental capacity of an eight-year-old."

"Two times he has been violent," Mai says. "Father have to use…" She looks at Samuel.

"Sleeper hold," he says, touching the sides of his neck. "Carotid constriction. Very sad. When Dung gets angry, he can be quite violent. Fortunately, it does not happen often."

"Mostly, he is kind," Mai says. "He is like a mother to the other men." She looks over at him. "*Chào* Dung!"

"Watch this," Samuel says. "He loves Mai."

Dung's posture snaps up straight, his head still turned away. He remains frozen for a moment, as if he isn't quite sure he heard correctly.

"*Chào* Dung," Mai says again, her voice melodic and full of fondness for the man.

He spins around, his knee striking the table leg, scooting it at least three feet and knocking askew a chair on the other side. "Mai!" he cries, launching his big self up. His walk is a bit of a lumber, his right leg stiff, giving him a gait like Chester on the old *Gunsmoke* reruns I used to watch with my grandfather. Still, he reaches Mai in three seconds flat, embracing her in an enveloping bear hug that lifts her off the floor.

Mai and Samuel both laugh. Samuel says something to him and he sets her down carefully. The big man beams and so does Mai. He takes her hand, leads her across the room to where he was sitting, and points at something out the window.

"They clicked the moment they met," Samuel says, smiling at them. "He is too childlike to do anything inappropriate. It is like she is his younger sister who he adores. Pity anyone who tries to harm her when he is around."

"I bet," I say. Actually, pity anyone who tries to hurt her when any of us are around. Or hurt us when she's around. What a family.

"There are separate quarters in this house so each man gets his own room. There are five bathrooms, an exercise room, kitchen, and a courtyard in the back with a heavy bag."

"A bag? Some men practice martial arts?"

"Four of them. Phouc, Phat Ho, Cong, and Viet. We will meet Cong and Viet in a moment. They have all trained a long time. It keeps them healthy and happy."

"Wait. There is a guy named Viet and another named Cong? Like in Viet Cong?"

Samuel smiles. "Funny, eh. Here is what makes it funnier. Viet is from the North, born in Hanoi. Spent years transporting supplies on the *Ho Chi Minh* Trail. Cong is from the South, Saigon. He fought against the *Viet Cong* for seven years before he was wounded and could no longer be a soldier."

"They get along?"

Over by the window, Mai is laughing with Dung about something.

"Viet and Cong are best of friends. Both are serious Buddhist. They want to put the war behind them."

"Incredible."

"They are amazing men. Phat Ho is—"

"Oh," I laugh. I quickly wave my hand apologetically. "Sorry," I whisper. "Didn't mean to… I heard you say that name a second ago but I thought I heard wrong."

"Yes, the English translation makes it funny."

"Sorry," I repeat, getting control of myself. "I probably sound like a thirteen-year-old boy."

Samuel smiles. "We all have moments of being a thirteen-year-old boy, no?" Tex, who has been outside doing something, hand walks up to us.

"You two have done an incredible job here," I say.

"I am very happy to help a little," Samuel says. "You see, the government does not take care of its old soldiers." He looks at Dung for a long moment before continuing. "Maybe in a year we can buy another building somewhere. I would like to open one in the country. We can get more for our money there." He looks at Phouc. "I want to help them." Then, barely above a whisper, "I *need* to help them."

*Tap... tap... tap...*

Coming from what appears to be the entrance to a hallway.

"Viet come," Tex says from below us. "Do not be filled with shock, Sam."

"Shock? Why would I..."

"Viet," Samuel calls as a horribly disfigured man limps around the corner, a broad smile across his face. He waves.

Oh my...

The right side of his face looks to have been melted, as does his right arm and his right leg. His left leg ends at his knee to which he has attached the bottom portion of a well-used crutch, the source of the tapping. His brown shorts and pale blue T-shirt appear too large for his thin frame.

He continues to smile as he walks up to us and shakes hands with Samuel, left hand to left hand. Closer, I can see that he's not smiling at all. The man has no upper lip and only part of a lower. "Viet," Samuel says. "This is my son, Sam."

"Oh," he says, extending his left hand. "Nuth to neet you."

"He says, 'nice to meet you,'" Samuel says, placing his hand on Viet's shoulder. "His English is quite good. Not having all his lips makes it hard to pronounce some letters."

Suddenly my concerns pale in comparison. "I understood perfectly," I say, smiling at him.

"Viet is a good kicker," Samuel beams. "He is in his sixties but if he kicks you with his peg leg, you will remember it for a long time, and you will have a round indent in your head." He laughs.

"Your 'ather is a 'under-ul teacher," Viet says, looking at Samuel with respect and love.

"Wonderful? You don't think he is too slow?" I ask, forcing my face to look serious.

Viet laughs, though his permanent smile doesn't change. "Yes, yes. He need to 'urk on his seed. Too slow 'or sure." His eyes twinkle at Samuel.

"Okay, gentlemen," Samuel says with a grin. "Viet, where is Cong?"

"In 'ack of house. I see hin out 'indow. He 'ractice kni."

"He is practicing with his knife," Samuel translates.

"And Phat Ho?"

I bite my lip.

"He go shaw-ing."

"Shopping?"

"Yes. Cuh' 'ack soon." He looks behind us, and points. "Oh, there Phat Ho already."

Phat Ho also looks to be sixty-something, with a pock-marked, chubby face, and a soft middle under his white T-shirt. He's carrying a large papaya in his right hand. He has no left arm, though I can see the impression of a stub against his sleeve. He acknowledges Samuel with a nod. There is strength in his bearing and an intensity in his eyes that convey danger, extreme danger.

Samuel says something to him while nodding at me. Without turning his head, Phat Ho glances my way, then looks back at Samuel. I wonder if Phat Ho translates to Mister Warmth. When Samuel speaks to him again, his verbiage is clipped, insistent. Mai turns and looks over at us. Phat Ho again looks at me, this time for about three beats before he nods slightly, his eyes like cold flames. I must have made a bad impression. He moves off toward what I'm guessing is the kitchen. A blue scarf protrudes from his back pocket.

"*Chào*, Phat Ho," Mai says as he passes. He nods with a snap of his head without slowing and disappears around the corner.

"He…" Tex says something to Samuel.

"Shy."

"He shy at Mai," Tex says. "Maybe shy all womans, all peoples."

That wasn't shyness I saw in his face. I don't think he'll ask me to share his papaya with him.

"Follow me," Samuel says.

"Nice to meet you, Viet," I say.

"Nice to 'eet you," he says, his mouth ever smiling. He peg-legs his way over to a chair in front of the television, plops down.

"I stay here, Samuel," Tex says. "I want to look at pipe in bathroom. Maybe fix if problem not big."

"Thank you, Tex," Samuel says. "Mai?"

"I will join you in a moment, Father." She and the big man have scooted their chairs side by side so they can look out the window together. "Dung is telling me about a pretty bird he saw in the tree yesterday. He thinks it was a yellow Greenfinch." She looks at me. "Dung knows the names of many birds."

Samuel smiles. "When you are ready. Come, Sam."

"Phat Ho doesn't say much," I say following Samuel down a long hallway toward a door that appears to go outside.

"He can talk," the doctors say. "But he chooses not to most of the time. The doctors think it is because of his war experiences. Something happened many years ago. He is from the North and fought for the Viet Cong. Living here in the house was very difficult for him at first, and still is at times. For many years after the war ended, it was still nineteen sixty-eight in Phat Ho's mind. He relived his many battles over and over in his head, sometimes when he was awake, sometimes when he was asleep, sometimes when drunk, sometimes when sober. He went to jail two times for fighting, once for almost killing a man with a *garrote*."

"*Garrote*? You mean like a rope or piano wire to strangle someone?"

Samuel stops a few feet from a back door. "Yes. You hold onto both ends and wrap it around someone's neck. Then you cross your arms to strangle your target. It was Phat Ho's specialty in the jungle. He would sneak up on a sentry and take him out silently, and in seconds. He prefers to use a scarf, a *rumāl*."

"*Rumāl?*"

"It is a long scarf used in India to wrap up a person's hair. Phat Ho sews a coin in one end to give it weight so he can swing the scarf around the neck of his target, grab it, and strangle the person. This is what the thuggees, the highway bandits in India, would do. He still carries one or two. Where he learned it, I do not know."

"There was one hanging from his back pocket."

"He always carries at least one. Oh, and he does not like Americans."

"Noticed. What about you?"

"I do not know. Maybe he accepts me because I have been here for many years and my wife is from the North. But I will not tolerate him being rude to you or anyone in this house."

I shrug. "It's okay. He must deal with his—"

"No, it is not okay, Sam. I am working to help the men come to terms with the war. The men here were trying to kill each other a few years ago, and now they are living under one roof. Sometimes it is a strain, but I work to teach them that we all live in the now, right here, right now. And we do it in harmony. That is what both sides fought for in the war, right?"

"I would imagine it's a slow process."

"Yes. War and all its horrors have a way of seeping into one's bone marrow. Phat Ho's kills with the *rumāl* were done so closely that he could smell their fear, see their eyes bulge, and hear their last choke. Only a psychopath could eradicate that from his mind."

"About the scarves, how does he do it? He has only one arm. Using a garrote is a two-handed technique."

"Not for Phat Ho," Samuel says. "He uses one hand and his mouth."

"He holds one end in his…"

"Mouth. Viet, who also fought for the North, told me that Phat Ho lost his arm in nineteen sixty-six, several years before the war ended. Although his superiors tried to muster him out of the army, he demonstrated his killing skills using his good hand and his mouth. They were so impressed, they allowed him to stay and specialize in sentry removal. Viet told me that during the war, Phat Ho killed twenty-six sentries and point men. I do not know how many were Americans."

"My God! I wasn't even in the war, yet I'm not sure how I feel about all this."

"Understood," Samuel says. "It took me a long time."

"I can imagine."

"But as I said before, things are simply the way they are. It is how we perceive them and label them, that causes us sorrow, anger, depression."

"What happened to Viet?"

"He is a true warrior. He suffered many years from depression but has been happy in the last two. His Buddhism has helped and so has living here. He was burned and disfigured fighting for his people, but many of those same people have been cruel to him. Some still are. Understand that the face is the first thing a person notices when talking to someone. It is also the person that one sees in the mirror at the beginning and end of each day. You and I cannot imagine how hard that must be."

I shake my head. "I can't even begin to. It's so sad. His face is…"

"Understood. It is bad. He says that it is his Buddhist practice—his efforts to look into the depths of his mind, to understand all the good and the bad that is there—that has helped him to accept who he is." Samuel shrugs. "So if he can accept it, we should, no?"

We continue the rest of the way to the door, where he turns toward me. "Do not feel sorry for him or any of these men, Son. Just honor their sacrifice because it was great."

"Yes."

"That is Cong," Samuel says, pointing through the small window in the door at a barefoot man out on the concrete patio. He is wearing only a pair of tan khaki pants, his finely-muscled upper body glistening with sweat as he moves about slashing and stabbing the air with a knife he holds in an ice pick grip. "He has only hinted about his war experience, but I have heard from his brother, who repairs motorbikes, that Cong killed many enemy soldiers with his blades." The man quickly lunges forward then glides back, bobs, and weaves to his left, and then leaps to his right, all the while filleting his imaginary opponent with great speed. "He does not talk about his experiences fighting with the South because of Viet and Phat Ho. Some things are best left unsaid for the sake of peace."

"He likes to target the face."

"Oh yes. He says it takes the man's spirit."

"Agree. It also takes his eyes, nose, and cheeks."

"Watch... there. Did you see how quickly he changed his grip?"

"He's using the fencer's grip now," I say, noting how he grips the knife handle between his thumb and forefinger, his other fingers wrapped loosely around the handle. "A very smooth and fast switch."

Now Cong is lunging forward and back, stabbing his imaginary target and retreating. Or maybe he is retreating as a ruse and then lunging forward when his suckered opponent follows. Only he knows for sure. He switches his grip again, smoothly, efficiently.

"Ice-pick grip again," I say. "But with the blade held along his wrist to conceal it a little. He's definitely fast."

With the blade held next to his wrist, he'll get less penetration but he can slash, which is exactly what he's doing now. As if sanding a wall with extraordinary speed, his hand slashes back and forth, slicing his opponent's head, torso and legs, all the while dancing in and out and from side to side with grace and deception. Sometimes his free hand blocks an imaginary hit and other times it covers his heart. This man has trained with a blade for a long time.

"He is seventy-one years old," Samuel says fondly. "He moves well, eh?"

"Yes!" I say. "He moves incredibly well for a twenty-year-old and what a beautiful physique he has. Seventy! Amazing. You train him?"

"I help with his footwork a little and help him to cover himself better with his empty hand. But he was a good knife fighter before. He has more experience with it than I."

"Was he injured in the war?"

"The war wounded Cong's soul. Ask him when he fought in the war and he will say, 'I still fight it, at night when I sleep.' He has never been able to separate himself from those years. He is intense and he has had violent outbursts from time to time, though only once since he moved in with us. He finds comfort here being around other soldiers, though they seldom talk about the war."

"Do any of the men have families?"

"Cong's wife and children left him a few years after he came home. He never hurt them but they never felt at peace around him. Once when a teacher told him that his daughter was having trouble with mathematics, Cong kicked the teacher in the stomach and stabbed his knife into the woman's desktop. His family loves him and comes to see him here; they just cannot live with him anymore."

Stabbing the desk strikes me funny but I manage to hold it in. "How about Viet?"

"The napalm burns still give him so much pain, even after these many years. He says it is like getting hit with electric shocks every day. It hurts him to walk, to sit, to read, and especially to be touched. He rarely complains, though. He has a wonderful sense of humor. You saw how he likes to tease me. He is a magnificent warrior."

Samuel looks back out the window, as if he doesn't want me to see his face. "Viet was married when his unit was hit with napalm. He told me once that his wife came to the hospital and when she saw how badly burnt he was, she removed his wedding ring and left, never to be seen again."

"Removed it?"

"She thought he was going to die, you see. She took it to sell."

"Oh man. And Dung and Phouc?"

"Dung's parents and siblings, six brothers, if I recall correctly, were all killed in the war. He spent many years either begging on the streets or in jail for stealing. Phouc lost his wife about fifteen years after the war ended. The doctors said it was natural causes but Phouc believes it was from her exposure to Agent Orange. She lived on a farm with her family, you see, and when our helicopters sprayed the nearby jungle, the chemical found its way into the farm soil. All of her family died young from lung ailments."

"Shit."

Samuel turns and looks into my eyes, the sadness in his profound. "War is indeed shit, Son. And it is wonderful people like these men that must clean it up and, in so doing, forever have their lives changed. War is shit, whether it is in a rice paddy in this beautiful country, in a rocky valley in Afghanistan, or in the streets of Los Angeles, or Portland. It has always been the warrior class, men and women, who must go toward the sound of gunfire while everyone else flees."

He takes a deep breath as if collecting himself. "Sorry, I think I got off track. What was your question?"

"Actually, I didn't have one."

He goes on as if he didn't hear me, the words spilling from his mouth as if held in for too long. "Those who are not in the warrior class do not always like us because we remind them that their societal graces are a thin veneer. When that veneer is threatened, it frightens them and they call upon us to make things better. They need us, you see, but they fear us. Sometimes they question our methods. That has always angered me, and I am a man who prides himself in being slow to anger. You saw *A Few Good Men*, right?"

"Yes, with—"

"There is a scene where Jack Nicholson, who plays a marine colonel, is being cross examined on the stand by Tom Cruise, and Nicholson says, 'I have neither the time nor the inclination to explain myself to a man who rises and sleeps under the blanket of the very freedom that I provide, and then *questions* the manner in which I provide it!' I almost cheered in the theater when he said that. In fact, I think I did."

I believe it, but what I say is, "I can't believe you remember that whole speech."

"I am passionate about this, Son. Kim says I get carried away. Maybe I do." He looks out the window at Cong slashing the air. "I am proud of these men and those I served with so many years ago." He looks back at me. "And I am proud of you. I know you have guilt and your guilt will be part of you for the rest of your life. But know this: You *will* survive."

Samuel and I stand side by side watching Cong. I'm watching the knife fighter, though it's Samuel's presence that I feel. His words have both depressed me and lifted me. As always, he never ceases to move me in some way.

"Dung seems lonely today," Mai says walking up to us. "It is so sad. Sam, did Father tell you that Dung's best friend died two nights ago?"

"Oh no," I say. "The man who died here?"

Samuel nods. "In his sleep. Heart attack maybe or just tired of living. We may never get an official report because he was of no matter, you see, at least to the government. But he mattered to us, and he especially mattered to Dung. Ngo Bao Chau lost most of his sight in a blast outside of *Củ Chi*. Dung was his eyes and Ngo Bao Chau was Dung's brain. They helped each other."

"They were a good team," Mai adds with a slow nod. "Such good friends. Dung is so sad by his death. I do not think he saw a bird outside that window. He just wanted me to sit with him for a while."

"It looks like you two have a wonderful relationship," I say.

Mai nods. "He is my very special friend."

Samuel touches Mai's arm. "Do you remember what Buddha said about friendship?"

"Yes," Mai says. She collects her thoughts for a moment. Then, "'Buddha said a friend will be a refuge to us when we are afraid. He will be there in our time of happiness and in our time of adversity and sorrow; he will not forsake us when we are in trouble. He will tell us his secrets, and he will not betray our secrets to others.'"

Samuel beams. "You see, Sam. She also remembers important quotations."

"I like that one," I say, thinking about my friend Mark. He is my lieutenant but we became fast friends the moment we met. He was there for me after my shootings, caring, sensitive, and on my side during the department investigation, and the media uproar. So how did I return his friendship? By putting his job in jeopardy, and worse, for not being honest with him about all that happened that terrible week. Yeah, I'm a real catch as a friend.

Samuel lightly punches my arm. "Then fix it."

Okay, he read my thoughts again. "Buddha say that?"

He shakes his head. "I say that." He pushes the door open. "Good one, no? You can quote me. Fix it. Come, meet Cong."

"Want to be my special friend?" Mai whispers close to my ear as Samuel calls out to Cong.

I stumble into the door facing.

"Cong, this is my son Sam. Sam, Cong. Cong's English is good. He worked with an American unit during the war and he has continued to study it since."

"Nice to meet you," I say, returning his bow.

"Glad to know you. I like to speak English and I like English movies."

"Sometimes I take Cong to see American movies at the cinema," Samuel says.

"*Platoon* my favorite," Cong says. "Your father and I see many times because they show Vietnam pretty good. "*Last Samurai* is good. Good sword fighting."

"Both good ones," I say. "You're fantastic with the knife. We watched you from the window."

"Oh," he says shyly. "Thank you. I like the knife. You cut anywhere—arm, finger, nose, hip, leg—hurts. You can cut him so he dies slow or you can cut him so he dies fast. It is all… pretty nice?"

"The expression is 'it's all good,'" Samuel corrects.

"Oh yes," Cong says. "Thank you. It is all pretty good."

"Close enough." Samuel points at Cong's knife. "Cong owns several, but he prefers the Marine Corps Ka-Bar and its eight-inch blade."

"Save my bacon too many times in war," Cong says, spinning the knife in his palm. "Opinions for knives like assholes. Everyone have one. That how you say it, Samuel?"

"Close enough."

Cong steps back two strides. "Ka-Bar good for far away." He jabs it toward me several times. Then he spins it smoothly in his palm so that the blade extends along his wrist. "This grip to cut open gut." He rips his arm back and forth horizontally, simulating cutting my stomach half a dozen times. "Also to ugly up face pretty good." He pumps his arm up and down in front of my face, making it clear how each swipe would leave deep, vertical cuts on my features.

"Are you glad he is standing back a ways?" Mai asks.

"Very glad," I say, impressed over the man's intensity and finesse.

"I end life many Viet Cong with Ka-Bar," Cong says, returning the blade to a leather sheath in his back pocket. He steps toward me and touches my throat, just below my Adam's apple. "Cut here first, so Cong cannot scream. Then thrust blade here"—he touches me just below my navel—"to give him long death." Cong smiles with some really bad-looking teeth, his eyes red, wet, and frightening.

"Ooooh boy," I say. "Any chance you entertain at children's birthday parties?"

Samuel laughs, and says, "Cong is a good warrior. He took lives but he saved lives too."

"I was just teasing, Cong," hoping that he got the joke, though he didn't smile. "Your skill is amazing."

He nods. "I hope you like my country."

"Thank you. It was nice meeting you."

"I go now, Samuel. Clean up and rest a little before meal." He nods to each of us and heads toward the building.

"You have done a wonderful job here," I say to Samuel after Cong goes in.

"Thank you. But I want to do so much more." To Mai, "What are your plans now?"

"It is almost five o'clock. We will go eat and then I will show Sam a little of Saigon."

"Okay," he says. "Stay alert and please check in with me every hour or so as long as you are out."

"I promise, Father."

# CHAPTER EIGHT

"What a great evening," I say. Mai and I are sitting on a cement bench by a huge, spouting fountain. "We've eaten at your favorite noodle stand, we had tea by the Saigon River, and we've strolled through a huge food market. I'm liking this very much. People look at us a lot, don't they? Some smile but a few have glared at us."

"I think people just look at other people. In Vietnam, people are more… overt?"

"Open about it?"

"Yes. If we went out into the country or to a small town, people would follow us, touch us. I told you before, in Saigon we are more accustomed to Europeans and Americans visiting. Out in the country, they are not so accustomed."

"The hate looks surprise me."

"Why?"

I think for a second. "You know, I'm not sure. It's not that hate looks are new to me. Hey, I wore a police uniform for several years and I got a lot of them." I shrug. "You know, I didn't know what to expect here, really. I didn't have a lot of time to read up on modern day Vietnam to get sort of a jumpstart on understanding you and Samuel more. I did read a piece in the Cathay Airlines travel magazine about how Vietnamese love the Americans, that many have forgotten the war. I mean, I know that was a blanket statement written by a travel agent, but still the hate looks took me by surprise."

Mai frowned toward end of my speech. Now she looks pissed.

"I see," she says tightly. "You knew that it was a blanket statement, but still you believed it, believed that *every* Vietnamese person has forgotten the war? That *everyone* in my country loves Americans? That *all* young people want to be like Americans? Is that what you think, Sam?"

"What? No, I was—"

"Do you think we are a simple people and that we are all made with one, uh, cookie cutter? We all have the same thoughts and opinions?"

"Mai, that isn't what I meant at all. I was just telling you what I read—"

"But it made your opinion, no? So you must have believed it because you said the stares 'surprised' you."

"I… yes, I did say that. But I didn't mean it to imply that I think Vietnamese people are simple or that they are all the same."

I want to say more, but I'll probably say something wrong or it will be misconstrued. So I don't say anything and neither does Mai.

Fifteen silent minutes pass when a couple stroll by, a male Vietnamese, about thirty, and a Caucasian woman, late twenties. They look at us, smile and continue walking slowly about the fountain.

"Did we just stare at them?" I ask, out of the corner of my mouth.

"You more than me," she says, out of the corner of hers.

We look at each other. "Mai, you know I don't think those things about Vietnamese people or any people for that matter."

She nods and takes my hand. "I am maybe too sensitive when it comes to my people, my country, especially racial insults. I heard many bad things about us when I studied in Paris and during my year in Portland. All of it was incorrect, opinions based on lies and exaggerations. In Paris, one time, I got so angry at a loud, drunk student who was saying terrible things about my people that I pushed her over a table."

"That's sort of funny," I say tentatively.

"It was very funny. Because when she get up she wanted to fight. So I kicked a chair, and it slid into her legs and knocked her down again. I left then, so I do not know if she got up."

"She might be still lying there," I say. "I got into a fight in middle school when a kid said that all soldiers who fought in the Vietnam War were baby killers. I punched him in the face and got expelled for a day. Kid was probably repeating what he heard his hippy mother say."

Mai smiles broadly. "You were defending Father and you had never met him?"

I smile. "I guess so."

"He will love to hear that story," she giggles.

We look at the water geyser for a moment. "So," I say. "Are we okay?"

She leans the side of her head on my shoulder for a moment, then stands. "We are more than okay. Want to see Saigon at night from the eighth floor?"

"I do indeed."

After a short drive, we're now ascending in the elevator of Vinh Tower One, the building she showed me the first day. Mai and I aren't talking because she has me pressed against the back wall laying a kiss on me that is making me feel tingly all oooover my body. We don't even notice when the elevator doors open. The noise of it starting to close brings us out of our tangle, and we saunter hand in hand across the vast, empty, carpeted room toward the floor-to-ceiling windows. The room is bathed in cool sapphire from Saigon's billion lights twinkling their way through all four walls of glass.

"Absolutely magnificent, Mai," I breathe, looking out onto the panoramic galaxy of stars and lights as far as the eye can see in every direction. "I can't get away from thinking how this city was torn by war just a few years ago."

"It is hard for me too. But Father remembers. He does not say too much about his personal experiences, but I think running the soldiers' home and seeing reminders like the war museum, and so many old men hobbling about the streets keeps it… what? Alive? Yes, alive in his mind."

"I can only imagine."

"Some dates make him be quiet. It took me a while to understand that on Christmas day, January fifth, January twentieth, and February twenty-eighth, he does not say anything, does not talk. Instead, he sits in meditation for many hours."

"You know why?"

"When I figured out the pattern, about ten years ago, I asked Mother. At first she denied that there was a pattern, but finally she gave in to my pestering. She swore me to secrecy that I was to never say anything to Father, which I have not."

"It had to do with the war, I take it?"

Mai nods. "Christmas day was the first time he had to kill. Three people, all with his hands. January fifth he killed seven people with a rifle. January twentieth he killed four people with a rifle. February twenty-eighth is when Father tried to kill an enemy soldier, but the man got away and came back later and killed Father's closest friend."

"My God," I say. "He's told me that he killed fourteen people when he was in the Green Berets, and I just thought that he had come to terms with it. It was stupid of me to think that he doesn't still suffer."

Mai turns her back to the window and leans against the ledge. "I am not sure, but I do not think that it is because he feels bad on those days. I think he holds them in... rev..."

"Rev? Reverence?"

"That means to show honor, right?"

"Yes."

"Father shows honor to those he killed and to the men he lost, especially his friend, the one who was killed by the enemy soldier that Father did not kill. That one bothers him the most, Tex told me. So Father meditates on those days and shows his respect to those who died on both sides."

"Powerful," I say, barely above a whisper.

Mai looks out the window for a moment. She turns to me. "Father have to kill one other time but I will tell you that story later. It is sad, and maybe I am selfish, but I do not want to be sad right now."

"That's fine," I say, reaching for her hand. "I don't want to be sad right now either."

She smiles and nods almost imperceptibly. We turn and look out the window without speaking for a long moment, our shoulders touching, hands clasped, my fingers lightly caressing hers.

"The first time we came here, you said that you imagined us here together, looking out at the view."

She doesn't reply, but her fingers begin to caress mine harder. It's a tad platonic and a whole lot sexual, at least to me. I wonder if Mai feels the same.

She moves into my arms, her body fitting into mine like a glove. Great answer. We stay like this for a long moment.

"Sam?" Mai says into my neck.

"Yes?"

"I like this."

I shrug. "It's okay, I guess."

She slaps my shoulder.

"Do you dance?" I ask.

"Of course. I have won many contests. I am the champion of Ho Chi Minh City."

"Wow! Really?"

"No. I lie. I do not dance."

"I don't either," I say, pulling her out into the center of the huge room. "That makes us a perfect dance couple. We're not *Dancing with the Stars*, we're dancing *in* the stars."

"Music?"

"There's music," I say, taking her hand and wrapping my arm around her waist. "There, do you hear it?" Only a faint hum of traffic penetrates the windows. "A waltz, I think. Beautiful"

Mai's eyes penetrate deeply into mine. "Yes," she whispers, and leans her head against my shoulder as we begin to wheel about the vast room. "I hear it and it is wonderful."

We glide and drift and soar and ascend and float on gentle melodies that only we can hear. It's as if we're part of the heavens, one body in perfect synchronization, adrift in a celestial ocean of clouds and sparkling lights.

An hour passes, or maybe just a few minutes, when Mai's whisper touches my ear like a kitten's breath. "Sam?"

I open my eyes as if awakening from a deep sleep and smile to see that we're now at the opposite side of the room from where we started. There are fewer lights below on this side of the building, but the view is still breathtaking. I lean back a little and look at Mai, at how the pale blue light accentuates the green in her brown eyes, the curve of her cheek, the fullness of her lips, the sensual way her blue-black hair frames her face, and falls over her shoulders.

"Yes?" I manage.

"Do you want to spar?"

I look at her as if she's been tongue testing car battery poles. "Spar."

"This room would make a wonderful school, do you agree?"

"Spar," I say again, with what must be a slack jaw.

"We could have two hundred people for each class in here," she says, gesturing around the room. "It would be the most wonderful school in—"

"Spar?"

"Yes," she says, laughing, "spar." She pushes me back with a two-handed shove. "Come on big boy. Put up your fists."

"You're a whacko woman."

"Okay, you tell everyone that a whacko woman kicked your ass."

I assume a stance. "You're biting off more than you can chew, you know?"

"Another crazy American expression," she says, moving around me as if looking for an opening. "Here is a Vietnamese one, 'It's better to eat salty food and speak the truth than to eat vegetarian and tell lies.'"

I sputter a laugh, turning with her as she circles me. "What does it mean?"

"How the hell do I know. I am not a philosopher."

"Oh, man. I used that one on Bobby in the flight over, and I think Samuel used it on me in Portland."

"Father taught me much. Things like this." She shuffles in and launches a fast sidekick at my middle, stopping her foot on the threads of my shirt. She holds her leg stretched out and bobs her eyebrows. "Got you." She retracts her foot and, without setting it down, whips out a hook kick that just misses my ear.

As she sets her foot down, I lunge in with a high roundhouse kick, snap it back before she can block it, drop it to the floor next to her lead foot, and sweep her leg out from under her.

She looks surprised for a whole second before she surprises me by grabbing my shirt and taking me down with her. She slaps the floor with her free hand to lessen the impact, while at the same time I yield to her pull and dive over her onto my shoulder. I roll back up onto my feet, facing away from her. She is already standing when I spin around.

"However sharp it is, the knife will never cut its own handle," she says, launching two punches at my head. I swat them away.

"Do you know what that one means?" I ask, snapping out a backfist, which she ducks. She scoots away and begins circling me while moving backwards, looking a little like Muhammad Ali in his prime.

"No," she smiles. "Oh look, your shirt is not tucked in now."

"Nor yours," I say, not letting her bait me into looking down. I point at her head. "And your hair is messed up." When she moves her hand up to move a loose strand away from an eye, I fire another roundhouse kick at her thigh, stopping it on the surface. "Got anything in your bag of quotations about being easily distracted?"

"No, but I…" Her face contorts in pain. "Sam!" She bends over clutching her midsection. "My stomach… Oh my…"

"Mai? What is it? Are you—"

She drops to one knee and spins her kneeling body about like a top, her extended leg catching me at my ankle. The room tilts and I'm falling. My butt hits first, and just as I start to tuck my chin to save my skull, Mai cradles my head in the crooks of her arms.

"Oh, I remember one," she says, her face over mine. She gently sets my head down. "'Even though you are competent, appear to be incompetent. Though effective, appear to be ineffective.' What do you think of that one?"

"Can't argue with success."

Mai swings a leg over my waist and lowers herself until her forearms are on each side of me, her breasts against my chest. She shakes her head so that her hair falls around mine, making a luxurious, perfumed cave for two. She holds each side of my face as her eyes move from mine to my mouth and back to my eyes again.

I wrap my arms around her, slip my hands under her loosened shirt, and stroke her lower back. Her skin is warm, soft, silky, heavenly. "This is what we call in America, a 'win-win,'" I wheeze.

"I think that is the best quotation of all."

"I would have to agree with—"

Her lips interrupt me. No matter, I don't remember what I was going to say anyway.

Sometime later, we come up for air and I find that I'm on top of Mai, her legs wrapped around my butt, her hands still holding my face. "How did you get into my mount?" she asks.

"Don't remember, but you must not have resisted." Her shirt is rumpled and pushed up just under her breasts. She has an amazingly long waist, stomach muscles lightly defined, skin the color of creamed coffee. And she's got an innie. I like innies best of all.

"Hmm," she says, thinking. "I know a couple ways to get out of this."

I shake my head. "Don't think so. You're pretty much mine, to do with as I wish, dontcha know."

She sighs. "You are right. But could you lift up a little for just a second? My right hip is pinched."

"Oh, sorry," I say.

When I move, Mai shoots her left leg up and around my head, then simultaneously thrusts her hip and pushes my head with her thigh to knock me off and onto my back. Just as she did in my school, she rolls up onto me in one smooth motion. In Portland, she pinned my arms and used her thumbs to force my mouth into a smiley face. This time she zaps me with a tongue-probing kiss that nearly sets my shoes ablaze. When we finally part, she sits back on my thighs.

"'Even though you are competent, appear to be incompetent. Though effective, appear to be ineffective,'" she says unbuttoning my shirt. "Did you forget that one so fast, Sam?"

"I guess." My voice sounds like loose gravel. I slip my hands under her shirt and slide them up and over her breasts. Soft, full, the bra sheer, nearly nonexistent.

Mai opens my shirt as if unwrapping lunch and commences to run her fingers over my chest and stomach. "Your muscles are beautiful," she breathes, her eyes devouring me. I'm liking this a whole lot. When she runs her finger tips across my nipples, I practically jackknife up. "Ticklish?" she smirks, her eyes never leaving my torso.

"Yeah, that's it. Ticklish." I push her blouse off her shoulders and pull her down onto me. We kiss as I unsnap her bra. She shrugs out of it, her breathing rapid, her eyes smiling as I take in the beauty of her breasts. "Oh my," is all I manage.

Her cell phone rings from her jeans pocket.

"No—Flippin'—Way," I say, panting.

"Probably Father. I have not checked in for a while." She called him once while we were sitting in the park and told him where we were. "I will call him after."

"After?" I say, pulling her hair out of the way so I can watch her tickling my chest and stomach with her breasts. "There's going to be an 'after?'"

She leans on one forearm and slides her hand down to my belt buckle. "Maybe two 'afters,' Buddha willing."

\*

"Wow!"

"I concur," I wheeze. "Wish I smoked."

We're lying on our backs next to each other looking up at the reflection of the city lights dancing on the ceiling.

"The top of my head is already smoking," Mai says.

I rise up on one elbow and look around. "We worked our way back over to where we started dancing. Good thing this carpet is here or we'd have road rash from the cement."

Mai rolls toward me, and lays a naked thigh across both of mine and rests her head on my chest. "Lots of scooting," she says.

I laugh at that, which makes her head bounce. That makes me laugh even more.

"Stop," she says, pinching my stomach. "You will give me a headache."

"Ow, no pinching."

"No bouncing your girlfriend's head."

"Deal," I say stroking her hair.

Outside the window, clouds with their bellies lit from the city lights, swarm by fleeing the northern winds. If we were in

Oregon, I'd say it was a pending storm, but here in this tropical climate, I don't know what it means, if anything. Mai's breathing deepens; she's asleep.

Four days ago, I was in my house in Portland, Oregon. Tonight I'm lying naked in the clouds over Vietnam with a goddess. Mai stirs and twists toward me. She kisses me and lays her head back on my chest.

"Are you a goddess, Mai?"

She nods. "Yes. Yes, I am."

"Thought so." We kiss again.

A couple of minutes pass, and she asks, "Do you think about what happened in Portland?"

"I do. You?"

"It saddens me. So many lives lost."

"I suppose you could think it to death and still not have it wrapped up in a nice, tidy package. Maybe the big things in life never can be. I killed people who would not have died if I had been somewhere else. People tell me that a man lived because I took another's life. Okay, I'm good with that. But the other... I can never be *good* with it. That will chew and gnaw and rip at me forever."

Mai reaches up and caresses the side of my face. It lulls me into the peaceful place I have been seeking.

*

"Sam."

I open my eyes and look into Mai's face.

"Hi. We've been sleeping." She lifts my left hand so I can see my watch. "Almost all night. It's half past five."

"You're kidding." I twist to see better out the window. "Oh man. It's getting light."

She sits up on her hip. I go for her breast.

"I would love to, Sam, but I am not sure when the workers get here. And we are both very, very naked."

"Gloriously so," I say, sitting up to take her in my arms. We kiss for a long moment.

"Come on," she says. "Our clothes are all over the room."

We stumble to our feet, hanging onto each other and nearly falling once, and begin walking across the room, kissing most of the way.

"We're walking and we're naked and we're kissing," I say. "This feel awkward to you?"

She giggles, her free hand partially over her eyes. I put my hand over mine.

"You're peeking, Mai. Your fingers are spread."

"Whoops. But you are too handsome for me not to peek."

"You are also too handsome for me not to peek," I say, spreading my fingers and looking her up and down.

She slaps my arm. "You are a baaaad man. I like that."

Giggling like happy little children, we slip on our clothes, bumping into each other as we hop on one leg to get into our pants.

Dressed, we kiss our way over to the elevator, pass through the already open door, and keep kissing a bunch more. A minute passes, or maybe it's two days, before we part. Mai pushes the button that closes the door. We begin our descent. I lean against the back wall and she leans against a side one.

"Did we just have our second date?" she asks, her breathing returning to normal.

"You know, I think you might be right," I say seriously. "How do you think it went?"

"Oh, I think it had its ups and downs."

"Yes, yes, I concur on your fine ass-essment in this matter," I say. Mai nods thoughtfully and we manage to hold onto our serious expressions for another moment before sputtering into laughter.

When the elevator door opens, she wraps her arm around my waist, and I droop mine over her shoulder as we walk down the hall side by side as if we've done it a thousand times before. Before we reach the door, we stop and embrace again.

"This is going to sound corny," I say, "but what's happening between us?"

Mai doesn't say anything for a long time. Then, "I think I know."

"I think I know too," I whisper.

She leans back and smiles. "I am very happy." When I tell her that I am too, she smiles again, and asks, "You want breakfast? I usually have *phở* and French bread. A good way to start the day."

"Will it help me recuperate?" I ask.

"I hope so," she grins, pushing open the door into a brilliant morning sun—and a dusty brown shoe slamming into her abdomen.

Mai catapults back into my hip, spinning me partly around. I don't see her collide with a corner of the scaffolding, but I hear her. Before I can turn back, something hits my lower back, hard, and a second blow collapses my right knee, sending me to the ground next to Mai where she is dry heaving into the dirt.

There are three of them standing over us, legs spread, hands fisted, all silhouetted against the glaring sun. The tallest man is on the left and the shortest on the right. I whip a roundhouse kick with my uninjured leg into the thigh of the tallest one, a technique I've used to break baseball bats in demonstrations.

His femur bone cracks loudly and he drops, screaming all the way into the dirt. I'd like to add to his misery, but the man in the middle is moving rapidly toward me. He knocks aside my side thrust kick to his knee and lifts his foot high. If he's planning on stomping me, he's holding the chamber too long, giving me a hair of a second to hook my ankle behind the knee of his support leg and jerk it forward, pulling him down next to me.

Close up and out of the sun's glare, he looks to be about twenty with a weight-trained physique showcased in a skin-tight black T-shirt. "Hello," I say, and backfist his brachial plexus, a pocket of nerves half way between the side of his neck and his Adam's apple. His eyes cross and he sags onto his side. That will give him a major headache and paralyze him for a few long seconds.

"Sam!" Mai's voice from behind me. "Stop!"

Out of the corner of my eye, I can see that the tall guy has gotten back up and is hopping toward me on one leg, holding his broken one behind him. Determined, I'll give him that. Since he's still a couple of hops away, I turn toward the guy lying on his side whose brachial plexus got slammed, and I hit the same cluster of nerves with a bottom fist. This time he doesn't cry out from the blow, but rather lets out a barely audible whimper, his eyes rolling like a Vegas slot machine. He's motionless now, at least his upper body. His feet, though, are churning in the dirt, pumping as if he were riding an invisible bicycle that's lying on its side.

"You! *Dừng lai*!" A man's voice from behind me.

"Sam!" Mai's voice again.

The hopper loses his balance and falls onto his side next to me with an "Ooomph" and a cloud of dust. A gift from the sky.

I'll take it. I scoot up quickly onto my good knee and lean on one hand as the downed hopper does the same. He punches first and I swat it aside. Since my swat hand is still out there in the air, I ram its thumb into the man's eye bringing forth that scream again. If a thumb into that eye got a good reaction, a thumb into his other one should—

"Sam, stop!" Mai. Scared.

"*Dừng lai,* you mutha fuck." That male voice, screeching.

I twist around to where Mai has fallen by the door. She's on her side, supporting herself on her elbow while the diminutive man stands behind her pointing a semiautomatic at the top of her head.

"You stop mother fuck! I shoot her brains!"

"Mai?" I say.

"Sam, look out be—"

Explosion of light.

Falling…

\*

My eyes are closed and the side of my face is lying in soft dirt. Breathing it in. Snorting it out.

Feet shuffling about me.

A car engine. Will it run over me?

I open my eyes a little.

I push myself up into a sitting position, eyes closed tightly against an excruciating pain in the back of my head that just might detonate my brain matter.

Footsteps. Moving toward me. I force my eyes open. It's the man whose neck I hit. He's recovered from the brachial stun blow, though he still feels the effects in his legs because he's walking like I do when I've done six sets of heavy barbell squats. The fact that he can walk at all means I've been out a few minutes.

He's holding a board, a two-by-four. He draws it back. I lunge for him, grabbing a handful of his groin and using it as a handle to yank him down to the ground. I let go of his cookies, grab the front of his neck with one hand, and slam a hammerfist into his nose, exploding blood like a popped water balloon. No whimpering this time. Instead, he bellows like a just-branded water buffalo and rolls onto his back, his hands flailing above his head. This guy has some strange reactions to pain.

Someone… pulling… my hair. I fall over onto my back.

Something hard pressing into my eye socket. Lots of yelling. Smell… gun oil. Rem Oil; I've used it for years. Got to be a gun barrel. With my one watering eye, I make out a car. Black. Mai's face in the back seat. Her mouth's moving but I can't hear her.

"Sam!" I hear her now. "Do not fight back. They will shoot you." She's sitting awkwardly, her arms behind her. "Lai Van Tan's—" The man I kicked hops in next to her and pulls the door closed.

They're Lai Van Tan's people.

The gun barrel remains pressed into my eye for a moment longer, then it's gone. Both my eyes are watering profusely.

"You stay," the gunman says from above me. "Stay down or I shoot your brains out good." I nod. "Look ground," he says. I do. "You stay. You no stay, I shoot brains."

Out of the corner of my eye, I can see the short gunman, swimming in my watering eyes, helping broken-nose guy into the car.

The door slams.

The car accelerates away.

# CHAPTER NINE

"Samuel most pissed," Tex says into my ear. "He no show it much but he pissed off big time." Tex and I are sitting side by side in the monitor room looking at Samuel who has opened the mini blinds and is looking out at the walkway as he talks on his cell. Lam is sitting behind the monitors keeping one eye on the screens and one on Samuel.

"He no go crazy when he most pissed," Tex says. "But he most pissed for sure."

"Who's he talking to?" I whisper, grimacing. I twist in the chair seeking a position that doesn't hurt my lower back. I don't think it was a kick that got me. It felt more like I was struck with one of the two-by-four boards lying around the construction site. The pain in the back of my head has finally subsided to a tolerable level. Actually, it's more in my neck, right where it connects to my head. I was out for I don't how many minutes so I don't know why it doesn't hurt more. But I'm not complaining.

Tex listens to Samuel for a moment. "Lai Van Tan friend. No not friend. Partner?"

"Someone who works for Lai Van Tan."

"Yes, yes," Tex says touching my arm. "Sorry. My English bad news."

"Your English is fine. What is Samuel saying?"

"He want to meet… no, he want to have meet with Lai Van Tan."

"A meeting?"

"Yes, yes, a meet-ing."

"But what about Mai? Is he negotiating for her release?"

Tex shakes his head. "Sorry, Sam. Too many words I do not know."

I space my words. "Is Samuel talking about Mai? Talking to get her back?"

"Oh. I do not think Mai is too much problem."

"What?" I say too loudly. "What does that mean?"

Samuel twists around and gestures with a finger to his lips for us to be quiet. He turns back to look out the window and continues his conversation. Okay, I'm getting a little mad now. Samuel has kept me in the dark since I called him from the construction site.

Tex touches my arm. "Sam, please tell me what happened."

I look at Tex and try to read his hard face to see if he has lost all respect for me. His eyes are intense, just as they were when I first met him, so if he thinks I'm as worthless as a dog turd, there is no way to know. I tell him about us coming out of the building, being taken by surprise, the fight, and the gun.

"Very good, Sam," he says. "You fight good. No sweat. But you cannot fight a gun that is in your eye. Okay?" When I don't respond, he lightly punches my arm. "Okay? It rule. Big rule. No fight gun in your eye."

"Yes, okay. You've got a point."

"Okay. So tell what happened."

I take a breath…

I wanted to chase the car, but I couldn't stand. The tendons behind my kicked knee were having a spasm fit, the slammed muscles in my lower back were contracting and threatening to bend me over backwards, and the back of my head felt like it would win a giant pumpkin contest. After a few minutes, the agony in my leg subsided enough for me to get up and lean against the scaffolding. My eyes were still watering, but not as much as when the short man was pressing the gun barrel into one of them. As soon as my lumbar muscles stopped contracting, I began hobbling my sorry self down the alley in the direction the car had gone. I made it all the way to the busy intersection, but my hopes that they had booted Mai out onto the street were dashed.

Without a clue as to which way they went, I went left. After a few yards, my eyes had stopped watering and my back had loosened up a little. Even my knee felt better, though my head was in desperate need of a half bottle of Excedrin. It was a typically nutso street with god-awful traffic, blaring horns, shouting pedestrians, and a myriad of vendors' carts. What could I ask? Excuse me, did you see a black car go by with people in it?

Why yes, you stupid American. Thousands.

I extracted my cell and poked in my prepaid, one eight hundred number, connected with international calling, and typed in Samuel's number from a piece of paper in my wallet. There was a series of beeps, clicks, and buzzes before Samuel's quiet voice said, "*Á-lô.*"

"This is Sam," I said, my voice a pitch higher than normal.

"Where is Mai?" he snapped, his ESP apparently in high gear.

"We got jumped, Mai and me. We were at that building that's under construction and—"

"Where is Mai, Sam?" His voice was so calm, so controlled that it was almost chilling.

"They got her. Three of them. No, four. There was a driver. Three jumped us and overpowered us before we had a chance. They forced her into a car, a black one."

"Was she hurt?"

"She got kicked pretty hard in the stomach."

"And you?"

"I tried to fight them, Samuel. I… failed."

"Were you hurt?"

"Some. I'll be okay.

"Did they find Mai's gun?"

I forgot about that. I remembered her removing it last night when she was taking off her pants.

"I see."

Oh man, he read my mind.

"Did she put it back on?"

'Yes," I mumbled.

"What?"

"Yes. She should have it."

Samuel didn't say anything for a long moment, then, "Okay. You have my address, correct?"

"I do," I said. It was on the same piece of paper on which I had his phone number.

"Flag over a taxi. Show him the address. You are only about twenty minutes from my house. I am here now. Tex will watch for you at the gate."

My hand was shaking so hard that I dropped the phone. I caught it somehow and lifted it back to my ear, holding my wrist with my other hand. "You there?" I asked. When Samuel replied, I said, "So sorry. I feel so—"

"We will talk when you get here, Sam. I must make some calls now." That's when the connection ended.

Tex was waiting at the gate when my cab pulled up. He paid the driver and gestured for me to follow him inside.

"Has Samuel called the police?" I asked.

"No call *canh sát*," he said, moving hand over hand up the stairs without effort, the muscles in his tattooed arms rippling.

"Tex?"

He turned around and faced me eye to eye. I was still a half dozen steps down.

"Any word on Mai?"

"No."

"I don't understand. Why no police?"

"Samuel say to you why." Tex lowered his voice and pointed toward the back of the house. "No want Kim to know about Mai. Samuel with Lam in TV room."

"You did good, Sam," Tex says. He was nodding as I was telling him what happened. "Hard to fight ambush. You hurt them in fight, right?"

I nod. "But not enough."

Samuel shuts his phone and sits on the counter in front of me.

"I heard your story, Son, and I agree with Tex. You did what you could. That is all anyone can do, right? Tell me, where did you go before you went to the high rise last night?"

"First, we went to your jewelry store, the one where Da`o worked and another lady… I don't remember her name."

"Hua. Did you talk with anyone else there?"

"No. Then Mai showed me around the city a little. We had noodles at a stand somewhere. Then we walked along the river, we sat by a fountain, and she showed me a busy market."

"You did not talk with anyone else?"

"No."

"Do you think you were followed?"

I shrug. "I wouldn't know. I mean the streets, the traffic. It's all new to me, overwhelming."

"Understood. I am sure that people looked at you two, but did anyone pay extra attention? Use your police instincts here, Sam."

"Coke, Sam?"

I look down and see Tex holding out a can of Coke.

"Thanks," I say. I take a deep breath and blow it out. "I just can't think of… wait. There was a young girl at the jewelry shop. A street kid. A little pimp. She asked if I wanted a girl."

"Too many street kids," Tex sighs, and then swings up into a chair next to a monitor. Lam has not taken his eyes off the screens since I've been in here.

"She couldn't have been more than ten or twelve…"

Samuel leans toward me. "What?"

"She had a cell phone. Before we left, Da`o shooed her out of the shop. She had been squatting at the entrance… listening to us talk. A few seconds later, she was talking on a cell. You don't think she—"

"Did she speak English?" Samuels asks.

"Yes. Lots of slang and curse words but she understood me quite well. She was listening when I was talking with Da`o. Actually, it was more like Da`o was threatening me that if I hurt Mai she would come after…" I look down, shaking my head, feeling like warmed-over caca. I look up at Samuel. "I didn't give a second thought to the kid."

Samuel shrugs. "She must have heard enough to understand your and Mai's relationship."

"So she called someone and they followed us? That fast? I mean, we left just two or three minutes after Dao`a shooed her away."

"Son, it is possible that you have been followed since you stepped off the plane."

He told me that before and it's still a whole lot uncomfortable. "Who? I mean, who?"

Samuel shrugs. "Maybe the police. Maybe the government. It is not that unusual for them to follow people, but since you are not an overt threat, they probably are just keeping track of your activities. But I can almost guarantee that Lai Van Tan's men have followed you, just as they have been watching this house."

"Shit."

Samuel nods. "As far as Lai Van Tan, it is likely that they used the kid because she wouldn't raise your suspicion. They know I own that shop, and they had the girl watching in the event you and Mai went there. They probably have people watching all of our stores. When the girl realized who you are, she called her contact, told them you were there, and described Mai's motorbike and what you two were wearing. They likely had people in the area so they were able to get a tail on you. Then it was a matter of watching for an opportunity to get to you."

"Assholes for sure," Tex says, his eyes burning.

I shake my head trying to grasp the whole thing. "So Lai Van Tan's people are following me and the government is at least keeping track of my movements. It would have been nice if the government had been watching when the goons jumped us. Or maybe they were and just laughed."

Samuel doesn't say anything.

For the umpteenth time since I've been here, I feel as if I'm on another planet. Okay, I understand Lai Van Tan's people following me, but the government keeping track of me? What do they think I'm going to do? I feel like I'm in a nineteen forties black–and-white spy movie.

I look at Samuel. "Why haven't the police been called? They could set up a watch at Lai Van Tan's for the car and—"

"Sam." Samuel says, scooting off the desk and stepping close to me. He puts a hand on my shoulder. Is he going to rip into me for losing his daughter? Kick me in the face? Well have at it. I got it coming. His eyes twinkle, as he says, "If I know Mai, and I do, she will be joining us for lunch shortly."

\*

Tex is on his cell. "Okay okay okay," he says rapidly, his smile huge. He snaps his phone closed. "Samuel," he whispers, louder than if he had spoken in a normal voice.

Samuel, who has been talking on his cell by the window for the last few minutes, turns.

"Mai call," he says lifting his phone. "She come home now."

"You're shitting me?" I blare.

"Tex no shitting on you," Lam says, pointing at a monitor where Mai fills the screen in living HD waving her finger tips at the camera. Other than a little dust on her clothes, she looks great. I bolt for the door.

"Do not make noise in house," Tex reminds me—I'm running and he's keeping up with me—as we head toward the back door. "No want Kim to know."

Mai steps through the glass doors just as I reach the top step.

"Mai," I breathe, enveloping her in my arms.

"Easy, easy," she laughs. "My ribs hurt. I—whoa!" She looks down at Tex who is embracing her leg, the side of his smiling face against her thigh, his eyes looking up at her. She grabs hold of the door facing and laughs. "Tex, it is good to see you. But I am going to fall over. You two! I think maybe I was safer with those men."

"We go to TV room," Tex says, holding Mai's hand. "Father there,"

"Okay," she says, smiling at both of us. "Lead the way, Tex."

"How did you get away?" I ask, holding her arm—I don't ever want to let go. "I'm so happy to see you. I tried to follow the car but I couldn't... I was so worried... My God, Samuel said that you would be home for lunch."

She laughs.

"But how did you get away?"

"Kung fu and Glock," she says, sounding like something Samuel would say. "Hello, Father."

Samuel is standing on the cobblestone walkway. "Mai." He grips her shoulders and looks her up and down. "You are not hurt?" His eyes glisten and his lips slightly tremble. Guess he wasn't as calm and collected as he appeared.

"I am fine," she says. We all move into the cool room. "Hello, Lam. My stomach hurts but I think it is okay. I do not think my rib broke."

"What happened?" I ask.

"At first I could not breathe because the kick was so hard. I could not even get up to fight with you. Father, the sun blinded us when we walked out the door and the men attacked us with surprise. I do not know what happen to Sam, but I saw him suddenly on the ground next to me. He was hurt but he fight hard. He broke one man's nose pretty good and another man's leg. When Sam started to beat everyone up, one man pulled a gun and pointed it at my head. He told Sam to stop or he would shoot me. They did not search me. They just shoved me in their car and I was between two men. Lucky for me, they did not have time to tie my hands. They just told me to keep my hands behind my back. I thought they would take me to Lai Van Tan, but after maybe ten blocks they turned into an alley where there is an old building. I think they were going to… rape me, kill me."

A ferocious wave of flight or fight juices surge through me, and it's not flight that I want to do right now. I'm guessing Samuel and Tex are feeling the same thing.

"My plan was to fight them before we got to Lai's, maybe when we were in a traffic jam. But it was better at the warehouse because there were no people around to get hurt. So I bend forward and pretend to cry, but I sneak my hand down and got my Glock. The man on my right saw me, saw what I did. He saw me with only one eye because Sam poke his other one out pretty good. Same man who had a broken leg bone." She points just above her knee. "This thigh bone, right?"

"Yes, thigh bone," Samuel says.

"Okay, thank you. Thigh bone poke through his pants. It was not fun to see with my eyes. Anyway, he yells, 'gun!' so I shoot him first."

"What?" I say. "You shot him?"

Mai nods. "I do not want to kill him so I shoot his… uh… here." She points at her knee.

"Kneecap," Samuel says matter-of-factly.

"Yes, kneecap. Father always teach that hitting the kneecap causes much pain."

"He was probably talking about kicking it," I say.

"Yes," Mai says. "So shooting it hurt him much more, I am sure."

"Cool," Tex says, from where he is perched on a chair, hanging adoringly onto Mai's every word. "Sam break his leg, you shoot knee. I think he most for sure fucked up now."

Mai nods. "When man on the left grab my head, I shoot him in his leg." She points at her thigh. "Right here. The thigh."

"*Beaucoup* cool for sure," Tex says. "Mai number one, eh Sam?"

"Oh, man!" I laugh, looking at Samuel who is leaning against the wall with pride written all over his face, and concern for her. "Definitely number one."

"Everyone was screaming in the car, and the two men in the front were trying to get out. The driver, who was real brave or real stupid, pulled out the screaming man on my left so he could get to me. I pointed my gun at him hoping I would not have to shoot him. When he backed up, I got out real fast and kicked him many times until he fell… unconscious. Unconscious is like asleep, right?"

The three of us nod.

"So I went around to the other side, pulled out the other shot man and threw him to the ground."

"Who had the gun?" I ask.

"The passenger. He must have been a big coward because he jumped out and ran away, and took the gun with him. So now, three men were on the ground and the fourth man with the gun gone. So I got in the car and drove away."

"You stole their car!" I laugh.

"Yes, because my motorbike was still at the building. I needed a ride and they were just laying on the ground."

That made Samuel laugh. "Where is it?"

"Two blocks that way," she says pointing. "I didn't want to drive it all the way here."

"Good," Samuel says, looking at her for a long moment. He takes a deep breath and blows it out. "I am happy you are safe, daughter. I'll have someone get your motorbike and bring it here."

Mai nods, smiles.

"Why don't you and Sam clean up and we will meet for lunch. There is much I want to talk with you about."

"I'm so sorry about this, Samuel," I say. "There was just no warning and the sun was piercing in our eyes when we came out the door." Man, can I possibly come up with more excuses?

"I do not hold you responsible, Son. A fighter cannot block what he cannot see. Well, I can, but others cannot."

Tex nods and smiles at me. "Your father pretty good."

# CHAPTER TEN

I feel better after cleaning up and changing clothes. I checked out my lower back in the bathroom mirror. The slightly red mark there, about four inches by twelve, belies how much it hurts. The skin is red behind my knee, as well, but that pain has mostly subsided. I got a tender lump on the back of my neck. There is no abrasion so I'm thinking the guy hit me with a hammerfist strike, a hard one. I've been knocked out before and had a headache that lasted a week. This one is starting to subside already with the help of the three pain pills that Samuel gave me.

I'm having trouble wrapping my mind around what happened. First, there was the glorious night with Mai. It was better than any dream. Then to be jarred back to reality so violently was simply overwhelming. What I told Samuel about the sun in our eyes and the explosiveness of the attack was true, but I think the fact that Mai and I were lost in ourselves slowed our reaction as well.

I've only been in Vietnam for three days and while most of the people I've met are warm and charming, the rest of my experience has been not just a little unsettling. Bobby's scuffle at the airport, the jerks at the tea café, and the kidnappers this morning—*dukkha* all over the place.

Mai meets me atop the back steps. She's wearing clean jeans and a red top. Jaw dropping sensational. Hard to believe she was fighting for her life a short while ago and pumping bullets into people's legs. As usual, her smile ignites my cardiovascular system.

"You feel better?" she asks. "I do."

"Yes, thanks. How is your stomach?"

"It hurts but I will be okay. I did not feel any broken ribs."

"Are you sure," I ask. "Want me to double check?"

"Triple check. But not now. Now we have spring rolls and fruit." She takes my hand and leads me into the dining area. No one else is here yet.

"I got to say, you just went through quite an ordeal and you look fantastic."

We sit next to each other. "Thank you," she says.

"And you don't seem to be too upset."

"I was before. Driving back, I had to pull over for a few minutes and have a good cry. At first, my cell would not work and then it did. After I was kicked and fell, the same man kicked me again in my hip and hit my phone. I will have a rectangular bruise, I think."

"I'm so glad you're okay."

"Your visit is not happening the way I wanted it to," she says, touching my hand. "Except for last night."

"Last night was wonderful," I whisper. "The rest of it, I am here to help. We're family. Please don't feel bad for me being here."

Mai's eyes twinkle. "You are the best half brother a girl could have."

Ly, wearing a beautiful tangerine *áo dài*, enters the room with a large tray of tea and fruit. "Hello, *Ông* Sam," she says. "*Gỏi cuốn*, I bring out one minute."

"Thank you, Ly," Mai says, leaning forward to distribute the cups. "*Gỏi cuốn* is the same summer rolls you have before. But this time you dip them in peanut sauce. I think you will like it better than the *nước mắm* sauce you have last time."

Two hours ago, I was rolling around in the dirt with kidnappers, and now I'm learning about Vietnamese dishes. "Sounds good."

Tex slaps his way up the back steps, into the dining room, and swings into a chair. "Feel good now?" he asks kindly, looking at both of us. "Your father worry you, Mai. He no show worry but I know him too long. I know him worry."

"Thank you, Tex," Mai says. "I will not tell him that I know."

He nods and turns to me, smiling. "Sam, Vietnam very fucking exciting, no?" he asks enthusiastically.

I sputter a laugh. "Yes, sir. It certainly is that."

"Hello, everyone," Samuel says coming in. He sets his cell on the table and pulls out a chair at the head. "Sorry I am late. I was with Kim. Hard day for her, so I am happy that she does not know what happened. She sleeps, so we must speak low."

Ly brings in the summer rolls and sets them next to the fruit and tea. Samuel begins filling our cups. "Ly, anything you might hear us discuss in here does not get repeated to Kim. I do not want her to worry. Okay?"

She bows slightly. "Yes. Of course." She leaves.

Samuel sips his tea and sits back in his chair. "Lai Van Tan has clearly gone to the next level."

"We attack him now?" Tex asks excitedly, fingering one side of his long braided Fu Manchu moustache.

Samuel smiles. "Hopefully never, my old friend. I am sure it is what he expects of us, so I have tried to take him off guard by asking him for a meeting."

"A meeting?" Mai repeats.

"Yes. I think that—"

The *Superman* theme.

"The monitor room," Samuel says, lifting the phone to his mouth. "Lam… *Cảm ơn.*" He sets the phone down. "Sifu is here," Samuel says, scooting back his chair.

I twist to look out the sliding glass doors as Samuel moves through the archway.

Mai stands and moves to where Samuel was sitting. "Sifu come through the front gate this time," she says. "Sometimes he does that. He likes to… what is the word…? Mess. He like to mess with Lam's mind." She scoots Samuel's plate, tea cup, and chopsticks over to the first seat on the table's long side. Tex hands her a clean cup from the tea tray, and she places it where Samuel had been sitting at the head of the table. She fills the cup.

"He no eat," Tex says. "Just drink tea."

"Sifu is joining us," Samuel announces as he enters the room alongside Shen Lang Rui. I quickly stand as Mai moves next to me.

The master is dressed in brown slacks and a white overshirt. His longish salt and pepper hair looks windblown. I wouldn't say that he's delicate looking, but he's not quite as healthy appearing as is Samuel, who is his junior by only three or four years. Incongruously, though, he radiates, for lack of a better word, an extraordinary life force. Samuel does too, but Sifu's almost vibrates with it. For a second I wonder if I squint my eyes a little that I might see balls of energy pulsating and crackling all about him. He stops before Mai and me.

Mai and I bow. He responds with his palms together.

"Happy," he says. His eyes, one green, one blue, penetrate first Mai's, then mine. After a moment, he takes each of our hands and holds them in his. I feel that same warmth as I did before when he touched me, just not as intensely. He rubs his thumbs on our skin and nods as if understanding something. He releases our hands and moves toward Samuel's chair. He speaks quietly to Samuel as we all sit.

Samuel looks at us. "Sifu says that your *chi* has been greatly disrupted this morning. Mai, yours the most. He says he cannot immediately restore it, but he has adjusted it so that when you rest you will recover almost one hundred percent."

Mai dips her head toward Sifu and speaks quietly to him. I only understand '*cám ơn*'. I tell him thank you too. Sifu nods once and again speaks to Samuel.

Mai leans toward me, and whispers, "Sifu apologizes for the interruption and asks that we continue our conversation. Now Father tell him about what happened."

Sifu nods and looks at Mai and me again.

Samuel sips from his tea. "Sifu understands what is going on now. Where were we? Oh yes. A meeting. Confucius said that 'life is simple, but we insist on making it complicated.' On that note, we can keep wondering what Lai Van Tan's mindset is, or we can go to him and find out. I just got off the phone with one of his men, a man named Phong Tran. Phong Tran is the man I spoke with four months ago about setting up a meeting with Lai Van Tan to see if he would back off demanding so much money from our stores. Phong Tran seemed like a reasonable man then, perhaps the most level-headed of the crew.

"I made it clear that Lai Van Tan's actions today were tantamount to an all-out war and that it is imperative that we talk so as to prevent that. Phong Tran said he would talk to Lai Van Tan about the possibility. I strongly urged him to make it happen."

"Do you think he will, Father?" Mai asks.

Samuel lifts his palm. "Let me translate what I have said to Sifu." Samuel speaks in a soft tone, all the while the master nods, and then speaks again.

Samuel looks back at us. "To answer your question, Mai. I hope Lai Van Tan will agree. Sifu also thinks that a meeting is a wise path to an understanding and agreement of some kind. He says that Lai Van Tan is clearly suffering great *dukkha* from having lost his son. He says we must have compassion for him, but we must do so with caution because in nature, there is nothing more dangerous than a wounded animal. And Lai Van Tan is clearly wounded."

I like that Sifu is philosophical without seeing the world through rose-colored glasses and secondly, that Samuel is thinking the same way. But I detect something in Samuel's face beyond his earnestness in wanting to find a peaceful solution. There is an occasional tightness around his mouth and an almost imperceptible flicker of that dead-eye look I saw in Portland just before he went into battle. Samuel wants peace but I think he's ready to rain hellfire if he doesn't get it. This could get ugly.

"What kind of a setup does the man have?" I ask. "Is he surrounded by bodyguards?"

"I do not know where he lives and Lu has been unable to find out. But I have been to his office, one of them. He occupies an entire upper floor of a building near the airport. There were six men in the room that time, all subservient to Lai Van Tan. All but one were in their thirties, hard eyed, tough looking. One man stood out. He was my age. Chiseled features, eyes that had seen violence, participated in it, liked it. I have heard rumors that Lai Van Tan has hired a few old Khmer Rouge soldiers to help protect him. I think that man was one of them."

"Khmer Rouge!" Mai blurts.

"Number fuckin' ten," Tex says, shaking his head.

"The Democratic Kampuchea," Mai says to me as Samuel catches Sifu up on the conversation. "For five years in the mid-nineteen seventies, they followed their leader Pol Pot to do, uh, gen… ocide. Genocide on their own people. The Khmer Rouge killed close to two million people. Their *own* people, Sam. Some say maybe it was more. That is one quarter of all the Cambodian population. They still find gravesites there, what you call… mass gravesites, put in ground by the Khmer Rouge. Even today many people are hurt and killed by the landmines they put all over back then.

"Mother has several newspaper articles she saved on it and I read all of them. I remember one was called "Year Zero," and it stuck in my mind. That is what Pol Pot called what he did to his people. He said Year Zero means all the culture had to be destroyed, so he could start a new one. Start it from the beginning, from year zero. Even the Cambodian history was declared not important anymore, and Pol Pot wanted it removed from the people. So the Khmer Rouge soldiers followed these orders with much brutality and much violence."

"Any idea how many Khmer Rouge he has working for him," I ask.

Samuel shakes his head. "I do not. Lu is checking into it, so I am hoping to learn something from him. Tell me, Son, what do you think of having such a meeting?"

"I think it's a good idea. We did it once in Portland with gangbangers after several weekends of fatal shootings." Samuel translates for Sifu as I speak. "Our chief was screaming for something to be done, and so was the community, especially those suffering from all the violence. So our gang unit met with seven or eight leaders from black and Hispanic gangs. The officers told these leaders that they would hold them directly responsible for any future shootings, and that the gang unit would come down on them with every bit of firepower they had, and every prosecutorial device they could use."

"What happened?" Mai asks.

"The gangbangers walked out. The leaders were enraged. I can't say that I blamed them. They knew that too many of their subordinates were loose cannons—uncontrollable, and they didn't want to have the turd put into their pockets."

"Why put turd in pocket?" Tex asks. Mai looks confused too. Sifu's face is neutral.

"Sorry. I mean we put the responsibility on them, the leaders."

"But they walked out," Samuel says.

"Yes. The shootings did slow down a little, but I don't know if that was just a result of the normal increase and decrease of gang violence that we see."

"Understood," Samuel says, sounding a little disappointed.

"Still, right now, I think it's your best option," I say. "You don't want the police involved, I take it?"

Tex is shaking his head. "No work for sure. Lai Van Tan too crazy for meeting."

After Samuel translates, Sifu gently says something to Tex to which the old warrior immediately responds with a bow, palms together. He doesn't look up.

Mai leans in. "Sifu say to Tex, 'People who say it cannot be done should not interrupt those who are doing it.'"

Good one. That should be on a poster or something. Tex lifts his head, apparently recovered from his gentle reprimand.

"I don't know who Lai Van Tan has on his payroll," Samuel says. "I have one friend on the police force, Vu Van Hien, but I think he is in Paris right now. That is what I was told last week, and the person I spoke with did not know when he is coming back. I will check again today."

"Okay," I say. "Let me see if I'm clear on everything. Lai Van Tan is into drugs, extortion, and now sex trafficking."

"Yes," Samuel says. "The sex trafficking we are just learning about."

"He has an unknown number of people working for him including the possibility of some old Khmer Rouge soldiers. We also know from what happened in Portland that he has people elsewhere at his beck and call."

Samuel nods. "Portland and Los Angeles that I am aware of. In Portland, though, I think he might not have any more people."

I nod. That's for sure.

"We don't know anything about weapons," I say, "but given today we can assume they have guns."

Samuel nods. "And many are martial arts trained."

"They seem hell bent on revenge."

Mai leans forward. "That would be, as you say in America, an understatement. Remember what I told you in Portland about how some criminals think about *Ba'o Th'u,* revenge? If they cannot get the person they want, they will go after that person's family. They want to revenge very much and they keep trying, even it takes a hundred years."

Tex has been eyeing me for the last few minutes. "Wish you be home, Sam?" he asks.

"No," I say immediately. "You are all my family."

He thrusts a fist toward me, stopping it a couple feet away. I bump it with mine.

"Can only do in chair," Tex says. "Do on floor, I fall over."

I smile a little, uncomfortably. But Sifu laughs. Guess he understands English better than I thought. He and Samuel exchange words, and Samuel laughs.

Mai whispers, "Sifu ask Father what do you call an Asian woman with one leg shorter than the other. I did not hear the answer."

"Irene," Samuel says, chuckling. "Get it? Sifu has got some good ones."

While Samuel and Sifu talk quietly, Tex, Mai, and I eat in silence. I'm not terribly hungry and I seem to be getting more tired each passing minute. I glance at Mai and see that she's sitting back in her chair, her face drained of color.

"How are you doing,?" I ask.

She rotates her head to the left and right, popping her neck. "I feel strange. Suddenly, I am very tired. Very, very tired."

"You should feel tired," I say, touching her arm. "I think the shock of what happened is starting to catch up with you. You've been getting progressively paler in just the last few minutes. If I may make a suggestion, you should lay down for a while."

"Sam right, Mai" Tex says.

"Three against one, daughter," Samuel says. "Go to bed for a while. Sifu says you will sleep very restfully."

She puts her hands on her stomach. "I will," she says somewhat feebly. "Excuse me." She stands and touches my shoulder. "Sam, I will talk to you later."

"Get some sleep," I say.

"Sifu, Father," she says weakly as she passes them.

"She white," Tex says after Mai leaves.

"It is normal," Samuel says. "The adrenaline has left her body so now she is tired and emotionally spent. How are you doing, Son?"

"Tired, but I'm mostly embarrassed that we got caught off guard. And I was so scared for Mai. I… I don't know. I don't have it all worked out yet in my head."

"A normal reaction," he says. "I think you might need rest right now." When I nod, he says, "You fought very well, and so did Mai, but *after* you two were taken by surprise. It is a hard way to learn, so it is important to analyze what happened and learn from your findings. Always keep learning, right?" Sifu says something and Samuel nods, and looks back at me. "Sifu says that 'pain is a wonderful instructor but no one wants to go to its classes.'"

I smile and nod to both men. "*Cám ơn.*"

"All of us here are martial artists, Sam, very good martial artists. But we are humans first. That makes us capable of mistakes." His eyes twinkle. "Even me, as hard as that might be to believe."

"Even Sifu?" I ask, smiling a little.

Samuel says something to his teacher and Sifu responds.

"Sifu says that 'the more masterful one is, the bigger his mistakes. We make them as do our enemies. When our enemies make them, do not stop them.' And to that I will add, do not let them learn from them either."

I nod to both men.

"You get some rest, Son, and we will talk after. Mai will probably sleep for hours. You should do the same."

"Thanks, Samuel, Sifu. If you will excuse me, I'm going to go hit the hay."

"Why you hit hay?" Tex asks.

"It means sleep." I say, lightly punching his shoulder.

"Hit hay same-same sleep." He shakes his head, shrugs. "Got it."

*

After leaving the dining room, I went back to my room, stretched, shadowboxed for about five minutes to burn off my remaining adrenaline, and took another shower. My plan was to do a little meditating, but a wave of fatigue pushed me down on the bed, which is the last I remember.

I'm awake now, sitting on the edge of the bed and feeling wonderfully refreshed. Wow, it's four in the afternoon. Four! I slept for nearly five hours. My lower back, behind my knee, and the lump on my neck are all tender, but I feel pretty darn good otherwise. I check my cell. No calls. Mai is probably still sleeping.

I'm still bugged about getting caught off guard. If we had had our heads on right, Mai and I would have at least considered that Lai Van Tan's people knew we were inside. We would have eased that door open instead of bursting out of it like school kids at three in the afternoon. As Samuel said, you can't block what you can't see, but if you're paying attention, if you're taking precautions, you can reduce the element of surprise.

Once when I was working uniform, I pulled over a car for a traffic violation in a quiet residential area. I gave the guy a warning and let him go. Walking back to my car, I felt a little antsy, though there was no one else out in the hundred and five degree August day. Still, I had a case of the creeps. It felt like someone with bad intent was watching me.

A few days later, the shift sergeant took me aside and asked if I had stopped a car on Southeast Lincoln a few days prior. When I said yes, he told me that a woman had called earlier and said that she and her boyfriend, an ex-con, were in their apartment and saw me pull over the motorist. Apparently, her boyfriend went psycho and got a rifle from a closet. At first, she thought that he was just showing off for her, but then he loaded it and thrust it out the window. She said she shouted at him, which made him look away from me. When he looked back, I was driving off, which angered him so much he smacked her around. That's when she came to the police to report how close I came to getting a pine box overcoat.

I had many narrow escapes on the PD, so I don't know why I'm thinking about that one right now. The Grim Reaper is always fluttering his cape in and out of our lives. The sniper would have turned my head into a red cloud if it hadn't been for his girlfriend's shout. Lai Van Tan's goons could have offed us as we came out the door, but didn't. I got the best of a couple of them, which probably kept me from getting beaten to death, still the guy who screwed the gun in my eye could have shot me. And Mai's situation could have turned out a whole lot different if Samuel hadn't trained her so well. Sometimes it seems like life is just a series of near misses.

Okay, enough of this line of thinking.

I walk out into the garden area and sit on the hard bench by the *koi* pond. Man, you could bake cookies in this heat. There's a bit of a breeze rustling the tops of the palm trees, but the solid, high walls around the house prevent the wind from reaching ground level. The *koi* have the right idea: They're lying motionless at the far end of the pond in the shade of a palm tree.

I close my eyes and take a deep, calming breath. I do another, focusing on drawing the air into my belly, holding it there for a few seconds before slowly letting it out. After a few exchanges, I return to breathing normally, or I try to. Funny thing is that I've been breathing for over thirty-five years, but now when I try to do it normally, the more erratic it becomes. I either breathe out too fast or too slowly, or I hold it in too long.

It's like trying not to think about purple elephants. Oh good, now I'm thinking about a giant grape-colored Dumbo.

"Listen to the wind, Son."

"Shit!" I half shout, snapping my arms up.

Samuel smiles at me. "Jumpy are we? One gauge of knowing that you are meditating deeply is that you cannot be startled. Calmness is one of the byproducts of meditation, you see. Keep at it. It is worth the effort, and it will affect your whole life in a good way."

"How is Mai?"

"Ly looked in on her about twenty minutes ago and she was sleeping soundly. I have seen Mai go and go and go and then sleep for twenty-four hours."

"She is amazing," I say.

"She thinks the same of you."

"Really?"

"How was your rest?"

"I feel wonderful." I look toward the glass doors. "Did Sifu leave?"

Samuel squats down Asian style at the shady end of the pond. "Yes, about two hours ago. You rested well because he, uh, adjusted is a good word for it, he adjusted your *chi*, and Mai's. He has incredible healing powers but some things he cannot fix directly. Like *chi* that has been greatly disturbed. But he can set into motion the healing by helping you to rest deeply."

"He's incredible."

"More than you know." He makes a little circle in the water with his finger. "Meditating can be difficult at first." The *koi* undulate away a few inches and then are motionlessness. Maybe they're meditating. "Focusing on your breath can be especially difficult after you have been agitated. But keep at it. Soon you will be able to do it easily, anytime, anywhere."

"I liked how I felt those times we did it in Portland."

"You took to it like," he flips the water again with his finger, "a *koi* to water." The fish don't move this time. They have either mastered meditation or they don't feel threatened by him. "You will enjoy the sense of calm you gain from it, and how your thinking becomes clearer and more focused."

I nod, sitting motionless, watching him watch the *koi*. I listen to the palms fronds whispering above us. The intense heat is starting to feel not so, well, intense, and the sounds of traffic outside the walls are sort of a low-volume white noise. An insect buzzes somewhere near, but not close enough to bother. I'm liking this moment a whole heck of a lot.

Time passes.

"I have been out of the American dating scene for a few decades," Samuel says, still watching the fish. "But I'm assuming young people still go to fast-food eateries and park down at the river."

"That might be a little dated," I say, wondering where he's going with this. "And I might be a little old for that scenario, but I guess in general terms that's right."

He chuckles. "But yours and Mai's courting is mostly about fighting other people."

I nod, then shake my head. "Yes, and I wish that weren't the case. Last evening, though, we enjoyed a normal date. We walked along the river, ate, talked." I'll leave out the all-nighter part of it, though I know he knows. "The normalcy of it was wonderful," I say quickly, so that I won't think about the eighth floor. Whoops, just did.

Still looking at the water, he smiles, either at what I said or at my struggle to not think about the eighth floor. Damn, I just did it again.

We sit in silence, Samuel teasing the *koi* with his trailing finger, me thinking about the fights Mai and I have been in. There is something that has tweaked my brain a little about them, and I was planning on talking to Mai about it. But since Samuel and I are having a moment here…

"May I ask you something about Mai?"

"If you want her hand in marriage the answer is no."

I feel my face flush blood red. "What? No."

"Good. You agree that it's too soon, then?"

"Yes. For sure. I wouldn't…" Even with his face turned away I know he's grinning.

"Just screwing with you, Son."

I laugh. "You're good at it."

"Okay, what did you want to ask?"

I take a deep breath, not sure why I'm nervous about asking this. So I say it quickly to get it out of my mouth. "I have a bad temper and I was wondering if Mai does too."

Truth is, I don't think I have a temper at all. I'm just trying to soften the question a little. While force was needed in each of our altercations—the one at the tea café here and the ones in Portland—the way she performed was… what? Over the top? Yes, that's it. Excessive. It was either rage, an explosion of temper, or, I don't know. Maybe that's just the way she fights. I'm falling hard for Mai, but I've made bad choices before and I want to know how she thinks.

Samuel looks up at me. Still squatting, he shuffles around and sits on the ground facing me, folding his legs into lotus, each foot on the opposite thigh. "I do not think so, not if a temper means she is out of control with anger. But there are things that make her angry. People who want to hurt her family. Bullies who prey on the weak. Ignorants attacking her because she is of mixed heritage. Injustice."

I nod. Maybe that's what it was. Or was it?

"What makes you angry, Son?"

"Same things, I guess. I definitely hate bullies and I don't like prejudice jerks. I'm not mixed, of course, but a cop in uniform is definitely in the minority. During the years I wore that uniform, I was hated by a lot of people, hated because of the color of my clothes. Many black people hated me because they saw me as the epitome of the oppressor: I was white and in a uniform that gave me power over them."

"Understood. People who did not know you still judged you negatively. You might be the greatest man in the world, but because you wore a uniform, they hated you."

"Exactly. I was doing my job. I put my life on the line, with the best of intentions, but that wasn't enough for some of them. I've been verbally and even physically attacked because of my damn clothes. Just before I left uniform for Detectives, I was coming out of a business where I'd just taken a call, and a hippy girl walked right up and spit on my chest. Called me a Gestapo. I'd never seen her before, never had any dealings with her. She told me when I was taking her to jail that she hated all cops. She was so riled by this time that she spit on the plastic shield that separates the front seat from the back."

Samuel looks at me, reading me. Soothingly he continues. "So you can understand a little of how it is with Mai. Of course, she cannot remove her mixed race like you removed your uniform. She wears hers, how you say in America, twenty-four-seven."

"I understand the difference. What got me thinking about this was the incident at the tea café with those two racist punks. I don't have a problem using force when there are no other options, but Mai went off before we had even tried to leave. I have to admit I was a little taken back by the explosiveness of her actions." I wait for Samuel to say something but he only nods. "Please don't think I'm being judgmental or that I'm being a girly man. Those two clowns needed some attitude adjustment and Mai gave it to them. But I still think that... I just want to understand her more."

Samuel looks across the yard, takes a deep breath, and eases it out as he looks back at me. "I was not there, but what I understand from what Mai said, they were trying to make her feel small and you as well. People cannot make you feel bad about yourself unless you let them, right? So she did not let them. I do not know if I would have chosen her way to accomplish that, but she chose it and I trust her instincts."

Hmm. Well, I'll give her the benefit of a doubt that she was giving them a lesson, and for sure they will think twice before picking on the seemingly weaker, as will those who were on the side of the bullies. Maybe she picked up on something culture-wise that I didn't, something that indicated that they were about to get physical. Maybe I should drop the subject. But then there was the fight in the massage parlor in Portland.

He looks at me. "You think she lost her temper in Portland because of what she did to that woman's arm?"

Okay, that was eerie. I didn't even get to ask the question. "I guess what bothers me a little is that after Mai knocked her down and the woman was hurting and having trouble getting up, Mai went for a *coup de grâce*." Did that sound like I'm accusing her?

"You are referring to Mai's kick against the woman's elbow joint."

"Yes."

"You thought it excessive?"

Oh man, I wish I wouldn't had started this conversation. "Uh, I think because the woman was already down, she was no longer a threat."

"Son, you sound like one of those left-wing liberal newspaper people I have heard you rant about," Samuel says, his look amused. "Worse, because you were there and you saw that we were in a desperate battle. Mai was not play fighting in a sporting event. The woman she hurt 'excessively,' as you say, would not have stopped attacking because the buzzer rang, or just because she was stunned."

I nod, but the argument in my head carries on. Part of my issue is that as cops we fight to get resisters controlled enough to get them into restraints. We don't fight them to finish them off.

"Here is what I believe," Samuel says. "I believe she did not lose her temper. She destroyed that attacker's arm because at that moment it represented the threat to our family. She felt she *had* to do what she did because you and I were in that room with her, and because of the danger to her family here in Vietnam. I do not believe she did it because she lost her temper."

Again he studies my face. "Let me ask you this, Sam. Do you think I lost my temper at Portland State?"

"I wasn't there when you did those things," I say quickly, with a shoulder shrug thrown in to imply that only he would know. But In the weeks since, I've often thought that he did lose it, and who would blame him? The three of us were being attacked in Portland, and his family was under threat here in Saigon.

"I did not lose it," he says emphatically. "I was being logical."

Logical. Like in reasonable?

"It was logical to take that shooter's eyes so that she would never use them again to harm others." He straightens his legs for a moment and refolds them into lotus again. "Understand that our world here in Vietnam is light years away from your world in Portland, Oregon, or any other place in the States. Life here is intense. Crime is monstrous, racism is widespread, feuds and revenge are practically an art form. Some of that followed me to Portland and threatened your life, Mai's, mine, and my family's here. That is the reality that we live in."

"Yes," I say, too confused to add more to it.

"Do you think it was wrong?" he asks, nudging.

I shrug. "No, I don't think… I'm not sure. Well, legal-wise, yes, it was wrong in Portland. But as far as the temper issue, I did wonder a little if these things were done out of anger."

"You have never responded out of anger, Son? Even when those people attacked you for wearing your uniform, for doing what they asked you to do, for doing what you thought was right?" One of the *koi* splashes water near Samuel's knee. He doesn't acknowledge it as he waits for my answer.

"Yeah, I have. But it made me feel bad after because I should have been better than that. Acting that way is not what I trained for both as a cop and as a martial artist."

"Yet you wondered about Mai and me."

I do an okay-you-caught-me smile. "Still, I weigh everything against what has been pounded into my head for fifteen years as a cop: We don't administer justice on the street. That is the job of the courts."

"Ah, the courts. What is that expression I hear on American television? Something like 'and how is that working out for you?'"

I chuckle. "Sometimes not too well. For the police, it can be hard not to want to administer justice on the streets. That's because cops get to the scene as it's happening or shortly after. So we are the only ones in the judicial system who see, smell, and taste the carnage up close. When the courts get the case months, sometimes years later, the facts, the reality, the horror, are reduced to legal arguments and suppressed evidence."

"And the bad guys walk," Samuel says.

I nod

"What if you destroyed the offending arm, or whatever, at the scene?"

"I get your point. But what if we did and we were wrong? Thank God when I overacted I wasn't wrong. But what if someone else did the crime and we destroyed an innocent person in error? Or what if at first what appears to be a crime turned out to be a situation where the person was justified to do what he did, but we punished him before we learned that? Or, what if we destroyed the so-called part out of rage, anger, or hatred because we didn't like the person who did it. Or we didn't like his race, his religion, that kind of thing? So not liking the person was really our motive for punishing him, not so much for what he did."

"And yet you shot those men. In one case an innocent boy died as a result."

"What?" Even without his mind reading abilities, Samuel must see the hurt in my face. "What does that have to do…"

"I am not trying to hurt you, Son. I know that you suffer from what you have had to do, and that you are a good man.

Clearly it has caused you to reassess your life as a warrior. You have been through a lot, even for a cop. But, perhaps it will help to remember that you chose to be a warrior. Maybe fate helped you along, but it was your choice."

Samuel smiles. "Mai did not choose to be a warrior, or maybe she did. Either way, it is her life now. And she accepts the choices she makes to stay alive and to protect her family. Perhaps that is what you need to do."

He studies me to see if his words are sinking in. I honestly don't know if they are. Maybe it's too soon right now.

"You said that sometimes it's hard for a police officer not to punish on the spot?"

"Yes."

"Do they ever?"

"The less disciplined do."

"You said that you have."

I nod slowly. "A couple times, yes."

"So does that mean you have a temper?"

I look at him, maybe sheepishly. I can't tell because my face feels numb.

He lifts his eyebrows.

Let's see, in the last few weeks I smashed my kitchen wall phone to bits, I attacked my heavy bag until my knuckles were literally skinned and bleeding, I pushed a vandal who had broken my living room window into a fight, and I tried to attack my partner in the Detective's Unit.

Some ass clown points a gun in my face and I'm suppose to decide in a half second the 'right' thing to do—of course the brass, the media, and the 'citizens' all have a different take on the right thing. Meanwhile, I'm trying not to stop a round with my forehead and trying not to shoot anybody else, including the whack job with the gun. And don't get me started on those GD liberals sitting in their safe little houses just waiting to stand on their liberal little soap boxes and… and when I see those perps, those vicious animals who prey on the weak… I want to…

Samuel gives me a look. "Listen, Son, maybe we all have tempers. For sure, it's something that we—our family and our circle of friends—must fight against since we possess lethal skills." He turns and looks at the white *koi* that has moved from the cool shade and wiggled its way into Samuel's shadow. "We are all a work in progress, no."

"Yes," I breathe. Then, "Thank you, Samuel. Much to think about."

He looks back at me, smiles. "Me too."

I watch the now motionless white *koi*, how it's found comfort in Samuel's shade.

I say, "I must have done something right, sometime, to have found you and Mai."

He looks into my face, the emotion in his nearly bursting. "I feel exactly the same way."

We both smile, probably looking like goofs.

"You ever played Chinese sticky foot?" he asks.

The abrupt change of topic takes me a second. Then, "Not sure I know what that is."

"Please stand." He straightens easily as if he hadn't been sitting in lotus for several minutes. If I'd sat that way I'd need a massage, a steam, and pulley system to get up. "Your back okay for this?"

"I can feel where they hit me but it's fine," I say.

"Chinese sticky foot," he begins, as we head over to the big bag, "teaches you much about which muscles you use when you kick. If you fail to stay focused or try to kick too hard, you lose your balance. Not safe to practice on a rooftop."

"Good tip," I say. I have seen his mind-boggling hand speed a few times but I haven't seen him kick. Wait, I did too. In my house, when he was demonstrating his style's Third Level of speed. Actually, I didn't *see* his kicks. I felt them, though.

"No demonstration this time," Samuel smiles. "Just a simple drill. Okay, my left leg is forward so you need to put your right one forward, so we are like a mirror. Good. Now we lift our front legs until our thighs are parallel with the ground and our lower legs are hanging straight down. I will place my shin against yours. Like that. We must keep our shins touching at all times. Ahh, you have excellent balance."

Right. I'm swaying and he's as still as a photo.

"The drill is to spar using only kicks launched from this shin-to-shin position. Just throw whatever kick you want without setting your foot down first. The other person's task is to use their leg to prevent the opponent's kick from landing."

"Like this?" I fire a sidekick at his support knee, stopping it against his pant leg.

"Yes!" he says. "And thanks for not actually hitting me."

I smile, though I know he let me do it.

"Okay, I will try to kick you in the groin and you use your shin to stop me."

He launches a medium fast roundhouse kick. I draw my raised leg in close to my groin to stop his foot with my shin.

"Good! You understand already. We can hop around if we want, but we must keep our legs raised and our shins always touching. Do not kick higher than the mid section and do not block with your arms. Try to feel my energy and balance, and understand how the two change when I kick. With practice, you will know which kick your opponent is launching."

I would have liked a warm-up, but oh well. I snap another sidekick toward his support leg, which he knocks off course with his shin, making me have to hop a couple times to regain my balance. He throws another roundhouse, this time at my support leg thigh. I'm too slow to react and it lands hard enough that I have to set my leg down to recapture my balance. I lift it again and touch shins with him.

"You cannot use momentum with these kicks," he says, hopping in a circle around me. Hard to believe he'd be getting Medicare if he were in the states. "Use only the muscles in your legs and core. It is good physical exercise as well as good for training sensitivity."

He smacks the ball of his foot solidly into my gut, then quickly withdraws his leg back to the shin-on-shin position.

I hop a couple spaces to my right and throw my world famous roundhouse at his abdomen. He hops back just enough for it to miss. I set my foot down quickly to keep from toppling over.

"Each time you need to touch the ground, Son, ask yourself what happened to your balance. Learn from it."

"Okay," I say, before snapping a front kick to his middle. He leans away so it misses him by inches.

"Very good."

"Thanks. So what is the worse case scenario with Lai Van Tan?"

His leg leaves mine and begins a roundhouse. When I lift my shin to block it, he snaps a crescent kick in the opposite direction that smacks into my stomach. "Worse case," he says, ignoring the fact that he knocked the wind out of me, "is that we will have a war."

"What does that mean?" I thrust a toe-out kick at his shin and the arch of my foot actually touches his leg. Score one for me. "A war? An all-out fight?"

"You see? You used a simple approach and you got me. Simple is best. Always do simple." He shoots his leg out as if to do a hook kick. When I lift my leg to jam it, he changes it to a low-snap sidekick into my inner thigh.

"That wasn't simple," I laugh. "That was a combo fake and kick."

He smiles. "But first I put an expectation of simplicity into your mind." The smile disappears. "What does anything mean with Lai Van Tan? I do not know. But I can tell you that should it look like war, I will take it to him. Your turn."

"My turn?"

"To kick. Your turn to kick."

"Oh, yes." I drop the ball of my foot hard onto the ground and bounce it up into a head-high roundhouse kick.

He leans away from it, but just barely. "That was pretty, but remember, you cannot touch the floor or kick above the waist."

"But you said simplicity was best. My plan was a simple one: to cheat."

Samuel laughs. "You are a good student. You listened and you improvised. Let us remember that simplicity, cheating, and improvisation are all important fighting concepts. Want to do another drill?"

"Sure."

"Tell me this, Sam. Is not most fighting improvisation? Maybe you have heard of this expression that we had in the army: 'No campaign plan survives first contact with the enemy.'"

"Yes. And cops say, 'All plans turn to shit when the first shot is fired.'"

"I like it. Crude and to the point. Okay, let us both put our left feet forward and place the backs of our left wrists against one another. There, good. Now apply just a little pressure. I think you have probably practiced this drill. The objective is to backfist the other person before they can block it. It is about sensitivity and speed."

I give him a you-got-to-be-kidding-me look. "Soooo, what chance do I have?"

He smiles. "It is about the exercise, about understanding reflexes, muscle control, and relaxation. I am not giving you a speed demonstration."

"Right. And the check is in the mail?"

"Feel my wrist, the pressure against yours. Do not let me hit you." He fires a backfist over my hand, which I block before it gets to my head. "Very good, Son. What did you feel?"

"I felt the pressure of your wrist disappear, and I saw the way your shoulder moved that you would backfist my face."

"Yes, yes, very good. The pressure was released, you knew I was going to hit, and your experience told you with what and where."

"I've done the drill before." That was smug. "Sorry. I didn't mean to sound—"

"No problem," he says, waving me off. "But I wonder how deeply you have gone with it."

"Deeply?"

"Okay, I said I was not going to do a demonstration, but allow me a little one so you can see the possibilities. This time, hit me with a backfist somewhere: stomach, groin, face, wherever. Do it fast, but don't knock me out."

We cross wrists and apply slight pressure against each other's arms. Although his eyes seem to be directed at our hands, they appear to be looking elsewhere. Knowing him, probably another galaxy.

I pop a fast backfist at his head—

His forearm blocks my blow, which incongruously sends a penetrating pain through my belly. "Ow," I blurt. "What the...? You blocked my arm but why do I feel a sting in my..."

"Your tum-tum?' Samuel asks, the corners of his mouth turning up.

"Yes, my tum-tum. My belly. What did you do?"

Samuel looks up at the palm tree. "The sun has moved," he says. "Let us move over into the shade. This is better. Okay, when it was my turn to backfist you a moment ago, you felt my wrist leave yours."

"Yes."

"That was the 'tell' that we talked about in Portland. My wrist leaving yours told you that I was launching a blow."

"Okay."

"This time when you snapped your backfist at me, I tapped your belly a fraction of a second before your wrist moved off mine."

"What? That doesn't make sense. Your wrist left mine *before* my wrist left yours? Even if that was possible, you cheated."

"I suppose one could argue that it's cheating, but I would not agree. And yes, it is confusing but only because the limitation of language makes it so. Okay, think of it this way. When I threw a backfist at you earlier, you felt my wrist leave yours." I nod. "It was your experience, skill, and speed that enabled you to block me. Was that cheating?"

"No."

"So when it was your turn to hit me just now, my experience, skill, and speed enabled me to *feel* your plan. *Feel* your thoughts." He shakes his head. "I know you're thinking that I read your mind. No, I did not. At least not in the normal way."

There's a normal way to read minds?

"You see, when the thought passed through your mind that you would backfist at my face, your brain sent an electrical current to your muscles. No, it was not a message to 'throw the backfist.' That one would be sent in a moment. The first message was to tell your muscles that the second command was on its way. In my layman's mind, I think of it as your brain telling your muscles, 'Get on your mark, get set,' and telling them in less than a nanosecond. Then the second message is sent to your muscles to go, that is the starter pistol: Bam! That is when you launch your backfist. All these things happen much faster than you can blink your eyes. Understand?"

"I think so."

"It's all about practice. With lots of it, you can develop the sensitivity to *feel* your opponent's plan an instant before he implements it."

"The hit to my belly?"

Samuel shrugs. "I did it to prove my lesson, to demonstrate what is possible. I tapped your belly with my backfist in the middle of that nanosecond between your thought and your physical backfist."

"So, you basically hit me twice. The first time between my thought and action and the second time to block my action. You do know I didn't even see the stomach blow?"

"Of course, because it was too fast, which is why I tapped you there in the first place. If I did not give you that little sting in your belly, would you have believed me that it is possible to move with such speed?"

I shake my head in disbelief. "It's hard to consider it even with the sting."

Samuel chuckles. "Right now I can do it when touching you. In this exercise, it is the wrist that is the conduit, you see. I feel your thought, your plan, through whatever point is touching. I was able to develop this skill through lots of sensitivity practice with my sifu. The next step for me is to do it when I am not touching the opponent." He sighs. "It will take lots more practice, I think."

"Damn!"

"Well said, Son. It is an example of attacking the enemy's strategy, just as Sun Tzu suggested in *The Art of War*. If the meeting with Lai Van Tan does not work and he wants war, that is what we must do: attack his strategy."

"You don't sound optimistic about the meeting."

"Mark Twain said that an optimist was a 'daydreamer more elegantly spelled.'"

*

I'm still feeling the effects of the thug encounter so I'm happy when Samuel soon calls an end to our Sticky practice. No sooner do we sit down—actually, I sit and Samuel squats Asian style, commenting that the hard bench hurts his rear—when my cell rings. With all that had been going on, I forgot that Bobby and I were supposed to meet today.

I tell him that I am really tired and ask if we could do it tomorrow. His voice cracks as if he were about to cry. "Please, Sam," he says. "Please meet me."

I tell him to hold on and give Samuel the condensed version of my contact with Bobby, and ask if he would work out the details of a meeting place since I haven't a clue where I am, other than the address.

After about five minutes of speaking in English and Vietnamese, Samuel says, "Okay, see you in a few." He closes the phone and hands it to me.

"What's happening?"

"He seems like a pleasant young man, except he is frightened."

"Of being caught?"

"Yes. And of being in Saigon alone."

"Where can we meet him?"

"It is walking distance. I did not want him to come here for security reasons. May I go with you?"

"Sure. You will be better able to advise him, anyway."

I fill Samuel in on what little else I know about Bobby while we walk toward the busy street. Mai and I turned left when we went out for tea; Samuel and I go right. It's almost dark now and the explosion of lights dazzle, and the frantic pace on the street and sidewalk has actually increased from when Mai and I were on it.

"Look," Samuel says, pointing at a two-story building across the street.

"Looks like a clothing shop of some kind."

"Not that. Above it, on the roof."

It's about fifty yards away, so all I can see against the darkening sky are about half a dozen people, no, there's more, maybe a dozen more, all wearing blue jackets. I can only see the top halves of their bodies as they punch and kick at each other.

"*Vovinam*," Samuel says. "Vietnam's martial arts style. It

combines hard and soft and uses many kinds of weapons. It is a very good system."

"I'd love to see it sometime."

"We will try to make it happen." He points toward the end of the block. "We are to meet your friend for noodles down there." He looks behind us and across the street, no doubt looking to see if we are being followed.

"Sounds good," I say, looking behind us as well. Not seeing anyone quickly stepping behind a lamppost or turning to window shop, I turn back and say, "Thanks so much for... Oh, I see him. There by that cluster of bicycles."

Bobby is no longer wearing his "Westminster, California" T-shirt, a wise decision since it stands out too much for a guy who is on the lam from the states. He's now wearing a white one with "I ♥ Vietnam" on the chest, with black shorts and running shoes. He looks like any other sixteen-year-old, one jerking his head all around like he's been popping paranoia pills.

"Bobby!"

He snaps his head toward us, smiles, and quickly walks our way. "Sam," he says, pumping my hand. "I'm so happy to see you. Thanks for meeting me." He looks at Samuel. "Hello," he says, and extends his hand.

"Bobby, this is my father Samuel." Wow, I said it again. Father. That's twice now. Samuel looks at me, his face beaming. He takes the boy's hand. "Samuel, this is Bobby, my airplane companion."

"Nice to meet you, sir," Bobby says. He looks behind him. "Can we get off the sidewalk?"

"Right here," Samuel says, pointing at an eatery the same size as the tea café Mai and I visited. Three of the four tables are occupied; we sit around the other.

"Sam, if you are tired of *phở,* you should try their noodle salad here. You get a bowl of cool noodles with cucumbers, lettuce, and mint, all topped with stir-fried vegetables and meat."

"Sounds good. Bobby?"

"Yes, that is fine," he says, nervously eyeing passersby on the sidewalk.

As Samuel tells the waitress what we want, I lightly punch Bobby's shoulder. "You doing okay, man? Want to tell me what's going on?"

He glances at Samuel.

"He's cool," I say.

Bobby's face scrunches. "I feel bad about lying to you, Sam. I don't lie but I was afraid. Didn't know who to trust."

"Your father filed a runaway report on you."

"Yes. He must have called the police here and asked them to stop me at the airport. They were suddenly on me. I just sorta panicked, I guess."

"Sam said you kicked them," Samuel says.

"You saw that?" Bobby asks, looking at me with surprise. When I nod, he looks down at the table, his face tight. "I saw you from the cab, but I didn't think you saw that happen."

"You drew a crowd."

He shakes his head. "I was just so scared and so focused. All I saw was those guys and they grabbed me so hard. I just like, reacted."

The waitress puts down the bowls of noodles and tea. Samuel thanks her.

"Why did you run away from the states?" Samuel asks.

"Because I'm stupid," he whispers, shaking his head as if in disbelief at how much so. "I met a girl online, a girl from here. She lied to me the whole time we talked. Said she loved me and all that, and begged me to come here."

"No dying grandfather?" I ask.

"He already died," he says softly. "That is why I came over with my mother and father two years ago." His eyes tear up, probably because he used his grandfather in his fabrication. "My mom read some of my emails to Cam, that's the girl here, and she saw the emails when I talked to her about coming here, how I already had a passport and everything. My mom got really mad, and when she told my father he got like even madder. Crazy mad. He slapped me. When he tried to hit me again, I blocked his hand and pushed him back. I didn't push that hard but his head hit our refrigerator." Bobby's tears are flowing now. "He wasn't hurt, but I felt terrible and my mom screamed and backed away from me like she was real scared. I tried to go to her, but she got like hysterical and covered her head with her arms. My mom... scared of *me*! Like she was afraid I was going to do something to her. I mean... shit!" He rubs at his tears with the back of his hand. "*Shit!*"

Samuel and I look down at the table for a few moments as Bobby tries his best, but fails, to stop weeping. It's a silent cry, the kind that makes his shoulders bob up and down. When he finally collects himself, he apologizes in a barely audible voice and empties his teacup in one big swallow.

"You should eat your noodles before they get cold," I say.

"They are supposed to be cold," he says, sniffling.

"Oh."

He looks up at me and notes my barely constrained smile. "So that's how it's going to be. Get the kid who makes the plane wait." We smile at each other.

"Inside joke," I say to a puzzled Samuel. "What happened

then, Bobby?"

"I apologized to my parents like ten times. They wouldn't accept it. My father told me to get to my room before he called the police. So I did, and I started getting my things together. I had my passport and visa, I had one thousand eight hundred and fifteen dollars, money I earned helping a friend of my dad's who owns a restaurant, doing dishes and stuff, and money I got selling a ton of CDs and some other things a few months ago. I was supposed to bank it, but I never did. I Googled flights out of John Wayne Airport that could get me to Vietnam and found one that stopped in Portland for a connection. It took almost all of my money but I didn't care. Anyway, Portland is where I met you."

"Where is… what was her name?" I ask. "The girl you met on line?"

"Cam. She wasn't who I thought she was. She was playing a game with me. She picked me up at the airport and took me to this place where there was like a ton of teenagers. All of them liked her and all the guys acted like they had been with her, you know? She talked to them more than she talked to me. When I told her that I was tired, she asked where I was going to stay. When I said that I thought I was staying with her, she just laughed and said that her parents wouldn't like that. I said I thought we had talked about this online and she laughed again, said she never thought I would actually come over. I mean, I told her the night before I left that I was leaving the next day, and she said she was like really excited. Then at the party she started talking with this other guy. I couldn't hear what she said because the music was so loud, but when he looked over at me, he laughed. So I just left. Man, I've never felt so stupid."

"So where have you been staying?"

"In *Phạm Ngũ Lão*. There are lots of cheap places where Americans and other people stay who are backpacking around the country."

"*Phạm Ngũ Lão*?" I say, looking at Samuel. "Isn't that where your store is, where Mai and I went yesterday?"

"Yes."

"Is it dangerous for Bobby?" I ask. I already know it's dangerous for Mai and me. Your honor, I present Exhibit A: Baby Cakes.

"It can be. Since you are Vietnamese, Bobby, you will have fewer problems than do Caucasians, but you have to be careful. You have been here before so you know that the locals can easily spot an American Vietnamese. Some don't like you."

"I know," Bobby says. "I've gotten the hard looks and stuff. And people have hit me up for everything, like dope, girls, free taxi rides, and other stuff. I had to knock a guy's hands off me yesterday when I was leaning against this wall just watching everything and wondering what I was going to do. I don't know what he was doing, maybe pick pocketing me or something. I smacked his hands real fast and I think it surprised him. He did a lot of big man talking then walked away."

Bobby slurps a mouthful of noodles and continues. "Then last night, I was sleeping in this place where there were like twenty other people sleeping. They had sleeping bags and stuff. I was just sleeping on the floor using my backpack as a pillow. One time I woke up, I don't know what time it was, and this big dude was going through one of the pockets in my pack. I grabbed his wrist and he like hit the top of my head." Bobby drops his chin and parts his hair to show us a small bump. "He said something to me but I couldn't understand him. He sounded like those Nazis dudes in *Saving Private Ryan*. Maybe from Germany or something."

"Good movie," Samuel notes.

"What did you do?" I ask.

"I kicked him. I spun around on the floor like a crazy break dancer and kicked his ribs. And I yelled for everyone to wake up because there was a Nazi dude stealing from us. A bunch of big guys grabbed him and threw him out. I thought he might be waiting for me outside this morning, but he wasn't."

"Bobby has a black belt in taekwondo," I tell Samuel.

"Good thing you have knowledge. Your visit has required you to apply it."

"What's your plan, now," I ask, struggling not to smile as Bobby tries to figure out Samuel, his accent and his demeanor.

Bobby shakes his head. "Not sure. I've shamed my family so much, I don't know if they would want me back. They were always so proud of me and just like that I ruin it. I don't feel worthy of… I don't know what I think."

Samuel studies him for a long moment. "Do you really believe that, Bobby?" he says, reaching into his pocket.

The boy shrugs and picks at his noodles.

Samuel looks at him for a long moment before extracting a crisp bill and dropping it on the table. "Tell me, would you like this two-hundred *đồng* bill?"

Bobby lifts his head and wipes his eyes. "Sure."

Samuel crumples the bill and pushes it a few inches in Bobby's direction. "And now? Crumpled. You still want it?"

The boy shrugs. "Yes."

"Now?" Samuel asks, wadding it to the size of a spitball. He sets it on the table and hammers it twice with his fist, flattening it. "Still want it?"

Bobby nods, leaning away from the crazy man.

"Hmm. So, no matter what I do to the bill, you still want it. Why?"

The boy shrugs. "It's still two hundred *đồng*."

"Indeed, sir," Samuel says. "It still has—value."

Bobby looks at him.

"There will be many times in your life when you make a bad decision and life crumples you, wads you into a spitball, and hammers you down. For a moment after you make those bad decisions, and you see the problems and the hurt they caused, you feel terrible, ashamed, worthless. But no matter what has happened, no matter how much you have been crumpled and wadded up into a spitball, and hammered down, you are still priceless to those who love you. You see, your value is not about your bad decisions, but about who you are. And I can see that you are a fine young man. Yes, you screwed up and that cannot be undone. That was yesterday. But you can fix it—now."

Bobby looks at Samuel for a long moment, slowly nodding as he digests the words.

"Thank you," he whispers, the tension gone from his shoulders and face.

Samuel looks at me and back to the boy. "'Yesterday is history, tomorrow is a mystery, but today is a gift. That is why it is called the present.' Do you know what that is from?"

Bobby shakes his head.

"*Kung Fu Panda*. Good movie. Lots of good messages." Samuel returns to his noodles.

Bobby looks at me and nods his head toward Samuel. "Should I be scared?" he asks with a smirk.

"Eat your noodles now," Samuel says, satisfied he's fixed the boy.

"So do I get the two hundred *đồng*?" Bobby asks.

"No way," Samuel says, slapping his palm on the spitball without looking up from his bowl. He pockets it.

*

Samuel keeps all exterior lights burning in the backyard at night, so even with the wooden shutter closed on my windows, bars of white light find their way through the cracks to fall unevenly throughout the dark room. One long rectangle of light runs across the floor and over the side of Bobby's sleeping face where he lies curled in a tight ball on a mat at the foot of my bed. I adjust the ceiling fan to low speed, flop onto the bed wearing just my boxers, and kill the lamp. The fan feels good.

Bobby must have gotten to Samuel too, because he invited the boy to stay with us. On the way back to the house, Samuel mentioned his *canh sát* buddy, who he learned had just returned from Paris. The mention of a policeman stopped Bobby dead in his tracks. I thought he was going to bolt, but Samuel quickly patted his shoulder and said that his friend would help him as long as he didn't kick the man in the face.

Once we got back here, Samuel found a mat for Bobby to sleep on, and the boy zonked out at the foot of my bed within seconds of lying down. No chatting, no shower, and no changing clothes. My shower didn't wake him and neither did my fussing around with my suitcase. Kid probably hasn't slept well since the plane trip.

He's really got himself in a jam. Reminds me of how my mother used to send me off to school each day with the same four words: "Make good choices, Sam." Sometimes I'd say it with her to make her laugh. Mom... Anyway, maybe I'll give Bobby a make-good-choices speech in the morning.

Tired.

Very… tired…

Very…

*"Where you been, Sam boy?" comes out of the rotten-mouthed tweaker, his head protruding from the tunnel under my bed.*

*The naked man's head pops up next to him. "Helloooo, deeetective," he says in that syrupy voice.*

*Now Jimmy's head appears, laughing. "This is cool!" the seven-year-old says. "It's kinda like Whack-a-Mole at Chucky Cheese."*

*"'Cept ol'Sam boy don't use no mallet," the tweaker says, his remaining blackened teeth falling from his swollen, cracked lips. "He uses a Glock 9. Right Sam boy?"*

*The three heads disappear into the hole and pop right back up. "Neener, neener," Jimmy says.*

*"Noooo shooooting, Sam?" the naked man asks. "Cat got your gun? Huh, Saaaam?"*

I awaken with a jolt.

I'm not at Chucky Cheese. It was that dream again. When will they stop? Please make them stop.

I'm on my back, my forearm across my forehead. The back of my head hurts from where I got hit. I just want to—

A hand on my chest.

"Sam?"

"Huh?" I sit up quickly, widening my eyes to force out the fuzz. Bobby? What's wrong with the kid?

"Sam, I am so sorry. I did not mean to startle you."

Mai. I sit up and swing my feet to the floor.

"I knocked but you did not answer."

She is standing next to the bed, her body lit only by the yard light that seeps through the shutters, and through what looks like white silk pajama pants and a white silk top held closed by a single button over her breasts. The pants ride low on her hips making her long, bare midriff look even more—

"I am sorry I slept so long today," she says. "I want to be with you." She drops her chin and looks at me with a combination of shyness and lust as she moves between my legs. "I have missed you." She releases the lone button and shrugs off her top in one smooth move. She picks up my hands and places them on her breasts. So silky. So full. So warm. So—

Bobby!

She bends down. "Mai," I say, but her devouring lips stop my words and inebriates my brain. She pushes me onto my back… the perfume of her hair… the silkiness of her skin… She moves a leg over me, and covers me with her hungry body.

Bobby!

"Mai—"

"Mmmm." She lifts herself enough to slide her hand down between us. "Wow," she whispers, then sucks my lower lip between her teeth.

"We're not alone," I manage.

"I would have to agree," she says, her hand busy.

"Mai," I say, sounding more like I'm coughing. "Bobby is here."

"He called?" she asks disinterestedly.

"Yes, and now he's here."

"Here?"

"At the foot of the bed. On the floor."

She looks at me for a moment, her hand no longer moving but still working its magic. "In this room?"

I nod.

"Sam!" She scrambles off me, leaning her weight on my—

"Ow!" I grab at myself.

—and lands on the floor, her top clutched to her chest. She peers slowly over the end of the bed; her mouth drops open. I roll up onto my knees and look. The boy is still curled into a ball, breathing softly, rhythmically.

Mai pushes me back onto the bed, and quickly slips on her top. "Why did you not say anything?" she whispers.

"I tried, but you kept interrupting and then for a few seconds I kind of forgot."

"You *forgot* a boy is sleeping right there?"

"Sorry. You mad?"

"Of course," she says. "I will see you tomorrow."

"Wait. It seems he's a sound sleeper. Maybe if we were careful not to make a sound—"

"*Trời ơi,*" she says in the same tone one would say 'what a pervert!' She picks up a silk bathrobe that matches her pajamas and slips it over her shoulders. She opens the door quietly, steps part way out, and turns back to me. The backlighting is bright enough to penetrate the layers of silk, revealing all the wonders I'm not going to get tonight. "You are a bad man, Mister Sam," she whispers. Oh man, the way she says it…

"Wait, Mai. Maybe if we were careful not to wake Bobby, we could carry him out into the yard…"

She closes the door.

Bobby starts to snore, quite loudly for a little guy. And annoyingly.

# CHAPTER ELEVEN

Bobby is fast, and his high kicks are done with well-trained muscles and flexibility, as opposed to swinging his leg up with momentum as so many do. He can chamber his bent leg as high as his chin and hold it there without any shake or obvious strain, then snap a kick out and hold his foot next to my ear for seemingly as long as he wants. He can do this with all of the basic kicks: front, side, round, and hook. He's got amazing power for a young man relatively new to the fighting arts. It's easy to see how he took the two cops by surprise at the airport.

It's midmorning, sultry, with low, dark clouds moving about in preparation of a downpour. We both awoke at the same time and chatted a bit about calling his parents. He told me that he had dreamed about getting a hold of them and they weren't angry; they just wanted him home. When I asked if that's how they would really react, he raised his eyebrows, shook his head, and said. "Not even. I'm *such* a dead man." When I asked what his plans were, he said that he had decided that calling them was the grownup thing to do.

No one answered his landline, though it was seven the previous evening in California. Bobby said he didn't understand it because his parents rarely went out on weeknights. He tried a couple more times without getting an answer, likewise when he called their cells. He left a message on all three.

I could see that he was bothered by his failure to make contact, especially after getting his courage up to call, so I asked him if he wanted to show me some of his kicks. His mood brightened instantly. "Wow! Show *you*. Oh yeah?" We've been playing around by the heavy bag for about twenty minutes now.

"Your kicks are fantastic, Bobby," I say.

"Thanks," he says, sliding his palm over Samuel's monstrous heavy bag. "Like I told you on the plane, I need to bring my hand skills up, though. They have been crappy like forever." He frowns at the bag as if just now noticing it. "So what's up with this gye-huge-ous thing anyway?"

"Samuel and his friends use it."

"Samuel? He any good?"

"Not bad," I understate, considering that my father is probably over qualified to be a superhero in a Marvel comic book. But I don't feel like going into his history and incredible skill right now. "About your hands, Bobby, seeing how good you are, I think they will easily catch up to your kicks when you find the right teacher."

"Like you."

"Like me. Unfortunately, the timing is bad and there's that whole thing about you living in California and me living in Portland. Oh, and one other thing: You're a runaway on the other side of the planet, fleeing the law, and likely to get the death penalty from your parents."

"Obstacles," he shrugs.

"Big ones."

"There are always obstacles and they are always big," he says with a shrug and an air of defeat.

"Isn't that the truth. The good news is that as time passes and you gather experience and wisdom, they get easier to handle. Well, not all of them, but a good many of them."

Bobby nods sagely, as he strokes the texture of the bag and probably thinks about what he's going to say to his parents.

"Do you ever kick low?" I ask.

"No, not really. My taekwondo style is all about competition and you don't get points for kicking low, like to the legs or something. In fact, they disqualify you for it."

"How about for self-defense?"

"I got into one fight in school and kicked the dude in the head, and then the other day I kicked those two cops in the head."

"You're batting a thousand. Did the kid in school know anything?"

"You mean did he have skills? No. Fat dude. A big, fat bully who used his size and lack of brains to scare everyone."

"So you kicked an unskilled person in the head."

"Yeah, but he was—"

"Unskilled. And you took two cops by surprise?"

"Yeah, but they wanted to take me—"

"My point, Bobby, is that high kicks worked for you because you used them on an untrained person and you caught two others by surprise."

"Is that bad?" he asks, no argument in the question, just curiosity. Unusual for a teenager.

"Surprise is always a good tactic, but in your two situations you had some luck going on besides your good skill. Just keep in mind that kicking high always carries with it a risk, especially when defending yourself in a real fight. It's hard to do in jeans, on slippery surfaces, and against a skilled opponent. Plus, a high kick starts losing speed once it passes the middle plane, your opponent's midsection. This might not be true with everyone, though it is with most. Thing is, that same flexibility and power needed to kick high will make your lower kicks fast and powerful."

"So, I shouldn't kick high?"

"I'm not saying that. You're good at it, plus your training and natural ability makes it easier for you than it is for others who use momentum and sloppy form to get their foot up high. What I'm saying is that you should include kicking low in your repertoire. Never put all your eggs in one basket. Plus, there are lots of nasty targets below the waist."

"Like the nuts?"

I chuckle. "The nuts are okay but they're often overrated."

"My nuts are overrated?"

"As a target, not for other stuff, loverboy."

"Whew," he says with a smirk.

"Cute. Tell me this, in class, people drop all the time from groin kicks, right?"

Bobby nods.

"Not always in the street, though. A person might be hyped up, excited, enraged, intoxicated on dope or booze, things that might make them tolerate a groin shot, or at least not react all that much to it. I'm not saying don't kick it, just don't count on it being a show stopper. Kick it and follow with hits to other targets until the threat stops."

"Cool."

"Let me show you some kicks that I like. You already know how to do them, so let's look at another way to think about them. Okay, stand so that your left leg is forward a little. That's it. Now, I'm going to hit it with about twenty percent of my power, okay?"

"No sweat, I can handle it," he says smugly, the immortal teenager finally coming through.

I pop a weak roundhouse kick against the outside of his leg, hitting it with my boney shin.

"Whoa!" he says, grabbing the bag for support as his leg wobbles like a drunk man's. "I mean, *whoa*. What did you do?"

"That's the peroneal nerve. It runs down the outside of both of your legs and it hates to be hit. It's most vulnerable about a third of the way down between the hip and the knee, right here. Feel it when I tap my knuckles into it?"

"Seriously!" Bobby says, jerking his leg away.

"The best weapon to use on this target is your roundhouse kick. You get the most penetration using your side kick and front kick, but when your adrenaline is cooking and your heart rate is thumping its way out of your chest, you might miss with those kicks. That's why I prefer the roundhouse. I don't snap my kick into it; instead, I slam it with my shin bone like it's an axe and the guy's leg is a tree. When the situation allows, I like to hit it at a slight downward angle. It seems to compress the tender point more.

"That's the physical. In your head, imagine that your leg is a two-hundred-pound-axe and that your shin bone is the steel blade. Don't just strike the surface with your axe, but rather visualize your shin blade hacking all the way through."

"Awesome. Can I do it on you?"

"Mmm, no."

"So that's how it's going to be."

"Yes. Want to learn another nerve center?"

"Definitely, still at twenty percent, right?"

"Smart man. No, this time I'll make it about fifteen."

"Uh oh. That must mean it's a nasty kick."

I smile. "This one can be done with a kick, but let me show you using a hand push. Okay, throw a front kick—"

He snaps out a head-high kick before I finish my sentence. Teenagers! I rotate my body toward the inside of his leg just enough that his kick misses, then I quickly press my fist just below his naval. I smile at him.

"Oh crap!" he says. "I was just funnin' you with the kick—" I thrust my fist downward at the promised fifteen percent force. "Aggh!" He snaps forward at the waist and half stumbles back. "Whoa!" he blurts, his face confused at the myriad sensations he's feeling. I wait a moment as the first wave of them begins to subside and a second wave hits. "Oh man! Like. What. Thehell. Wasthat?"

"That's your bladder, homeboy. Feels strange, doesn't it, kind of like you have to go to the bathroom, but you don't know if it's to go pee-pee, poo-poo, or throw-up. Or all three."

He tries to straighten. He almost makes it then bends forward again. "Wow. The other eighty-five percent must be majorly naaas-teee."

I laugh. "It is. Impact there sparks all kinds of sensations in the many sensitive nerves just under the surface."

He finally manages to stand upright, his hands gingerly covering the spot. "Who knew?"

"Who knew? Few do, and now you do."

"Cute," he says rolling his eyes.

I chuckle. "Just be sure to hit it at a forty-five degree downward angle. You can use your fist, fingers, or your foot."

"I'm betting I can't try that on you, either."

"You'd do well in Vegas. Want one more? It's the easiest of all."

"Okay. What percentage?"

"Fourteen and a half, maybe closer to thirteen. Walk toward me as if you're going to hit me or grab me."

"Any attack, huh?"

"Yes."

The boy crosses the space quickly, his arms extended like the Frankenstein monster. He going to try a trick on me but it doesn't matter. I pop the ball of my bare right foot into his closest shin.

"Ooow!" he yelps, lifting his leg and grabbing the kicked spot. "That hurts. That's a mystical technique? An old girlfriend did that to me once." He sets his foot down and gently touches his shins with his fingers. "You sure that was only fourteen percent?"

"Yes to both questions. It doesn't matter if the person is buff or fat because all those highly sensitive nerves are right there just below the surface. And the beauty of this target is that you don't have to over commit your kick like you do when kicking someone's ear."

"That's cool, Sam. Painful and cool. And simple."

"Combat should be."

"Simple?"

"Yes. Always seek the simple way."

He nods.

"Sam."

I turn toward the house. Samuel is standing on the landing, his face hard.

"Lai Van Tan has agreed to a meeting. One o'clock today."

*

We're sitting around the dining room table—Samuel, Mai, Bobby, Tex and Lu—sipping tea. Only Bobby has touched the fruit. Samuel looks as relaxed as ever, but his eyes… There is a hardness there that's chilling. It's the old "windows to the soul" thing, and through his windows I can see a hint of the raw essence of a man who has come to terms with all that he has seen and done. I can also see, and it's more than a hint, a willingness, if necessary, to do it again. Maybe I'm reading that into the situation. For sure, those eyes could strip old varnish off wood furniture.

Samuel said that as soon as he got the call from Phong Tran, Lai Van Tan's contact person, he called Lu and told him to meet us here. While we talked before about not letting him come to the house anymore, I'm guessing Samuel allowed it this time because it was easier then everyone meeting somewhere else. And if all Lu sees is the living room and dining room, it shouldn't be a problem.

Then there was the question of what to do with Bobby. Samuel invited him to the table. He said that as long as the boy was here, he should know a little about what is going on.

Bobby nodded politely when I introduced him to Lu, giving no indication that he was savvy that Lu was a transsexual. In fact, the kid was ogling him a little, his sixteen-year-old testosterone indifferent to the fact that the oversexed "woman" is over fifty. The lad is going to be mortified when I break the news to him later. He probably has never heard of such a thing as a shemale.

I introduced Mai and Bobby to each other a few moments ago at the door. They had seen one another at the airport, but they didn't meet since Bobby was busy thumping cops. The boy offered his hand and bowed slightly to her as he spoke in Vietnamese. She smiled and replied. When she turned to lead us to the table, the boy looked over his shoulder at me, and mouthed 'Whoa dude!' and gave me a thumbs up. He didn't say anything about hearing or seeing Mai in the room last night, so I think she and I are safe. That would have been in the red zone on the ol' embarrassment meter.

"Okay, folks," Samuel says. "Let me begin by telling you that Phong Tran told me that Lai Van Tan not only agreed to the meeting, he wanted it. I asked if it was because of what you two did to his people or some other reason, but Phong Tran did not know. Lu has filled me in on the location of the meeting and the way Lai Van Tan likes to seat the participants. I will explain that to you later."

"Any chance there could be violence?" I ask, remembering shouting and pushing matches when my police department sat down with the leaders of the Bloods and Crips gangs. Fortunately, officers had patted everyone down for weapons before they were let in.

"I really do not know, Sam," Samuel says, with a shrug. "Are you thinking a setup?"

"Yes, or that things could deteriorate during the meeting given his rage."

"Anything is possible with this man, of course, but my gut tells me it is not a set up. I must add that my thinking as to how he operates has changed. Now my instinct tells me that he likes to work the same way the enemy does in Afghanistan and Iraq. And like the Ninja's did. His people sneak and hide and attack when we least expect it. That is how they did in Portland and that is how they attacked you and Mai yesterday. Happily, they do not seem very effective at their ninja skills. Of course, their luck could change anytime, or their skill might improve. Lots of unknowns." Samuel looks at Lu. "Anything new?"

Lu is wearing a peach *áo dài* with white silk pants and peach-colored high heels. His flawless makeup gives him a slightly flushed look, and his raven black hair falls long and curly. How early does he have to get up in the morning to put this together? Is he taking estrogen and whatever else transsexuals take to help them look female?

"Since last time we talk, I hear that he have two more Khmer Rouge people. They are old soldiers but still good fighters."

"Do you think Lai Van Tan brought them in because of us?" I ask.

Lu shakes his head. "I do not think so. I think maybe it is to protect his new business, the kidnapped children."

"Sex trafficking," I say.

"*Dạ*. I mean yes."

Mai's face is grim and tight, probably thinking of their friends' daughters who were lost to sex trafficking. She looks at her father. "I want us to stop Lai Van Tan's *business* before it gets too far." Before Samuel can say anything, Mai looks back at Lu. "Can you get us more information? Find out where the children are held? How many there are? How many guards?"

Samuel nods. "Please get that as soon as you can, Lu."

"How will the meeting today go down?" I ask.

If the PD was doing something like this in Portland, we would have officers with rifles on rooftops, cops at the ready on every block within a square mile, a couple of helicopters buzzing around, and undercover cops outside the building pretending to sweep the sidewalk and wash windows.

"You, Mai, and me will go," he says.

"Three of us," I say, incredulous but not surprised.

"I go," Tex says.

Samuel smiles. "I need you here to watch the house and Kim and Bobby. That is a big responsibility, my friend, and you are my first choice as always."

Tex nods, already steeling himself for the task and Bobby looks at him with unabashed curiosity. Tex came in a minute after we had all taken our seats so I didn't get a chance to introduce them. When Bobby heard the legless man's name spoken, he tried not to smile, but failed.

"To answer your question more, Son, they will have three people on their side of the table, including Lai Van Tan. They have asked that we not bring weapons but they said they will not insult us by searching us. I think they are not concerned about insulting us at all. It is because they do not want us to search them."

"Are we going to take weapons?" Mai asks.

"I want to discuss two things with the man," Samuel says, ignoring Mai's question, probably not wanting to reveal too much with Lu here. "First, I want us to settle the issue of his son's death. He has got to understand that it was his son's doing, not mine. And I want the extortion of our businesses to stop."

"What if he tells us to stick it?" I ask.

"We will talk about that later."

I nod, looking at Lu out of the corner of my eye.

"We will leave in a few minutes," Samuel says. "Can you two be ready by, say, eleven-thirty?"

Mai and I nod.

Samuel looks at Bobby. "You have called your parents?"

Bobby coughs and sits up straight. "Yes, sir, several times. No answer. I left messages for them on our home phone and their cells. It's weird that they don't answer."

"Maybe they are visiting friends or relatives," I say. "They are probably so worried about you that they need some emotional support." Might as well throw some salt on his wounds.

Bobby nods. "We have lots of relatives in Westminster, but my parents would still have their cells with them."

"Well, just keep trying," I say. "Call every twenty or thirty minutes while we're gone."

"I do not have time to call my policeman friend now," Samuel says, scooting back from the table. "But I will after the meeting."

"Thank you," Bobby says, clearly not thrilled about a policeman coming to visit.

"By the way," I say. "Bobby meet Tex. Tex, Bobby." Bobby stands and leans across the table to shake his hand.

"I saw you kicking outside," Tex says. "You better than me."

Bobby smiles uncertainly and glances at me. I shrug, trying not to smirk.

"Lu, thank you as always," Samuel says.

Mai stands and walks around the table to Lu who is getting to his feet. "Please learn what you can about the kidnapped children."

Lu takes Mai's hand in both of his and pats it. His peach-colored nail polish matches his *áo dài* perfectly. "I will. I promise." He turns and nods to Bobby and me.

"Thank you again, Lu," Samuel says. "Mai, would you help Lu with a taxi?"

"Yes, Father." She and Lu head out of the dining room.

"Bobby, would you like to help Tex do some yard work?"

"Sure," the boy says smiling at Tex.

"Just until two or two-thirty. Then you two can watch TV together. Bobby, your choice: Chinese opera or Tai kickboxing matches."

"Hmm." Bobby pretends to think hard about it.

"Really?" I say. "I thought you would have jumped all over that opera thing." Tex and Bobby laugh. "By the way, Tex is a hell of a fighter. Maybe he can show you some things."

"Really? Cool," Bobby says excitedly. "Some hand moves?"

"What else?" the legless man says with an affected sad shrug.

Samuel stands. "Tex, please take him in the kitchen first and get the lad some breakfast."

"We go get grub, Canyon Bob," Tex says, swinging down from the chair.

"Canyon Bob?" Bobby says, glancing at me.

I'll have to remember to tell the boy later about Tex's affinity for cowboy movies. Canyon Bob follows Tex out to the kitchen for grub at the same time Mai walks back into the dining room.

"Lu got a taxi," she says.

"Good," Samuel says heading toward the archway. "Follow me out to the living room you two. The sun is not on that side of the house yet so it is a little cooler."

Samuel lowers himself into the leather chair and looks up at Kim's painting while Mai and I get situated on the sofa.

"Mai," Samuel says, "I want you to take your ankle gun. I am guessing, and this is just a guess, that they will be less likely to think that you are the armed one. Sam, you and I will be unarmed."

Not a problem. If I won't carry a gun in Portland, I sure as hell am not going to carry one here.

"Mai, Lu said that you should sit on my right. Sam, you sit back from the table this first time. Understand that because he is from Hanoi and fought for the North, Lai Van Tan hates Americans. I have heard that his mother, father, and siblings were all killed by American bombs."

"No need to explain. Where I sit isn't important."

Samuel nods. "If there are more meetings you will sit at my side. But this first one is critical and a very sensitive one.

Someone once said 'don't wait for people to be friendly. Show them how.' I will try to do that and try hard not to antagonize him."

"Good plan," I say.

He looks at his watch. "We should meet back here in about twenty minutes."

After Samuel leaves, I say, "Short meeting. We moved out here for that?"

"I think Father might be nervous, full of, uh, anxious. Anxiety." She looks up at the painting. "And I think he wanted to be by Mother for a moment."

"Understandable."

"Are you nervous?"

"Of course," I say. "Very. You?"

"Terrified. I so badly want my family to be safe. But I am worried because Lai Van Tan is a mad man."

# CHAPTER TWELVE

We've rode mostly in silence, Mai driving the Volvo, Samuel riding shotgun, and me in the back. About twenty minutes into the journey, Samuel said that Mai and I should not speak at the meeting. "Even if you are asked a direct question, let me answer. The exception would be if I indicate that you can."

Mai turns down a side street and brakes hard to avoid killing a bike rider. That spiked my heart rate up to about one-eighty, though I'm guessing the bicyclist's reached two hundred. Or maybe he's used to near death experiences.

"That's the building," Samuel says, nodding his head at what looks to be a fairly new structure that occupies the whole block. "First, I want to go around the block once."

"Is it his?" Mai asks.

Samuel nods. "Unfortunately. I wanted a neutral location, but he said that since I was the one asking for the meeting, he would say where. I've seen this building before, but I did not know he was associated with it, or owned it. I do not know which. I agreed to meet here, reluctantly, but only if we met on the ground floor. Easy to get out should there be a problem. Lu said it will be in that end room right there."

It's a basic building, gray, three stories, lots of windows, and an entryway with two glass doors. Mai drives to the end of the block and hangs a right turn.

"Hey," I say, looking at an armless man leaning against the corner. "Isn't that…"

"Phouc," Samuel says. "On post." The old veteran winks at us as we pass. Mai makes another right, this time onto a pothole-riddled dirt road behind the building. "It is about to rain," Samuel notes, looking skyward. "These holes will be filled shortly." We take another right. "There is Phat Ho. See him, Sam? Sitting at that noodle stand there."

Yup, there he is, the one-armed *garrote* master sitting at a little stool and chopsticking a clump of noodles into his mouth. Silk scarves dangle out of a back pocket, one blue, one red. He doesn't react to us other than to give me a hard stare. My best friend, Phat Ho.

"The men are positioned to see two sides each," Samuel says. "I got them on speed dial should we need them."

So we got two guys for backup: one with no arms—how will he answer the phone?—and the other a one-armed man packin' pretty scarves. Maybe we've been overdoing it all this time in Portland with a SWAT team that can reduce a small city to ruins.

Mai rounds one more corner and we're back on the street that passes by the front of the building. She parks at the curb.

"Turn your eyes not your head," Samuel says, "and look at those two guys across the street sitting on motorbikes. I am sure they are Lai Van Tan's people. Same with that woman and man leaning against the side of the taxi in front of the door. See how the woman looks toward one end of the building and the man toward the other?"

"They missed the class on how to look nonchalant," I say. Light rain begins dotting the windshield.

"Very true," Samuel says. "Consider them armed."

Armed. Wonderful. Us? Well, we've got two old guys with one arm—total. One gun between Samuel, Mai, and me. There are no cops running the show, no high-tech communication, no hovering helicopters. Oh, and we got one guy who doesn't speak the language and has no clue where he is—me.

When Samuel says "Let's do this, folks," like a crazy person, I nod.

We're about twenty-five feet from the door when the rain starts falling harder. We pick up our pace and by the time we scurry under the overhang, it's falling like the wrath of a vengeful God. Probably is. This must be the infamous monsoon I've heard about.

The couple acting as a lookout have moved under the overhang, making things a bit crowded and awkward. Samuel says something to them—probably that they should keep their day jobs because they suck at undercover work—and they both try to look hardass and like they haven't just been spanked by their daddy.

The lobby is typical: tile, gray walls, two elevators in the far wall, a hallway to the right of them, and doors in the left and right walls. I saw three doors on the backside of the building. Maybe the hall leads to one of them. The only exit I know for sure are the doors we just came through. A tall man of forty stands in the center of the lobby, wearing an expensive charcoal gray suit that compliments his distinguished bearing. I hear Samuel say Phong Tran, so this must be his contact man. They exchange bows and words before the man gestures toward the door on our left. Pleasant enough guy.

"Lai Van Tan is waiting for us," Samuel whispers over his shoulder. He pushes the door open into a large room, complete with a long, highly polished mahogany table, and chairs all around. Two men sit on the far side, one who looks to be Samuel's age, who I'm guessing is The Man himself, Lai Van Tan.

The other, sitting at the older man's left, is a granite-faced guy probably in his late thirties. Both are dressed in expensive, dark power suits, white shirts, and dark ties. Granite Face checks out Mai with predator's eyes, while Lai Van Tan looks at me as if I were a six-foot-tall dog turd.

Samuel and Mai pull up chairs at the table across from the big boss, and I sit near the wall slightly behind Samuel's left side. Phong Tran pulls up a chair and sits at the old man's right.

Outside the rain roars. Inside, the room drips silence.

The old man's eyes move from mine to Mai's and, as if cued, the younger man's eyes leave Mai and move to Samuel. Phong Tran looks straight ahead, his fingers interlaced on the table. Seems a tad uncomfortable, like he would rather be in Philadelphia.

"Thank you for agreeing to this meeting, Mister Lai," Samuel says, taking the lead. "I have two requests—"

The old man rattles something off in Vietnamese, his eyes never leaving Mai's.

"No," Samuel snaps. "One of my requests is that we talk in English. You requested the venue. I request that we speak English."

Lai Van Tan's eyes don't waver from Mai.

There's that dripping silence again.

Lai Van Tan is a handsome man in a scary sort of way: iron-gray hair combed straight back, thin moustache over thick lips that hint at a snarl, square jaw, and eyes like mud puddles. The mud puddles move to me.

"Everyone speaks Vietnamese, except *him*?"

Nice to meet you too, Viet Cong dude.

"Yes," Samuel says, as if asking what's his point.

Long pause, and then the old man says, "Okay." He looks back at Mai, the skin around his mouth impossibly tight.

That was easy. Too easy?

"My second request," Samuel says, "is that my son sits at my side at the table."

Oh man, Samuel. Don't push it. It's okay, I'm all comfy and good sitting right here.

The old man's hard eyes move to Samuel's. "Meeting about *my* son," he says, his voice like the low growl of a motivated-to-kill pit bull. "Not *your* fuck-head son."

Even through his shirt, I can see the many small muscles in Samuel's back knot up, then relax. Amazing self-control, my old man has.

The sound of the Niagara Falls outside stops just as quickly as it began. A chair squeaks. I'm not sure whose since everyone is as still as a room full of statues. Phong Tran continues to appear uncomfortable, his fingers interlaced, knuckles white. Lai Van Tan looks like he could eat coal, and the younger man is grinding his jaw so intensely that he's probably filling his mouth with enamel dust. Mai grips the edge of the table as if she were about to spring over it.

If this were happening in Portland, I'd play Phong Tran as the weak link in Lai Van Tan's organization. I'd try to talk to him by himself and see if he's amendable to moving from the dark side to our side. Or at least be an informant.

Samuel probably feels that his power was somewhat weakened by yielding to Lai Van Tan's request to meet here in his building, so getting the big man to agree that the conversation be in English is one building block toward regaining it. But asking that I sit at the table seems a little antagonistic. Back at the house, he said that he didn't want to do that.

"Your son may sit at table," Lai Van Tan says, his words uttered as if chipped from the cement-hard silence, "when your daughter be one of my whores."

Mai leaps to her feet shouting something and knocking her chair over backwards. Granite Face responds quickly, standing up and slamming his chair back against the wall. He takes a protective step closer to Lai Van Tan. For a second, Mai postures to jump onto the table, but Samuel, still sitting, touches her arm. "Sit down, Mai," he says calmly. I put her chair upright and she sits without looking behind her.

The corners of Lai Van Tan's mouth turn up a little in what might serve as his smile, but his eyes still have that dirty water thing going on. He says something to Granite Face, and the guy sits, his hands out of sight seemingly in his lap. Phong Tran has remained seated during the outburst, his hands flat on the table.

Master puppeteer, this Lai Van Tan, and he just had Mai dancing at the end of his strings. I can't see Samuel's face but I'm guessing he's not too pleased about that.

After a half minute of eerie silence, Samuel speaks first, his voice tight as if struggling to restrain himself. "I have come today… to talk to you man to man… and you insult my daughter."

"I insult your daughter," Lai Van Tan says gruffly, "but you kill my son!"

"I did *not* kill your son and you know this."

Lai Van Tan's quivers as if he, too, is fighting to control his rage. "I know nothing of the kind."

"Do not insult my intelligence, Mister Lai. I came to you that night to ask you to reduce your demands for money from my stores. You insulted me and tried to intimidate me. So I left. Then you sent two men to confront me in a narrow street."

"You lie! I sent no—"

"One man lifted a gun toward my face," Samuel continues, ignoring the accusation, "just as the second man moved into the bullet's path. The shot man was your son, shot by one of *your* people. The second man continued to fight me. He died when his head hit a railing."

Samuel told me in Portland that he tried to meet Lai Van Tan after the incident but he was refused. So Samuel wrote a lengthy letter to him explaining what happened that night, but he got no response.

I'm not sure, but it looks like Lai Van Tan's eyes might be tearing.

"That night haunts me." Samuel says. "Two lives gone unnecessarily. A waste."

"Waste," Lai Van Tan grunts. "My son's life was a waste, you say."

"I am saying that his death was unnecessary. An unnecessary death is a waste."

Lai Van Tan is quivering. I can't tell if it's because he is trying to control his anger or his sorrow. Maybe both.

"Do you know my son's name?" Lai Van Tan asks quietly.

"I am sorry, I do not."

"Duc."

"It means good," Samuel says softly.

Lai Van Tan nods, his eyes looking off to the side for a moment.

"I am sorry this happened, Mister Lai."

"Duc was most precious to his mother and to me. He have important future. In one year he would be doctor."

Doctor. Then why was he doing strong-arm work for the old man? Not sure if I'm buying this. Phong Tran still looks like he'd rather be anyplace else but here. Granite Face looks like he was born to be here.

"I am sorry this happened," Samuel repeats.

"I send him to get you to come back. To talk more."

Right. Next he's going to offer to sell Samuel a bridge on the River Kwai. This guy is the worst kind of dangerous. He's in denial and he's nuts.

"Lai Van Tan," Samuel says, sounding more like, *come on, knock off the crap.*

"You do not take responsibility?" the old man suddenly shrieks. I jump a little; Samuel and Mai don't.

Okay, he's not just crazy, he's a whole lot crazy.

"Sir," Samuel says, his voice low and subdued, no doubt trying to calm the man. "We both survived those dark years of the war and we are old men now. We are no longer enemies. Have we not earned a peaceful life?"

He looks at Samuel for a long moment. If I were betting, I'd wager that Samuel's words just bounced off the old man's stone-carved head.

"Do you take responsibility for my son's death?" he asks.

I would have won the pot.

"If that is what it takes to have peace between us, then yes, I take responsibility. I am sorry it happened."

Lai Van Tan sputters a laugh. "Your words are like a whore's whispers of affection. Empty, meaningless, self-serving."

Samuel has to be exasperated, but he isn't showing it, at least from my view of his side profile. Mai has been sitting motionless, except for her left hand that I can see clearly from my position. Since Samuel encouraged her to sit back down, her fingers have been continuously curling into a ball, first the little finger, then her ring finger, middle, index, and thumb.

When they're fisted, they reverse the action and straighten. Then they curl again.

"Tell me what you want from me," Samuel says.

"What I want," Lai Van Tan says in a voice as cold as an icicle through the heart, "is my vengeance."

The quiet in the room earlier was like a Mardi Gras compared to now. I'm guessing that Samuel and Mai are thinking the same thing I am, that this man cannot be placated. He is in another world where the sky is a different color.

"Revenge is not the way, sir," Samuel says.

"I thought you a learned man," Lai Van Tan says, his mouth doing that curl-up thing. "I am not seeking revenge. That is an act of passion and I am not acting passionately. My actions are deliberate because vengeance, you see, is about justice. I *will* have justice."

This is one of those "oh shit moments" when you know that everything from here on out is going to turn to caca.

"What can I do to make this better?" Samuel asks.

Lai Van Tan lays his palms flat on the table. "Simple. You can die and your family can die."

A slight movement from Mai catches my eye. Using my peripheral vision, I see that she is maintaining her upright posture as she ever so slowly lowers her knee down as far as it can go. Now she is curling her foot up... a little more... there. She slowly slides her Glock 26 out of her ankle holster, then lowers her foot back to the floor and brings her knee back up to its normal position. She did it all without giving away her action to those on Lai Van Tan's side, and while appearing to have her hands in her lap the entire time. That's where they are now, but the right one is holding a Glock loaded with eleven rounds, ten in the magazine, one in the chamber. That is, if she reloaded after shooting her kidnappers.

"I am sorry we could not come to a peaceful agreement, sir," Samuel says, still sitting calmly. "So we are leaving now. I request that the man on your left lift his arms out to his sides, shoulder high. I want to see his empty hands."

Granite Face has been sitting through the conversation with his hands out of sight, his eyes looking at Samuel, his body motionless, coiled. In fact, I haven't seen him move at all for the last several minutes, but maybe he's as subtle at unholstering a gun as is Mai.

The rain starts again, slamming the windows hard.

"Ngai," Lai Van Tan says, his eyes darting to Granite Face, then back to Samuel. Granite Face starts to bring up his hands.

"Stop!" Samuel says, then says something in Vietnamese, probably "move slowly."

The man does slow for a moment, then stops moving all together, his hands still not visible, his eyes boring into Samuel's. Lai Van Tan, still watching Samuel, talks to his man out of the corner of his mouth. Again, Granite Face's arms begin slowly moving. His left hand clears the tabletop first, empty. Then his right hand.

It's holding a gun, a revolver, big. Three-fifty-seven.

The three of us are instantly on our feet. Samuel side-steps so that his body covers mine. Mai is thrusting her Glock at Granite Face, shouting something. Still in his armed crucifix pose, the man is speaking to Mai, his voice eerily calm. If he swings that weapon around toward us, Mai will turn him into burnt toast.

Phong Tran, still seated and looking terrified, pushes his chair back against the wall as if the extra four feet would make a difference to a bullet. His eyes meet mine, he frowns, slowly shaking his head. Is he sending me a message? About what? I don't understand.

Lai Van Tan remains cool, his mouth turned up a little into a sick smile, eyes watching, excited. He's having a good time.

Without turning around, Samuel reaches behind his back and grips the front of my shirt. "Stay behind me," he says over his shoulder. He begins side-stepping behind Mai who is keeping her weapon trained on Granite Face. Half a dozen more steps and we're at the door, Samuel still in front of me. "Open it, Sam."

I reach behind me, fumble for the knob, find it, turn it. "It's open."

"Mai. Come," Samuel says, nudging me to keep backing out.

Mai moves in front of Samuel, her gun trained on the three on the other side of the table. The last I see as we back out into the lobby is Lai Van Tan still sitting passively, looking at his nails, that vicious smile curling up the corners of his mouth. Mai pulls the door closed. Surprisingly, Granite Face doesn't shoot through it.

"Keep watching the door, Mai," Samuel says, as we move quickly across the lobby.

The same "undercover" couple are still under the shelter of the outside overhang, probably because another downpour is slamming the street and sidewalk. This time the man and woman don't move out of our way in the tight space. The male is making an Elvis sneer and the female is doing an outlaw biker chick pose. She can't nudge the scale to more than a hundred pounds, even with her boots on. It's hard not to laugh.

Bad for them that this time Samuel is no longer in the mood

for their nonsense. He grabs Elvis's shirtfront with both hands and sweeps the man's left leg to the side until he's teetering in a half split, his foot out in the rain. Then he sweeps the man's other foot to the right, dropping him into a deeper split. Elvis is yelling something quite loudly and struggling to stand upright, but Samuel is preventing that by pulling down on his shirt.

When Biker Chick screeches and reaches for Samuel, Mai grabs a wad of her hair, whips her head back and forth a couple of times, and flings her out into the monsoon. Mai does this with her left hand because she still has her Glock in her right. That's my girl. The shake job must have jarred the woman's brain because now she's staggering about in a small circle as if she were drunk.

Samuel kicks the man's left leg out a couple more times, until his crotch is about a foot above the sidewalk. I'm guessing he doesn't normally do the splits because he's screeching like an actress in a bad horror movie. Samuel does one last kick and the man goes all the way down. I think I hear his muscles tear, but I can't be sure because the rain's din is so loud. All this took place in about ten seconds.

Then the rain stops.

Half a minute later, we're all in the Volvo and Mai is driving like a crazed person—even considering her regular style.

\*

With a Southern twang, I say, "You sho doo know how to show a feller a good time."

Samuel, sitting on the passenger side, twists part way around and looks back at me. "I thought Lai Van Tan and I could settle our problems, but as you can see I was naïve."

I shake my head. "The guy is a madman. I don't think it's

possible to penetrate his warped brain with logic and truth. Did you see how he smiled when Mai got upset at him? He was enjoying every second of it."

"I wanted to hurt him," Mai says, no doubt understating what she would have done if she had actually vaulted the table or began pumping rounds. She slows to the speed limit and hangs a right onto another busy street.

"You responded to his insult the way he wanted you to," Samuel says gently. "Lai Van Tan wanted to… push our buttons? Sam, is that the right expression."

"Yes."

"He was pushing our buttons," he continues, "saying things to make us angry."

I agree, but don't say anything.

Samuel punches in a number on his cell. He has a brief exchange with someone, signs off, and pokes in another number. Again he speaks briefly and signs off.

"I told Phouc and Phat Ho to stay on post for a little while. See if anyone else comes to the building or, if Lai Van Tan leaves, try to follow them."

"Do you think his man would have used his gun?" I ask. We're sitting in a traffic jam now, the car's hard-working air conditioner losing the battle with the oppressive humidity.

Samuel shrugs. "We will never know. But I would guess that if Lai Van Tan would have told him to shoot, I am sure he would have. Tell me, Son, what are your thoughts on Phong Tran."

"A couple things. He didn't seem comfortable in the meeting. He certainly didn't seem invested in what Lai Van Tan was saying and doing. The other thing is that when all the guns were out, he looked at me and shook his head."

Mai looks into her rearview mirror at me. "Shook his head?"

"Yes. You two were looking at the gunman so his only choice was to look at me. He kept frowning and shaking his head. I don't know him, of course, but it was like he didn't want you to shoot or any of us to do anything."

Mai looks at Samuel.

"Okay, this is a stretch," I say. "It was like what my grandfather would do behind my mother's back when she was chewing me out for something. When I'd start to sass her back, he'd shake his head as if to say 'let it go.' I know that's probably off the wall, but that was my immediate thought when he did it."

"I did not see him shake his head," Samuel says, "but I did watch Lai Van Tan while all that was happening. His face could not hide that he wanted a fight."

"I saw that," I say. We're stopped in a traffic jam.

"But why would Phong Tran shake his head?" Mai asks, closing the space vacated by a truck that bullied its way into the next lane.

"Not sure," I say. "Don't know these people like you do, but is there any chance that entire scene was an act, a device for Lai Van Tan to establish his dominance? Earlier there was that power play over what language to speak and where I should sit. He lost the language issue and did some name calling on the other."

"Are you saying all that was a bluff?" Samuel asks.

"I don't know. Like I said, you know him and the culture better than I do. It would seem to be a very dangerous and hard to control bluff, for sure. For all he knew, Mai could have shot his man dead. Or if he was winging the whole thing, his man with the gun could have shot us."

Samuel nods. "But only if the man did not know about his plan."

"Exactly," I say. We're moving again, though traffic is still thick as syrup. "Seems like a crazy stunt if that's what he was doing. If so, maybe Phong Tran understood and was trying to warn us not to take it to the next level."

Samuel nods again. "I think maybe the gunman did know. Why else would he agree to place his arms into such an awkward position."

"Right," I say.

Samuel looks out his side window. "It all sounds like a crazy premise, but if I learned anything about Lai Van Tan over the years it is that he *is* crazy."

"Maybe talk to Phong Tran as soon as possible?" Mai suggests.

"I plan to. When I called him to arrange a meeting, he and I had a chance to talk. He told me that he is an accountant, educated at Columbia in New York in the mid-nineteen nineties. He is Lai Van Tan's nephew. The more he talked, the more I sensed that he wanted to be doing something else. If I had to guess, I would say that he was being forced to work for the man."

"Excellent," I say.

"I will try to talk to him later today."

We're moving now and once again Mai is doing a good job of zipping through traffic. If she is bothered by what just happened she isn't showing it. Yesterday she shoots two men in the legs and today she was ready to fire a bullet into a man's face. Tough gal, but I'm betting that she needs a mental break. Will she get one before all this is over?

"What now, Father?" Mai asks.

"I will call Ly and tell her to have *phở* ready when we get home."

\*

Tex and Bobby are in the living room, the boy sweating profusely as the legless man throws medium-speed punches at him. The boy parries with a blend of skill and desperation. They have brought a dining room chair out into the living room, and Tex is perched on it so that the two are equal in height. The boy is clearly having a good time bobbing and weaving and swatting aside the short man's big fists. My mother used to say, "Smile, Sam, sunshine is good for your teeth." She'd love this boy.

"You look good, Bobby," Samuel says as he leads us into the house. "Tex working your hands?"

"Oh, hi," the boy says, stopping abruptly, his face red from the exertion. "Yes, sir, he's amazing. He's got some crazy skills. He's so fast and strong. He can move like a monkey and…" He turns to Tex and touches his shoulder. "Sorry, I didn't mean that to be disrespectful."

Tex shakes his head, trying hard not to smile. "No sweat, Canyon Bob. Say fast and strong not disrespect."

"No, I meant the monkey part… you messing with me?"

"No messing," he says, snatching the boy's hand and applying a wristlock. "Making wrist hurt." He laughs uproariously as Bobby dances on his toes. "Now you monkey's uncle."

Mai laughs. "You two have become friends, I see."

"He's pretty cool," Bobby says flexing his freed hand back and forth.

"Canyon Bob tell truth. What happen meeting?"

"First things first," Samuel says. "I will tell Ly that we are all here, and then I want to check on Mother. We can meet in the dining room in ten minutes."

After Samuel leaves, Bobby says that he and Tex repotted two plants out front, had a Pepsi, and watched three muay Thai kickboxing matches on the tube. For the last half hour,

Tex has been giving him pointers on offensive punching, counter punching, and blocking. The boy is as high as a kite, truly enjoying himself and his new friend. Judging by how Tex is acting, the feeling is mutual.

A few minutes later, we're all settled around the dining room table, each of us digging into a steaming bowl of *phở*. Bobby and Tex are sitting next to each other, and I'm sitting between Samuel and Mai. So as not to frighten the boy, Samuel tells Tex about the meeting in French. I know that many Vietnamese speak it but I didn't know Samuel did. Tex nods throughout, his mouth a thin hard line. When he responds, I hear Kim's name. Samuel says something and Tex nods. They both dig into their soup.

"Try your parents again?" I ask Bobby.

He sucks a long noodle up until it disappears. "Yes, twice. I don't understand where they could be."

"Think they might be coming over here?" I ask.

"Whoa," Bobby says, his eyes big. "I never thought of that. Maybe that's why they aren't answering."

"If that's the case, they would get your messages when they lay over in Japan, or wherever."

Samuel looks at me. "If I may suggest, you should leave a message on their phone. Tell them that you are a policeman and that the boy is staying with us."

Bobby's head jerks toward me, his chopstick frozen half way to his mouth. "Wait. You're a policeman? *You're* a policeman? In Portland?"

I smile at him. I couldn't remember if that *Black Belt* magazine article had mentioned it. Apparently it didn't.

"Yes, I am—I was—I am—why don't you dial your father's number and let me talk with him or leave a message."

Bobby extracts his cell, shaking his head. "How bizarre is this? I was hiding from the police, I call you, and you *are* the police. So much for that thing that they're never around when you want one." He hits his speed dial, still shaking his head.

I laugh. "Ironical, isn't it. But I'm not a cop over here." He hands me the phone. "Phan, right?"

Bobby nods. "David Phan."

I take the cell into the living room. Ringing, ringing, the Phan's recorder picks it up and Mister Phan, with just a hint of an accent, tells me to leave a message.

"Mister and Missus Phan, my name is Sam Reeves," I say in my police voice. "I met your son on our flight to Vietnam three days ago. At that time, he told me he was flying to Saigon to meet his father. We hit it off and, fortunately, I gave him my phone number because he contacted me two days ago. He is now staying at my father's house in Saigon, and we have been attempting to contact you. I am calling to reassure you that he is safe and we are looking after him. My father is Samuel Le. He has several businesses in Vietnam, and I am a police detective on leave from Portland, Oregon. You can contact me at five zero three—"

Damn, the recorder cut me off. Looks like Bobby has one bar left. I click redial. The screen changes to "dialing" but then clicks off. Got to be the battery.

"Bobby," I say walking back into the dining room. "Tell me your father's number. It cut me off before I could leave him mine, and it looks like your cell is dead."

"Ahh," he groans, scrunching his face. "I didn't bring a charger. I'm so dumb." He gives me the number and I poke it into my cell. Lots of clicking and clacking, then nothing. Great.

"Phone service is not always good here," Mai says. "Try later. And we can buy a charger for Bobby's near the tea café."

"Okay," Samuel says. "We need to discuss things. Bobby, please excuse us for a while. You can go to Sam's room, or go out in the back, or go in the living room and watch some television. Channel nine has muay Thai matches all day and channel sixty-four has American movies in English with Vietnamese captions."

"Cool. I'll check out the tube." He starts heading toward the living room, stops, and turns back to Samuel. "Thank you, sir, for helping me out. I messed up big time and, uh…" He shrugs. "I don't know. Just thanks for helping me."

"*Không có chi*," Samuels says with a smile. You're welcome, I'm guessing.

"One more thing," I say. "When will you be seventeen?"

"In three months. Why?"

"Just wondering. Go on and check out the tube." I wait until the TV comes on in the other room, then in a lowered voice, "Fantastic kid."

"He number one," Tex says.

"It makes me uncomfortable that he is here," Samuel says. "It might get dangerous and Bobby is a responsibility that I did not count on. But I do not know where we could send him right now."

"I agree," I say. "We are lucky he isn't twelve years old. In fifteen months he'll be an adult. That, and he's more mature than most his age." I smile, adding, "But when he does make bad choices, he makes big ones."

"I called Linh," Samuel says. She and An are my half sisters I have yet to meet. "She and her husband live in *Phan Thiết*, about two hundred kilometers from here. Linh and An alternate coming down every ten days or so to help with their mother, usually for a day or two. They were both planning to come with their husbands on Saturday to meet you, but Linh is coming this evening to get Kim and take her back to *Phan Thiêt* to stay with her until we know what is going on with Lai Van Tan."

Mai nods, grimly. "I do not like Mother to not be here, but I agree it would be safer for her not to be here, and it would be less for us to worry about."

Samuel nods. "Ly will be going to stay with her parents until Kim returns." He shakes his head, probably because of the disruption to his family's life. "I hope all this is overreaction, but I do not think—" His cell plays *Superman*.

He smiles broadly at the voice on the other end, converses briefly, and signs off. "That was Vu Van Hien. He got my messages and is coming over in a few minutes."

"He same-same sheriff," says Tex, the western movie buff. "Number one."

This should be interesting. I read a little online about the Vietnamese police. One story said that Human Rights Watch had documented fifteen cases of police brutality in which the victims died. One man died after he was arrested for arguing with his mother and another man after he was taken into custody for riding without a helmet. Both received severe head injuries and miscellaneous broken bones. Samuel says that his friend is one of the good guys. Hopefully.

"What will happen?" I ask. "I mean about Bobby?"

"Hien, he goes by Harry, said no sweat about the boy. He and I will make it go away. Also, I want to tell him what is going on with Lai Van Tan."

"Will it cost money to make it go away?" I ask.

He waves off the question, which probably means the answer is yes and that he's paying out of his pocket. "Harry has been a good friend for many years. He has helped me avoid the government's microscope many times, and helped minimize their harassment and extortion of our businesses."

"All the stores are in Mother's name," Mai says. "But the government causes us problems anyway. Sometimes officers watch the stores and when they see Father there or me there, they stop us in our cars when we leave. Because they know we have a successful business, they, uh, pressurize, no, pressure us to pay more than other people to get out of a ticket." Mai waves her hand a little. "But not all police are bad. Some are our friends. Harry has been a good friend of our family for a long time."

"Does he know about the sex trafficking?" I ask.

"I would say yes," Samuel says, "but how much, I'm not sure. I will ask him when he is here."

"What we do now?" Tex asks, his eyes as dark and deadly as the ends of a double-barreled shotgun. "We attack Lai Van Tan? Kill every swinging dick, let Buddha sort out."

Once a warrior always a warrior. Could use a dash of subtlety, though.

"There is always the possibility that our visit had an effect on Lai Van Tan," Samuel says, smiling patiently at Tex. "Or maybe he wants peace but wanted to control us first, show us that he is in charge. I do not know for sure yet."

"No attack," Tex says, with irritation. "He send assholes attack Mai and Sam yesterday. You no think we must revenge?"

"I understand what you are saying, but I do not agree that revenge is the answer. We saw what that did in Portland."

"Revenge important to do," Tex says.

Samuel settles his palm on Tex's shoulder. "Confucius said: 'Before you set out on the road to revenge, dig two graves.' Things that were done by me in Portland were not done out of revenge but to keep Sam safe after we left."

I'm not sure what I think about this. The police academy trained me fifteen years ago to function and survive in a dangerous situation and I've been doing okay on my own. Samuel might have acted in Portland because he felt he needed to keep me safe, but he didn't ask me about it. If he had, I would have told him not to do anything, to return to Saigon, and let me worry about my safety just as I have always done. But now is not the time to bring this up. It's also not a good time because I'm guessing that Samuel is still processing in his mind what he did.

"What do you think, Son?" Samuel asks. Whoops. Did he pick up on my thoughts?

"About…"

"How to proceed."

Whew. "Well, asking for a meeting was a good plan, a good way to see where his head is." Tex gives me a confused look. "To understand his thinking," I clarify. "But we left the meeting not sure what's in his head. He wants to control us, we know that much, which makes him a dangerous man. On the other hand, some things happened there that might, *might*, indicate that he wants peace."

"So we go get him?" Tex asks.

"Sometimes taking the fight to the enemy is a wise plan," I say. "But I'm wondering how we would do that? Would we ask for another meeting and then beat everyone up who comes? Should we jump them in a café? I don't think so. I'm in the dark as to how you do things here, but for sure I would do surveillance on these people."

Samuel nods. "Phouc and Phat are watching him for a while today. I need to put someone on his primary office where I tried to talk to him a few months ago. Lu is getting us the exact locations of any other place he frequents, including where he lives and," he looks at Mai, "the locations of where he is holding children."

"Good," Mai says.

"I will also increase security outside the walls here. The man on the second floor across the street can see the front and the north side of our property. There are only the back sides of homes in the rear so I cannot post anyone up high there. But I do have a man who watches from his car and strolls the alley, paying special attention to the south side where that tree is. By the way, the earliest I can get someone out here to remove the tree is four days from now."

"Shoot," Mai says.

Samuel says, "I am thinking I would like to have two men at street level, one in the front and one more in the back."

"Who are these people?" I ask.

"They are all trusted, men I have known for many years. All are old soldiers but do not let their lined faces fool you. They have kept up on their skills. They are slower than they were during the war years but they are still good. The only problem is that I have less than a dozen people. And of course some are more able bodied than others."

"They are from the soldiers' home?"

"They are friends I have known for years. I hire them from time to time when I need extra protection, like when a store gets in a new shipment of expensive jewelry."

I wonder how many of the men I've seen back home wearing "Vietnam Veteran" baseball hats are still keep up on their skills? Here, at least among Samuel's friends, even guys with missing limbs at the veteran's home are ready and willing.

"You have weapons?" I ask. "Aren't weapons strictly controlled over here?" I ask. "You can't even have fireworks, right?"

"Yes to all three questions," Mai says. "But we have guns."

"How? I mean, aren't you worried?"

Samuel shrugs. "Like my friend who dug the tunnel under your bed, I have old habits, maybe, and a strong desire for security for my family. I bought three handguns a few years ago from a friend of a friend of a friend." Tex's frown indicates he doesn't understand that. "Mai has one, Lam in the monitor room has one, and I have one in my bedroom. Yes, it is dangerous to possess them. A Caucasian owning a gun in Vietnam would not be looked upon favorably. If it was discovered, I would get some serious jail time because—"

The *Superman* theme from Samuel's cell. He speaks briefly and closes the lid. "Lam says Harry is here."

*

Mai, Tex, and I follow Samuel through the living room. "Come meet my friend, Bobby," Samuel says.

The boy tenses but doesn't budge from the sofa. "The policeman?"

Samuel laughs. "It is okay. He will help us." Bobby climbs to his feet slower than an old man. Samuel pats his shoulder. "No worries. Besides, worry is as useless as a breast on a snake."

We go outside to the parking area where Harry has just been buzzed through the front gate. He is barely five feet tall, wearing an asparagus-green uniform with red and yellow shoulder straps, an old-style bus driver hat trimmed in red and yellow, and a small thirty-eight caliber pistol on his hip. I had a gun like that once. A friend teased, "That's sort of like a gun but smaller."

The man looks to be as old as Tex and Samuel, and a clear exception to my observation about how all of Samuel's veteran friends seem to be fighting fit. Harry's sporting a rotund belly so large he can rest his forearms on it. Oversized-framed glasses cover a third of his red, fleshy face, magnifying his eyes making him look like an owl, and he has cartoon-fish, thick rosebud lips. The poor man is an unpleasant mix of fish and fowl.

Samuel pumps the policeman's hand and slaps his shoulder. Harry beams happily. The two friends converse for a moment in Vietnamese, laughing heartily.

"Harry doesn't speak English," Mai whispers behind my shoulder. She pats my butt.

I turn toward her, and mouth, "What are you doing?"

She frowns at me like I'm the one violating some kind of etiquette and nods toward the two men, her eyebrows bunched as if listening intently. When I turn away from her she pinches my butt.

"Ow!"

Samuel looks toward me. "Oh, sorry, Son. This is my friend Harry." He speaks to the policeman and gestures toward me.

"*Chào ông*," I say, bowing. With those glasses, I'm betting he could look at a map and see all the little people running around.

"*Chào ông, Chào ông*," he says, his big lips spreading into a smile.

"Mai," Samuels says, "please help to translate."

"Yes, Father, she says, shooting me an innocent smile. "It would be my pleasure."

Harry shakes Tex's hand.

Samuel gestures toward the door inviting Harry to enter. To us, he says in English, "Let us go inside, everyone."

"Let us go inside, everyone," Mai mockingly interprets.

"Got it," I say mockingly, in turn. "Wise ass," I whisper into her ear.

"What?" she asks with raised eyebrows.

Samuel shoots us a fatherly frown over his shoulder. Mai covers her mouth to keep from laughing as we move up the steps.

"Ly is getting Kim ready to leave," Samuel says, gesturing for us to sit. "Mai, would you please get us some tea?"

"Yes, Father," she says. She excuses herself to Harry with a slight bow and leaves.

Harry eyes Bobby for a long moment, which makes the boy drop his eyes to his interlaced fingers. The policeman and Samuel talk amongst themselves.

"He asked about Bobby's parents," Samuel says. "I told him that we have tried but have been unable to contact them and there may be a possibility that they are coming here."

"I see. What about the assault on the two policemen."

Samuel shakes his head. "In time, Son." He returns to talking to Harry.

"No good ask favor too fast," Tex says.

"Whoops. Sorry."

Samuel and Harry chat amiably for a few moments. At one point, Tex shrugs at me, and says, "Talk about Paris. Harry like Paris womens too much."

Ah yes, I can see how he'd be a chick magnet.

"Tea," Mai says, carrying in a tray. She sets it on the low, black table and fills the cups. No one speaks until everyone has theirs. Mai sits next to me on the sofa.

"I will begin with Bobby's situation," Samuel says. He speaks for a long moment in which Harry nods several times and laughs once.

"Father tell him about you meeting Bobby on the airplane and Bobby kicking the policemen in the head. That is what make Harry laugh. Father says Bobby is a good boy but made a big mistake. He says that he was frightened and is very sorry about the policemen."

Harry sips from his cup, his magnified eyes watching the boy. Bobby looks at the floor, his tea untouched. Harry begins speaking.

Mai speaks softly in my ear, which I'm liking for other reasons beside her translation. "Harry says that the two policemen are not friends of his. I think he means that he does not like them. He says he is glad Bobby kicked their heads. He say they have too much… con… conceit?"

"Yes."

"Before they have big heads but now their heads are small."

"And hurting."

"Yes." Mai smiles behind her hand. "Other policemen tease them too much and now the two policemen want to forget it happened. Harry say their boss, he is like a captain, needs money to make the case disappear."

Samuel is speaking now.

"Father say no problem, he will take care of it. He say Bobby will be back with his parents in a few hours."

I shake my head. "No, no. Tell Samuel that I will take care of the money. He shouldn't have to pay it."

"Wait," Bobby says. "*I* did it. *I* will pay, somehow. I will send you the money or something. I work in a restaurant sometimes, a friend of my father's."

LOREN W. CHRISTENSEN

"That's commendable," I say. "But this needs to be taken care of now. I'll pay it and you can owe me."

Embarrassed, the boy looks down at his cup. "Thanks," he breathes.

"I am sure Father will not let you, Sam. It will probably be one hundred fifty dollars. Something like that."

Harry looks at Bobby, who is still looking into his tea. The policeman says something and the boy looks at him for the first time, nods.

"Harry say, 'sometimes our actions are far reaching.'"

Isn't that the truth.

"Now Harry ask what career he wants to be." Mai listens to Bobby's response. "He says he wants to be a martial arts teacher like you. Teach taekwondo."

The boy flushes when I smile at him.

"Okay," Samuel says. "I think the airport issue is settled now as well as Bobby's runaway status. Bobby, I hope you understand that both of these issues were quite serious and could have resulted with you going to jail. They do not coddle violators here as they do in the United States. Jail would have been terrible for you."

It wouldn't be easy for him in the states, either. A good looking boy like him would be every con's girlfriend in a week, and if he fought it, things would be even worse.

"Thank you very much, sir," Bobby says softly. He converses with Harry. The policeman smiles and winks a magnified eye at Samuel.

Mai whispers, "He thanked Harry, and apologized for being a problem."

Samuel leans toward the boy. "We are going to talk about something else now that does not concern you. If you do not mind, go on out to the kitchen and get some more to eat. Ly always has pastries made."

"Yes sir," Bobby says, standing. He extends his hand to Harry and they shake. The rotund policeman says one more thing.

"Harry say he does taekwondo too," Mai translates, fighting a smile.

After Bobby leaves the room, Samuel says, "Sam, when Mai and I returned from Portland, I told Harry about my incident with Lai Van Tan's son, and the other man. He told me that he looked up the report by the location where it happened and found one that told of two anonymous deaths, one by gunshot and one by blunt force trauma. He says there was very little investigation because there were no witnesses. Harry thinks that the responding officers probably called Lai Van Tan as soon as they recognized his son's ID. Lai Van Tan probably paid them off. The reports said that the victims did not have identification, which means the police removed it. It would be assumed that the two men were unknown street thugs who met a violent death. A very common occurrence here. Bottom line is that there was no follow up."

"Good lord!" I say.

"It is good, Son, because I would be sitting in jail if the police knew of my involvement. So right now, I am going to tell Harry about you two getting jumped and about the meeting today. Mai, please translate as before."

Harry listens intently to Samuel. At one point Harry smiles, looks at Mai, smiles, and makes a big owl-eye wink.

"Samuel must have just told him what you did to those two guys."

"No," she whispers. "He laugh because Father say I escape when they stop the car. Father say they were not good kidnappers." She lowers her voice even more. "Father did not tell about the shooting because that could cause problems for me."

"But you were defending yourself," I argue. "Fighting to get away."

"Because I have gun, it could cause big problems. Father does not want to tell that even when Harry is his friend. Harry would not do anything but he would not want to know about it."

Mai listens for a moment. "Oh yes, now Harry tell Father that he does not know how he can help because Lai Van Tan pay the… I do not know English word. Like big bosses of police."

I nod. "Okay, I understand. The top officials. He paid off the police brass."

"I am sorry, I do not know the word 'brass.' But Harry say Lai Van Tan pay the big bosses so he can do what he wants. He say that one man, a businessman in *Cholon*, get mad at Lai Van Tan about a month ago and attacked him in a restaurant. Lai Van Tan's bodyguards beat the man almost to death. Then police came and took the man away. The man's wife came to police station and complain that she has not seen her husband since that day. The police tell her that they do not know where he is, that maybe he, uh, run away. Like, leave and not tell her."

"The man disappeared after the police took him away?"

"Yes, disappear. That is the word I mean."

"Damn."

Mai pauses to listen to Harry. "Harry say that he will talk to some policemen, but he worries that we might have to solve our problem ourselves. He say we must be careful not to cause attention to ourselves."

This is starting to piss me off. "This is nuts," I say loudly. "I'm sorry, Samuel, but this is wrong. You're telling me that the police won't protect your family?" Samuel raises his palm to calm me. I ignore it. "What the hell good are they? Is their only purpose to take payoffs?" Mai is pulling on my forearm. "Maybe I should call a couple of newspaper friends in Portland and tell them about this. I'm sure other big papers would pick up the story."

Harry's giant eyes bore into me.

"Son, calm yourself," Samuel says, lifting his palm. "This is not the United States. America does not have a monopoly on how things are done. There is a way that we do things here, a certain protocol that must be followed."

"Protocol?" I snap. I really need to shut up. "You mean like etiquette? Well, where was the etiquette when those shit-heads jumped Mai and me? One of them had a gun. They could have easily shot us dead as we walked out that door. And what about Portland? After everything that happened there, which wasn't the way we do things in America, by the way, we still have to worry about protocol here? How about the damn cops show some etiquette and do their job?"

Loooong uncomfortable silence in which Mai looks at the floor, Samuel looks at me with disappointment, and Harry stares at me with eyes the size of hubcaps. I'm sitting motion-less, except for my left foot, which is tapping the floor.

"You done, Son?"

I sniff, nod.

"Your mother had a quick temper. Really ripped into me once. Do not remember why."

I start to apologize but stop because I'm not sorry.

"No need," Samuel says, picking up on my thoughts. "Your

protest is noted, and I understand it, but if I may continue with Harry?"

"Of course," I say, bowing my head. "Please tell him I am sorry for the interruption. But I still feel that—"

"Stop while you are ahead, Son."

"Okay."

"Sam," Mai says, "never apologize and then say 'but.' Because the 'but' takes away from—"

"*Okay.*"

Samuel resumes talking to Harry, probably explaining that the boy has a short fuse. Mai raises her eyebrows at me and makes a zip motion across her mouth. I nod.

"Father say to Harry that you are worried about our safety," Mai says. "Then Harry say that there are policeman that might help, but he has to, uh, figure it out who they are." Mai pats my forearm. "Do not get angry, okay?"

"I won't. I have it under control now."

"Harry say it is not the officers that are the problem; it is their bosses. They get paid by Lai Van Tan. Not all of them, of course, but some, maybe only one or two. The problem is that Harry does not know which one or which two."

I force my hands to unclench. I hate police corruption. The Portland Police Bureau is one of the cleanest law enforcement agencies in the United States. In my fifteen years on the job, I saw only one crooked thing and that was when a guy I was partnering with for a week pocketed a small ornate figurine when we raided a drug house. I got in his face, he put it back, and I refused to work with him again. Every agency gets complaints about stealing and bribes, but usually the complainers are disgruntled suspects wanting to strike back at the arresting cop. Most drop the accusations when they are told that if Internal Affairs discovers that they were lying, they will get charged with filing a false police report.

This is pissing me off, but I need to shut up, grow up, and man up. This is Vietnam and I'm a guest here. Samuel's right, the United States doesn't have a monopoly on the right way to do things.

"So how much of this refusal to help your family is racially motivated?" I ask. Damn me and my mouth.

"Mai, take Sam into the kitchen and—"

"I'm sorry, Samuel. Not another word, promise."

Samuel shoots me a glare and resumes talking with Harry.

"Sam," Mai whispers. "Please be quiet."

"I'm under control," I say. When she lifts her eyebrows again, I say, "That was the last outburst. Promise."

"Father is telling Harry about the sex trafficking. Father say that he thinks it is a new, uh, business for Lai Van Tan. Father say that we have a person who is looking into it to learn what is happening. Harry say that because he be in Paris for four weeks he has not heard about this. But he might not hear about it anyway since the warehouse Lai Van Tan is using is in Biên Hòa, twenty miles from here. He say his, uh, jurisdiction? Yes, his jurisdiction is only in Ho Chi Minh City. He said he will try to learn about it and tell Father."

Samuel looks at me. "One of the big problems about sex trafficking is that while so many people have experienced their daughters, and the daughters of their friends, suddenly disappearing, it's rare that the police or anyone else knows where to look, and once they are transported out of Vietnam, it is impossible to do anything. Knowing about the warehouse as a holding place is rare information."

"A big break?" I ask.

Samuel nods and returns to talking to Harry.

"Okay, now Father and Harry talk about family," Mai says. "I think the serious talk is over." She turns all the way toward me. "Sam, I told you when Lu was here that sex trafficking is a very big problem in Vietnam. Thousands of children are taken and sent to other countries. Keep in your mind that there is much corruption in the government about sex trafficking. So do not be angry. It is the way it is and it will not change soon. But I think it will change someday. I am ashamed of my country for this, but we just have to work with the way it is."

My jaw starts to cramp and I realize I've been grinding my teeth as Mai spoke. We have to work with the way it is, she says. This is so diametrically opposed to everything I believe about law enforcement and the police code of ethics to protect the innocent and the weak. It gnaws at me, though that same code says I'm not supposed to let personal feelings, prejudices, and animosities influence my actions. Even so…

I look at Mai. "You ever see the movie *Death Wish*, with Charles Bronson?" Samuel, the movie buff, turns and looks at me.

"Understood," he says.

# CHAPTER THIRTEEN

Bobby is sitting cross legged next to the *koi* pond and I'm perched on the end of the cement bench. When Samuel said he wanted to talk with Harry in private, Mai excused herself to do some work in their office and I took Bobby out into the backyard. For the last couple of hours, we've talked about everything from martial arts, to school, to work, to girls.

"So how has this running away thing worked out for you?" I ask.

"It hasn't worked out so good," he says softly, looking down at the wiggling fish.

"Lesson learned?"

"To always keep my phone charged?"

"Cute."

"Just playin'," he says. "I learned that sometimes my parents really know what they're talking about."

"Very good. You sure you're only sixteen?"

"Almost seventeen."

"Ah ha, that's why you're so wise. Are your parents strict with you?"

"Not much. I mean there are lots of rules, which I understand, and I'm okay with, but there are some that don't make sense."

"Think they make sense to your parents?"

"Don't know, probably. I mean, sometimes they—"

"So the rule makes sense to them, just not to you."

"Yeah."

"Would they explain their reasoning if you asked them nicely?"

"Yeah, unless they were mad or something."

"What if you asked them later when they weren't so mad?"

He doesn't answer for a few seconds, then, "I hear what you're saying."

"Look at me for a moment, Bobby. Thank you. From what I've seen during our time together, you got yourself some outstanding parents. Want to know how I know?"

"Yes."

"I know because they got themselves one hell of an outstanding kid."

"Yeah, right."

"I've seen a lot of troubled kids on my job. Some were that way because they had turds for parents and some were troubled in spite of having good mothers and fathers. Maybe they were born with a bad gene, I don't know. I leave that to the shrinks to figure out. But I think... no, I know that I'm a good judge of a man. Looking at you, I see a wonderful young dude—smart, funny, respectful, physically fit—who is quickly maturing into a fantastic man."

Bobby loses his struggle not to smile.

"I'm not blowing smoke up your ass, Son."

"I always thought that was a funny visual," he says.

"I'm telling you what I see based on my experience, and big city cops get more life experience in three months than most people get in their entire lives. With you, I see the makings of a good human being."

He lowers his head into a slight bow. "Thank you."

"No charge. But now you've got to fix your screw-up with your parents."

He widens his eyes with a combination of mock and real fear. "I'm so busted."

"Why, because they're spending thousands of dollars to fly over here to get your sorry ass?"

He lowers his chin to his chest. "I didn't think of the money thing. I'm so seriously, royally screwed."

"No doubt," I say. "But part of being a man is to first admit you screwed up, take your punishment, and then strive to do better. Pushing your father and inadvertently making your mother afraid of you is huge, but it's fixable—with time."

Bobby nods and moves a piece of palm leaf through the water. The *koi* streak away from it, but return just as quickly. At Bobby's age, kids start pulling away from their parents. They do it in many different ways. Bobby just added running away to the other side of the world to the list. I haven't met the parents, but I got a gut feeling all is going to be fine after they kick his behind.

"May I ask what the secret meetings have been about?" Bobby asks, looking up at me. "I've been asked to leave the room like twenty times."

"Not quite that many times, to be accurate. Family stuff that they want to keep private."

"I got that, but I've been getting vibes that something is majorly wrong, like everyone is worried, or something."

"Very perceptive. Samuel wants some privacy so I need to respect that. But what I can tell you is that there is tension with some people over an incident that happened a few months ago. Samuel has tried to make peace but the other people aren't receptive, we don't think, anyway. He is going to continue to try to make things better, it's just iffy right now."

"That's intense," he says.

"Nothing for you to worry about. We'll get you hooked up with your parents and you'll be out of here. On that note, let me try them again." I poke in the number.

I like Bobby's company but I want him gone before anything happens. We're damned if we go outside the walls and we might be damned if we stay here. Of the two, Samuel thinks staying behind the walls is the safest. I'm not so convinced and I'm not sure why I think that. Maybe it's because being in here is a little like being a rat in a barrel. I close my phone.

"Nothing?" Bobby asks, moving to sit beside me.

"Bunch of clicks and burps. You got a return ticket, right?"

"Yeah, for next Monday. I was planning on staying a week with her."

"Then you were going to fly home to receive your punishment?"

He shrugs. "What can I say? Pretty dumb, huh?"

"There is a saying in police work that any plan is better than no plan. I think you just made that untrue."

"Gee, thanks."

I bump his shoulder with mine. "Suck it up, troop."

He scoots his foot in the gravel. "Yeah."

"Hey, want to hear my biggest blunder?"

He looks up at me and grins. "Definitely."

"One time I wore a raincoat and... you ready?"

"It didn't rain?"

"That's it."

Bobby sputters a laugh. "*Shiiii*. Okay," he says standing. "You, me, we spar to the death. Now."

"Well, all right. But you should know that yours will be a slow one with lots of groaning, writhing, and coughing up green gunk."

"Gentlemen," Mai says walking across the yard toward us like "a soulful flower in the garden." My man Sting sang that. This flower is carrying a tray of fruit and pastry. "Are you two enjoying the evening?"

"Hi Mai," Bobby says enthusiastically. "You just saved Sam's life. We were about to duel to the death."

"Really? But I made food for three. Oh well," she says with a shrug. "Looks like there will be leftovers."

"We just made up," I say. "Here, sit between us. Bobby, move over and give the lady a spot."

"Cool," he says, sliding over, but not that much. He fires Mai a toothy smile as she sits.

"Do you know the names of the fruit, Bobby?"

"Some of them," he says, scooting even closer to her, to better see the fruit, I'm sure. He looks at me with a goofy grin, and looks back at the plate. He points at a star-shaped slice. "That is *trái khế*. In the U.S. we call it star fruit. That one is *quả chuối*, banana. That one… I don't remember."

"*Quả đu đủ.*"

"Doo doo," I say. "Don't think I want to eat anything called doo doo."

Mai elbows me. "Sorry, Sam, I did not mean to do that. There are accents on the… doo doo. It is papaya."

Bobby takes a piece of the fruit and a croissant. I retrieve a banana and some kind of pastry I've never seen before.

"That is *bánh pâté chaud*, Sam," she says. "It is a little bit Vietnamese and a little bit French. They are filled with pork."

"Mmm, good," I say around a mouthful, spraying crumbs onto my legs and onto hers. "Sorry."

Mai laughs. "That was gross but I understand. I love them too. I made them."

303

"You did? When?"

"This afternoon. I finished work fast in my office, so when I see you two out here enjoying yourself, I made these. Ly is busy with Mother and so is Father."

I shake my head in wonder and imitate a carnival barker. "She cooks, and she fights. Ladies and gentlemen, the amazing Mai."

"You practice martial arts?" Bobby asks, munching his pastry.

"Yes, my father teach me."

"What belt are you? I just got my black belt in taekwondo."

"You did? That is a special accomplishment. Congratulations. You must be *very* strong."

"Thank you," he says blushing. "Pretty strong, yes."

"Oh, very good. I do not have a belt. Father does not believe in them. But he trains me hard."

"How long?" Bobby asks, picking up a piece of banana. "I've been training for four years."

"I start when I was six, no, seven. So that is twenty-six years."

The boy's eyes widen. "Daaaamn! Almost as long as Sam."

"Yes," she says looking at me. She smiles, bats her eyes, and tilts her head in mock sweetness. "See anything you want, Sam?"

I swim in her eyes, backstroking, breast stroking. "Oh yeah," I say, forgetting for a hair of a second that the kid is sitting on her other side.

She lifts her plate a little. "Try the đu đủ?" Oh man, it's not what she says but how she says it that stirs my—

"That's the papaya, Sam," Bobby says, leaning around Mai to interrupt our moment.

"Uh, yeah. Thanks. Let me try your parents again, Bobby."
I pretend to reach for my phone.

Mai smiles with fake innocence and retrieves some *quả đu đủ* for herself.

"Mai," Tex calls from the top of the stairs. We all turn. "Linh here now."

"Oh, good. Come, Sam. Meet your half sister."

# CHAPTER FOURTEEN

"Sam, this is Linh," Mai says, pulling away from a gentle hug with a slightly younger woman who bears several similarities to Mai, though she is about six inches shorter. "Sister, this is the brother you never knew you had."

Linh bows slightly and smiles, which makes her look even more like Mai. "Good to meet you," she says, in lightly accented English. "You are very handsome man." She giggles. We're standing in the living room. Tex goes out front to tend to something.

"It's wonderful to meet you. It is so amazing that I have a sister. I'm not sure what to say other than it's obvious that you and Mai got your beauty from your mother."

"That works," Mai says.

Linh nods. "Yes it does. And you got your wisdom from Father." We all laugh. She obviously has a mind that is as quick as Mai's. She takes Mai's arm.

"This is Bobby," Mai says. "Sam met him on the airplane over and he is staying with us for a short while."

Bobby flushes as they bow to one another.

"Nice to meet you," they say in unison.

"I understand you will be leaving right away," I say.

"Yes. Father wants Mother to be away as soon as possible. I hope when problem is, uh, fixed, we can spend time together. An is most excited to meet you. This Lai Van Tan is a son-of-a-bitch, no?"

Mai smiles at Linh and I snort a laugh at her bluntness that

306

she no doubt inherited from her mother. "I think that is a perfect way to think of him."

"Mai tell me you kill people in the United States. I am sorry that happen."

My jaw drops.

"You killed people?" Bobby asks, looking at me.

"Linh," Mai says sharply. She speaks rapidly to her in Vietnamese. Linh quickly covers her mouth with her palm and bows to me.

"I am so sorry, Sam. My English... I do not mean to be rude how I talk."

"Not a problem. Your English is excellent. I am sorry that I don't speak Vietnamese at all."

"What happened?" Bobby asks. "Why did you kill—"

I wave my palm at the boy. "Later. Not the time now." The boy nods, but continues to look at me with big eyes. To Linh, I say, "I'm sorry that your mother is so ill. She is a wonderful lady and I'm sure she will be fine."

"Thank you. We are very worried."

"Linh!" Samuel says entering the room, a white mask hanging from his neck. He's got a few more in his hand. "I am happy to see you." He envelops her in his arms. She hugs him back, speaking in Vietnamese. "You have met Sam?" he asks rhetorically.

"Yes. It is wonderful to meet him."

Samuel moves between Mai and Linh, and slips his arms in theirs. His face always brightens whenever Mai is near; now it practically radiates.

"I have been truly blessed with these young women, Sam. And with you. Only when you have children will you understand how they make my old heart sing."

Linh slaps his forearm. "You are not old, Father."

Mai shrugs. "He is a little old, Linh."

Linh frowns and looks Samuel up and down. "Yes, I believe you are correct, wise sister."

Samuel laughs heartily. "Maybe I overstated the being blessed part." He waits until everyone stops laughing, and says, "Mother is ready. Linh, I am so sorry you can't stay, but it is important for her to be away from here as soon as possible."

"I understand, Father. I want to clean up a little and then I am ready."

"I have packed some food for you, sister," Mai says.

"Thank you." Linh nods to me and leaves the room.

"I am going to leave with them," Samuel says. "I will ride to just outside the city to ensure they are not followed. I will take a taxi back."

"I should go with you."

He shakes his head. "I need you here, Sam. I have four people outside but we need capable people inside." He looks at the boy. "I do not know how much Sam has told you."

"He said you were having a problem with some people. Will everything be okay?"

"Have you contacted your parents?"

Bobby and I both shake our heads. "No contact, yet," I say. "Something is wrong with the connection. We think that they might be on their way here."

"I hear Mother coming," Samuel says. He hands the bundle of masks to Mai. "Please hand these out."

"Masks?" Bobby asks, taking one.

"Mai's mother has TB," Samuel says. "It is communicable so we wear these to protect our nose and mouth."

"You guys live interesting lives," he whispers into his mask.

"Oh, yeah," I whisper back.

"Hello, everyone," Kim says from behind her mask. She's wearing black satin pants and a white top. "Youngest," she says, holding out her hand as her daughter enters the room. Linh takes a mask from Samuel, slips it on, and scurries over to greet her mother. Kim looks more fragile than the last time I saw her. Probably from all that's going on and the stress of having to leave. Still, her bearing is regal and her beauty undeniable. She looks over at me. "Sam. How are you? Are you enjoying your visit?"

I bow. "I'm fine, thank you. I'm sorry you're leaving. I was looking forward to more talks." Samuel leaves the room.

"I was as well," she says. "I hope things will improve and we can have those conversations."

"I look forward to it."

"Has Mai showed you the view from the new building?"

If I were drinking tea it would be shooting out of my mouth right now.

Kim shakes her head with disappointment. "I have not been able to see it, but I understand that it is mind blowing. Is that the right term?"

"I showed him, Mother," Mai says. "And I believe 'mind blowing' is exactly what he said."

I could fry an egg on my face.

"Wonderful." She looks at Bobby. "This young man is your friend?"

"Yes, this is Bobby," I manage. The boy bows.

"Welcome to our home. You have come at an interesting time."

Bobby and I exchange a look. "Thank you so much. I am enjoying being with your family." Kid never fails to amaze.

"As much as I hate to say it," Samuel says, half staggering into the room carrying two large suitcases, "we must get going. Mother, you packed your barbells, I see." Kim smiles and winks at me. Samuel sets the luggage down. "Sam, Bobby, I need to check with security. Would you carry these out to the car. And lift with your knees, not your backs."

He taps in a number on his cell and begins talking to someone as Bobby and I lug the suitcases out to the front. It's dark now. When did that happen? Tex is by the front gate, perched on a five-foot-high flowerpot so he can see over the wall, a cell in one hand, a flashlight in the other. To anyone on the other side, he must look eight feet tall.

Bobby and I load the suitcases into the Toyota's trunk and help Samuel maneuver the wheelchair down the stairs. Mai and Samuel assist Kim out of it and into the front passenger seat. The poor woman's legs tremble at the exertion and she releases an audible sigh upon sitting. She doesn't utter a complaint, though. I see where Mai gets her grit.

"I will be back in an hour or so," Samuel says. "Keep your cells close."

Mai is kneeling next to her mother and holding her hand. She looks up at her father long enough to acknowledge him and for me to see a lone tear rolling over her mask. She whispers to her mother, to which Kim nods and pats her hand. Mai stands and shuts the door.

Samuel is talking on his cell again and looking at Tex, who gives him a thumbs up. "Okay," he says to Linh. "We are clear to go." He climbs in the back.

"See you soon," Linh says to me.

"I look forward to it."

She looks at Mai, nods her head toward me, and says, "Good job, big sister." Mai gives her a quick hug and shuts the car door behind her as the gate slides open. A moment later, they're gone and the gate clanks closed.

"Why do I think stuff is more serious than what you said?" Bobby asks as we remove our masks. Tex uses the gate to swing down to the driveway.

I smile and punch the kid's shoulder. "Because you're a suspicious dude. You'd make a good cop."

He brightens. "Really?"

"I'm sure of it. Let's go inside, officer."

"Wait," Mai says. "Tex, would you and Bobby watch television while I show Sam our security?"

Hoorah! I think I know what she means by "security."

"Sorry, no can do, Canyon Bob," he says seriously. "It is six-thirty. Time I polish my shoes."

Bobby laughs hard at that.

"You think funny, eh" Tex says. "No need feet to kick your little ass."

"Okay, they are fine," Mai says, gesturing for me to lead the way into the house. "Father wants me to introduce you to the night man in the monitor room."

"I've been curious as to how many people you have watching the screens," I ask, playing along as we walk through the house and out into the backyard. We slip on sandals. "I've only met Lam."

"There are three most of the time. Lam for daytime, Ngai for afternoon until midnight, and Trai from midnight until Lam comes to work at eight o'clock again. But Ngai got sick three days ago, so Lam and Trai have had to work twelve hours at a time."

"Ouch. That's too long to spend on a post."

"It is just for a short time. Father will get someone from the old soldiers' home to come help. Right now, Tex relieves Lam and Trai during their shift so they can rest their eyes and walk around a little."

She stops in front of my bedroom door and turns to face me. Oh yeah. I can handle this. I rotate my head a couple times and shake my arms loose. I'm warmed up now.

"Before you meet Trai, it is important for you to know about him."

"What?" Not exactly what I was expecting.

"Actually, not so much to know about him but to understand more about Father."

"Okay." I look at my door. Longingly.

"I know that this might not be the right time to talk about Father. But because everything is crazy, I must tell you things when I can."

I shrug. "No problem. I want to know."

"Anyway, Trai is not the same age as Father's other friends. He is the same age as me."

"Not a veteran?"

"No. But his father was in the war."

I wonder… "Is Trai an old boyfriend or something?"

"No, but he likes me."

"But you don't like him?" Suddenly we sound like we're in high school.

"Not like that."

"Then what are you telling me?"

"Father have special relationship with Trai because he… knew his father."

"Okay."

"In war… Father kill his father."

"What? You're kidding."

She shakes her head. "Not kidding. True."

"Incredible. But how did he… I mean, did Samuel somehow find out the enemy soldier's name and look up the family after the war ended?" That sounds like something he would do. But to befriend the fatherless boy?

"His father was not the enemy. He was Father's friend. A scout for the Green Berets."

"I don't understand."

"I am sorry, Sam. I do not mean to be mysterious. It is because I am uncomfortable telling you this about Father. I… " Mai watches a half dozen insects flitter about the overhead light. The evening is hot; the sound of traffic far off. "Okay, his name was Dai. He fight the North for many years and became not right in the head anymore. All Green Beret soldiers say he was *điên cái đầu*, which means crazy in soldier slang, and they named him 'Dinky.' Father said he loved to kill the enemy; he killed many of them and he loved to do it too much. Father was very sad because he and Dinky were friends, and Father was saddened to see how crazy he was getting.

"Every time they came back to their camp after a mission… oh, mission mean the soldiers would go out and fight with the enemy. Sometimes a dozen men would go, other times only a scout and one or two men. Sometimes Green Beret missions were very secret and very dangerous. Sometimes they would fight only with hands and knives. Anyway, when Dai and other soldiers would come back from a mission, Dai would disappear into the jungle for an hour. Father saw him do this three or four times, and other soldiers told Father they saw him do it other days when Father was not there. And Dai always carried a bag.

Some thought that he might have a radio and he was calling the enemy.

"Father knew that Dai hated the VC too much to be a double agent, but he still needed to know what his friend was doing. Plus, Father was getting worried because Dai was becoming crazier and crazier. One time, Dai went out on a mission with other soldiers for two days. When they radioed that they were coming back to the firebase, Father went into the jungle the same way Dai always did when a mission was over. He followed the broken vines and smashed grass.

"The... uh, trail stopped at a small creek. But before he could hide, Father saw something under a pile of vines next to a big tree. It was raining very hard, so at first he did not understand what he was seeing. When he got close, he could see what he thought was a dead person. So he pulled the vines away, and that is when he knew what Dai had been doing for the last six weeks.

"It was not a dead VC; it was a man with, uh, parts not attached. The body was lying there on the ground but the head was placed on top of the, uh, what do you call? Oh, torso. One arm, the right one, was next to the torso's shoulder. There was no left arm. The legs had been placed below the torso, but one did not have a foot and had rolled away a little."

"My God," I breathe.

"Father said that he was so shocked that it took him a moment to see that the parts—the arm, the head, the torso, the legs—were from different people. Some had... decomposes? Yes, decomposes, no, decomposed very bad while some were fresh, like they had been added not long ago. He saw that Dai had replaced one leg because there were bones in the creek that looked like a leg skeleton. A body... rots very fast in the jungle and animals take parts. Father think maybe he had replaced a lot of parts to keep the body… fresh.

"When he could not look anymore he turned to leave, but Dai leaped on him. Father did not hear him because of the hard rain. Dai had a knife and fight Father like crazy, like an animal. He cut Father's arm very bad. Maybe you remember the scar when he had his shirt off at your house."

I remember seeing a lot of scars that night. Including scars from a whip.

"So he and Dai fell on top of the different body parts, and Dai got on top of Father with a knife at Father's throat. When he start to cut, Father got one of his arms free and he hit Dai here, at the temple. It killed him." Mai snaps her fingers. "Just like that."

As Mai wipes her tears away, it dawns on me that I've been holding my breath. I've been a cop for fifteen years and thought I'd seen and heard it all, but this tops the list. First to have to see such a thing and then to have to kill your friend, even one that had gone mad.

How has Samuel remained sane?

"Father say that the bag Dai carry that day had an arm inside, but a right one. Dai made a mistake because the torso needed a left one."

If it wasn't such a gruesome tale, I'd laugh at that.

"Unbelievable, Mai. It's so unthinkable. Did they ever figure out how he did it, how he got the parts?"

"Not for sure. Like I said, many battles were hand to hand, and it is possible he would take something when no one was looking. Father say it is also possible that after they would return to the base, Dai would go back out to the battle place and get a part he needed. The only thing they know for sure was that poor Dai had gone crazy and was trying to build a man. Father said that maybe he wanted to make up for all the men he had killed."

Mai and I stand for a long time, side by side, leaning against each other and looking down at the cobblestones. After several minutes, I ask, "Do you think Samuel would have told me about this?"

Mai shrugs. "He did not tell me. One night before I went to Paris, I overheard him tell Sifu about it when they were sitting on the balcony of the condo where Mother and Father used to live. I was staying with them for a week and my window was open a little. When I thought about it, I remember Father was very quiet for several days before he tell Sifu."

"What did he say?"

"Sifu said, 'You have two choices: You can either lose hope and fall into depression, or you can use the terrible memory as a way to find the strength inside you to go on.'"

"Use it," I say aloud. I like that. Don't be a victim to the memory. Instead, use it.

"I wanted you to know this horrible thing that Father experienced because it helps you to understand him a little more."

"Thank you, Mai." Her compassion humbles me. Her pain for her father was in every word of the story, and it helps me not only understand more about Samuel but also about myself.

She smiles and says, "We go meet him now."

"Okay. First, about him liking you. You mean, like-likes you?"

That heart stopping smile laughs as me. "Yes, he like-likes me. But no worries, Sam. I like-like you."

She said it emphatically, as if to get that out of the equation. Nice. I've had a couple girlfriends who liked to play the jealousy game. Glad she's not one of them.

"But Trai has been watching the monitors at night. I forgot about him when we kiss here by your door and when I came to your room. I remembered about him after, but I forgot before because I wanted you so very, very bad."

I gulp audibly at that last comment, then, "Do you think he might not like me? Do you think he is watching us right now?"

"I guarantee it. That is the right expression, no?"

"Yes," I sigh. Guess that means a little lip action is out of the question.

"It is still important to meet him because Father wants you to see the additional security. He say it is important for you to, uh… 'know the players.'"

"Okay, no problem."

"Good. You know," she says, lowering her chin and looking up at me in that way that heats my blood, "I would prefer to be in your room right now instead of going to the monitor room."

"Please stop. You're making this hard."

She giggles and pats my chest. "That metaphor pretty damn hot. Come on big boy." We move down to the next door. Mai raps on it twice and says something before opening it.

Trai is a tad shorter than me, skinny, with shoulder-length black hair, wearing a green T-shirt and black shorts. He has eyes only for Mai as he moves around the monitor station to greet her shyly in Vietnamese.

"Please," Mai says, we can speak English. "Trai, this is Sam, Father's son. Sam, Trai."

His eyes dart to me and back to Mai. He didn't just look away, he dismissed me as if I were irrelevant. I wonder if he knows Phat Ho. He says something to her in Vietnamese.

"Trai, we will speak English," she says adamantly.

He gives me another glance, as if I were a bug on the wall, one not significant enough to worry about. He looks back at Mai.

"Lam showed Sam this room before so he is familiar with the monitors. I would like you to show him the additional security outside." When he doesn't respond, Mai adds, "Father says it is important that he knows everything."

Trai's eyes flit toward me and then to the monitors. An "Okay" finds its way through his tight lips. I'm pretty sure I can scratch him off my we're-becoming-fast-friends list.

"You know already monitors see outside walls, front, back, side, gate?" His voice is monotone, deliberately so to show that he isn't about to give me one ounce of energy.

"Yes."

"Look this one," he says, moving over to the far left screen, "Lam put more cameras here." He pokes a button on the bottom of the monitor and I immediately recognize the street along the front of the house. The camera must be mounted somewhere high because it shows a long stretch of the street in front, including the property's far corner, the closest corner, and a couple of feet of the south wall. I see the gate to the house about halfway down the street. "HD," he says. "Very good, uh, very clear."

"Yes," I say. "Good work,"

"See, man?" Trai says, tapping his finger near the top of the screen at a small image of a person on the far side of the front gate. "He sit on sidewalk across from house. That man Vien. He work for Samuel. Sell motorbike parts to fool people."

"Outstanding," I say. "He can watch the place and pick up a few *đồng* at the same time."

Trai shakes his head and looks at Mai. She translates. He looks back at me, nods without acknowledging the hilarity of my observation. I think he's loosening up a little, though. He barely sneers at me this time. He pushes the same button and the screen shot changes to show another street, actually, a dirt road.

"Back house," he says, pointing at a view that affords a long shot of the back wall. There are fewer lights back there so things are a little hard to make out. It looks to be an alley with ruts and potholes full of water. There is a wall of bamboo on the other side that appears dense enough to actually serve as a wall. It's probably the backside of another high-end home.

Trai taps the lower part of the screen that shows the front end of a dark-colored car. "That Danh, he work with us. He old but have good eye."

Judging by Samuel's other friends, Trai probably really means eye, singular.

"You have done a good job, Trai," I say, kissing up a little. "Everyone has done a good job on security." He nods, then looks toward Mai like a lovesick puppy. Poor bastard. But not really. "Are these the people Samuel was talking with when your mother was about to leave?"

Mai nods. "Have you heard the saying…" she pauses to think for a second. "People sleep peaceably in their beds at night… only because rough men stand ready to do violence on their behalf."

"I have. George Orwell, I think."

"I do not know him. But Father say it all the time." Mai smiles. "He told me he made it up."

*

Trai again looks away when I extend my hand. The guy is in his thirties but he has some growing up to do.

Mai and I head back to the house—both of us look at the door to my room longingly as we pass—to see what Tex and the boy are up to. There is a kickboxing match on the big screen in the living room, a noisy one with drums, cymbals, and what I think is called a Javanese clarinet. Tex is perched on the sofa and pointing at the boy's hips. Must be teaching him about the importance of rotating them when punching. The kid snaps out a couple rear crosses. Looks good.

Tex looks our way and nods toward Bobby, as if to say, "What do you think of my protégé?" When I say that his hands are improving, the boy immediately gives all the credit to Tex, who smiles and punches the kid in the chest. Bobby rubs the spot and laughs.

It isn't until Mai and I sit down to watch them that I realize how tired I am. Between the heat and all the drama, I seem to conk out quickly over here. When I see Mai yawning, I lean in close and whisper that we ought to go to bed, bobbing my eyebrows like Groucho Marx. She laughs, smacks me, and suggests we go get a snack.

The kitchen is what I would expect in a nice home in the states: modern appliances, lots of chrome, hanging pots and pans, and a huge chopping block. Mai removes a papaya from the refrigerator and we enjoy a few slices without speaking, both of us comfortable in the quiet. She picks up the last piece and gently places it between my lips. While I splash around in her eyes, she nibbles the exposed end of the fruit down to my mouth, then gives me the juiciest most erotic kiss ever exchanged on the planet Earth.

She apologizes that we can't spend the night together since Bobby is sharing my room and her parent's room is just below hers. She says we'll have to "put it on hold" until Bobby's parents collect him. I stomp my feet like a spoiled child, which makes her laugh, and say, "I know, riiiight?" I tell her they need colder showers in Saigon, making her laugh again, and mimicking me adds, "I concur."

We enjoy one more lip lock, minus the papaya, though I suggest she bring it when we do have time alone. I tell her goodnight, get Bobby, and we head to the room where I'm hoping the shower spits out ice chunks.

# CHAPTER FIFTEEN

*My head is filled with the roar of pounding rain and howling wind. In the dark swirls I see little Jimmy, the tweaker, the naked hostage taker, and Trai, who has joined the ranks of people who want to shoot holes in my face.*

*"Yoooou tooook my liiiife frommmm meeee, Deeeetective," the syrupy-voiced naked man says.*

*"And my life," the tweaker says in a slighter higher-pitched voice.*

*"And my life," Jimmy says in falsetto.*

*Trai stretches his arm at least three times its normal length to press the end of his gun barrel against my nose. "And you took my life—my Mai!" he says, in voice so cold I can see his breath.*

*"We're going to shoooot you in the faaaace now, deeeetective," the naked man says. "Kissss your assss gooood byyyye."*

*BOOM!*

I jerk awake.

"Sam, what was that?"

I sit up, blinking against a brilliant light piercing through the now open shutters. It disappears, followed by an explosion that sets my bed trembling.

"It's okay," I say, shaking the dream out of my mind. Bobby's on his knees at the foot of my bed. "Storm. Forgot to shut the window. The wind must have blown the shutter against the wall. Man, listen to that rain out there."

Lightning blinds us again, followed by a thunderclap that just might rip open the earth.

"I've never seen or heard anything like this in Westminster," Bobby says. "What time is it?"

"Three a.m." I move over to close the window and shutter. "Nothing like this in Portland, either."

Then the rain stops. Just like that.

"Can you believe that?" Bobby says, laughing. "Awesome! Like God shut off a giant faucet."

"Maybe he did, homeboy." I fall back into bed. We've got air conditioning and the ceiling fan, neither of which are doing much against the awful humidity. Feels like we're inside an Elmer's Glue bottle.

Elmer's Glue. Reminds me of… third grade. Pasting fall leaves… on…

Shouting awakens me. Someone cursing angrily in English. I can see Lam through the window's slats moving toward the monitor room. Most of what he's spewing is in Vietnamese with a dash of English potty words. I hear the monitor room door open and slam shut. I wonder if Shen Lang Rui, Samuel's teacher, just defeated the security again.

I sit up. Seven forty-five on my watch and the humidity is still as thick as mud. Except for waking up at three to what I thought was the end of the world, that was the best night's sleep I've had since I've been here. Make that the second best night. The one I spent with Mai will forever be *numero uno*.

The swelling on the back of my neck is gone, though it's a whole lot tender to the touch. Bobby is still sleeping in a tight ball, his single sheet kicked off onto the floor. I strip out of my wet T-shirt, put on a dry one, a pair of cargo shorts, and quietly slip out the door.

Except for damp soil under the shrubs along the walkway, there's no sign of last night's clamorous storm. Overhead, though, full, dark clouds churn threateningly. I'm guessing another is on its way. I slip through the hedges to see Samuel and Shen Lang Rui over by the heavy bag.

"Son," Samuel calls with a wave. "Come."

I make my way over to them noting once again how still Sifu stands. I've noticed the same trait in Samuel, but the master makes my father look hyper.

"*Chào ông*," I say, bowing slightly to both men. It doesn't hurt to try to impress the man. The sifu is wearing a black Chinese jacket and tan slacks. He nods his head slightly and looks at me for a long moment, his multicolored eyes peering intently into mine as if reading the fine print on the inside of my skull. His voice is gently melodic.

Samuel nods and turns to me. "He said not to worry, that the bad dreams will fade." I jerk my head toward Sifu. "Best to close your mouth, Son. There are many insects in Vietnam.

"But how did he—"

Sifu says something to me. His eyes... they are at once stern, kind, frightening, full of... love? Yes, that's it. Love.

Weird.

"Sifu says that the people in your dream want to harm you because they are angry about what you did."

"My God, Samuel..."

"He says that you must think about these dreams during the day and change how they end."

"Change them? I don't understand."

"Sifu says to give the people flowers."

I wait for the punch line.

"Give each person a flower and walk away from them. It changes the ending, you see. Do this several times a day and soon your bad dreams and their bad endings will become less."

Change the outcome of the dream. Okay, that sort of makes sense. But a flower?

"Hippy generation," Samuel says, apparently reading my thoughts. He listens to Sifu for a moment. "Sifu says that giving yourself a flower when needed is also helpful."

"I don't understand."

Samuel smiles. "I think you will know when it is needed."

This is a whole lot weird coming ten minutes after awakening and before breakfast.

"*Cảm ơn*," I say to Sifu. He lowers his chin a couple inches. I look at Samuel. "How was the trip with Kim?"

"Uneventful, thank goodness. Linh called this morning and said they got home about ten o'clock. Mother has been sleeping since."

"I know she will be better," I say uselessly. When Samuel doesn't say anything, I ask, "Are you training?"

"A little. Our training is mostly on hold because of all that is going on. We have been talking a little about ripping hits. Are you familiar with them?"

"Maybe. I call a ripping hit one that sinks into the target just an inch or so, then rips along under the surface a short distance before extracting."

"Yes, that is it." He says something to Shen Lang Rui. The old man doesn't say anything. "Sifu is very good at it. He has taught me to rip nerve points. The idea is to hit them and rip them out of position. For example, may I see your arm?"

"Uh, okay. But please remember I am a visitor in your country and you're supposed to be nice to me."

Samuel shakes his head. "Sorry, that does not apply here." He smiles, grasps my left wrist, and points at a spot just below the inside of my elbow. "You are familiar with the two nerves here?" I nod. "When struck lightly like this," he strikes the beefy part of my forearm with the edge of his hand, "you feel a sharp tingling in your lower arm and a numbness in your hand."

"Yes, sir." Even the light impact makes my arm twitch a little and my hand feel slightly numb. "I struck a guy there once who was threatening me with a screwdriver. It numbed his hand and he dropped it."

Samuel translates for Sifu and the master smiles.

"Okay," Samuel says. "If I may, I will rip your arm just a little so you get a feel for what happens to the nerves."

"Uh, I'm not sure what I think about 'rip' and 'your arm,' being in the same sentence."

"Medium speed only," he says, holding my wrist so that my forearm is parallel with the ground. He strikes it with the four middle knuckles of his other hand, retracting his blow about three inches from where he made the initial contact.

"Hello!" I say, as an electrical current travels down to my fingertips and simultaneously shoots up to my shoulder. Five seconds later the initial pain is mostly gone but my hand feels dead and useless.

"Sifu says that by ripping the impact—see, I hit this spot here and ripped it over to here—the target nerve is displaced." Conspiratorially, Samuel tells me, "I do not think that the nerve actually moves, but for sure it is shocked by the force of the rip." Using a normal voice again, "It is important to penetrate into the target before ripping. On your forearm, I could penetrate only about two centimeters, about an inch. It would be about the same on your cheek, but less on your forehead where there is not much flesh. On your stomach, even though yours is strong, I would sink my strike in several centimeters before beginning the rip."

I shake my arm. "It's starting to feel normal. Delivers an amazing shock."

Samuel catches Sifu up on our conversation. Then to me, he says, "Yes. The master can do it quite well." He says something to his teacher and the old man nods. "He will demonstrate to show you the potential of ripping."

"Not on me."

"Yes, of course on you. On your face."

"Wait. There is no way—"

"Kidding, Son. He will show you on this palm tree."

"A tree?"

"'Watch and learn.' That is from the movie *Batman and Robin*. Batgirl says it to Robin. I did not like the movie much."

Uh, okay.

Shen Lang Rui steps over to the tree, a particularly large one that curves outward a ways, then about fifteen feet from the ground it straightens and continues up for another fifteen feet. At about five feet from the ground, where Sifu is pointing with his right index finger, the trunk looks to be maybe eighteen inches thick. I have no idea what palm tree bark is called, but by whatever name, it's rock hard and gnarly. Judging by all that I've heard about him, I'm guessing Sifu is going to smack the tree hard enough to shake loose a coconut.

Just as I wonder if these trees even have coconuts, Sifu's hand whiplashes out and back with a pronounced sound similar to a damp towel being snapped, and something arcs through the air, landing near the *koi* pond. It looks to be about six inches long and maybe three inches wide. Sifu steps away from the tree, his hands clasped behind his back.

"Did you see what happened, Son?" Samuel says excitedly, as he always gets when demonstrating his art. He points at the tree. "His knuckles first impacted here—"

"Wait!" I say, moving slowly forward, my eyes locked on the tree. There is a chunk of bark missing. "What the…"

"Yes, Son, what you see is true. Sifu hit the tree here with his big knuckles and ripped across the trunk about two centimeters, that's about six inches, to this point here. That's where he stopped the rip and snapped his hand back. That's the piece his punch tore away over there. Keep in mind that the skin of a palm tree is many times tougher than a human's."

No flippin' way, I think, touching the raw wood with my fingertips. Sifu's ripping punch penetrated into the palm tree at least three quarters an inch.

"Imagine what he could do to an adversary, Son."

"I would never have believed it if I hadn't seen it," I say, in total awe. "Even still, I'm still not certain that I believe…"

Again, Sifu's voice is just above a whisper. Samuel nods to him and turns to me. "Son, he says that your mind does not know the difference between what is and what could be. Let your mind be free. Free to believe, believe that you can."

"Hi," Bobby says, walking up sleepy-eyed and yawning. "Did I miss something?"

*

"How much trouble are you in?" I ask.

Bobby exhales a gush of air. "My father told me once how his uncle was caught by the Viet Cong. He was beaten for several days, given only lettuce and dirty water, and he was locked into a metal crate with snakes tied to the ceiling."

I nod over dramatically. "Your punishment is going to be worse than that?"

"Oh yeah," the boy says. "I'm a dead man and some."

After Sifu went into the house with Samuel, the boy and I went back to the room just in time to grab my ringing cell on the nightstand. It was David Phan, Bobby's father. He immediately asked me to tell him again who I was and how I knew his son. I explained in a little more detail everything that I had previously said on his phone recorder, and I gave him my friend Mark's number back in Portland to vouch that I wasn't a pedophile or kidnapper. Mark might be mad at me right now, but I don't think he would tell him that he's figured out that I was more than likely involved in the death of Tiger Woman and Do Trieu.

Sounding relieved at my explanation, David explained that he and his wife were indeed on the way over to get their son, but a terrorist threat on the plane sidelined them for several hours in Taipei. They weren't allowed to use their cells until the authorities had cleared everyone. When they could call, they got the messages from their son but they couldn't connect with Bobby's phone. It wasn't until they called their home phone that they got the message from me.

I assured the father that Bobby was in good hands, and while I didn't know him all that well, it appeared that he had seen the error of his ways and was wanting to get all this behind him. I don't think that helped the boy's case because when David Phan asked to talk to his son, his voice was that of a hooded executioner. My last words to him were to call this number when they landed and we would arrange to meet for the handoff.

"I don't know exactly when they are getting here," Bobby says. "My dad wasn't sure when they were leaving, and because they had to change planes they don't have a straight flight anymore. Now they got to go to China first, Shanghai, I think he said."

"I'm thinking your dad was really pissed about that and now you're most assuredly a dead man."

"I'm so porked."

My cell rings. It's Mai.

"Fire department, you set 'em we wet 'em."

"Too funny. I am laughing so hard it is causing injury to my ribcage."

"Oh, hi, Mai. It's you. Did you sleep well?"

"Alone. What are you guys do… hold on, Sam. Father just came into the kitchen." Low murmuring, then, "Sam, can you come over here. Father just talked to Lu."

Big, fat raindrops are beginning to fall as we head across the yard toward the house. When we reach the steps it's falling so hard we have to shout our greetings.

"Hi," Mai and I say in unison, smiling like goofballs.

"Hi, Bobby," she says, guiding him through the door. "You guys hear the storm last night?"

"It was awesome, like in a Bible movie," he says, moving next to her.

"You mean the movie about Noah Nguyen?"

"Yeah," Bobby laughs. "That one."

"Someone woke up full of piss and vinegar," I say.

She smiles at me. "I don't know what that means but Father is in the living room. Bobby, you—"

"Lemme guess," the boy says disappointed. "Go to the kitchen for milk and cookies."

"More like spring rolls and tea," Mai says.

"That's better. Hey, you want to come have some with me?"

"I will have some with you later," she says, turning him about by his shoulders and nudging him toward the kitchen. "I have to go with Sam to see my father."

Samuel and Tex are sitting on the sofa talking. Samuel looks up as we enter. "Please sit down, both of you. What did you think of Shen Lang Rui, Sam?"

"Amazing. How old did you say he is?"

"A little older than me but I am not sure by how much."

"He good, eh?" Tex says. "Master for sure."

Samuel points at a tea setup on the black lacquer table. "Pour yourself some. We need to discuss something and make some decisions. First, have you contacted the parents yet?"

"I just spoke with them," I say, as Mai pours two cups and freshens Samuel's and Tex's. "They are stuck in China and aren't sure when they can get out." I tell him about the rest of the phone conversation.

"So they might not arrive until tonight at the earliest," Samuel muses. "I'm betting tomorrow morning. Bad timing."

Mai and I sit in a couple of chairs with our tea. "Why?" she asks. "What did Lu say? Did he have information about the children?"

"He did, and that is what I want to talk with everyone about. Lu said that in the last few weeks, Lai Van Tan has kidnapped twenty-seven children, all girls. Lu does not know their ages but thinks they are probably around twelve. Some a little older, some younger."

"Bastard," Mai grunts.

"Twenty-seven!" I say, shocked at the number.

"A glass of water out of the ocean," Mai says bitterly.

"All the girls are being kept in a warehouse until Lai Van Tan gets his target number to sell. Lu even learned the location of the warehouse."

Mai squirms, her anger barely restrained. "Did he say how they are being treated?"

"Look at me, Mai," Samuel says. "This is a bad situation and you must keep your anger in check. Understand?"

She glares at the floor.

"Mai?"

"Understood, Father," she says tightly.

"Okay," Samuel says, satisfied that Mai has collected herself. "Lu says that the children are beaten and drugged."

Mai and I aren't touching but I can sense her body tense. "Son of bitch!"

Samuel shoots her a look and raises his eyebrows. I'm guessing Samuel and Kim didn't tolerate any disrespectful talk from their girls when they were growing up, and that still seems to be the case now and Mai is pushing thirty-four.

She raises her palms. "I am fine, Father. But we must do something." she says with more pleading than anger. "We cannot wait for Harry to find out if there are police who will go against Lai Van Tan. Lu says they are hurting the girls now. They are there *now*. We must save them before they are shipped out."

"They go Cambodia, to Phnom Penh," Tex says.

"Lu said that?" I ask.

Samuel nods. "He said they might be shipping tomorrow night even if they have not gotten their goal number. They have been in the warehouse for a week and he is getting anxious to move them."

Mai leans forward, nearly spilling her tea. "Tomorrow... Then we must *do* something!" More anger than pleading this time.

Samuel lifts his palms to calm her. "I have made some calls—"

"And what, Father?" That was total anger.

Samuel shoots her a look that makes her sit back a little, only to lean forward again a moment later.

"I called Harry and he said it would be impossible to find the right cops in such short notice but—"

"*Right* cops!" She sloshes her tea cup on her thigh but doesn't seem to notice.

"Mai!" Samuel says sharply, his stern eyes letting her know that his patience is waning with her. I bet that same look got her back on course when she was a rebellious teenager.

"Sorry," she says, gesturing for him to continue. Samuel says she doesn't have a temper but I don't know what else to call it. Passion, maybe.

Tex winks at me. I think he gets a kick out of these father-daughter clashes.

Samuel looks over at me. "Harry has a sister and brother-in-law in Bien Hoa who operate an orphanage there. Mai and I have known them for a long while; they are wonderful people. Anyway, Harry is arranging with them to have a bus at the ready if and when the police can get the kids out. The friends will take them back to the orphanage and work to get the girls back with their parents or other relatives. But right now, the problem is the police."

"I can't begin to tell you how this issue with the police pisses me off," I say. "I have always—"

Mai slams her fist on the arm of her sofa. "You know how much it angers *me*, Father. I want to go to the warehouse. We can do it if the damn police will not."

Samuel shakes his head. "I have more information."

Mai lifts her hands impatiently, as if to say, Bring it on.

Samuel waits until she lowers her hands, then looks at me. "I spoke with Phong Tran a short while ago, the man you thought might be the weak link, the one who shook his head at you in the meeting. You were right. He said the meeting yesterday was mostly a sham. He said Lai Van Tan did not say that to him, but Phong Tran has been around his uncle long enough to understand his actions."

"Did he agree that his boss was trying to confirm his control?"

Samuel nods. "Pretty much, but not for the reasons we were thinking. Phong Tran thinks the loss of his people's lives in Portland as well as his loss of face there, and his loss of face yesterday with what you two did to his people has changed his thinking. Of course, he is not convinced that Lai Van Tan has suddenly gotten religion, but he thinks the old man wants to spend his energy on his new enterprise, sex trafficking."

"He want peace?" Tex asks, sounding a tad disappointed.

Samuel shrugs. "At least peace the way he defines it and at least for now. Maybe he is putting us on hold until he sets up his business or, hopefully, he has seen the futility of, and maybe the ridiculousness of, seeking revenge for something that he brought on."

"Or maybe Phong Tran is lying to get us to lower our guard?" I ask.

Samuel shakes his head. "Anything is possible but that is not my read of the man. I think it is as we discussed before, that Phong Tran does not agree with his uncle's enterprise and he does not want to be part of it. So until he figures out how to get away from it, he is willing to do what he can to keep people from getting hurt. Like us."

"So we have a détente?" I ask. Mai and Tex frown. "For how long?"

"That is the question," Samuel says. "Lai Van Tan is so crazy I do not think it would take much to set him off again." He shakes his head. "It still amazes me how crazy people can attract followers."

"What did Phong Tran say about the warehouse?" Mai asks.

Samuel looks at her for a moment, as if weighing how he should answer. "He said he does not know much about that operation because he has been involved in other aspects of Lai Van Tan's endeavors. He confirmed that it is in Bien Hoa and is somewhat hidden in plain sight, as the saying goes. I think Lu and his contact might know more about this than Phong Tran."

I follow Samuel's eyes to Mai's hand where she is white knuckling her teacup. He hesitates as if weighing his words. Then, "Mai… I know how you feel about the children…"

She sits up, her beautiful face hard as stone. " I 'feel about the children' what, Father?" she snaps. "Finish what you were going to say."

Oh man. For a second I think about picking up one of the sofa pillows and using it as a shield. But Samuel just looks at her, his face neutral.

"Mai," he says. He takes a deep breath, eases it out. "We cannot act this time. I will do everything I can to work with Harry to get the police involved, but we, this family, cannot act this time."

She stands quickly. "Are you shitting me?" she says loudly. Must have picked that expression up at Portland State. "We are going to do nothing?" She moves quickly toward the big screen TV, looks up at her mother's painting, then spins about. "Nothing?"

"Mai," Samuel says calmly. "For the first time in months we might not have to constantly look over our shoulders. We might actually have peace from Lai Van Tan. I do not want to jeopardize that peace and once again put my family at risk."

"For the children," Mai says, her hands trembling at her sides.

Samuel tilts his head a little to indicate he doesn't understand.

"What you are saying is that you do not want to risk the peace for children. To save the children's lives. Have you forgotten my friend's daughter, Qui? And Nhung's daughter, Tuyet? Nhung worked for us and she was almost family. The girls were taken and—"

Samuel leans forward. "I care about Qui and Tuyet and the children in Bien Hoa. I care about all children, Mai. Do not insult me. And so does Harry. He and I are doing what we can through the police."

"We have this house, Father. All the security. Mother staying at Linh's."

"Those are Band-Aids, daughter. The best prevention is peace."

Mai looks toward the front door and clasps her hands in front of her abdomen, but still they tremble. She looks up at the painting again, then at her father. She is controlling her emotions but at the risk of imploding. She takes a deep breath, lets it out, shakes her head.

"I uh… need to go for a drive. I will go to the downtown store to check on things." She looks at me. "Sam, I would like to go by myself. To think."

I stand. "Of course," I say, hiding my disappointment. "I understand."

She looks at me for a long moment, nods. "Father, Tex, I will talk to you later."

"I think that will be best, daughter," Samuel says as she crosses the room toward the front door. She opens it and closes it behind her without responding. A moment later I hear her motorbike start, leave.

Samuel smiles uncomfortably at me. Clearly, he is bothered by how things went. "Like her mother, Mai has a strong will and a passionate sense of right and wrong."

"I like that about her," I say, sitting back down.

"Me too," Tex says. "She tough womans, for sure."

"She is right about the children, you know," Samuel says.

I nod. "Yes, she is. But so are you."

He raises his eyebrows. "Are you being political or do you really believe that."

"I believe it."

"It is like that expression six of one, half a dozen of another."

I nod; Tex looks puzzled.

Samuel moves over to retrieve the teapot. "Lu said he learned that the warehouse is guarded." He freshens our cups. "There are two, sometimes three people outside, and he thinks maybe four inside. He said there might be a couple of others inside who keep the girls drugged and cook food for them." He returns to the sofa.

"Weapons?" I ask, noting that he knows more than he indicated to Mai. I'm also wondering why we're discussing it.

"My old soldiers will bring M-16s and an amazing set of close-quarter-combat skills."

"I don't understand," I say. "You're going there?"

"Of course I am going to go to the warehouse, Sam."

"Samuel tough damn soldier," Tex says. "Green Berets."

Samuel sips from his tea.

"But you told Mai that… You intended on going the whole time?"

"Of course. Like you, I am a protector. Who do you think you got it from?"

"But Mai was so angry. You let her storm out of here."

He shrugs. "I would prefer her to be angry at me than for her to get hurt. As I said earlier, Mai is a passionate person, too much so to go on a mission like this. As you know, a warrior must focus on the objective. Mai is well trained, but her passion can cloud her thinking."

"She no be happy camper when she find out, Samuel," Tex says. Isn't that the truth.

"I know," Samuel says. "It will be hard for her to forgive me."

Oh man, I'm feeling divided here. Before Mai left, I was seeing her side of the argument and I could see Samuel's as well. Then when she said she was leaving, I felt I should go with her, but then I thought if I did that Samuel might think I was against his way of thinking. Then she told me to stay here. Why? I don't know, other than she needed some space to cool down. Whatever the reason, it took the pressure off me to take sides. Now I find out we're going to the warehouse after all, just not with her, which means I'm now involved in a conspiracy behind Mai's back.

In short, it sucks to be me right now.

"I am assuming there will be weapons on site," Samuel says, looking up at Kim's painting.

"Khmer Rouge mother fuckers be there for sure?" Tex asks.

Samuel nods. "Lu thinks Lai Van Tan has hired four of them but only two are at the warehouse, maybe three. He does not know if they would be posted inside or outside. I am guessing that the remaining ones guard Lai Van Tan wherever he is. Lu does not know about weapons at the warehouse, but if they have old stuff it will likely be M-16s and AK-47s. He also says that he has seen some of the guards practicing martial arts, *vovinam*."

"Like those guys in the blue *gi* I saw practicing on the roof when we went to get Bobby?"

Samuel nods. "It is a very good art. As I said the other night, it combines hard and soft empty-hand techniques, and they specialize in fancy but highly effective takedowns."

"Use weapons too," Tex says. "Like axe. Axe hit face is a number ten day for you, for damn sure."

"I can imagine," I say.

"I studied it for a while," Samuel says, "when we lived in Snake Village. *Vovinam's* takedowns are called *dòn chân,* a type of twisting technique where the fighter uses his legs to grab the opponent's head, torso, or legs, to twist them down to the ground. They also use their hands to twist their opponent's legs to take them down. It can be done very fast. *Vovinam* has many *dòn chân*."

He looks at me, at Tex, and then back at the painting. Samuel is like a chameleon. Sometimes he looks like an average sixty-five-year-old man, average height, slight frame, graying hair. Other times he looks like General Patton: large and in charge. Move out, get 'er done. Right now, though, I'm not sure. His profile looks worried but determined. Like he's got an eye on the prize but concerned about the means to get it. He looks at me.

"Do you know what a warrior is, Sam?" Before I can answer, he says, "It is one who does what needs to be done. It is one who moves toward the gunfire while everyone else flees it. That is who we are. It is what we do."

I remember Mai saying similar words in Portland. She talked about being trained in the warrior ways by her father, about being prepared, about protecting others, and going toward what others run from. She once told me in one of our webcam talks that although she never met her biological father, and Kim has said little about him, she thinks he must have been a great soldier. She said, "With his blood in my veins mixed with Mother's strong blood, and with my stepfather's guidance over the years, I had no choice but to follow the warrior ways."

When I first met Samuel in that park in Portland, I remember thinking that while his face showed his years, maybe even more than his birthday, his stature and bearing were that of a military professional. I forgot about that when I first got here because I didn't see it in him, probably because he is relaxed around his family and home. Today it's back.

"So what's our plan?" I ask.

"I want to pick up the old soldiers. By then I should have information about the warehouse and how it is laid out. I also asked my friends to see if there was a similar warehouse nearby that I can look at to determine the best approach. I would…" He looks at me for a long moment, before saying, "Sam, you do not have to be involved in this."

'What? You've been telling me all these things about the warehouse and now—"

He lifts his palms, shaking his head. "I know, I know, and I am sorry. I was thinking of you as a policeman, just a policeman… I… I was in the moment and not thinking of you as my son." He shakes his head. "There is no way to know what is there. We will have firearms and as I've said before, an American with a gun in Vietnam is a most serious charge. Plus, this could be extremely dangerous. I do not want my children involved in something so—"

"Wait," I say, then take a moment to gather my thoughts. "Okay, hear me out, please. I came over here knowing that things weren't settled with Lai Van Tan and considering the tactics he employed in Portland—well let's just say I knew that and I came ready for it. I came accepting that danger. On the matter of firearms, I will not carry one, even if it were allowed. The last time I pulled a trigger was the last time I will ever pull a trigger. I will go with you," I say, clenching my fists and holding them in front of me, "but armed only with these."

I feel my face flush. I was doing all right until that bit of hokey dramatics. "Okay, that's corny, but my point is that we're a family. You yourself have said that several times since we've known each other. To me, that means I lay it on the line with you, especially for something that is as important as this."

I don't know how much of that Tex understood but he's nodding.

"Also," I say, wound up now. "I haven't spent the last fifteen years bagging groceries. I've been in two shootings, I don't know how many physical force situations, high-speed chases, riots, and I've been ambushed twice by gangbangers. I've trained cops on hand-to-hand combat, and I was assigned for a while to work with SWAT on close-quarter combat."

"No sissyboy, you," Tex notes.

"Yes, sir," I say.

The *Superman* theme. For a half second I think it is the sound track to my soliloquy. Samuel pokes his cell. "Lu?"

I look at Tex and he lifts his thumb up without moving his hand off the sofa.

Samuel closes his cell and stands. "Lu said they changed their plans. They are moving the girls tonight, around nine. We have to get ready, Son."

*

"Both Lam and Trai will be on duty tonight," Samuel tells Tex. "Trai will watch the monitors and Lam will be on foot outside the walls checking all sides of the house. They might rotate their duties; I leave that up to them. That gives us one set of eyes watching from the second-story window across the street, one set watching the front at street level, one set, er, make that one eye, watching from a car in the back, and one set of eyes on foot patrol. What do you think, Sam?"

"The set of eyes at street level in front, is that the man selling motorbike parts earlier?"

Samuel nods. "About nine o'clock, he will fold up his goods and pretend to sleep in a doorway."

"Sounds good."

Samuel looks toward Tex. "My friend, please uncover the tunnel in Sam's room and show it to Bobby. Just make him think you are showing him something fun. But I want him to know that it is there should he need it. Then take him into the monitor room and tell him to stay there until we return."

"I make happen," Tex says.

"If I may comment, Samuel." He looks at me. "Bobby is a smart kid and he knows something's up. I think we need to clarify that there is a risk. If, God forbid, something does happen while he's here, it's not fair to him to have to play catch up. I would like to tell him in general terms what is going on so that he can be alert and quick to respond to whatever Tex tells him to do."

"Okay. I keep thinking of him as a child, but he is nearly an adult." His eyes suddenly look faraway. "Before I went into the Green Berets, I knew two soldiers who were both seventeen. They had lied and said they were nineteen so they could join up. They were fine troops, at least in training. They went to

Vietnam before I did," he says, saying 'Vietnam' as if it were a different place than where we are right now. "I heard that they did not…" He blinks a couple of times and shakes his head. "Sorry, I'm just an old man with too many memories. Will you talk to him, Son?"

"Of course."

"Thank you. Tex, after we leave, call all the posts every thirty minutes to see that they are alert. Once we finish in Bien Hoa, I will call you and we will get back here as soon as we can. Lai Van Tan will not be happy when he finds out what we have done."

"No sweat. I do," Tex says, his face tight with determination.

"Lai Van Tan might want peace now in his strange way of thinking," Samuel says, "but if we succeed in freeing the girls, I am sure he will see it as an attack on him and his livelihood and by a man he hates. He just might go over the edge."

He checks his watch and looks at me. "Okay. It is twelve thirty now. I want to call the home to get the old soldiers on board, and I want to call my friends in Bien Hoa. Sam, do whatever you have to do to get ready. Before we go, we will eat something and meditate for a few minutes. It is important to feed our bodies and our spirits."

"Sounds good," I say, smiling to myself as I try to imagine an old police sergeant telling the troops to eat and meditate before serving a warrant on a drug house.

"They should," he says, looking at me. "It worked for the Samurai."

I will never get used to him doing that.

He smiles, probably at my reaction and Tex's confused look. "We meet in forty-five minutes."

Samuel heads toward his office, Tex to his room, and I go looking for Bobby. He's not in the kitchen, but a thumping sound coming from the backyard tells me where he is. Through the kitchen window I see him throwing kicks at the heavy bag.

"You getting tired of being sent to your room every time the grownups talk?" I ask, as I approach.

He shrugs. "Maybe a little. But it's none of my business. Besides, your family has been so nice to me I can't complain."

"Good answer, troop. Your sidekicks look great. That's not always an easy kick for people, but I can tell you've worked on it. Plus your parents gave you a good hip structure for it."

"Thanks," he says, beaming. "But what do you mean my parents gave me... Oh, I get it. Thanks for the mental image."

I laugh. "My pleasure. Listen, There are some things you need to know."

"This doesn't sound good."

I point at the bench. "Let's sit."

For the next several minutes, I bring Bobby up to speed with an edited-down version of the Lai Van Tan saga. I tell him that Samuel had a confrontation with the man's son a while back that started the ball rolling. I skip all of what happened in Portland. Mostly, I impress upon him Lai Van Tan's erratic personality, the intensity of his need for revenge, the possibility that he might want peace now, and the remote possibility there could be an attack on this house. I assure him that there is a lot of security in place, outside and inside, and that Tex will show him even more after Samuel and I go to take care of another problem.

I can tell that the idea of me leaving the house scares him, so I assure him that everything will be okay and that we won't be gone long. I'm hoping that's true anyway. I also tell him that I'll leave my cell phone with him in case his parents call. And if by chance we're still tied up in Bien Hoa, Tex will get a taxi and take him to the airport.

It's obvious he doesn't like that option, either. I explain that this isn't ideal, but since it's the situation we find ourselves in at the moment, we're doing all that we can to make it as safe as possible. I turn on my inner father and tell him that there will be lots of times in his life when he finds himself up to his ears in a pit full of alligators and all he can do is the best he can. It's a more manly take on that old "when life hands you lemons you make lemonade" thing, and somewhat better than the old "whenever you have kill-crazy Khmer Rouge soldiers guarding kidnapped girls, you got to get them first" thing.

I tell Bobby to go into the house and check with Tex about getting us something to eat and that I will be in after I change my clothes.

Back in my room I rinse my face and brush my teeth. I haven't a clue why I feel a need to do these things but doing them makes me feel better. I change into a pair of pants that gives me more freedom to move. A few arm and shoulder stretches, and some hulas get the kinks out of my upper body, and a few stiff leg raises to the front, side, and back loosen the leg muscles a little. I smile, remembering a "Far Side" cartoon that depicted a castle in the background, and in the foreground, a company of medieval soldiers warming up with jumping jacks and leg stretches before they attacked.

My mother used to say that we never know where life will take us, although I doubt that she imagined that in one six-month period her son would use lethal force, meet his long-thought-to-be-dead father, fall for his father's stepdaughter, go to Vietnam, and within four days be brushing his teeth in preparation for attacking a warehouse in which children are being sold into the sex-trafficking trade. What next? A zombie invasion?

I've never given much thought to destiny and what if anything I'm supposed to be doing. Such thoughts have always been way too new age for a meat-and-potatoes kind of guy like me. Whatever I've done—martial arts, police work, and the relationships I've had with people—I've done because that's what I wanted to do, at that time. I never thought that it was something I was supposed be doing.

Two times on the job in Portland, I yanked people back to safety a hair of a second before they leaped off the Fremont Bridge, the highest one in Portland. Another time I knocked a woman's gun arm aside just as she fired at another cop. The bullet hit his uniform sleeve instead of his gut. One late night, I pulled an old man out of a car that was upside down and sinking in the Columbia River.

I felt good about these things; I just never thought my actions were written in the stars.

Then a while ago, while listening to Samuel's plans, I had an epiphany. Maybe, just maybe, I'm supposed to help free those girls at the warehouse. Samuel said once that we can't change the wrongs we've done in the past, but we can strive to do good now and in the future. I will never be able to make up for what happened in Portland that day, but I can do this good thing for children right here, right now.

Okay, if I think about this much longer, I might convince myself that I was, indeed, destined to save those jumpers on the bridge, save the policeman from a heck of a stomach-ache, and rescue the man from swimming with the fishes. Slow down, big boy, before you start believing you're really a guardian angel, with big arms.

I wonder where Mai is? She is going to be so upset that we are doing this without her. Will she forgive her father?

Damn, will she forgive me? Should I call her? Would that make Samuel mad? I have to call her. I won't tell her what we're doing for Samuel's sake, but I need to know what she's thinking. No. I better not. Okay, I will.

I retrieve my phone and tap in all the international long distance numbers and then hers. Static, clicking, ringing. Ringing some more. She's not picking up. It goes into voice mail.

"It's me," I say. "I just wanted to make sure you're okay. Call me back."

I poke End Call and start toward the door. My cell rings. Got to be Mai. No. The screen reads "Unknown."

David Phan asks if Bobby is there, and I tell him that if he can hold for a few minutes I'd go to the house and get him. Mister Phan says there isn't time because he and his wife were just informed there were two last minute cancellations and they were dashing down the jetway, the last to board. He also tells me that it's been a nightmare trying to get a cell phone connection since they've been in China, and that he finally got through but with only a minute to spare. The plane has to make another stop before it heads to Ho Chi Minh City, and he thinks they will land here tomorrow around midmorning, but he isn't sure.

Before Mr. Phan hangs up, I tell him that I'm anxious to meet him, but in the event I can't, a friend will take Bobby to the airport. I say that while Bobby did a bad thing, I think he's a great kid and I've really enjoyed getting to know him. I leave out the part that there is a chance that we might get attacked by a Vietnamese gang and that we're about to leave to attempt to free some kidnapped girls.

I head back into the house where Tex is directing Bobby as to how to lay out the rice, chicken, and vegetables on the dining room table. I fill Bobby in about the call from his dad. He's obviously happy.

Tex says that Samuel told him that we should all eat without him. I try to eat some, but I'm more tense than hungry. Tex might be, but he hides it well by bantering with Canyon Bob. They are going to miss each other when Bobby has to leave. I'll miss the lad too.

"Everyone feel better?" Samuel asks, coming into the dining room. He's changed into loose fitting tan khaki pants and a dark blue overshirt. "Sam, did you get enough to eat?"

"I did, thanks." I decide not to mention that I tried to call Mai.

Bobby leans across the table to push the dishes toward Samuel.

"Thank you, laddy," Samuel says, patting the boy's shoulder. "You and Tex did a fine job preparing things."

"Canyon Bob do," Tex says. "Some day he make someone a good wife."

Bobby makes as if he is going to push Tex off his chair, which makes us all laugh. A little levity before the storm.

"Do you have a quote about food," I ask Samuel, noting that he actually seems in good spirits considering what we're about to do. Maybe his exterior is a camouflage for all that's going on inside him. Nerves? Of course. An intense focus honed from his time in combat and his decades of martial arts training? Yes.

"Hmm," he says, bunching his eyebrows. "Yes. A nickel will get you on the subway but garlic will get you a seat."

"Good one," I chuckle. Tex and Bobby don't get it.

The *Superman* theme.

"Lam?" Samuel answers. "Okay. *Cám ơn.*" Then to us, "Sifu is here."

I turn toward the archway.

"This time he is coming in the back way," Samuel says, scooting his chair back and heading toward the sliding glass doors.

"I didn't see a gate back there," Bobby says to me.

"Cause there isn't one." I shrug when he gives me a quizzical look. "Don't ask."

Samuel pushes open the door and bows as his teacher climbs the steps and toes off his blue Converse. I indicate for Bobby to stand.

"Sifu," I say, bowing.

"Happy," Shen Lang Rui says, moving toward me, pressing his palms together under his chin as I bow. He acknowledges Tex with a smile, and bows to the boy when introduced by Samuel. The two look at each for a moment before Sifu gestures that he wants to look at Bobby's hand. The boy looks at me to see if it's all right. I nod and, with some reluctance, he extends his hand. Sifu takes it by the wrist, rotates it palm up and places it into his own hand. He studiously traces his finger over the boy's palm as Bobby looks at me, not sure what to make of it. I again nod that it's okay.

The master looks into Bobby's eyes and speaks softly, so intimately that I almost feel like I'm intruding on them. Whatever he said, makes the boy tremble a little and suck in his breath.

Samuel leans toward me, whispering, "Sifu says to the boy that if he looks deeply at his palm, he will see his parents, his grandparents, and all those before them. They are all living in him, right now, in his body and mind. Sifu told him, 'You are the continuation of each of these people.'"

"How does he…" Bobby stammers, retracting his hand as

tears erupt from his eyes. He turns his head away from us and wipes them with the back of his hand. Sifu smiles at him as if to say, "It will be all right."

Incredible. I was impressed when he picked up on my jet lag that first day and then did whatever he did to make me feel better. Now he picks up on Bobby's issues. Mai said he does this all the time with the family, but it's still beyond amazing.

I flash to a kata I learned when I studied *goju ryu* for about a year in my early twenties. Since I was already a black belt in another style, the teacher taught me an advanced form called Sanchin. It originated in China but is the core of several Okinawan karate styles. The word means three battles, usually referring to one's struggle to unify the mind, body, and spirit. Sifu Shen Lang Rui appears to have conquered this battle in spades, not only within himself, but in a way that enables him to look into the internal struggles of others.

Sifu is talking to Bobby again and Samuel translates. "He is telling the boy, 'If you train very hard…'" Shen Lang Rui gently lifts the boy's chin. They look at each other for a moment. "'If you train very hard, you will be very good.'" Samuel looks at his teacher with deep admiration. "He likes simple lessons like that."

His eyes still wet, Bobby smiles and bows, his palms together, the way Sifu does.

As Samuel situates his teacher at the head of the table, Bobby looks at me, and breathes, "Whoa!"

"Couldn't say it better myself," I whisper.

"Did he know I ran away from California and that I do taekwondo?"

I shake my head. "I didn't tell him and I doubt Samuel did."

"Freakin' eerie," Bobby says, shaking his head.

"He master for sure," Tex says.

Sifu listens while Samuel, I'm assuming, brings him up to speed on what's happening. It's interesting watching the dynamics between these two. There is a teacher/student formality, yet it's an immensely comfortable one that is also like father/son, or two close brothers. What an amazing experience Samuel has had with this true master, one that most martial artists would give up their first born to have. I don't know what Samuel was like before, but I know how he is now. He is also a master, not in the way of meaningless master ranks given to thirty-year-old martial artists, but a consummate warrior who has conquered himself and in so doing, risen far above the norm. He has become the ideal that others can only hope to become. Over the top? I don't think so.

When Samuel concludes, Sifu says no more than a dozen words. Samuel nods and looks at us.

"If you are done with lunch, let's all go outside and sit in the shade. Sifu will guide us through a meditation. Bobby, this one has been passed down from the samurai."

"Awesome!" the boy practically shouts. "Too cool."

Samuel laughs and translates for Sifu. There's probably a word for awesome, but too cool?

"That it is, Son," Samuel says. "And you will like the results."

We all head outside where the humidity is still a soggy blanket that wilts our clothes in seconds. The heavy skies have turned the early afternoon into twilight.

"A storm is coming," Samuel says, looking up at the agitating clouds. "Thunder and lightning tonight."

We move over to the pond and sit on the ground facing the water. Bobby and I sit cross-legged, Sifu sits in lotus before us, and Tex balances on his torso stump. Samuel sits in lotus next to me and slightly to my rear, probably so he can translate.

Sifu and Samuel are instantly still, as Tex, Bobby and I adjust ourselves several times to get comfortable on the hard ground. Sifu's eyes are closed, his face relaxed, instantly at peace. He reminds me of a four-hundred-year-old Chinese painting titled "Sage" that I saw in the Portland Art Museum. It depicted an aged Chinese man dressed in a shabby robe meditating, sitting in lotus position, in a grove of bamboo. The dominant color was gold in its many hues with some green in the leaves. I felt that the artist was depicting every Chinese sage from the beginning of time to the present. He could have been painting Sifu as he looks right now.

Samuel speaks first to all of us, his voice gentle, melodic. "Place the back of your right hand in your left and allow your thumb tips to touch. Good. Now take a few slow, deep breaths… and settle your body into the ground, feeling it touch your legs, your rear, your feet. Feel the warmth of the day… feel the thick humidity… hear the distant traffic… hear the wind high in the palms… and feel your breath pass into your nose and out again. Breathe naturally… do not force it."

I already feel loose from the little bit of stretching I did in my room, and now I can feel the tension oozing out of me with each exhalation. Samuel's voice instantly soothes and hypnotizes. He ought to make audio CDs of his meditation techniques.

"Thank you," Samuel says, picking up on my thoughts. "Now let us sit quietly for a moment. Sifu will guide us when he knows we are ready."

Interesting. Not when he's ready but when we're ready. I like that. Sort of like, "When the student is ready the teacher will appear." Okay, I'm thinking too much. Need to just follow my breath, in… out… in… Feels good. Very peaceful. Very relaxing.

Sifu speaks.

Samuel translates in a whisper. "He says to you, 'do not judge your meditation with words like peaceful and relaxing. Just breathe. In and out.'"

Oh man. He can mind-read English. Okay, follow my breath into my nose. Let it collect in my abdomen, then ease it out, feeling it pass across my lips. Sifu speaks.

Samuel translates. "Sifu says that this is a meditation method used by the samurai before they went into battle. They used other methods during peaceful moments. This one they used before battle because it instantly heightened their awareness, perception, and readiness, while helping them to remain calm. You will also experience this. Most feel it within a minute or two.

"To begin, choose something to look at just above your eye level. Something small, like a mark on a palm tree trunk, a spot on the far wall, or the tip of that Japanese lantern. Put all of your attention into that one single point. Do not look at anything else, just that point. Notice its shape, texture, the colors. Keep looking… keep looking… until it seems… to be coming toward you."

Sifu's voice is as melodic as Samuel's, even more so. It's as if his voice is the breeze that ruffles the palm trees and caresses my face.

"Do not judge it, Son," Samuel whispers. "Just experience it."

What chance do I have with both of them reading my thoughts?

"Now Sifu says to soften your gaze. Notice that, without moving your eyes from your spot you can see things to the left of it… to the right of it… below it… and above it. Allow your field of vision to expand until you can see as far as you are able in the four directions. Breathe in… breathe out… naturally.

"Now move your eyes to another point and focus on it. Notice that you are instantly able to look at that one thing, while still seeing far and wide in all four directions.

"Now as you breathe, exhale twice as long as it takes you to breathe in. So if you inhale to a count of two, exhale to a count of four. As you do this, relax your tongue to dissolve the tension in your face and to help you focus. Just breathe now… focus on your point, as you expand your visual plane."

We continue to sit for another five minutes, maybe longer. It's hard to tell because I feel like I'm floating on one of the overhead clouds. Floating… floating…

Samuel's soft voice slips gently into my brain. "Sifu says, 'open your eyes when you are ready. Take with you this new sense of calmness… and this new heightened awareness of your personal perimeter. Let it be with you the rest of the day.'" I keep my eyes closed for a few seconds longer, wanting to float in the dark forever.

When I open them, I'm startled to see Sifu rising to his feet without effort, without unfolding his legs first, without pushing off the ground with his hands. He just rises, like a puff of smoke drifting up from a fire.

I know Bobby and Tex didn't see it because they are looking at each other and giggling about something. I turn to look at Samuel, and he is also standing, though I didn't hear him make a sound. Did he rise the same way? Am I sure that's what I saw? I saw something and I got some serious goose bumps going on.

"It is a little after three now," Samuel says, as if nothing bizarre had just occurred. Maybe it's not bizarre to them. "Sam, we should meet at the car at three-thirty. Tex, would you and Bobby please fill a few bottles of water for us."

"Sam." Sifu's voice. I look over at him. He presses his palms together and says something, his voice gentle, kind.

"Sifu thanks you for helping," Samuel says. "He says you are doing the right thing. Lai Van Tan is evil. Sifu says, 'You cannot shake hands with a clenched fist.'"

"*Cảm ơn*," I say. "I love Vietnam already, and I love my new family. I'm honored to help in whatever small way I can."

Samuel squeezes my shoulder, looking at me with an encompassing warmth. He looks away, clears his throat, and says, "Bobby, Tex is going to show you some things while we are gone, including a tunnel."

"Whoa, a tunnel," Bobby says. "Where?"

"In ground," Tex says, shaking his head as if the boy were a helpless case.

# CHAPTER SIXTEEN

I'm sitting in the passenger seat of the Volvo with my door open to combat the stifling humidity. Samuel is standing in front of the car calling each of his outside security people to make sure all is copasetic for us to leave. Satisfied that we're good to go, he closes his phone just in time for the *Superman* theme to sound. He takes the call, pacing in front of the car, nodding to whatever the caller is telling him. He snaps the phone closed and hurries to get in.

"That was Lu," he says, starting the car. He nods to Tex who is sitting on his perch by the gate. Tex pushes the button on the post and the gate slides open.

"Updates?" I ask, as we enter the street. His man selling motorbike parts acknowledges us as we pass by holding up what looks to be a carburetor. We pretend not to see him.

"Lu said earlier that the kids were going to be moved out around nine o'clock tonight, but now he says that the time has been changed to seven-thirty. No reason given. We are still okay, but we must not waste time. I called Viet at the home but he did not pick up. He might be at the market or some other place where it is noisy."

"You plan on squeezing everyone in this car?"

"No, no. There is a van there that will carry all of us."

"Sounds good. It's dark by six, right?"

Samuel pulls onto a busier street and immediately we're swept into a fast moving current of thousands of motorbikes. "Normally, it would be almost dark around six," he says. "With these clouds, I think it will be all the way black."

"Our SWAT guys like to say 'darkness is our friend.'"

"I agree. Lighting conditions was one of the things I asked my two people scouting the warehouse to check on." He takes a deep breath and releases it. "Sam, I understand that you are used to having a set way of carrying out a mission. I was too, when I was in the Green Berets. But like us, I am guessing that you executed some missions spontaneously, with no time to prepare."

"Not 'some missions,' probably the majority. I discovered early on that real situations tend to be more fluid than any plan a sergeant draws out on the chalkboard."

"Understood," he says. "Still, rehearsal is good, even if it is just to talk about what everyone's role is. I hope we can do that. But my instincts tell me we will be flying by the seat of our pants on this mission."

Like Mai, Samuel is a master of maneuvering through the heavy, erratic traffic.

"Not knowing how we're going to do this is the worst," I say.

He nods as he takes us into a busy traffic circle that's fed by five, no, six vehicle-choked streets all raging into the loop, the drivers making up road rules as they go along. Much like we're doing.

"You know, Sam, it is said that fear is based on something that we think might happen in the future. Because we try to predict what it will be, our fear becomes a projection of our mind."

"Makes sense." I watch an old woman perilously walking against the traffic flow, a puppy clutched in each hand. She's trying to give them to people in vehicles, but they either ignore her or wave her away. I look over at Samuel. "No offense, but knowing that projection thing doesn't help much."

He laughs. "No, not much." We regurgitate out of the traffic circle onto yet another crowded street. "How about this: At the warehouse there will not be time for fear because we will be in the moment, each of us following our training."

The power of being in the moment. I do know that feeling. There were many times on the PD when I responded to violent situations without conscious fear. My police and martial arts training kicked in, in the moment, but after the dust had settled, I'd tremble like a newborn fawn.

"This mission is the right thing to do," I say. "I'm proud to be doing it with you."

"Back at you. As Mai discussed, sex trafficking is a huge, sad problem here."

"Made worse by the corrupt police."

Samuel frowns. "I wish we were saving twenty-seven thousand girls instead of only twenty-seven. But every little bit helps, no?"

"Mai called it 'A glass of water out of the ocean.'"

"Yes. Still, it is less water than before."

"Speaking of Mai, how angry do you think she is going to be?"

Samuel nods as he slows for a cluster of about fifty motorbikes roaring out of a side street into our lane. I wonder if he's starting to second guess his decision about leaving her out of this? I'm not a parent, especially a parent of a warrior daughter, so I don't know what I would do. On second thought, I would do exactly the same thing Samuel is. In fact, I probably wouldn't take my son either.

I recognize the front of the home as we turn into the parking area. "Now we pick up the troops," he says. "We will get everyone in the van and…"

"What is it, Samuel?"

"The van. It is not here."

*

"Did one of the men drive it somewhere?" I ask, as we get out of the car. He shakes his head. Because he doesn't know or because…

He calls out as we walk through the front door. The room is empty except for Mai's friend sitting by the far window. Dung, wasn't it? Samuel lowers his voice as he walks toward him, his words spaced, as if talking to a small child.

The big man shakes his head and looks back out the window at the empty tree limb. I remember that he likes to watch birds there. He looks sad.

Samuel speaks to him and Dung shakes his head again. Samuel walks over to a large clock on the wall. He repeats what he said before, pointing at the clock's big hand. It's four fifteen. He looks back at Dung, who scrunches his face in thought, then lumbers to his feet and limps over to the clock. He scrunches his face once more, then abruptly smiles. He points at the twelve.

Samuel turns to me, his face a strange mix of anger and… pride? He retracts his cell from his pants pocket.

"It is partly my fault," he says. "I raised her, taught her, guided her, supplemented the warrior genes she already possessed." He taps in a number, looks back to me. "Mai took the van. And the troops."

I bite my cheeks to keep from smiling. I thought I saw her motorbike outside parked with the others, but then I thought it must be one that's similar to hers. "She came and got the men and they just went with her?"

"She is not answering because she knows it is me. Yes, the men went with Mai because they love her and will do anything for her. They probably thought she was going to meet up with me. Dung indicates they left about fifteen minutes ago." He pokes his cell again and once more pokes in a series of numbers. I assume he's calling Mai over and over.

Samuel speaks with Dung, and the big man's face brightens even more than when he remembered where the big hand was on the clock when Mai left. He tells Samuel something, turns and hobbles quickly down the hallway.

"I am taking Dung with us," Samuel says. "He was upset because Mai would not take him. I am sure she wanted to protect him." He shoots me a sheepish look, probably thinking how he wanted to protect Mai. There's a lot of protecting going on of people who don't want to be protected. He shrugs. "But if this plays out as I think it might, we can use him." He taps in a number again.

"Where did he go?" I ask.

"To use the bathroom."

"Would you like me to keep trying on your phone while you drive?"

"Yes, please," he says handing it to me. "If she has not shut her phone off maybe we will wear her down until she answers. She has a black belt in stubborn, but I have two black belts in it." He speaks to Dung as he rejoins us and the big man nods. "He says the men took their weapons. Let's go. Keep trying Mai."

Samuel is driving like a crazy man. Dung is in the back holding on for dear life as he's thrown against one door and a few seconds later thrown against the other. He's so big he might rip out the door hinges. I'm still trying to reach Mai using the redial button. After about ten minutes, she answers.

"Father?" She sounds agitated.

"Mai! It's me, Sam. Where are you?"

"Sam? Why are you on Father's—"

Samuel pulls the cell from my ear. "Where are you, Daughter," he says tightly. "Tell me right now… Okay. Stay there. We will be there in a few minutes and I will talk to them. Do you have all the men?… Okay… No, Dung is with us… It is my decision. From this point forward, I will make *all* the decisions. Any part of that you do not understand?… Good… No, there is no time for that now. We will talk about all that later. Here is Sam."

"Mai?"

"Sam. I am sorry I did not talk to you. I was just so crazy angry at Father. Were you two going to go to the warehouse?"

"Uh…"

"Without me?"

"Uh…"

Long silence. "Okay. No worries. I was going to go without you. Sorry. It will all get worked out later. Is Father very mad?"

I look at Samuel's profile as he rockets us along the busy streets. I can't get a read on him right now, but if I were to guess it would be that he's proud of his daughter's intestinal fortitude to go against his wishes to do the right thing. If he had his druthers, he wouldn't want either one of us involved in this, but he probably realizes now that he's dealing with a woman he raised to do exactly what she's doing and a man who has his blood. He didn't have a chance against us.

"I think all will be fine," I say. "What's going on there?"

"The men are not getting along. Father will fix it."

"Are you parked somewhere?"

"Yes, in front of a KFC."

"What's that?"

"Kentucky Fried Chicken, silly."

"You have that here?"

"Yes. That is how I am able to park in front of it."

*

The gray van is indeed parked in front of a Kentucky Fried Chicken, with people moving in and out of the eatery and sitting at small tables under green umbrellas. This appears to be a high-end neighborhood, judging by the many upscale shops and the expensively dressed passersby. Mai is standing at the rear of the van with Cong, the seventy-year-old knife fighter, and Phouc, the armless man. Phouc is puffing on a cigarette that protrudes from the center of his mouth. I can only assume that Cong lit it for him and put it between his lips.

Viet, the badly burned napalm veteran is sitting in the front passenger seat, his half leg, half crutch bracing the open door to keep the hot air circulating. Phat Ho, the coin-in-the-scarf *garrote* master, man of few words, and the guy who took an instant dislike to me, sits in the back seat. All are dressed as they were the last time I saw them.

Samuel leans in the van's open passenger door and speaks to Viet and Phat Ho. "North and South division?" I ask Mai out of the corner of my mouth.

"I think so," Mai says. "It has been very tense in the van. They are not fighting but their lack of words, as you say in American, speaks volumes."

"Samuel said something about them bringing guns."

Mai nods. "Two old M-16s from the war. They are on the floor in the back. Cong has his knives and Phat Ho his scarves. Oh, and I have my Glock in my ankle holster."

Samuel, suddenly thrust into the role of mediator, moves from the van over to Cong and Phouc, who have stepped into the shade of a curbside tree. No doubt the mission has brought back some old feelings between the one-time enemies. If a smell or the sight of something can stir up emotions from our past, how quickly can a dangerous mission stir confused thoughts and feelings?

"How much do they know about the warehouse and the girls," I ask.

"Everything I know," Mai says. "I told them that the girls are there, there are armed guards, and that our duty to the girls, to ourselves, and to Vietnam, is to free them."

"I bet they didn't hesitate."

Mai shakes her head. "Not one of them. But after five minutes on the road they began snapping at each other as to who was going to do what. It got so… in… intense? Yes, so intense that no one would talk anymore."

"I think you did the right thing by pulling over."

"I tried to talk to them but no one was listening," Mai says, frustratingly. "They were like angry children."

"But not as cute."

Mai smiles a little. "No, not cute at all. I think Father will fix things."

"No doubt. Did you know the girls are now being moved at seven-thirty? Samuel talked with Lu before we left."

"So did I. I do not know who he talked to first, Father or me. Maybe he thought that Father and I were busy and had not talked to each other, or something." She shrugs and smiles uncomfortably. "He was right."

What a mess, and I don't even want to think about the lack of manpower we have. But I do. There are eight of us. Unarmed Samuel and me, armed Mai, and four aged dudes, albeit tough old geezers with two Vietnam War era rifles between them. And one giant of a man who is mentally impaired. Oh, and we got knives, and killer scarves. Can't leave out the scarves. With our geriatric troops and our high-tech killing tools, our mission is to raid a warehouse that's patrolled by well-armed guards, free a bunch of kidnapped girls, and rush them off to an orphanage.

"If you only do what you know you can do, Sam," Samuel says, walking up to Mai and me, "you never do very much." He moves on to the men in the van.

What? All right, Samuel once again knows what I'm thinking and has a ready quote, though I don't think this one applies. We're not talking about switching from martial arts to pilates here, we're talking about raiding a warehouse with minimum resources.

I take a deep breath and blow it out. Okay, that's my ten seconds of whining. I'm done and I'm back on the job.

"Good," Samuel says, as he turns back to us. He motions for Cong and Phouc to get back in the van. To us, he says, "The men think they are in the war again and fighting for their sides. I talked with both pairs and I think the momentary animosity has cooled a little. I am going to talk to everyone now. Mai, please translate to Sam."

"Yes, Father." She waves at Dung who is still sitting in the back of the Volvo. When he starts to get out, she gestures for him to stay.

"He was sad that he didn't get to go with you," I say.

"I did not want him to get hurt. Father probably will have him watch the vehicles. Come, Father is talking to the men now. We need to move closer so I can hear."

The men are either looking out the windows or down at their hands. The tension isn't palpable but it's thick enough to be obvious. Samuel barks a command and all four men snap their heads toward him. He begins talking.

"Father say that this is not the American War," Mai says in my ear. "He say that we are all going together to save children from a terrible fate. We must go because those charged with protecting them will not do it. He says that we might be old warriors who once fought each other but that is long in the past and this mission now is our destiny. 'Helping others is the rent we pay for our room on Earth.'" Mai smiles. "Father say Muhammad Ali said that. The troops love Muhammad Ali."

At first blush, these guys look like characters out of a dream powered by a late-night dinner of spicy meatballs and sour tapioca. But when you look past the broken bodies, you see in those tired eyes a warrior spirit that has not faded and is still raging hot. It is what keeps them alive.

I remember sitting in a coffee shop at the courthouse. Dean, the officer I was sitting with, pointed at a table where four sheriff deputies, old timers, sat quietly eating breakfast. All the other tables around us were occupied by younger cops boisterously telling funny war stories, guffawing at ribald jokes, and bantering with each other. Dean asked if I knew the four salty dogs and I said that I'd only seen them around.

My friend shook his head, his eyes large. "The two guys with graying hair fought with the Delta Force in Vietnam. The shorter guy was a tunnel rat with three tours, and the bald guy served with the Navy Seals." Dean, a Vietnam veteran himself, paused for a moment as he looked at them with total admiration. Then he summed them up in one short sentence: "Those guys have seen some serious shit."

Likewise with Samuel and his troops. They've been in some serious shit and they still know how to bring it on. I can feel it radiate off them. I pity any adversary who fails to take note. Samuel is talking again, Mai translates.

"Father say, 'Sex trafficking is an ugly blight that is hurting our country. Those who profit from it are forever damned, and their karma will give them misery for many lifetimes. Those who deny and look the other way will also be haunted. Hoping that it will go away is not a strategy. Hoping is the dream of sheep.'"

Good stuff.

"Father say, 'As warriors, we have worked hard to prepare ourselves for the day we are needed. Each of us chose to be a warrior, a decision made many years ago when we were young men fighting for our countries. And that is the life we continue to live. Today, we are called to end a wrong and protect the innocent because there is no one else who will.'"

Samuel looks in the face of each man for a moment. "Father say, 'You are a frightening bunch. You look a lot like evil. You have fangs and the ability to be violent. The difference, though, is that you do not harm the weak. You defend them. You fight for them even at the expense of your own life.'"

Samuel pauses for a long moment.

Mai whispers, "Can you see how the men are changing?"

I nod.

"'Phouc, Viet, Phat Ho, Cong. We are one now, older and wiser, yet we still move *toward* the guns while others run away or look away. We do it because that is what we do. It is who—we—are.'"

Samuel does an about face away from his wide-eyed troops and moves back to the front of the Volvo. The men look at each other as they ponder Samuel's words. I look at Mai.

"What do you think?" she asks, her face beaming with pride.

"Well, I feel like a girlie man for whining to myself a few minutes ago. Actually, I feel like joining the army right now. Special Forces. Navy Seals. All of them. Ooorah!"

She nods enthusiastically. "I knoooow, right?"

# CHAPTER SEVENTEEN

"Father tell me that this road between Saigon and Bien Hoa was very dangerous during the war," Mai says, following close behind the van so that no one gets between us. "Many Viet Cong snipers shoot at vehicles during the day and night. At night, the enemy shoot rockets from the rice fields into Saigon. It was all rice fields then. As you can see, it is changed now."

After Samuel gave his pep talk to the troops, he took Mai's arm and guided her to a spot under a tree. They spoke for maybe ten minutes, their voices rising, then falling. Once, Mai wiped away tears. I took the role of backup, watching as passersby looked at them with curiosity while others stopped a few feet away and openly gawked. A Caucasian man ripping into a pretty Vietnamese woman probably isn't all that common on the streets of Saigon. I was ready to move in if someone tried to interfere. At one point, two rough looking men stopped no more than four feet away from them and looked as if they were about to interfere, but a sudden, sharp look from Samuel sent them scurrying off. I haven't asked Mai about the conversation nor has she volunteered what was discussed. I'm glad they got it settled between them and Samuel got the troops squared away. Now we can all focus on our anxiety.

"It's hard to tell we left Saigon," I say, turning my head like a barnyard chicken to look out all the windows. Dung, sitting in the back, is doing the same. Mai whispers a concerned comment that he doesn't get out often.

"Yes, they are sort of connected by restaurants, nurseries, theme parks, small businesses. But Bien Hoa is really about thirty kilometers, that is about twenty miles or so from Saigon. Many times it is a slow drive like today because traffic is hard... heavy. Father say Bien Hoa was dangerous during the war. He say there was an American base there but many people in the city sympathized with the North. Also there were people there who were secretly Viet Cong. That is why the air base got so many mortar attacks, bombs shot from the, uh, res... residential areas."

"It's so hard to imagine now. A different time, almost a different world."

We drive in silence for a few minutes. At one point, when we're creeping along at a walking pace, she says, "I was hoping your visit would be a time for us to be together more, to learn about each other."

"Me too. I guess our courtship is destined to be about fighting."

"At least it is about fighting other people," she says, scooting up close to the back of the van to prevent a motorbike loaded with ceramic pots from squeezing in between us. The van's windows are dirty, but I think that's Phat Ho's intense eyes looking back at us. Mai's defensive driving and Phat Ho's look are a metaphor for our courtship.

I say, "I read an article on relationships once in *Cosmo* magazine that said you need to be with another person for at least four seasons to see if it's the one you want to spend your life with."

"Seasons? You mean like summer and fall?"

"Yes, but all four. In other words, at least a year so that you're able to see the other person when they're happy, angry, moody, depressed, sick, and so on. If you still want to be with them after experiencing all those things with them, then that person is a keeper."

Mai laughs. "A keeper. I heard that before in Portland. It's a good one." Another motorbike with four people on it wants to squeeze between us and the van, but again she won't budge. "We have not seen each other in four seasons yet."

"No, but we have seen each other in some intense situations that combined are the equivalent of at least one season, maybe two."

"We have seen each other injured but not sick."

"I'm a big baby when I'm sick," I say.

"Ooooh," she groans with mock compassion. "I thought you might be."

"Hilarious. I just need to be held then I'm better."

"Okay, I can do that."

"Good."

Mai slows because the van is slowing. Neither of us say anything for two or three minutes, then she asks, "So what did we learn by having this talk? Are you trying to tell me that you are falling asshole over teakettle for me?"

"What?" I sputter. "Asshole over…"

"Is that the wrong phrase?"

"I think you mean head over heels."

"Oh," she laughs. "Yes, that one."

"Okay, then… yes."

Dung has twisted onto his side, which has quieted the foghorn in his nose.

After a few seconds, she asks, "So how many women have you been with?"

"Subtle," I say with a grin. "Are you asking because you have also fallen asshole over teakettle for me?"

"Maybe." Her cell rings. "Hello, Father. Yes. Oh no. Okay, we will." She drops the phone on the dash. "Checkpoint ahead. The police are waving the van over. Father said for us to go around and keep going. He will catch up."

"I don't understand. Why are they stopping him?"

"Police do that a lot here. They check your papers and want money to let you go."

Samuel slows and guides the van to the shoulder where an officer in a brown uniform and white helmet is stopping him with a raised palm. A few feet away, two other officers are talking to a motorist in a brown sedan. Just as Mai steers around the van, the sedan pulls away and the two officers wave us to the side of the road.

Mai utters something that I assume is a curse and stops in front of the van.

"Do you have your passport?" she asks, angrily.

"I do."

"Get it out."

In my side mirror, I see Samuel handing the policeman some papers. He looks at his watch, at us, and back to the officer. So far the twenty-mile trip has taken an hour, and we're not there yet. He's got to be worrying about the time.

One officer moves toward my side and the other gestures for Mai to get out. When I open my door, the officer quickly pushes it shut. Glad I didn't have my leg out. He twirls his finger for me to roll down my window.

"Passport," he says, palm extended.

Mid-thirties, fit, skin leathery, probably from many long days pulling checkpoint duty in the sun. His eyes are piggy and wet, like those of a cranky man with about three beers in him. He flips through my passport, glares at me, looks back at my photo, glares at me, looks back at the passport. I'm starting to feel guilty.

"ID more," he says, clamping the passport under his armpit and extending his palm.

I open my wallet, which displays my Oregon driver's license on the left side and my police ID card on the right. I hand him both. He looks first at the driver's license and then at the ID card. His eyes widen. He looks up at me and points toward my chest. "You. Same me?" I nod and shoot him an uncertain smile. He looks back at my wallet, minus a return smile.

In front of the hood, Mai giggles at whatever the other policeman is saying, patting his arm as if he were the most dashing man she had ever seen. It's a good act and it seems to be working. He hands her license back, blushing and gushing at Mai's batting eyelashes, and unaware that at the end of one of those mile-long legs is a holstered Glock 26, its barrel dirty from shooting two men a couple days ago.

My policeman hands back my wallet and passport. He points at my arms, and says, "Strong very."

"*Cám ơn.*" I point to his badge and give him a thumbs up. He looks at his partner and back to me, smiles, salutes. I force a smile and return the salute. Whew. Once again my charm wins the day. Mai gets in, faking a big laugh at something the policeman said.

"*Trời ơi!*" she says, shaking her head as the officer walks back toward the van. "What a creep."

"You are quite the actress," I say. "I thought you were going to feel his biceps and swoon."

She adjusts her mirror to see Samuel's van. "It worked. But I gave him money too."

"You did? How much?"

"Same as about thirty dollars American. Ten for you, ten for me, and ten for Dung. He signaled your officer that he got it. You did not see him?"

"No. I thought I was charming my guy."

"Cannot buy *phở* with charm."

"That pisses me off."

"It is the way it is," she says, looking at something in the rear view mirror. "Uh oh. You stay in the car."

She is out before I can ask what's going on. I twist around in the seat, but Dung's big frame is blocking the back window.

"Mai friend me," he proclaims. When did he wake up?

"What?" I lean right then left trying to see around him, but he tracks me like a cobra. "Oh, yes, yes. Mai your friend."

"No friend you. Mai friend *me*."

"Okay, Dung," I say, giving up. I get out, but stay by the open door.

The two policemen who checked Mai and me are laughing at Viet as the badly scarred old soldier tries to stand on the sloped dirt shoulder. The partial crutch that serves as his lower leg keeps sinking into the wet soil, making it even more difficult. His smile, made permanent by napalm that burned away his lips, looks as if he's laughing with their cruelty.

Samuel is showing his cell phone to the third officer as Mai stomps up to her father and points toward the two harassing Viet.

*There are things that make me angry, like bullies…* This could get ugly.

Mai listens for a moment and then starts to move toward Viet, but Samuel's quick-arm grab restrains her. The officer looks at the cell, at Samuel, nods his head, and exchanges words with his two compadres. The one who checked my ID says something that agitates the one with Samuel into waving his arms about. A couple seconds later, the two idiots move off toward the back of the van, presumably to coerce another motorist out of money.

Now the policeman with Samuel is bowing and smiling a lot. Samuel ignores him and gestures to Mai to return to our car. The policeman continues to kowtow as Samuel gets into the van.

"We go," Mai says tightly, as she slips in behind the wheel.

Dung pats Mai's shoulder. "Mai friend me," he says, looking sternly at me.

Mai pats his hand and says something that makes him sit back. The van accelerates around us into traffic and Mai gooses our car until we're once again behind it. In my rear mirror, the policeman continues to look after us.

I wait a half minute until Mai's breathing appears to be back to normal. "So what happened?"

"Father pay the policeman, then the other two opened the van door and made Viet get out. They make fun of his face and his leg." She takes a deep breath. "I thought about scarring *them* for life."

"I would have helped."

"Viet is the sweetest and nicest man. He fight for Vietnam and he sacrifice his body and a normal life, and his wounds hurt him all the time. These three bastards are worthless and just take from people. They do nothing to help anyone, nothing to help their people."

"What was Samuel doing?"

"He say that he was going to call Vu Van Hien, our policeman friend, you know, Harry. Harry is a captain. The one Father was talking to knows Harry and did not want any trouble. So he told us to go. It makes me angry to think how many people these three terrorize everyday."

"This is just incredible," I say, shaking my head. "So wrong. You do know that it isn't like this in the United States? The police don't do this sort of thing."

"I know. But they do it here and it makes me ashamed."

We ride in silence for a while. All Dung knows is that our voices are agitated and I'm the reason. I lower the visor, as if to shelter my eyes from the sun. The real reason is so I can keep an eye on the big guy in the visor's mirror, while I mentally review my defenses against a neck break attack from behind.

We creep along for several minutes, so slowly that an elderly woman walking along side us, with a large basket strapped to her back, passes us.

Dung disturbs the silence. "Mai friend me."

"Mai would you please tell him I'm not a threat."

"But you are," she says innocently. Feeling her old self again.

"I just don't want him wadding me up like a piece of paper."

"Okay, understood."

I watch him in the mirror as she rattles off something. He relaxes, smiles.

"What did you tell him?" I ask.

"I told him not to kill you now, but it is okay later."

"What?"

She smiles. "I told him not to worry that you are my brother."

Her cell rings.

"Father? Yes." She looks at her watch. "Right, not much time. Maybe we should... oh, okay. Call me back."

"What's going on?"

"Father was worried because he had not heard from the two men who were going to look over the warehouse. Then he got another call. He will call us after."

"It's five-fifteen now. As predicted, it's getting dark fast."

"Yes, it will be sooner because of the storm coming. Look at those clouds up—"

The car jerks to the right and the back end begins wobbling hard. Mai hugs the wheel.

"You got a flat tire."

She utters what I can only assume is another curse.

"Better guide it to the side of the road. Look, there's a flat dirt area coming up."

The van continues down the road as Mai expertly steers the car onto the dirt to the angry accompaniment of a full orchestra of blaring horns behind us. She honks back at them. I wonder for a moment if they have the middle finger gesture here. The car settles to a stop, leaning to the rear right.

She pokes her phone. "Father, we have a flat tire. That is okay, no need to come back here. Yes, I will let you know. We will hurry."

"Is he going on?"

"He did not see us pull over so now he is looking for a place to get off the road and wait. We must hurry."

We forage about in the trunk finding only a spare tire, a lug wrench but no jack.

"Damn."

Dung touches Mai's shoulder, his eyebrows scrunched with concern. The two converse for the next few seconds.

"What's going on?" I ask. "Should we call Samuel?"

"Dung says he used to work in a garage where they fixed

cars. He cleaned up for them. He said one time he lifted the back of a car off a man, a mechanic."

"You're kidding," I say, eyeing the behemoth.

"You think you guys can lift it?" Mai asks. "Dung is sixty and he has a bad leg. Maybe he lifted that car when he was young."

I shrug. "Volvos are heavy but we can try."

I position the spare so Mai can easily slip it on, then I loosen the lug nuts.

"Okay," I say, as Mai drops to one knee. "When we lift the car—that is, when we hopefully lift it—spin the nuts off fast and quickly slip the tire over the bolts, and tighten—"

"Uh," Mai says pointing behind me.

"Mai friend me," Dung says, bending to slip his hands under the bottom right panel. He straightens, the car creaks and groans, and the back tires clear the ground. "Not friend you." There is no strain on his face nor are his muscles trembling.

Who lifts a Volvo and their muscles don't tremble? "Tell him to keep holding it up," I shout, spinning the bolts free. Who lifts a Volvo, period?

Mai keeps repeating the same words, probably "hold it, hold it" or maybe "don't drop it on Sam as much as you want to," as I strip off the flat. We quickly slip on the new tire and twist on the nuts. I spin the lug wrench on each one until all four are tight.

"Okay, tell him to lower it." She does and the new tire settles into the dirt. I tighten the nuts again and stand. "In-flippin-credible," I say, looking at Dung who is looking at me to see if I got his not-so-subtle message. "Has he forgotten that you told him that we're brother and sister?"

"Maybe."

I point at the big man's chest and at mine. "You, me, friend."

"You sound like Tarzan," Mai says. She says something to Dung and he slowly smiles at me. He holds up his palm.

"Is he going bitch slap me?"

"He wants to do a high-five with you."

"Oh, okay. He's not going to lift me up or anything?"

She shrugs. "Maybe later if you ask him nicely. Come on, we got to go."

Dung and I high-five—he does it a little harder than what is required and with just a hint of an evil smile.

"The tire is fixed," Mai says into her cell as she honks her way out into the bumper-to-bumper stream. Everyone is running with their headlights on now as dark clouds bring on an early night. "Where are you, Father? Okay." She hands the phone to me. "He wants to talk to you."

"I am about half a kilometer ahead of you," Samuel says. If he is getting anxious about the time I'm not reading it in his voice. "You changed the tire faster than I thought you would."

"Yes, a story to tell another time," I say. Rain begins pelting the windshield. A young couple on a motorbike zip around us, both of them laughing. "How far are we away from Bien Hoa?"

"Twenty minutes in this traffic. But that is just to Bien Hoa. I have an address of the warehouse, which we still have to find." Lightning streaks across the distant sky. If a thunder clap follows it, I doubt we'll hear it over the commotion of traffic. "This storm is going to get bad, a blessing to cover our movement at the warehouse."

"There he is," Mai says pointing.

"We see you. You see us? Behind the green bus."

"Yes, yes. Tell Mai to let me in."

"Slow down so he can get in."

"Put me on the speaker phone, Sam," he says.

"Done."

"Can you both hear me?"

"Yes," I say, holding the phone up between us.

"I talked to my friends after they scouted the warehouse area. They said the building, number Four Twelve, is in an area where there are many warehouses and factories. Four Twelve is at the end of a street. There is a high fence behind it about ten feet away from the building. The warehouse itself is over a hundred fifty feet long by about eighty feet or so. There is one outside light bulb on each end and one guard on each end. The one in front has an M-16. The guard watching the back was wearing the red and white checkered scarf of the Khmer Rouge, holding an AK-47.

"He is in his sixties," Samuel continues. "Formidable looking, intense." He doesn't say anything for about half a minute, then, "You two still there?"

"Yes, Father."

"Okay. I was just thinking. My friends said there is another building that is exactly the same. It is three buildings south, building Four Nine. I'm hoping we will have enough time to stop and look at it and make loose plans as to how to hit the target. Sam, what do you think?"

"A rehearsal would be good."

Actually, several rehearsals would be better so that all of us know our specific tasks and what the others are doing. The old "any plan is better than no plan" doesn't apply here since we don't have any plan at all. Police officers say that a cop's job is to fix the problem not to become part of it. I just hope we aren't risking becoming exactly that. I understand and agree with the need to free the girls, yet I wonder if we're moving too fast.

What if we screw this up? What if in our fervor to save them right now it costs a little girl her life? Or more than one?

In the sky ahead, the bellies of chunky, low-moving clouds shine bright from the direction of Bien Hoa. Above those, a broader layer of light gray clouds and others that are blacker than black are moving in the opposite direction. Just as I think how strange that is, a single bolt of lightning streaks from right to left and is swallowed by a giant mass of blackness.

*Tommy, Mitchell, and I are outside the bedroom door on the second floor of the upscale home. Inside is a beast of man, an escapee from hell. The beast bellows, a deep, tortured guttural sound so awful, so demonic that my skin prickles and shivers, and my heart punches painfully against my chest.*

*I know the outcome of this moment because it has played out a thousand times in my head. I know so well that within seconds we will burst into the room, but…*

Mai's hand is on mine. I look down at it. I like it there. Makes me feel… safe.

"Are you okay?" she asks, not taking her eyes from the back of Samuel's van. "Are you with me?"

"Yes," I barely manage. "Yes, I am," I say louder. "Sorry."

Traffic is heavy, noisy. Mai shoots me a quick look before looking back out the windshield.

Sifu told me to imagine giving a flower to the people in my dream. Okay, here's a daisy, beast. I hope you got allergies. And here's another, this one for me.

"Father said your name two times."

"Oh, Sorry Samuel. Uh… yes, the plan sounds about as good as we can do under the circumstances."

"Yes, the circumstances are not good but… Another police checkpoint."

Mai utters something under her breath.

"You've got to be kidding," I say. "How many of these are we—"

"Okay," Samuel says sounding relieved. "They are getting in their cars. They probably do not want to get wet. We keep moving."

Mai points at the three police cars as we pass. "There, see them? The officers are all in their vehicles."

"Listen, Sam, Mai. We will talk again as soon as we get off this highway and into Bien Hoa. I need to call about the bus and call Lu to see if he has heard anything new. *Chào.*"

Mai chats with Dung, and I look out at the blurred lights of the roadside stands, and establishments offering food, gas, and beer. The rain continues to fall harder each passing minute. Right now, it's like the rain we get in Portland. Ahead, lightning continues to rip across the dark sky. We're getting close enough now that I can hear the thunder's deep rumble, even over the traffic noise.

Mai taps a number into her cell. She looks over at me, smiles, and looks back to the road. How incredibly beautiful she is, inside and out. If she even uses makeup, it's subtle, nearly imperceptible. I like that. And I like that I have yet to see her wear anything to deliberately show off her body, though one can't help but notice it no matter what she's got on. That makes her even more beautiful in my mind. Add in that she's funny, smart, family oriented, and she can fight like a demon, oh, and she likes me. How cool is that?

It isn't until she closes her phone that I notice her eyes glistening in the lights of passing vehicles.

"You okay?" I ask.

She wipes the back of her hand across her eyes. "Linh said

Mother is not doing well. The trip was hard on her and she worries about us. I think she knows what is going on. She told Linh that she wanted to return to the house. She has been sleeping a lot because she is so weak. Very, very weak, Linh say."

I start to reach for her hand then remember Dung in the back. "Sorry to hear that, Mai. Soon all this will be over and you can get back to a normal life."

"Maybe. But I am not optimistic about her health. She has grown so frail in the last few weeks. All that happened in Portland, the tension here, moving to the new house, and then traveling to Linh's house have been bad for her."

"She knows about Portland?"

"Yes. She and Father have always told the truth to each other. The exception is this time when she went to Linh's house. Father did not tell her of the danger we are in now. But like I said before, I think she knows."

Mai points at a road sign. "We are here. Bien Hoa."

# CHAPTER EIGHTEEN

We're straining to see one end of Four Nine, our rehearsal warehouse. Lightning illuminates everything in flashes of white light and a continuous, rolling-type thunder shatters the skies and jars my skull. While the rain isn't at monsoon level, it's difficult to see even with the windshield wipers on full speed.

The rain, thunder, and lightning stop. One moment the deluge is a deafening roar on the car roof and a second later all that remains is heavy dripping.

I look over to my right and see Viet, in the front passenger seat. For a moment I forget that he has no lips and I think he's giving me a big smile. I smile and nod. Mai leans across me so she can see Samuel.

"One story high, a double door on this end," he says, looking out his windshield at the warehouse. "No windows in the front and none on the right side of the building. I wonder... Mai, see that pipe that extends up the right corner to the roof?"

"Yes."

"Think you can climb it?"

"Climb it?" I say.

"Yes," she says. "It is not high. I can jump half way up and climb the rest of the way easily."

"Good," Samuel says. "If there is one on the target building, I want you to get on the roof as soon as we remove the guard. Phat Ho and I will do that."

*Remove the guard.* A thousand butterflies riot in my gut. What if I have to kill again? Oh my God, what if I have to kill again? What if I can't do it? What if one of us gets hurt because I can't—

"Son?"

I look up at Samuel's face framed in the van window opening. The single light bulb above the warehouse door provides just enough dull illumination to reveal his face in shades of orange, though his eyes seem to have a radiance all their own. They look into mine.

"The past is past, Son. Use the experience you have gained to help these children. The only thing important *is* now. These girls need our skills and our experience right here, right now."

The butterfly war dissipates a little. I take a couple deep breaths, nod, and give myself a flower. "I'm good to go," I manage.

He smiles. "*De oppresso liber*. To free the oppressed," he says. "Follow me around to the other end, Mai."

"You okay?" she asks, guiding the car along the left side of the warehouse. No windows on this side either.

"I'll be fine. My worst enemy is my head. Sometimes I let negative thinking overcome me."

"We all do that. Hey, look how quickly you fixed it. You will be good."

"Thanks to Samuel—again. And Sifu, and a bouquet of flowers."

She follows the van around to the back and parks along side it so that it's again on my side of the car. The back of the building looks the same as the front: a double door and one single window. Samuel and I roll down our windows. He scans the building before he speaks.

"No fence behind this one, but there is one behind the target warehouse. Hold on a second." He talks to the old soldiers for a couple of minutes, then looks down at us. "Let's get out of the vehicles," he says opening his door. "It will be easier to talk."

He leans his hip against the fender of the Volvo and looks at the warehouse. "Now that we see the structure, we have to change our plans a little. The boys thought there would be windows on the sides but that is not the case. So our entries will have to be through the front and rear doors. We do not know where the living quarters are but we can guess that they would be at this end, at the rear of the building. There is probably a kitchen in this back half and a restroom. There must be other rooms but we don't know where or how many. Phat Ho and I will take care of the sentries. Once the guards on both ends have been eradicated, Mai will go to the roof and check on access from there. There are likely skylights or something similar to let out rising heat and humidity."

"How we going to work communication?" I ask.

"All but Phouc and Dung have a cell," he says.

"Phouc has no arms," Mai reminds me. "And Dung does not need one." The big man hears his name and sticks his smiling face out the window. Mai touches his cheek affectionately.

"Call only me, not each other," Samuel says. "Doing otherwise might cause confusion. Okay, Phat Ho and I will take out the front guard, and then we will take out the one in the rear. We will enter the building and maintain a post as you sweep through the warehouse from the front. In the event of shooting, crossfire will be an issue. So stay behind cover as you sweep through."

"Sounds good," I say. "So many unknowns. It would be nice if before we make entry Mai could get on the roof to report back what she sees through the skylight."

"Agreed," Samuel says. "Of course, we could talk all night on what would be better than the way we are doing it."

"Right," I say, wishing I hadn't made the dumb comment.

"Not a problem," he says. "So once we take out the guard in front, you, Phouc, Cong, and Viet will enter. By that time, Phat Ho and I will have taken out the guard at the rear of the building. Mai, if you cannot see anything or do anything from the roof, come back down and join Sam in the front. If you can do something from the roof, call me.

"Yes, Father."

"Dung?"

The big man sticks his face out the window. Samuel talks to him for a moment, his tone gentle.

Mai whispers, "Father say that he has the most important job here. He is to watch the van and this car." Mai looks back at Dung, and smiles. "Dung say he is happy he has such an important job and he will do it good."

"Any last thoughts?" Samuel asks.

"I have one, Father. Do we know anything about the children? Are any hurt?"

Samuel shakes his head. "Lu knew nothing about that. I am sure he must be careful of what he asks. If he looks to be too curious they might get suspicious. Personally, I think they would want to keep the girls healthy but that might be naïve thinking on my part. Hopeful thinking. Lu did say that some or all of them are kept drugged." Samuel looks at me for a moment. "I think our earlier suspicions about Lu were wrong."

Before I have a chance to agree with him, the *Superman* theme sounds and Samuel extracts his phone from his pocket. "That reminds me," he says. "Set your phones on vibrate." He looks at the screen. "Speaking of Lu… *Chào* Lu."

Mai looks at me.

"Want to get a hamburger and a milk shake when all this is over?" I ask.

Her eyes smile into mine. "And a movie."

For a moment, as I look at her, nothing else exits, not the storm, not the awful humidity, not the others, and not the frightening mission we are about to go on. All I can see, all I can feel are her eyes and my thumping heart.

Her lips make a sweet smile. "Do you remember what I asked you in the tea café?" she asks.

I glance toward Samuel, who is listening intently to Lu as he rolls a round pebble back and forth with the toe of his red Converse. "You asked if I wanted to touch you as badly as you wanted to touch me."

Her smile widens.

"And the answer is still yes."

"Actually, you said, 'more,'" she says.

"And you said, 'Impossible.'"

A sudden flash of white light, followed a heart beat later by a blast of thunder, slams my chest and vibrates the gravel under our feet.

"Damn!" I half shout.

Giant drops of water begin to smack into us, the vehicles, and the gravel. Samuel gestures for us to get into the car. He climbs into the back with Dung.

Again the world lights up followed by a window-shaking peal of thunder. Mai gestures that she can't hear Samuel's conversation because of the downpour, but judging by the expression on his face, something's up. He closes his phone, leans back against the seat, and looks at the ceiling.

"Something happen, Father?" Mai shouts.

He doesn't answer for a moment. Finally, he leans forward and says loudly, "Lu said their plans changed. They are moving the children tomorrow night. Not tonight."

\*

"Did Lu have an explanation?" I ask.

Samuel shakes his head. "He said his contacts were positive that it was going to be tonight at seven-thirty, but something happened and the people involved in moving them have to postpone. He did not know why, but he thinks it might be a problem of transportation. He also said that he cannot talk to them about it anymore because someone was getting suspicious about his questions. He said a man hit him."

Mai's eyes widen. "Did you say 'hit him?'"

"That is all I know," Samuel says, tightly.

No one speaks for a moment as rain slams the roof. Then it subsides, just enough for us to hear one another without shouting.

"I think we should do it now anyway," Mai says. "I want to get those girls out of there."

"Agreed," Samuel says. "We are here, the bus is a short distance away, and there might—*might*—be fewer guards tonight since they are not moving the girls. Sam?"

I exhale a long breath. Terrible traffic all the way here, harassed by the police, a flat tire, a scary storm upon us, and now the move bumped to tomorrow night, which was their original plan before all the changes. Bad signs? Bad omens?

I did a little theater my first couple of years in college. The director used to say that a bad dress rehearsal meant a brilliant first night performance, and she was always right. It might be a stretch to make that apply here, then again maybe not.

"Let's roll," I say.

"Let 'oll," Dung parrots.

Samuel smiles at Dung, pats his thigh, and says something that makes the big man laugh.

"Father say to Dung that he is a good man."

"Okay, listen up," Samuel says to us. "My friend said that all of the warehouses in this row are army green except the beige one before our target. We will park at the front of the beige building. Follow me and keep your headlights off. I have not seen any traffic around here, which is good. The noisy storm should cloak our approach."

He leans forward and places a hand on my shoulder and one on Mai's. "You know how I feel about you both," he says, looking at each of us. He looks out the window. "We are going to get drenched." He scoots out the door and slips into his van.

Mai takes a deep breath, releases it. "Here we go," she says, dropping the shift lever into drive. "Hard to see in the rain and without lights. And hard to see with lights." She hugs the wheel and follows the van down the side of warehouse Four Ten. The next one is beige, Four Eleven.

Samuel parks the van next to the front door and gets out, patting the air with his palm for us to debark quietly. Mai holds her index finger over her lips and says something to Dung. The men in the back of the van climb out just as the rain begins falling harder, cloaking what little noise we make and drenching us within seconds.

Samuel points at me and then at the light bulb over the door. I'm the only one who can reach it. I twist it off and cross over to Four Ten to loosen the bulb over its back door.

Samuel pulls Mai and me into a huddle, our foreheads nearly touching, as the rain beats on our backs.

"Here is the plan we discussed in the van. Phat Ho and I are going to walk down the street pretending to be drunk. The rest of you move along the wall of this building until you reach the end, or just before you are exposed. Do not let the guard watching Four Twelve see you. After we remove him, we will go to the rear and take out the guard there."

We nod.

"By the way," Samuel says, "The building number? Four Twelve? Ecclesiastes 4: 12, says: 'A person standing alone can be attacked and defeated, but two can stand back to back and conquer.' Then it says, 'Three are even better, for a triple-braided cord is not easily broken.' There are seven of us. We got it made in the shade. That still a saying, Sam?"

I shrug. "Dated, but it still works."

He squeezes our shoulders. "See you inside." He gestures for Viet, Cong, and Phouc to join us, and gives Dung, who has moved behind the wheel of the Volvo, a thumbs up.

Samuel wraps his arm around Phat Ho's shoulder. Three scarves hang from the one-armed man's back pocket, a red, black, and orange one. Part of a white one dangles from his right fist. He's no doubt preloaded each one with a coin. He's good to go with locked and loaded scarves.

They move away from the building over to a paved one-lane street probably used by delivery trucks and such. It's still raining hard, but I can hear Samuel singing loudly like a drunken sailor. The two stagger and stumble down the street as if they've been doing this act for years.

The five of us flatten ourselves against the side of the warehouse. I'm in front, behind me is Mai with gun in hand, then seventy-year-old Cong holding his Marine Corps Ka-Bar, the blade along his wrist, a position he explained the other day that's good for opening up stomachs and to "ugly up face pretty good." Next is the armless Phouc, who Samuel claims is a good fighter with his stubs. He's pinned one of the M-16s under his right one. I point at the weapon and raise my eyebrows at Cong.

"Like knife better," Cong whispers, lifting his blade. "He give gun to me if I need."

Wonderful tactics. Next, and certainly last in our warrior circus squad is napalm-burned Viet, with his permanent grin and part of an old crutch for a leg. I'm relieved to see that he's actually carrying his M-16.

As Oliver said to Laurel, "Well, here's another nice mess you've gotten me into."

Now I'm quoting movies.

Thinking that the weapons should be leading us, I motion for Viet to move up and take the front, Mai next, Cong behind her, then Phouc and me at the rear.

We begin moving down the side of the warehouse. Fortunately, there are no lights here and the rain is making visibility even poorer. I can see a dim glow at the far end, probably from the light bulb at the rear of this building and the light on the front of the target warehouse a few feet away.

Samuel and Phat Ho are at the halfway point now, staggering and singing up a storm, at least Samuel is singing. Phat Ho must be acting the part of a quiet drunk.

Still no sign of a guard. They progress a few more steps and stop. Maybe they've spotted him and they're waiting for him to see them. Samuel sings louder and fakes an even louder laugh as he pounds Phat Ho's back. Quite the thespian, Samuel.

Someone shouting now. Our line freezes in place.

Samuel and Phat Ho look toward what would be the front of the target warehouse, though I know Samuel has been watching it all along out of his peripheral.

One person's voice. Barking short sentences.

Samuel waves a greeting in the direction of the shout.

More shouts, though not as intense this time. It seems they've succeeded in fooling the guard into thinking they are a couple of drunks. Samuel raises his hands and Phat Ho raises his one, though he doesn't open his fist.

The guard, in silhouette, passes the edge of our building, crouching and pointing a rifle—looks like an M-16—at Samuel and Phat Ho who are moving slowly toward him. Samuel is pressing his palms together now, making short, subservient bows. He's saying something. Probably telling the man that they have been drinking and got lost.

The tension in the armed-man's silhouette dissipates a little, though he keeps his rifle trained on them as he crouch-walks closer, stopping about ten feet away. If the guard knew Samuel, he would stay right there. He doesn't know him, though, so he doesn't stay.

Samuel is still talking, probably asking how they can get out of this warehouse district. The guard, I can't tell how old he is by his silhouette, says something, maybe telling them to turn around and walk the other way. The guard advances to within about six feet of the pair, his rifle still trained on them. He jerks his head in the direction they came from, probably indicating for them to stagger back.

Samuel's on him.

I don't see him lunge, jump, or launch himself. One instant he is six feet away and the next he is in front of the guard, his hands a blur, the sound, even at this distance, like playing cards being shuffled.

A pained whine, like the bleat of an injured animal, penetrates the downpour, followed by the man's rifle flipping end over end away from him, as if fleeing the fury launched on its owner.

I expect the guard to be sent flying through the air like his rifle, but instead he crumples as if his bones had suddenly turned to dust and were no longer able to support his body.

I would have thought that the old soldiers would have seen Samuel move before, but they look at him just as awestruck as I am. Mai's eyes are huge. She has probably never witnessed her father having to kill—I'm assuming the guy is dead. Phat Ho stares at the lifeless body at his feet, his scarf hanging impotently from his only hand.

The rain increases, along with its roar. To add insult to injury, the five us are now under a waterfall pouring over the gutterless roof edge. It's falling so hard that it hurts my head and that tender spot on the back of my neck.

Samuel walks quickly over to the rifle, bends to pick it up—

Movement out of the corner of my eye.

A man running toward Phat Ho, his arm over his head, a large curved knife in his hand. Samuel doesn't hear him but Phat Ho sees him.

The *garrote* master sidesteps at the last second, whips his yellow scarf around the man's neck, catches the coin-end in his mouth, braces the side of his face against the man's back, and yanks the other end tight.

All that in a second, second and a half, tops. The hapless guard makes a feeble, flailing attempt to stab back at Phat Ho, but the pressure of the scarf against his two carotid arteries instantly restricts the blood to his brain.

The first stab misses Phat Ho's thigh by an inch and when the progressively groggy man tries again, he accidentally punches the blade into his own leg. He's unconsciousness before the pain message reaches his brain.

I've applied carotid artery constriction many times against resisting suspects, most of whom passed out four or five seconds after I had caught their neck in the V of my arm. It's a relatively safe technique that restricts only the arteries. Phat Ho's *garrote* restricts the man's arteries *and* his windpipe, a deadly technique unless it's released as soon as the recipient passes out, which I'm guessing isn't going to happen.

The strangled man collapses to the pavement as the old soldier finishes his job. Phat Ho unravels the deadly scarf from the man's neck and makes a subtle flip of his hand that folds it back into his palm. I think he's done this a few times before.

In the few seconds it's taken Phat Ho to take the man out, Samuel has been covering him by pointing his M-16 in the direction of the warehouse. Now he's looking our way, though I doubt he can see us in the dark and through the downpour. He points in the direction of the target warehouse and gives us a thumbs up. The front is clear.

He and Phat Ho cross diagonally over to the building and begin moving down its side to take out the other guard. Samuel probably figures that the drunk act won't work again because the rear guard would know that the first sentry would have stopped them. He holds the weapon along the far side of his leg as the two disappear into the darkness, their bobbing heads intermittently appearing as silhouettes against the dim, yellow light coming from the far end of the warehouse.

I hold my fingers to my lips, and wait until everyone sees me and nods. Just as I motion Viet to move toward the corner, a sudden flash of white illuminates everything for a second, making all of us turtle our heads a little, as if that would prevent the lightning from hitting us or anyone from seeing us. If Mother Nature decides to send lightning down to this metal-sided wall, we're all going to look like crispy bacon. Thunder follows, a detonation that nearly stops my heart.

Over to the right, hard rain splatters off the dead faces.

Viet, first to the edge of the building, holds up his hand for us to stop. Gripping his M-16 with both hands, he quick-peeks around the corner, once, twice, three times. He gives me a thumbs up. I motion for the others to stand fast while I move up next to him, and peak around the corner. Twenty feet away, the front of the target building looks the same as the one we looked at a few minutes ago, including the pipe at the corner that extends from the ground to the roof.

I turn to Mai and whisper in her ear. "You ready to climb?" She nods. "Okay, tell them that we will move together toward the door. As soon as we get there, you go up the pipe and—"

*Bebebebebebe!*

Automatic gunfire from the back of the warehouse. We drop as one into a crouch. Cong snatches the M-16 from Phouc and Viet flattens himself against the wall, pointing his barrel in the direction of the gunfire. Age, deformity, and a partial leg has not slowed the man.

*Bubububububu!*

No one moves or makes a sound.

After about ten seconds, Cong whispers, "First, AK-47. Second, M-16."

Lu said the rear guard was usually a Khmer Rouge armed with an AK-47. Samuel had the Sixteen. If Samuel fired second that means he wasn't hit, or maybe hit but still able to return fire. Mai looks at me, her eyes asking me if Samuel is okay.

Before I can respond, she plunges her hand into her pocket and pulls out her cell.

Her shoulders relax.

Lightning and thunder hit simultaneously, shaking the ground and illuminating everything in brilliant light. We all lean toward Mai.

"Father and Phat Ho are okay," she says. "Khmer Rouge not killed; he ran inside the warehouse. Father say for us to go in now."

I nod to Viet. "Lead the way. One behind the other. Mai, tell them."

Viet hobbles away from the corner, his M-16 leading. Mai follows, her Glock thrust forward in a two-handed grip. Cong is behind her, his M-16 covering the other front corner of the warehouse should someone step around to surprise us. Phouc follows Cong and I follow him. As Cong moves off to quick-peak around the left corner, I stop at the end of the beige warehouse and twist off the light bulb over the door. Cong gives me a thumbs up that the side is clear. I quickly move over to twist off the light bulb over the target warehouse. Now the area is in darkness except when lit for a couple seconds by the heavens.

Mai moves to the right corner, jamming her pistol into the back waistband of her pants. Without hesitation, she leaps high up the pipe, but the tin is rain slick and her hands begin to slide back down. Fortunately, her running shoes have good traction and she's able to stop herself.

She pushes off with her feet and gains twelve inches. She does this three of four more times until she is high enough to grab the edge of the roof. There must be a ledge of some kind there because she has no problems holding on. She swings free for a moment, then pulls herself up far enough that she is able to grab something on the flat roof and hoist herself the rest of the way. Her feet disappear over the edge.

At the door, I gesture to Viet to go left and for Cong to go right, and I pantomime to Phouc to follow Cong. I'll go in low behind Viet. Everyone nods. I motion to Phouc to open the right door as I pull open the left one. He looks at me funny and lifts his stubs. Whoops, forgot about that. I signal to Viet to open it.

The doors are huge, each about six feet wide and eight or nine feet high. I'm hoping to hell that they're unlocked. I take hold of the door handle—lightning flashes…

*I'm outside the bedroom door, my gun out, my shoulder to the wall…*

No! Not now. I push the intrusive thoughts away. There is no time to reminisce about those doors. I mentally drop a tulip in front of them. Done. Now it's all about these doors here and what's behind them.

That's the thing about doors; it's always about what's behind them.

"Thow tine," Viet whispers.

I lift my eyes from the door handle to Viet's ever-smiling lipless mouth. Did he just say "Show time?" He pantomimes opening the door. Guess so. We simultaneously turn the handles. The doors release.

We pull them open just enough for us to enter. Viet curls around his and peg-steps left, his M-16 covering his half of the dark room, and Cong moves quickly to the right in a deep crouch, his weapon covering his half. Phouc follows. I dash in and crouch behind Viet.

The rain hitting the metal roof is deafening.

It's dark, but I can see that we're in a large room, probably the storage portion of the warehouse. There's a puke-yellow light source at what appears to be the back wall, about sixty feet from where we're crouched. I can just barely make out a door back there on the left and some cardboard boxes against the wall. In between that wall and us are silhouetted shapes. One, two… Nine of them. They are about six feet high, rounded. My mind flashes on a photo I once saw of Easter Island at night, those giant heads in eerie silhouette against a full moon.

*Bam!*

Gunshot! From overhead. A Glock pistol, I'm sure. Got to be Mai. "Mai," I whisper to myself. I should be with her, protecting her. I should call her to be sure she's okay, but I'd have to find the scrap of paper in my wallet, the one with the long distance numbers on it. It's too dark to read it anyway.

Again, the only sound is the rain battering the roof.

Viet is looking back at me. Over to the right, barely visible faces in the darkness look at me, as well. Come on people: look and listen. I point at my ears and eyes and wave my hand at the darkness before us. They understand and turn back to the room and those shapes.

The metal roof and sides act as a low-tech sound system that amplifies the rain's roar—its vibrations so intense it feels like it might flatten us into the concrete. A giant hand of thunder spasms the metal, an all-out assault on the senses that's nearly overwhelming.

It's dark, but I still feel exposed without some kind of cover in front of me. There are three rows of the dark "Easter Island" shapes, three across, three deep. The front one closest to Viet and me is about ten feet away. I assume if there were people hiding behind the big shapes they would have already made their move.

Must never assume. One of my academy instructors would say that an assumption is the mother of all screw-ups.

I twist around to see what's behind me: a hand truck near the door and a rectangle shape, probably a light panel above that. If there are people behind the shapes, I would assume that they know their way around better than we do. That's another assumption, but this time I've got to assume it's a good one and it would be better for us if I turn on the lights. I point to the light panel and gesture for everyone to align themselves behind the monolith closest to them. Cong moves over behind the closest one to him and Phouc follows. Viet does the same on my side.

Screams from somewhere in the warehouse. My hand stops just inches from the light panel and I drop to my knees. More screams, at least three different ones—children. Got to be coming from the other side of the far wall.

*Bebebe!*

Gunshots.

*Bebebe!*

The AK-47.

Shouting—men this time.

Then silence, except for the Armageddon of rain.

Five seconds pass. Ten. Thunder explodes overheard and shakes the metal building again.

A crunch behind me. A foot step on gravel?

I stand and step toward the door, my hands up. Ready.

"It is me," Mai whispers.

I grab her arm and pull her in away from the doorway so she isn't silhouetted. We kneel in the shadows off to the left.

"My God, Sam," she breathes. "I saw… I saw children… they were…" She shutters. "They were…"

"Tell me later," I say. "Right now we need to focus on this room.

"I shot a man. He had a snake."

"Snake?"

"He… I know I hit him, then he ran into a little shack."

Mai is near hysteria. I've never seen her like this before. I don't understand what she's trying to say.

"Have you heard from Samuel?"

She nods. "He said they were inside the door. He tried to call you but got Bobby."

"Aggh! I forgot I left my phone with the boy. Did he say what he was seeing?"

"Only that they were in a small space behind a wall or something. He said he can hear children on the other side."

We've got the children and the bad guys boxed in. The kidnappers can't get away, but that might mean we're forcing them to decide whether to fight or to give up. Or, to take the children hostage. I want to call in hostage negotiators, SWAT, and stall for time. The first two aren't an option here, and I'm not sure about stalling. I definitely don't like functioning in the dark.

"Listen," I say. "I'm going to turn on the lights. Go over with Cong and Phouc and be ready for anything."

"Okay." She touches my chest for a moment, then turns and runs in a crouch into the deep shadows. I wait a beat, stand quickly, and hit the light panel.

Scrunching my eyes shut against the pain, I run in a crouch toward where I last saw Viet, nearly tripping over his crutched leg when I find him. I drop to my knees, forcing my eyes open.

The old veteran is lying on his stomach, pointing his rifle at…
It takes my eyes a second to adjust… to see what he's…

Buddhas. Brilliant, gold Buddhas, all at least six feet tall.
The three in the left column are fat and laughing. Those in the
middle are painfully emaciated, and the three in the right column are more ornate and detailed than the others. The sculp-
tor has somehow carved their faces to appear wonderfully calm,
peaceful and—

A man, gripping a long curved knife, springs out from
behind the Buddha near Mai and her group, and charges
toward them. Still prone, Cong snaps up his M-16… it doesn't
fire. He drops the weapon clattering to the cement and leaps
to his feet as agile as a teenager. Mai raises her gun, but Cong,
swiftly removing his knife from his hip scabbard, is in her line
of fire. Two paces away from Cong, the attacker stabs his blade
downward, ala caveman style. The knife master steps diagonally, and snaps his Marine Ka-Bar out and back as quick as a
serpent's tongue.

The attacker takes two steps past him, hesitates for a second, then falls straight forward onto his face, his knife bouncing on the cement a few feet beyond his outstretched arm. He
writhes, twisting in my direction. Blood arcs from his neck
at least three feet into the air, splattering onto the floor near
where Mai is kneeling, her Glock and her eyes focused on the
Buddhas. The attacker quivers for a moment, then his movements cease.

That's their second suicide charge. Is that their idea of
defense?

"Kay-er Rouge," Viet says.

"Khmer Rouge?"

"Yes. Nu-er ucking ten."

I'm staring at the Buddhas so hard that my eyes begin to water. For a second, I think the middle statue in the center row moved, but it's just my watery eyes tricking me. I wipe the back of my hand across them. That's better.

A metallic noise to my right.

Cong is trying to fix his M-16 with Phouc looking on. Cong looks at me and shakes his head.

Didn't anyone check these guns before they brought them?

Noise on the other side of the far wall again: shuffling feet, low voices. At least with Samuel and Phat Ho over there, no one from that side can go out the back and circle around to this end to ambush us. But that doesn't mean they can't call for reinforcements to hit us from this side.

I look at the door behind me. Talk about having your butt hanging out. We need to keep Mai's Glock and Viet's M-16 in here, assuming that Viet's isn't broken. I can't send armless Phouc out there and I need to be inside. This is bad. Got to keep watching the door and let Mai or Viet know if we get visitors. Also have to watch the small door in the wall ahead of us. If someone comes out of it and at the same time someone charges through the door behind us, we're pretty much scre—

*Bebebe… bebe!*

I flatten myself onto the cement. Came from behind the wall. Sounds like the AK.

Screams. Running feet. Silence.

I tap Viet's foot to get his attention and point that I want us to move over to the wall and advance from there. When my wave gets Mai's attention, I gesture the plan. She nods, scoots in front of Cong since she has the only workable gun, and gives me a thumbs up. I hold up one finger, two, three, and nudge Viet to start moving.

"Stay even with her," I whisper, hoping Viet understands. He shakes his head. I move my hand, palm down in small slow motions. He understands that. He crawls just fine with his partial crutch-leg, but he's wearing shorts so the cement has got to be chewing up his knees.

We're exposed next to the wall, but it allows us to see the room a little better and lets us see behind the Buddhas sooner than if we had to crawl around each one. It's the best of two bad scenarios, but not by much.

We crawl until we're in alignment with the three lead Buddhas. I gesture for everyone to hold up and to look about and listen. Nothing new. I gesture for everyone to advance again, slowly, until we can see the backside of the front row of Buddhas. Crawling... crawling... and... all three are clear.

Again, I gesture to look and listen, then move. We have about ten feet of crawling until we're even with the second row. As I move, I look behind me at the double doors, over at the man bleeding out on the cement, and back to my front where we're almost even with the second row of smiling gold Buddhas. How ironic that Buddhism's symbol of peace, love, and compassion is stored in a place where such horror is being carried out. These terrorists kidnappers are going to be struck with some bad karma.

The pounding rain on the roof stops abruptly. Thunder grumbles in the distance.

We're even with the second row now. I gesture for Viet and Mai to stay put, and point to my ears for everyone to listen before we advance and expose ourselves to the backsides of the second row of statues.

*Drip… drip…*

Water drips somewhere to my front by the wall that separates us from the other part of the warehouse. Each little splatter—*drip… drip*—punches into my brain like a chisel tapping—*drip… drip*—into the walls of my head.

About five years ago while still working uniform, the neighboring beat car and I went to a shabby apartment in Southeast Portland to serve a warrant on a guy for not showing up in court on a domestic violence arrest. We knocked on the door and when the man saw us through a side window, he screamed at us to go away. We told him that that wasn't going to happen and that he needed to come out.

All was quiet for about two minutes, and then a skull-rattling boom, a shotgun blast, nearly gave us a cardiac. We shouldered in the flimsy door to find the man sprawled awkwardly over a dinette chair, the majority of his brains splattered over his kitchen counter and a partially made sandwich, the shotgun braced against one leg.

A couple years later, the other officer told me that he was still haunted by the horrific damage to the man's head. Oddly, I kept thinking of the man's still burning cigarette resting in a glass ashtray in front of him, an inch and a half of gray ash curled out from its end. I can still picture it. Funny what darkens our minds.

Right now, it's the sound of dripping water—*drip… drip*.

The column of Buddhas closest to us are robed figures with sedate, fleshy faces, elongated ears, and peaceful smiles. One bare foot is posed slightly ahead of the other; the back of the right hand resting in the palm of the left, thumbs touching. Walking meditation, maybe? The skin, hair, and robe are a brilliant gold, maybe paint, maybe the real thing. The Buddhas in the middle column have been carved to look as if the poor man just got out of a POW camp, the chests, depicted bare, show the ribs well defined. The hands are positioned by the abdomen, the arms skeletal thin. I don't know what the emaciated look is supposed to depict—

Something appears from behind the center skeleton Buddha, then disappears. An arm? Viet must have seen it because he's swinging his M-16 toward it.

Seconds pass. A half minute. I quickly wipe my hand across my right tearing eye. I glance at Mai. She's kneeling on one knee, extending her Glock forward in a two-handed grip. I gotta assume she saw it too. Phouc and Cong are lying on their bellies behind her.

No. Mai is aiming at the other Buddha, the one closest to her.

Movement out of the corner of my eye; the center statue again. A hand… an arm. Little. Viet raises his rifle. I push the barrel down, shaking my head.

A girl steps all the way out from behind the figure. She can't be more than ten years old, wet, muddy, her long hair hanging in wet strands. Eyes lifeless.

Across the way, Mai is gesturing at me.

No, not at me. At another little girl standing on the other side of the Buddha that's closest to her. She, too, looks wet and muddy.

Movement from behind the last emaciated statue in the back. A man! He's walking backwards toward the wall and holding his hands up. Viet watches him over his barrel. The man turns quickly and reaches for something on the wall. It's another electric panel.

The lights go out.

# CHAPTER NINETEEN

The little girl, silhouetted by that one low-watt light bulb on the back wall, stands as motionless as the statues.

"Tell her to come to me, Viet," I whisper, though I doubt she will. The last thing she saw before all went dark was a big wet ape—me. "Tell her it's okay. Tell her we're here to save all the girls. She's going to be fine. Tell her to come to—"

A bright flash from my right. *Bebebe!*

Sparks fly from the metal wall just above Viet's prone body. "Aaaaaa!"

"Viet?" I scoot towards him. "You hit?"

When he doesn't answer, I grab his arm and pull him back a few feet so that he's no longer where the shooter last saw him. I look toward the small door in the dividing wall. Still closed.

"Viet, are you—"

He mumbles something in Vietnamese and rolls onto his back. "Uddha," he manages.

Buddha, I think he said. I look at three Buddhas in the last row. Out of the corner of my eye, I can see Mai jabbing the barrel of her Glock toward the back wall. Which one does she mean? The center one?

Viet groans.

"Where are you hit?" I ask. Then I see his bleeding calf, where the round hit the side of his lower leg.

"Lay," he groans, which looks strange coming from his permanent smile. "Good lay."

Oh man. He's saying his good leg.

"No set," he says, straining. "Li-el hur."

No sweat. Little hurt.

"Geh gul."

Get the girl, I think. She's still standing motionless next to the statue. Viet rolls back onto his stomach and points his weapon at the last Buddha in the center column.

"Here," I say stripping off my shirt. I quickly wrap it around his calf and cinch it tight. "To stop bleeding. Understand?"

"O-ay," he says. "Go geh gul."

She's only about ten feet away but it's a long ten. I drop onto my belly and low crawl as fast as I can across the open space, scuffing my elbows and stomach on the raw cement. The girl remains motionless until I'm three feet away then abruptly disappears behind the Buddha. Without hesitation, I spring to my feet and curl around to the other side of the big statue, hoping for the element of surprise.

A man, his head facing away from me, pushing the girl against the Buddha's back.

*I'm in the bedroom, my gun trained on the naked—*

"No!" I shout.

The man startles, spins, and lunges toward me. I slam my palms against his shoulders to stop him, then push one and pull the other to spin him about until his back is against my chest. Using his face as a handle, I yank his head back against my shoulder, shoot my right arm out in front of him, and then whip the thumb side of my fist back into his Adam's apple. Repeat for good measure. The blows won't kill him—I don't think—but for the next few hours he will wish they had. I fling his limp body aside, hearing something clatter as he thumps to the floor. Maybe it's one of those big curved knives or a gun. Too dark to see.

Got to get out of the open because there's still someone behind one of the statues in the back row. I scoop up the comatose little girl and slip around to the other side of the Buddha. I'd like to take her out the back door, but then what? Leave her there? Even if I knew how to tell her to run down the road until she sees big Dung, she's not responding to anything. Better to stay right here in the dark behind the statue.

I strain to see Mai across the way. She's huddled behind the Buddha in the center column with her little girl crouched behind her, the girl's arms encircling Mai's waist. Cong and Phouc crawl over to get behind Mai. Four people in a line taking refuge behind the Buddha. I try to nudge my statue with my shoulder; it's solid, made of stone or concrete. Good cover, fair concealment.

"Viet," I whisper, "tell the girl to stay with me. Tell her not to step out from behind the statue."

Viet's voice is tight, pained. No doubt the nerves in his leg are rebelling now.

The poor bedraggled girl doesn't react to what he says. She's got to be in shock. I make a cursory check to see if she's been hurt, all the while she stands motionless, her eyes in some far off place. Then, without a word, she squats and wraps her arms around her legs.

I'm a little closer to Mai here and better able to see her. I shrug a What-do-we-do-now? She shrugs one back. We can't advance and we can't go back toward the door where we entered. We need to help Samuel and Phat Ho on the other side.

Got an idea. I reach into my pocket, pull out two quarters, and hold them up, hoping Mai can see them in the semidarkness. She nods. I wave to get Viet's attention and he manages a nod. I pantomime throwing them against the back wall. Mai gives me a thumbs up.

I launch the coins as hard as I can at the far corner. If someone reacts with gunfire, I want the rounds to go away from us. The coins clatter loudly off something that must be metallic.

*Bababaclankclankclank!*

A deafening burst of automatic weapon fire lights up the back of the last Buddha in the center row as bullets rip into the metal wall where my coins fell. Mai's girl screams and tries to climb onto her back. Mine still squats behind me, staring at the floor.

The gunman didn't reveal himself and no one came through the door off to the left. All that was gained is that we now know for sure that the man is armed. Is there anyone behind the other two Buddhas in the back row? If someone is behind the last statue on Mai's side, the clatter of the coins and the incoming rounds had to have scared him to death.

Silence now, except for that dripping in the corner.

We wait. One minute passes, three, ten. Mai extracts her phone, pokes a button and holds it to her ear. Even in the relative silence, I can't hear her. A moment later, she closes the lid and nods to me. Things must be going better where Samuel is.

*Bebebe!*

AK-47 from the other side of the wall, followed by a loud groan on this side and another piercing scream from Mai's girl. Mine still stares at the floor.

That dim light bulb on the back wall hangs a little to the left of the center statue, illuminating just enough that I can see a silhouetted hand from behind it grab the Buddha's boney right shoulder, the fingers bent, trembling. They struggle for just a moment longer before slowly sliding down the skeletal arm. A man's silhouetted head extends out from the side. I sense more than see Viet take aim. The head drops and hits the cement with a sickening crack. In my gut I know the man's dead. Viet must think so too, because he doesn't fire.

The guy took refuge behind the Buddha but on the wrong side. The AK burst punched through the back wall and hit him in the back. Friendly fire that wasn't so friendly.

Are there more men over here? Cong brought one down and I put another out of commission. What were the two little girls doing on this side? Being used to slow us down? Or maybe the men were up to no good with them before we interrupted.

We know the center Buddha in the back row is clear so that just leaves the two outside ones. My gut tells me they're clear, but we need to be sure. I'm unarmed and Viet's mobility is limited. It has to be Mai who moves up.

"Sam," Viet whispers. I look over at him. "I 'o there," he says, pointing toward the wall. "Lay no prah-lem."

I think he said that he will go up, that his leg is no problem.

"Tell ai to no o." Tell Mai not to go. With that he begins scooting himself along the wall, leading the way with his rifle, dragging his wounded leg behind him. Hell of a troop, this guy.

Pointing at Viet, I motion to Mai to stand fast. She nods.

Pushing himself with his crutch-leg, Viet crawls about three feet before giving me a thumbs up and clutching his neck with one hand. I take that to mean the guy I throat punched is still down. Then he starts crawling to check out the partly lit back row of statues. That gives Viet an advantage since he's mostly in the dark.

He slow crawls for another painful minute until he looks to be flush with the last row of Buddhas. He leans out a little, a little more, and a little more. On the PD, we call this slicing the pie. Each time Viet leans out a couple of inches, he makes a visual wedge. He doesn't lean back because he'd lose what he gained. He continues doing this until he stretches his body out one last time to see around the statue. Another thumbs up. The closest Buddha to him is clear.

He inches forward, looks, and gives me another thumbs up that the center Buddha is clear, except for the man lying on the floor. Viet makes a cutting motion across his neck with his fingers. Dead. He slices the pie three more times before giving me one final thumb. The back row of Buddhas is clear.

Mai, clutching hands with the little girl, darts over to me. Behind her, Cong and Phouc get to their feet and go to check on the man Cong cut.

"Whoa, whoa," I whisper loudly. "Get behind this statue with us, Mai. We're still down range here. An AK punched through the wall and got that guy. The shooter may still be over there. Tell Cong and Phouc."

No need. The two men have already figured it out and aligned themselves again behind their statue.

"I want to get the girls out of here," Mai says. "I will show them the way back to Dung."

"Okay, and I want to check on the man I throat punched. Keep yourself aligned with a Buddha as best you're able."

She nods. "You are bleeding."

"Cement burns. No problem."

"Do you want my gun?"

"No."

She speaks to the little girl who has been squatting behind me. When she doesn't get a response, Mai gently takes her hand and pulls her to her feet. She glances at the back wall, at me, and then bolts with the girls across the room. At the door, she places my girl's hand in her girl's hand and nudges them out.

"Lights?" she whispers.

I hold up a finger for her to wait. I start to tell Viet to get behind the statue closest to him but he's already crawling behind it. The guys might have been rusty but they're getting back into the groove.

I nod my head to Mai, then squint against the sudden brightness. Once my eyes have adjusted, I dart up to the next statue in my column and peer around it. The man I punched is still lying in the fetal position holding the front of his neck, his breathing raspy. I've been hit there a couple times in training, and for hours after it felt like a pickup truck was caught in my throat. I hit this guy twice. I look around and spot some nylon rope on a bench near where I'd thrown the coins. Cong has moved up behind the center statue in his column and looks where I'm looking. He darts over to get it, moves back behind his Buddha for a moment, then dashes over behind mine.

I step around my statue and grab my squirming and whimpering man by his collar and drag him around to the so-called safe side. Armless Phouc moves over with me and kneels on the man's head as Cong and I tie his legs and arms. The guy has probably never felt so miserable in his life. Instant karma.

One by one, the three of us move up to the next and last statue. I quick-peek around the emaciated Buddha's shoulder to see that the man is lying twisted, though mostly on his belly. Blood seeps from a back wound. Rope not needed.

Mai runs up to help Viet. The Buddha in that row is laughing and in a mad mimic, so is Viet.

"Stay here," I tell the men. I dash over to Mai. "How's he doing?"

Mai was a nurse's assistant for a while a few years ago. "The bullet hit the calf muscle," she says looking down at an ugly bleeding hole, "but no come out. I want to get him out of here, but he wants to stay and watch the door. He insists."

"You sure, Viet?" Actually, it would be good if he could stay and cover the room.

"No set. Li-el hur," he says, repeating what he'd said earlier.

I look over at Cong and Phouc who are crouching with the tied-up man. Cong is tapping the butt of his knife on the bridge of the man's nose. Toying with him. I look back to Mai.

"How are you doing, Mai?" Her clothes are dusty from lying in the cement; her face flushed. We've witnessed four people die in the last half hour.

A mental image of the ocean flashes through my mind: tropical beach, white sand, gentle warm wind, Mai and I on a blanket. There are beautiful beaches somewhere in Vietnam; I saw photos online. Maybe we can go there when this is all over.

"I am okay. You?"

I look about the warehouse. "Let's get this done. Call Samuel and tell him that this side is secure. And ask what he wants us—" I jab my finger toward the small door near the corner. "Viet! Door!" I pull Mai down with me behind the Buddha.

Viet, still on his belly, raises his M-16 toward the back wall door that's no more than fifteen feet away.

It remains closed.

I peek around one side of the Buddha and Mai peeks around the other. "Sam, what is it?"

I blink rapidly and shake my head. "I don't know. I just... I just suddenly knew that the—"

The door swings open and slams against the wall and, for the next two seconds, everything moves as if it were a slow moving slide show.

A man with a rifle appears in the doorway. Young. Tan shorts. Red T-shirt.

Eyes searching. Scared.

Viet fires a deafening single round.

A hole appears over the man's right eye.

Red mist sprays from the side of his head.

His weapon fires a burst at the ceiling as he falls back into the other room.

His feet sprawl awkwardly in the doorway.

One foot spasms for a moment, stops.

Quiet. Except for that far off dripping.

*Drip… drip…*

\*

Viet remains in the prone, his rifle trained on the doorway. Kneeling now, Mai braces her gun arm against the side of the statue. Phouc and Cong crouch behind the emaciated Buddha that's just diagonal to the door, Cong aiming what looks like a carbine at the doorway. Must be the dead man's weapon.

My heart is beating so rapidly that my chest hurts. I take a deep breath to a count of four, hold it for a count of four, and exhale it for a count of four. I do it a couple more times until my heart rate slows and reduces my chance of blowing a heart gasket across the room.

How did I know about the door?

I signal everyone to stand fast and listen. I glance back at the other door, the one we all came through and the one the girls just went out. It's opened just enough that I can see the double doors of the beige warehouse a few feet away. It's raining again and now that I can see that, I can hear it on the roof. I guess my senses are picking and choosing what I need. That's a good thing.

Two dead on this side of the wall, one tied up, and one of us wounded. I haven't a clue what's happening on the other side, but with all the shots fired and with Samuel over there, who knows?

This is nuts. Never in my wildest imagination did I think I'd be involved in something like this.

Mai plunges her hand into her pants pocket and retrieves her phone. "Are you okay, Father?" she whispers desperately. She nods to me that he is. "Next to me," she says. "Okay. Yes, I will." She hands me the phone.

"Samuel?"

"Anyone hurt there?"

"Viet. Took one in his leg. But he's good to go. He took out the guy at the door. We have two enemy dead and—"

"Tell me later. This is the layout here. Just inside the door is an open area, fifteen feet by fifteen. That's where the guard by the door is lying. Looking straight ahead from there is a tan-colored wall. That is probably where the girls sleep and probably where they are now. Some of them. There might be more in a room of sorts on the right side of the building about halfway down. I can hear crying in there. To the right of the door where the dead man is are two rooms: an office and a kitchen. Phat Ho and I have cleared them and the three people in them are no longer a threat. We have also cleared a restroom where we first came in. The guard there is no longer a threat. That leaves the sleeping quarters and the other room for us to clear. There will likely be a threat in one or both places."

"Where are you now?"

"We are in the office looking out. We can see the door to the sleeping area and to the other room. I can also see the man Viet downed."

"Mai said she is sure that she shot someone."

"I know. But we don't know if there are other guards in the unknown room or how many are in the sleeping area other than the Khmer Rouge man. He ran inside after we exchanged shots."

Oh man.

"The best strategy is for us to wait outside these two doors, stall for time, talk them out. But I do not know if anyone has called Lai Van Tan. There may be reinforcements on the way. I want these kids out of here and us out of here as soon as possible."

"New rules."

"What?"

"Nothing." An old uniform partner used to say, "new rules," whenever a situation dictated that we threw out the procedural handbook. It was new rules when we entered the warehouse a while ago and it's new rules again.

"One more new rule," Samuel says. "You and I will go in the sleeping quarters unarmed. Too many friendlies there. Tell Mai that I want her and the others to go into the other room without guns. You disagree?"

"No."

The troops on the PD would say it's crazy, and it is. A cop never gives up his gun, even if a bad guy has the drop on him. Still, I agree with Samuel. There is no way I would go into that room with a firearm and I'm glad Samuel won't have one. As far as the old vets are concerned, they're good, but are they good enough and disciplined enough after all these years to control their emotions and their trigger finger in a room full of kids? I don't know and neither does anyone else.

"Good. We will improvise as we go along. Ready?"

"Expect us in two minutes."

I quickly fill Mai in on the conversation. She doesn't bat an eye when I tell her that Samuel says no guns.

"Put yours in your waistband," I say. I look over at Cong. "Unload and leave the Carbine in here. There are many children over there."

"Okay," he says without hesitation. "I have knives." He unloads the weapon, lays it down, and pockets the magazine.

"You okay?" I ask Viet.

He nods without looking away from the doorway. "Lek urts, ut I okay.

"We are going to go inside. You stay here and watch the door. Understand?" He nods. "That wall behind the man is where the children are. You understand?" He nods. "A bullet could penetrate it. Samuel and I will be in there. Understand?" He nods. "If you have to shoot, aim high. Head shot only. If you miss, the bullet will hit the ceiling, not go through the wall."

"I un-er-sand. Shoot like e-ore. Through head." His permanent smile seems a little larger.

"Yes, sir."

I move over to the wall next to the door and forcefully push out the thought of an AK round punching through my back. Mai joins me. Cong comes next followed by Phouc. Call us a poor man's SWAT stack. I make a curve in the air with my finger, indicating that we go around the door and to the right.

I look down at the dead man and the pool of blood haloing his head, his AK-47 lying across his chest.

"You familiar with that weapon?" I ask Mai.

"Yes."

"I'm not. Strip the mag and eject the round in the chamber as you pass."

"Yes."

I cut the pie around the door facing, which reveals the open area Samuel mentioned, and a sort of hallway between the room on the right and the one on the left. Samuel and Phat Ho are in one of the rooms to the extreme right. I curl around the door opening and move rapidly to the right until I see Samuel peeking around the door facing of the closest room. He moves aside so I can duck in. Phat Ho looks at me with dead-fish eyes. His arm stump is bleeding.

"Hurt?" I whisper. He shrugs.

"The Khmer Rouge man nicked him," Samuel says, watching Mai strip the AK. "But it is not his good arm."

Looks like we're in an office. Samuel said they took care of three people. They aren't in here so they must be in the kitchen. Mai slips in, followed by Cong.

As Phouc approaches, the door straight across from us opens and a soaking wet man steps out, along with the sound of rain spattering in water, a gush of humidity, and the rich smell of mud. He shuts the door before I can see in.

Without missing a beat, the armless Phouc whips a fast roundhouse punch with his right arm stump into the man's face, knocking him to the left. Before the guy completely loses his balance, he's hit with a left roundhouse stump that's even faster. That one knocks him upright. Phouc hooks his right foot behind the man's left foot, and head butts the hapless fellow's already bleeding nose. He falls back onto the cement with a splat.

Mai grabs the downed man's arms, drags him into the room with us, and pats him down for weapons.

She nods to her father. "He is—"

The man grabs Mai's leg and starts to pull himself up. I step in that direction just as Cong's hand snaps out at the man's leg and snaps back just as quickly, and at the same time Mai hits his face with a quick palm-heel strike. The guy lets out an awful scream and curls into a tight ball, his trembling hand reaching toward his bare, muddy foot.

Mai hit his nose, so why is he—

"He no get up now," Cong says, wiping his knife on the writhing man's pants. It takes me a second to understand that the guy isn't reacting to Mai's palm-heel strike. He's fussing about the muddy blood just above his heel, his Achilles' tendon. It's been sliced all the way through.

Phat Ho, a red scarf dangling from his hand, looks at it intently. This time Cong might have reacted quicker than the g*arrote* master, but I'm guessing there are bodies lying around this part of the warehouse with purple faces and protruding tongues; he has only one scarf left.

"Drag that man back into that corner," Samuel says to Cong and Mai. "Sam, we go now. Mai, secure that other room."

*

Samuel and I cross the open space to the door that leads into what we believe is the girls' sleeping quarters. I don't like dividing our manpower between two rooms. I'd prefer if we all went into this room, squared it away, and then all went into the mystery room. But that just isn't doable given the volatility of our situation and our small numbers.

Just as I think that entering the room without a firearm is another less than desirable tactic, albeit the best given the circumstances, which includes the necessity to act fast, and just as I wonder how we're going to do it—knock, charge in, call the gunman, or gunmen, out—the door opens a little and a set of eyes peer through the crack.

Samuel front kicks the door so fast that I see only a flash of his red Converse slamming it into the set of peepers. He slips through the opening before it bounces back off the man's skull and I rush in behind him in a low crouch.

*Bebebebe!*

I turtle my head against deafening gunshots and chunks of wood showering down on me. My peripheral vision detects a man to my left, about fifteen feet away, working desperately to clear a weapon jam. I start to rush him when something streaks over my head and whacks into the armed man's face. A shoe, Wingtip, redish-brown. The man yelps.

Screaming coming from somewhere in the room. Lots of it. Girls.

"Get him now, Son," Samuel says, in the same calm voice he used at dinner when suggesting that I try the spring rolls.

I lunge toward the gunman, who has now lowered his weapon and is covering his bloody mouth with his free hand. He raises the rifle, but I knock it aside with my closest forearm. Samuel's shoe-fu must have weakened the man's grip because the AK flies out of his hands and strikes the wall. When he lunges for it, I whip in a roundhouse kick to his gut, dropping him to his knees.

He looks to be in his fifties, dark skin, small stature, with lean, hard muscles wrapped in a dirty white T-shirt. He's got a

419

red and white checkered cloth wrapped around his neck. Got to be a Khmer Rouge guy.

I sense more than see Samuel rush by me.

I whip another roundhouse at the Khmer Rouge Man, this one at his face, but he bobs his head out of the way and catches my leg in his arms. He whips both of his arms in a circle, as if he were trying to manually turn an old airplane propeller. The action sends a shock of pain through my hips as I go airborne, horizontal with the floor, and spinning three sixty. I tuck my body hard and hit the cement on my butt. A shock wave of pain streaks up my spine, but at least I didn't land on my head. I'm terribly dizzy, though.

Kids. Girls. Screaming. Running by me.

I push myself up just in time for the man to scissor my neck with his legs. I try to grab them, but I'm wrenched off my butt and jerked forward into a somersault. I manage to tuck my chin into my chest, so the landing isn't bad, but my neck feels like a stretched, three-foot column of pain, including the spot where I got hit when Mai and I got jumped.

"*Vovinam*, Son!" I hear Samuel call out from the door. "Leg specialist. Do not fight his fight."

Advice is nice but help is better. Man, my neck hurts.

When I sit up, the man, now on his knees, grabs my right ankle and yanks it toward him, which slams me onto my back again. That hurt and this is getting old. How I long for soft mats.

My head fuzzies clear enough that I can see his ugly grimace—bleeding black teeth on top and a couple of dark ones on the bottom—and that he's about to crank my ankle until it breaks. It also occurs to me that the guy isn't trying all that hard to kill me. No, he's toying with me. That's just plain dumb and a whole lot mean.

I fast-scoot my butt toward him. "Eat this, pal," I say, chambering my free leg. My heel slams into his ugly mouth, which frees my caught foot and sends him sprawling. He sits up on his elbows and makes an even uglier face when he opens his mouth to release some of the blood that's pooling inside. Two of his top teeth are gone. Must have swallowed them. He shakes his head back and forth, spraying blood in the air like a hound dog's slobber.

I look over where his AK landed. Gone. Samuel must have picked it up. Where is he, anyway? I start to get up but Khmer Rouge Man jumps to his feet, lunges toward me and scoops up my right foot with one of his. Before he can do one of his *vovinam* tricks with my leg, I push myself toward him on my rear, chamber my free leg again, and ram my foot into his closest shin, impacting all the tender nerves just under the skin. He grimaces, drops my foot, and stumbles back.

I rock forward to come up into a squat, but the guy takes a fast, limping step toward me and launches himself into an aerial somersault to land butt-first on my chest, slamming me once again onto my back. Before I can process how amazing that move was, he begins wailing on me with his fists.

I do a double shield with my forearms to protect my face, though his blows are hurting my arms. After the fourth or fifth bone rattling hit, I see an opening between his shots, it's just his nose, but I'll take it. I thrust my right index finger deep into one of his nostrils, then whip my hand to the side. He's too busy screaming to notice me draw up my leg. I hip bump him off me and onto the floor.

On my feet now, I can see that Samuel is gone, as are the girls. The guy he force fed the door is squirming and trembling on the floor, his mouth silently opening and shutting like one of the *koi* back at the house. Whatever Samuel did to him is giving the man some kind of a seizure. He's also missing a Wingtip.

Khmer Rouge Man grabs my ankle with one hand, his other still covering his bleeding nose. Man, this guy has no off switch. I stomp his wrist with my other foot to shred his hand off my ankle. He spins around on the floor and tries to kick, missing me by three feet.

What do I do with this guy? I need to get out of this room, but I don't want to kill him and I don't want him to follow.

As if on cue, he removes his hand from his nose, and struggles to see through his pouring tears. He scoots toward me and tries to do a scissoring ankle trap, but falls short by a foot and a half. All those tears are affecting his depth perception. He pauses, his labored exhalations shooting blood out of his trashed nose. He's lying mostly on his right side, his right leg bent, his left lower leg resting on top making a little bridge. In its center, his kneecap.

If I think about it too long, I won't do it.

I lift my knee as high as I can, and slam all two hundred pounds of me down onto the bridge.

He loses consciousness before he can complete his scream.

I peek out the door. Samuel and the girls aren't in the hall. No one is. There's crying coming from the mystery room, at least two kids, maybe more. I look into the office to see if Samuel might have ushered the freed girls in there. Nope. Just the moaning man with the severed Achilles tendon. In the next room is a cooking stove, refrigerator, preparation counters, and three dead bodies. The purple-faced man was clearly the target of Phat Ho's *garrote*, and the other two, judging by how badly they have been mauled, tried to fight Samuel. A cleaver and two handguns lie on the floor next to the bodies.

He must have taken the girls outside. No doubt he's calling in the transport bus. I take a deep breath to oxygenate myself. I'd like to do more but there's no time. Hopefully, there will be later.

I step over to the door, push it open, and walk into hell.

# CHAPTER TWENTY

For a moment, my brain isn't computing what I'm seeing. It's a room of sorts, maybe twenty feet by fifteen, no roof, and the same metal walls as in the room of statues. The storm has turned the dirt floor into ankle-deep mud with pools of brown water fed by small running streams. The only light, an incongruously warm tungsten that falls across the mud, comes from the open door of a shack in the corner to my right. The structure looks to have been made with scrap wood, complete with a small window where someone, I'm assuming, can stay dry as they look out at the—

"Sam!"

The Buddha statues had been lined up in rows that were three across and three deep. In this room, there are three rows of... my God...

"Sam!

... heads. Each a young girl... protruding from the mud.

The room seems to tilt; I feel like I'm under water.

Four girls in the back two rows, only one in the first. Phat Ho and Cong are digging around the heads of two girls. Digging so... very... slowly. The rain... each silver drop falling... falling... falling so slowly... hitting the dirty water... the sound like gunshots... each one making a little geyser.

"Sam! Snap out of it."

Mai's voice. There, down on one knee, consoling three muddy, crying girls, her beautiful face filthy with the mud she desperately claws.

"Help us get the girls out of the earth, Sam. Quickly."

"I'm... not understa..."

Then, as if someone snapped their fingers, I'm back in real time: rain falling hard, Phat Ho and Cong digging madly with their hands, heads protruding from the ground, some crying, some silent. Mai stroking the head of a muddy girl.

"Yes," I say. "Yes, of course." I drop to my knees by the closest one. The poor thing can't be more than ten or twelve. She looks at me and screams, mud spraying from her mouth.

Mai speaks to her calmly, soothingly. The girl looks at her with eyes that are impossibly large, impossibly terrified. She's breathing hard, erratically. The pressure of the dirt on her overworked chest must be tremendous. She gags on mud and spits up on my digging hands. Mai says the same words to her again. Then two more times. The girl calms; her eyes never leave Mai's.

"I am going to move my girl out into the hallway," Mai says on her way to the door. Mine begins hyperventilating.

"It will be okay, sweetie," I say gently to her. "Look, I've cleared your shoulders. In just a moment your arms will be free." She looks down at my digging hands and back up at my face, tears rolling over her muddy cheeks. "I almost have your right arm out now. There. Okay, let's try." She pulls and I pull, and her arm releases from the mud's grip with a sucking sound. Her eyes look at me, the fear in them dissipating. I smile at her as I vigorously rub her thin limb to stimulate circulation.

Mai returns and lifts the second girl into her arms. The third one stands like a newborn fawn and, with a little support from Mai, walks with her on wobbly legs out the door.

My girl's left arm is free now. Her eyes smile, only a little, but I'll take it.

"*Xin*," says a thin, weak voice from a young girl in the next row back. Mai hurries back in, drops to her knees next to her, and begins digging hurriedly.

"What did she say?" I ask, hoping that once I free my girl's waist, I can pull her out.

"She said, 'please,'" Mai says, clawing the mud away from the girl's chin. I dig faster.

Cong sloshes by, a whimpering girl held tightly in his arms. He returns a moment later to begin digging out another.

"Where is the person you shot?"

"In that little house," Mai says. "He is not dead, but the bullet made it so he cannot move."

"And the snake?" I pull my girl by her armpits. She cries out. "Sorry, sweetie." I dig some more. "Almost there, almost there." She hasn't a clue what I'm saying, but I think my voice reassures her.

"The cobra is by the house." Mai frees one of the girl's arms. "Dead." When her girl begins crying, Mai whispers something that calms her a little.

Phat Ho, holding a muddy little girl in his one arm, moves by us heading for the door. I hear a vehicle just over the wall. Sounds like a bus.

The rain is coming down hard again so that every two scoops of mud I remove, one slithers back into the hole from the collapsing sides.

After a couple of minutes, my little friend and I try again, and this time her hips and legs slurp out. She's free and she's laughing. I lift her into my arms and carry her out into the hall. Phouc is there watching the girls.

"Bus come," he says. "Samuel take girls bus. Now he do same-same these girls."

I nod that I understand. I point at the garden door and hold up six fingers. "Six more."

"Yes," he says, squatting by my girl. She reaches out and touches one of his arm stumps. He smiles at her and looks up at me. "Okay. Get six more." He sits on the floor next to the girl.

I almost bump into Mai at the door. Her girl barely looks ten, her head hanging limply over Mai's arm.

I touch her face. "Is she…"

"She passed out. She smiled at me when I pulled her out and then went limp."

Phouc says something to Mai, holding out his stumps and crossing his legs. She lays the girl gently in his lap, and he holds her as best he can. The girl I dug out pats the unconscious girl's head.

Mai straightens and looks at me. "The man in the little house," she says, her beautiful eyes now as glassy as marbles. We look at each other for a long moment, her arms and legs dripping mud, my arms and bare chest covered with it. I know what she's thinking. In my head, I want to kill him too. But in my heart… no. And I know in her heart the answer is no as well.

I touch her arm. "Let's get the rest of the girls out of the ground and get them to that orphanage."

The coldness in her eyes dissolves as does some of the tension in her body. "Yes… Yes."

For the next several minutes, the four of us dig frantically to extract the last girls. Four are so weak and stiff that we have to carry them out; two are able to walk with our help. By the time we get the last one out, the rain is crashing to the ground so hard that the puddles from that downpour are overflowing and feeding streams that zigzag around the now empty holes. Three holes on one side are nearly full of water. It's a miracle that some of the girls didn't drown or choke to death on the moving mud.

Out in the hall, Mai sends Phouc to tell Samuel that we're ready to move the rest of them out. I cross over to the doorway where the man with the AK-47 is sprawled.

"Viet?" I call out, keeping my body behind the door facing. "It's Sam."

"Saa?"

"All is okay over here. I'm stepping into the doorway, okay? Don't shoot."

"Yes, no shoot."

I move into the opening, feeling a little naked. Viet leans his smiling face out from behind a Buddha statue, his gun barrel off to the side.

"You okay?" I ask,

"I enn etter."

I think he said I've been better. Ain't that the truth. "Everything is okay on this side. You understand?"

"Yes."

"Watch that backdoor and we will come get you when we load the rest of the girls into the bus."

"You ut girls on us and get e."

"Yes, we'll get you after we get them on the bus. You are a great soldier, Viet."

"*Cảm ơn.* You same."

"Can I have my shirt back?"

"No."

I give him a thumbs up. He returns the gesture, his "smile" ever present.

*

The rain is coming down hard enough that it's washing much of the mud off my bare shoulders, back, and arms as I help carry the girls to the bright red bus. Although only five of us are able-bodied enough to do the task, we still get everyone loaded in quickly.

When Mai and I go back to get Viet, we find him still lying in the prone watching the door, his face white as rice.

"Viet? How are you?" I ask, kneeling by his shoulder. There's a substantial pool of blood around his lower leg.

"He loosened your T-shirt," Mai says, retying it. "There. I tied it good around the bullet hole."

She says something to him that sounds like a scold. His barely audible response shocks Mai.

"No!" she practically shouts.

"What, Mai?"

She shakes her head. "He say he want to… I do not know the English word. Like bleed a lot. Bleed over"

"Bleed out, you mean?"

Viet speaks to her for a long moment, his words making her shake her head with disbelief. When he stops, she looks at me, her eyes glistening.

"Viet say that he must have had much bad karma in a life before… a previous life, because he has been punished too much in this one. Now there is a bullet in the only part of his body that is good. He say it is better that he die to end the karma, end *dukkha*, suffering."

"We need to get him to a doctor quickly. The pain and the blood loss is messing with his mind."

"Yes," Mai says. "Take his other arm so we can get him up on his crutch."

I remember when I was recouping from a broken knee, every pain receptor in my leg screamed in protest anytime I stood after sitting for a while.

"Viet," I say in an attempt to distract him as we get him up. "Mai, please translate what I'm saying." She nods. "Viet, you are a great soldier. I am sorry you had to shoot that man, but you saved my life, and Mai's, Cong's, and Phouc's."

We wrap his arms around our shoulders and support as much of the slight man's weight as we can. His injured leg trembles as he struggles to hold the foot off the floor and shift his weight to the half crutch. His moaning makes my knee hurt. Mai and I take a step, then wait as he drags his crutch up even with us. We do it again and again as we move toward the door. I continue with Mai translating.

"By stopping that man, you allowed us to go into the other part of the warehouse and rescue those poor girls. You are the true hero today. You earned much good karma by helping the rest of us." Mai smiles warmly at me. By the time she finishes translating, we're at the door.

Cong is already waiting with the van and is sliding open the side door. Happily, the rain has stopped. After we manage to get Viet in the back seat, Mai checks that my T-shirt is still secure over his calf wound. When I look up from watching her work, I find Viet looking at me, his eyes smiling as well as his frozen mouth. When I take his extended hand, he covers it with his other one.

"Sam, number one," he says.

The big bus lumbers to a stop next to us, the double doors swing open, and Samuel steps out, his shirt muddy from carrying the girls. A heavy-set woman sits behind the wheel, her eyes looking up at her mirror, scanning the girls in the back.

"*Chào* Chi," Mai greets the woman, who waves back at her.

"We need to get going," Samuel says. "All but two of the girls are on board; the men too. Cong will take you down to the

Volvo. Then we will take all of the girls to the orphanage and get them settled. Chi says they have medical supplies so Mai you can help the injured."

"I will, Father."

"You two okay?" he asks.

We nod. I'm not sure what to say about the experience so I don't say anything.

"I doubt if they have a shirt that will fit you at the orphanage, Sam," he says.

I shrug. "Maybe a small blanket or something."

Samuel looks in the van. "Viet?" The smiling man gives Samuel a thumbs up. He's regained some of his color.

"Okay," Samuel says. "Meet you at the Volvo."

After Mai and I squeeze into the front seat, Cong drives down to where the car is parked. I'm not sure what I expected to find there, but for sure I didn't think I'd see the girls we rescued from the statue room sitting on Dung's big shoulders as he sings and dances about on the gravel, a rough ride, given his gimpy leg. The girls are having a blast. Even mine who had been in shock earlier is laughing uproariously, her hands clutching the big man's head the same way she would if she were riding a water buffalo, which they sort of are.

Samuel is laughing as he steps out of the bus. "Mai, Sam, I think you have lost your passenger for a while." He speaks to Dung and the big man moves over to the bus where Mai and her father help the girls down. "Okay," he says. "The orphanage is about twenty minutes from here. The bus will lead, then the van, then you two. Watch all sides to see if we are being followed. Call me if you see anything and I will do the same."

Just after we leave the warehouse area, a pickup and a motorbike pull in behind us and follow close for three or four minutes until the truck makes a left onto a side street, and a minute later the motorbike takes a right. It's close to midnight as we drive through Bien Hoa proper, so traffic is light and the sidewalks are sparse with only the occasional food stand in operation. Mai and I must look like two nervous chickens as we jerk our heads about, watching our mirrors and looking out windows.

After driving through a residential area for a couple of minutes, we turn into a tree-lined courtyard that is several times larger than the one at the soldiers' home. The orphanage is a rectangular structure of plaster and wood covered with beige paint. Colorful flowers and cartoon animals have been painted over the front wall and door. Mai says she heard that during the war, the American Army used the structure for clerical operations. Twenty years later, around nineteen ninety-five, Chi and her husband, Danh, acquired and remodeled it to serve as an orphanage for as many as forty-five homeless kids at a time. Sadly, they've never lacked for occupants.

Chi is quite the earth mother. She directs all the males to go around to the other side of the building with her husband, Danh, and rinse off with a garden hose. Armless Phouc, the cleanest of us, does guard duty out on the sidewalk. Mai and the dozen girls who had been buried in the garden stay in front to clean off with another hose, and the rest who are not dirty are directed inside to get some food. All the girls, even those from the garden, are in amazing spirits considering what they had been through before our rescue, and during it.

Dung helps Cong and Phat Ho rinse off first, with Cong stripping all the way naked. When it's my turn, Phat Ho, the *garrote* master who took an instant dislike to me, takes the hose from Dung and pins it under his stump. He cants his body right and left so the water pours over all of my bare torso while he wipes the caked mud off with his hand, being especially careful when washing around the abrasions on my stomach and back. The ones on my front I got when low crawling over to the girl behind the Buddha and those on my back I got fighting Khmer Rouge Man.

I point at the dried blood on his T-shirt sleeve. Samuel said his stump had been grazed by a bullet. He shrugs and keeps washing. About a minute later he stops, and moves his eyes up to mine. He's not looking at me with disdain, as he did when we met at the soldiers' home.

"He say in bus, he think you good fighter," Cong says, ladling water over his head from a wooden barrel.

Really? "Cong, please tell him that he is a great warrior."

Phat Ho listens to Cong, then looks away, nodding almost imperceptibly. When he looks back at me, there is no pride in his face from the compliment. Instead, I see sadness, the kind that comes from carrying a great burden. My gut tells me that he might be good at killing, but he doesn't like doing it.

It's been over thirty-five years since all of these old soldiers have had to fight, to kill. But how quickly it came back to them. Men with one arm gone, two arms gone, half a leg gone. They had a mission tonight, a rescue that no one else was going to do. So they did it and they did it well, and they didn't let their so-called handicaps slow them down even a little.

By the time we're cleaned up and move around to the front, all the girls are inside eating and finding their beds. Mai, her face and arms clean but her jeans and top filthy, is in the van tending to Viet's leg wound. She said the bullet might have struck a bone and that a regular doctor who tends to the soldiers' home will look at it after they get back. She gave Viet three Tylenol for his pain. Who knew? Get shot in the leg, take an over-the-counter pain pill. He's smiling.

Mai checked Phat Ho's stump and confirmed it a graze. She put antiseptic on it and a large bandage. She also dabbed antiseptic here and there on my scrapes and applied small bandages on two of them. Danh brought out a red T-shirt that he found inside. He said it belonged to a worker, an especially heavy-set man. I manage to wrestle it on though it's a size small for me.

When we first pulled into the courtyard, Samuel went straight into the house. He's out on the porch now looking grim.

"Father?" Mai says.

He moves down the stairs. "We need to get back. I just talked to Phong Tran. He said that Lai Van Tan just got word of what happened at the warehouse and he is on a rampage. He stabbed a man who is in charge of the sex-trafficking side of their organization, and he threatened to shoot someone else. We need to get back to our house now. Tex said everything is okay there, but that could change in an instant."

# CHAPTER TWENTY-ONE

It's one in the morning and we're moving fast down the highway back to Saigon, passing the occasional truck and motorbike. Samuel again leads in his van with Mai, Dung, and me following in the Volvo. At fifty miles per hour in this light traffic, we should get back into the city in thirty-five minutes or so. Mai and I haven't said much to each other in the ten minutes we've been on the road. It's not an uncomfortable silence, just one that I think we both need for a few moments.

The warehouse was the stuff of future nightmares. I'll never look at Buddha statues the same way, and I will certainly never think of that awful mud room, that… that "garden" and think of tomatoes and peas.

How many people were killed? Two outside the warehouse, two in the statue room, one in the doorway, three in the kitchen, and I don't know how many Samuel and Phat Ho had to remove to reach the girls.

This would be a monstrous news event back home. Here, I don't know. It will be news, but what kind of an investigation will it get? Will my involvement, Samuel's, Mai's, and the troops' be discovered? Will those left alive tell? Do they even know who we are?

Thank God I didn't have to kill again.

"Tell me what you are thinking, Sam."

"I'm thinking we both need showers."

"Want to save water?"

I laugh. "You know what that means, huh?"

"I saw that on a poster or something at the university," Mai says smiling. "I have not thought about it until now." She looks at me. "But that is not what you were thinking, right?"

The lights of Saigon are a glow in the night sky ahead of us. Out my side window I can just barely discern the sensuous curves of distant hills. How awful it must have been to have been a soldier—American and Vietnamese—crawling around out there in the absolute darkness. Snakes, mines, bugs, tracer rounds, shit-covered punji sticks, wild animals. Fear. Death.

I look at Mai. "I was thinking that as bad as it was at the warehouse, we accomplished our objective with minimum injury to us."

She doesn't say anything for a moment. Then, following a long exhalation, she says, "It will be in my mind forever."

Big Dung is fast asleep in the back, his mouth open, his head slumped against the window. I reach for Mai's hand. "Mine too."

Oh what power there is in the simple act of holding her hand. Our two palms pressed together, the pad of my thumb idly caressing the back of hers, her index finger rubbing the back of my hand. How can such a small area of contact be so comforting?

"Those girls are free now," I say, looking out at the night. "They're clean, and fed. An hour after they were freed, they were carrying on like kids."

"Yes, but they will suffer in their heads, some of them for all their lives. I feel good that we got them out, but I feel bad that it was just a… drop in the bucket."

"A glass of water out of the ocean?"

"Yes."

"You know, young cops come on the job with big ambitions about saving the world. They discover quickly, though, that it isn't going to happen. They arrest this rapist, and there are ten thousand more of them out there hurting people. They bust this dope dealer, and there are a hundred thousand more running free. They save this troubled kid, while a million more are getting into trouble. As the young cops get older, they're happy to get what they can. They feel good about the one kid they can save. They feel good about the one drug dealer they get off the street. They've come to realize that it's all about the one drop in the bucket because every little drop is important."

Mai doesn't say anything for a long moment. "Thank you," she says softly.

"No charge," I say, lightly bumping her shoulder with mine. I look back to see if Dung saw that. He's still sleeping.

"That warehouse was so horrible," Mai says. "Sex trafficking, the way it destroys girls lives, has always angered me. I have always wanted to do something to fight it. But I did not know what to do because it is a big secret here, a secret crime with many people making huge profits off the girls, off their suffering. I am sad and angry that our government does little to fight it. And now that I have seen it, uh, close…"

She shakes her head as if trying to rid the image from her mind or maybe put it into some kind of framework. "The garden was terrible, but I think that if those girls had been sent off to other countries… to men… it would have been even worse for them. I wanted to shoot the one with the knife who tried to stab Cong and me. I wanted to shoot the one in the doorway. I wanted to beat the one that Phouc fought, beat him to death. I wanted to kill the one in the shack. I wanted to watch their evil lives end, watch it leave their eyes."

Mai is squeezing my hand so hard it's hurting my little finger. I can't tell her it's wrong to have such thoughts because

I've had them. About ten years ago, I investigated a child abuse case that was so abusive, so cruel, so traumatic that the little boy stopped growing for two years. When we went to arrest the vile stepfather, he glanced toward the corner of the living room where a shotgun leaned against a small table. Instead of going over and securing the weapon, I moved aside so he had an unobstructed path to it. Maybe he saw the look in my eyes that I wanted him to go for it, because he didn't, which is why he still lives. And why I have one less killing on my soul.

I say, "Maybe the closer you are to evil, especially when the victims are children, the more you're tempted to do evil back." I shrug. "Does this make us bad people? I like to think not, but I'm not sure. 'Vengeance is mine, sayeth the Lord,' and all that."

"But what if the Lord is busy? I did not see him at the warehouse."

"Maybe he sent us there," I say, not sure if I'm arguing with her or trying to convince myself.

"And because he is so busy, maybe he would want us to kill those men to keep them from ever hurting another child. Do you think he works that way?"

I shrug. "What would Samuel say?"

"He would probably quote Gandhi. Something like 'An eye for eye ends up making the whole world blind.'"

"Nice one."

"But Buddha, Gandhi, and God didn't keep the girls out of the garden or would they have kept them from being sent to a life of hell in Cambodia."

I shrug. "Religion! All I know for sure is that the older I get the more questions I have and the more confused I get."

Mai exhales a long breath. "I do not know either, Sam. I just know how I felt. I am sure that in a day or two I will be glad that I did not take anyone's life. But right now…"

After a couple minutes of silence I bump her shoulder again. "Right now maybe we shouldn't overthink it. We did some good and the girls are safe. Let's think about that."

"Okay."

We drive in silence again. Mai's crushing grip on my hand lessens with each passing minute until once more it feels warm and wonderful.

"Sam?"

"Yes?"

"Do you think we will fall in love?"

I sputter a laugh. "Wow, that came out of left field."

"Left field?"

"Baseball reference."

"You want to talk baseball?"

"Uh, no. I don't follow it anyway."

"So?"

"You and your mother never beat around the bush, do you?"

"Beat around the—"

"Just another saying."

"You want to talk about bushes?"

"No!" I say loudly.

"Why are you getting mad at me, Sam?" We're still holding hands.

"I'm not getting mad. I just—"

"So what is your answer?"

"Yes! Yes, I think we will fall in love." I have already.

\*

The van's taillights suddenly brighten and Mai brakes sharply to keep from rear ending it.

"What's going on?" I ask.

"I see lights ahead, all over the place." She turns out into the oncoming lane a little, then jerks the wheel back as a motorbike in the oncoming lane whizzes by us, its shrill horn blaring. "Accident, I think."

We slow for a few seconds, then stop. Another motorbike goes by in the oncoming lane and two that have been following us, putter around each side of our car. The one on the left zips between us and the van, and follows the other bike down the shoulder.

"We do not need this right now," Mai says. "I hope no one is hurt here but we need to get back."

I lean out my window. "The motorbikes got around it okay. Maybe it's just a matter of a few minutes until we can get going."

Mai gets out and steps over into the oncoming lane.

"It is a truck up ahead," she calls out. "About five cars in front of us. The truck crashed; it is on its side. The cars coming this way have stopped too."

"Mai?" Dung calls out, leaning forward to see out her door. She speaks soothingly to him, and he leans back and closes his eyes.

I walk over to her. It's the truck trailer that's on its side, the cab tilted about half way over, the tires on the driver's side in the air. Unless it hit something or someone, I'm guessing there are no injuries.

Just as I start to wonder if Samuel is still in the van, I see him up by the truck trailer, illuminated by headlights as he walks back. "No one hurt," he says as he nears. "But the lanes are blocked. It looks like we can get around the right shoulder as soon as they get the gawkers out of the way."

"Glad no one is hurt," I say. I've seen more than my share of fatal traffic accidents, and we've all been around enough pain and death for one night.

"Mai, would you mind driving the van, and I will take the car so Sam and I can talk a little?"

"I will," she says, with a tad of disappointment in her face. "I think Dung is asleep so he should be okay."

"I do not like this delay," Samuel says after we're back in the car. "We need to get back."

"You think an attack on the house is an absolute now?"

He doesn't answer for a moment, then, "I did not like leaving Tex and the boy at the house, but it was the safest of two bad options. Sending them outside the walls would have been worse. If I had taken Bobby to a friend's house and Lai Van Tan's people followed us, they could have gotten to the boy and exposed my friend to danger, as well. I could have left a guard at my friend's house but that would been one less at my house."

Samuel has obviously been thinking about this and now he's second guessing himself. "I think your decision was the only one. The third option would have been for us not to have left the house at all and just let the twenty-seven girls go to their awful fate."

"True, but I left a young boy at a place that might be a target."

"*Might*," I say. "And we saved twenty-seven that were *definitely* a target. Look, you talked earlier about warriors doing the right thing. That is what you did. You got people watching and guarding the outside of the house, you got security monitors inside, weapons inside, and a safe room under my bed."

He knows all this, but maybe he needs to hear it said aloud. We all need assurance from time to time, I guess even Samuel. When he doesn't say anything, I continue.

"When I worked uniform, I rode with an ex-Navy Seal for a while. He posed this situation to make me think. Say you're driving an empty bus on a single-lane dirt road high on the side of a dangerous mountain when suddenly the brakes go out. As you come careening around a sharp curve, you see a toddler standing in the middle of the road. A little boy. What would you do? The warrior answer is that you would crank the steering wheel away from the kid and drive over the side of the cliff. You would die, so the boy could live.

"Let's say you're driving that same clunker of a bus and the brakes go out again. This time you got a load of kids riding in the back. You round that dangerous curve and there's that little guy standing directly in your path. What do you do? Do you drive a bus full of people off the cliff to save the one? A warrior makes the tough decisions. If it were me, I'd run over the toddler so that the bus load of kids could live."

Samuel guides the car around the tipped over trailer and begins to accelerate before he speaks. "Thank you, Son. It is not an easy choice, even after you have made it."

"For sure."

"After the war ended, I hoped that I would never have to face a gun again and that I would never have to kill again. I truly believe that every life is precious, you see. But as you well know, life has a way of taking us on journeys that we don't plan. Like your bus driver, we who have chosen the warrior way, or have had it chosen for us, must be forever ready for potholes, stones, and the dangerous curves life puts in our path."

"I agree," I say. "But let me ask you this. Does that mean we can never remove ourselves from the way of the warrior? Don't you want to retire in that sleepy ocean side village you told me about? For me, I no longer want to live a warrior's life. I don't know what I want to do instead, but whatever it is, I want a peaceful existence. I'm not even sure where I want to live. Back in Portland? Here, maybe? Could I live here in Vietnam? Judging by the last week, no."

Samuel smiles at that and so do I.

"I think that would be wonderful if you decided to stay here, Son. During that violent week in Portland, you told Mai and me not to judge your life by that week. I can say the same thing about the past few days here. My family's life was quite peaceful before Lai Van Tan sent his son and his henchman to harm me."

I look out the side window at the darkness. My stomach and chest burn where I scraped myself on the cement in the warehouse. My mind flashes to the back door where the guy with the AK-47 tried to come in.

"Speaking of unpredictable events," I say. "When we were in the room with all the Buddhas, I got this feeling… No, not a feeling, it was more like I suddenly knew that the gunman was going to open the little door." I look at Samuel's face, the passing headlights strobing off his features. "I *knew* it was going to open." His eyebrows bob once. "You told me, didn't you? Mentally, I mean. You saw the guy heading toward the door or something and you sent me—"

"Buddha said we are all interconnected. Faster than instant messaging, no?"

Oh man. I mean, oh man!

"Much for us to explore, Son. Right now we are about to enter the city limits. You and I will get back to the house, and

Mai will return to the soldiers' home and drop off Viet and Phat Ho so the *bác sĩ*, excuse me, the doctor can look them over. Then she will bring Cong and Phouc back to the house to help provide security. Thankfully it is the middle of the night and the traffic is light. Let me call Mai."

The streets are brilliantly lit, but most of the storefronts are closed, their roll-down doors in place. There seems to be a lot of people sleeping outside. Some are camped against the closed shop doors, some in hammocks slung between two vehicles, and still others are curled up under trees that line the boulevards.

As our two vehicles rip through the near empty streets with the occasional red light stopping us, Samuel tells Mai that he got a hold of the doctor when we were at the orphanage and he will meet her at the home. After she drops off the injured Viet, she is to bring the other two men with her to the house. At the intersection, she hangs a left and Samuel and I continue on.

"The home is not far from here," he says. "But my house is on the other side of the city. Fortunately, the traffic will be light for another two hours or so." He glances at me. "Tired?"

"Not really. It's been a pretty relaxing day."

"Like a walk in the park. That still a saying?"

I smile. "A little dated, but it still works."

"I need to call Tex," he says. "Tell him we are coming in."

\*

Samuel closes his phone and sets it on his lap. "Tex says all is well at the house. He had a quiet evening with the boy and they trained a little. He said Bobby loved the tunnel and wanted to sleep down there. That is where the lad is now. My friend is going to miss him when he leaves."

I chuckle. "Canyon Bob, you mean?"

I expect a smile out of Samuel, but he frowns. "Back in about nineteen sixty-five when the war was gathering steam, Tex was a teenager living with his mother, father, and three sisters in a home just outside of *Cholon*, the Chinese section of Saigon. One night the Viet Cong came to his home and told the family that they would have to work for them, gathering intelligence and feeding people who passed through, people working the underground for the North. Tex's father was a big, burly man by Vietnamese standards and he refused them.

"The father was very loyal to the Saigon government, in fact, he worked for them. On the surface, he was half owner in an ice distribution company, but unknown to his family and probably the Viet Cong, he occasionally supplied the South Vietnamese Army with information about suspicious people in the community. Even when the Viet Cong threatened the father, he still refused to do as they commanded him. Tex says that his father was a stubborn man; he would never be a double agent. The Viet Cong were angry but they left without further ado. Two days later, they came back, two of them, and again he refused. In fact, he became angry and overpowered them, disarmed them, and threw them out of the house into the night.

"Some days later, Tex was away visiting a friend when a crying little girl, about ten years old or so, came to his family's house. It was raining and Tex's mother put her arm around the little girl's shoulders and guided her inside, probably to dry her off and give her some food. About a minute later, the house went up in a huge explosion. Everyone died, the father, mother, three sisters, and the little girl. Even a neighbor man who was parking his pedicab died."

"Oh man! The VC rigged the little girl with an explosive device? Like they do in the Middle East?"

Samuel nods. "Yes. The neighbors said she was wearing a big coat, an adult's coat, big enough to conceal something. There was quite a bit of that sort of terrorism during the war. How much? Who knows? I doubt if anyone kept records, and if they did, they were probably lost or destroyed when the North swept in. There were lots of stories about kids walking up to American and South Vietnamese vehicles under the ruse of talking to the soldiers inside. While some kids distracted the occupants, another would drop a grenade into the gas tank. The pin had been pulled, you see, but tape had been wrapped around the handle. After a few days, the gasoline ate through the tape and the grenade exploded taking anyone and everyone who had the misfortune of being in the vehicle that day. Tex witnessed that happen twice during the war. Even his uncle, his father's older brother, was a victim. Fortunately, Tex did not see that happen.

"Here in Saigon, little street urchins would go up to GIs in bars or on the street and ask to give them a boot shine. When the troop would put his foot on a shoeshine box, which had been wired with explosives, the box would explode and the GI would lose his leg. He would be lucky if that was all. Tex saw that happen in Cu Chi to his sergeant."

"That's insane," I manage. "Would the little kid know?"

Samuel shrugs. "My point telling you these awful things is that Tex told me that because he was around so much of this during the war, he developed a paranoia."

"About kids?"

"Yes. He said that snipers, rocket attacks, and the VC did not bother him as much as the sight of a kid. Strange, no? He told me he would start shaking and sweating whenever one was near. I think his paranoia finally passed twenty years ago or so, or maybe it just became manageable. I do not know for sure because we have not talked about it in a long time. This is why I am happy that he likes Bobby."

"I'm glad he does. I liked the boy within a couple minutes of meeting him. Maybe Tex picked up on whatever that quality is that he has."

"Whatever it is, he has been good for my friend." Samuel guides the car around a large traffic circle and takes a side street to the right. "Okay, we are almost at the house. I am going to check on Mai and see how she is doing. I will feel better when she and the boys are all back." Just as he lifts his phone, it rings. "Oh, Mai? I was just going to—"

Samuel's smile disappears. "When?" His face suddenly hardens, his eyes blaze. The fluctuating lights and shadows bouncing off of his profile add a theatrical touch to the intensity of his expression. "Where are you now?" he asks, his voice tight. "Alright. Go to the store, and take Cong and Phouc with you."

"What is it?" I ask.

Samuel holds up an index finger. "Okay," he says to Mai. "If he is up to it then let him come. But don't let any of them take firearms. Yes. We are on our way."

Samuel begins accelerating, his hands white knuckling the wheel. "What's going on?" I ask. "Is Mai at the soldiers' home?"

"She got a call. Our jewelry store on *Phạm Ngũ Lão* street… " He takes a corner fast, then gooses the car even faster down an empty two-lane street.

"What happened? Isn't that the one that Mai and I went to the other day? A woman ran it, uh, Do`a."

"Do`a was beaten."

"Beaten. How? I mean, it's three a.m. Why was she at the store this time of night?"

"She lives in the back of the business; many people do that. She was closing the big door about eight o'clock tonight when three men forced their way in and beat her. She was unconscious for a long time."

"Will she be okay?"

"She is hurt badly. She could not call until just a few minutes ago. Mai called an ambulance and the police."

Samuel screeches around another corner, nearly clipping a parked truck. I'm glad that there is no traffic right now because if it were congested, we would be leaving a wake of destruction.

"Robbery?"

"I did not ask. But I know it is Lai Van Tan."

# CHAPTER TWENTY-TWO

*Phạm Ngũ Lão* street is not the festive carnival it was the last time I was here. It was the middle of the day then, but now the street is virtually empty except for a white van with large universal red crosses on its front and sides, and a red light strobing on its roof. A white police car and a police motorbike are parked next to it, their lights flashing. Nine or ten rubberneckers have gathered to watch what's going on.

Mai is a few seconds ahead of us and stops the van in the middle of the street. She's out the door in an instant, followed by Cong, Phat Ho, and Phuoc. The three troops take up sentry positions on the street and sidewalk, their backs to the jewelry store. They must be thinking of Lai Van Tan. Reminds me of how street gang officers set up a perimeter when another gang enforcement patrol unit stops a gangbanger's car. Samuel is out of ours almost before he shuts off the engine and I'm close behind.

Do`a lay on a gurney, her neck in a brace, her torso strapped in snuggly. Her cheek and lips are swollen, there's blood around her mouth, and a little trickling from the one ear I can see. Samuel says something to the two men about to lift her into the ambulance. They nod and step back, allowing Mai and Samuel to move up on each side of the woman. Samuel speaks first, touching Do`a's arm as Mai takes hold of her hand. The injured woman's words come slowly and painfully.

The big pull-down door is about half way up and the lock mechanism doesn't appear damaged. The lights are on inside and I'm not seeing broken glass or smashed counters, which would indicate that the thieves didn't do a smash and grab. Maybe it was an armed robbery? I look back at Do`a. She's in bad shape; the blood trickling from her ear could be an indication of a concussion.

Mai walks over a few minutes later. Behind her, Samuel is talking with an officer. "Is Do`a going to be okay?" I ask.

She exhales and shakes her head as if to rid herself of her anger. "I think so. She said two men forced their way in just as she was lowering the big door. One man beat her in the head until she was knocked out. But the men did not rob us. They only wanted to hurt her."

"Maybe someone scared them off," I suggest, watching Samuel lock the big door.

She shrugs.

The ambulance pulls away, its red lights pulsing down the street.

"Did she describe the men?" I ask.

"Only one. He was quite tall and his head was shaved bald. She said he was not old, but his face was broken, like a fighter's."

"Good description. I hope we can add to the damage."

"Yes," Mai says under her breath.

"I locked the big door," Samuel says, walking up. "I called Hoa and told her to come here in the morning and check the inventory. Then go home. I do not want her here very long by herself."

"Are we done, Father?" Mai asks, as if fighting to restrain herself.

He gestures for us to head to the vehicles. "Yes. Let Dung ride with you, daughter. He wants to be with you."

"No problem," she says, heading over to the Volvo to get the big man.

Samuel shakes his head. "Do`a is a special friend," he says. "She is part of our family and has been for many years." His face is tight, as if his features are crowding together. I have yet to see him show anger, but he has got to be boiling over inside. I wonder if sometimes too much self-control can be bad. It's called venting for a reason.

Mai walks Dung over to the van, helps him inside, and slides the door shut. "We go to our house now, Father?"

"Yes. We need to get moving. I do not know what this attack on Do`a means, but I have my suspicions. I called Tex a few moments ago and told him—"

The *Superman* theme emanates from Samuel's pocket. So far, none of tonight's incoming phone calls have brought good news.

"Doctor," Mai whispers after listening to Samuel for a moment.

"At the home?" I ask.

She nods.

Samuel snaps the phone shut his face drained of all color.

"They attacked the home," he says. "Viet is dead."

*

Samuel calls out to the guys watching the street and they all head toward the van.

"Wait here," he says to Mai and me. He moves over to speak to the officers for a moment, then heads back. "The soldiers' home is between here and our house," he says, machine gunning the words out. "The *canh sáts* will follow us over and call for more officers to meet us there."

"What happened, Father?"

"We need to move. I will call you from the car."

We form a small and desperate train careening through the increasing traffic of the predawn streets. We're behind a police car, its lights and siren going, and the van is behind us. Samuel taps in Mai's number.

"It is happening the way I feared," he says. "Earlier, I was remembering that Lai Van Tan was involved in the *Tet* Offensive in nineteen sixty-eight. He was part of the planning, or he commanded a North Vietnamese unit. I do not remember for sure." He looks over at me. "*Tet*, is our New Years. During *Tet* of '68, the North Vietnamese simultaneously attacked cities, towns, hamlets, and American military installations all over the South. I think Lai Van is trying to do that to us. He attacked the jewelry store earlier and waited until we got there to attack the soldiers' home. If I'm right, and I think I am, he will attack our house very soon."

Mai growls something in Vietnamese over the cell's speakerphone. Curse words, I'm sure, several of them. Now I think she's crying.

"What is happening, Father? Why is this bastard doing this to everyone we love?"

"Psychological warfare," Samuel says. "He is trying to shock us, instill fear in us, confuse our thinking."

"He's screwing with our minds while hitting us physically," I say unnecessarily.

Samuel nods, his lips tightly pressed together.

"He would be happy to know that it is working on me," Mai says angrily.

No one speaks. The air between us is choked with our rage and fear for loved ones. Samuel continues his mad race on the near empty streets, desperate to keep up with the speeding police car, and almost gives me a coronary when he takes one corner so fast we nearly roll over.

Then he says, "Fight it, Mai. Fight it."

I look at the hard edges of Samuel's determined profile in the fluctuating street lights. No psychological babble for him. No warm kitty hug. Just suck it up and fight it.

When Mai doesn't respond, I ask, "Why do you think Lai Van Tan will hit your home, especially right now? If he knows we were just at the jewelry store, he must know that we heard about Viet and we're on our way to the soldiers' place. So he knows we aren't at the house. Tex and Bobby are, but Lai Van Tan might not know that and think it's empty."

"Lai Van Tan knows that house is not our real home," Samuel says. "He knows we moved there out of necessity to find temporary refuge and protection. He knows I moved my daughter there, my wife, and my dear friend Tex to keep them safe. Now you are there. He knows all this, and he knows that all of you, and my other daughters are most precious to me, more precious than my own life. So even if the house were empty, and I think he knows that someone is there now, his people invading it, ransacking it, burning it, would deliver a powerful psychological blow to us. It would show that we are not safe anywhere and that he can harm us anytime he chooses."

Many burglary victims have told me that knowing someone evil had invaded their homes, touched their belongings, defiled the objects that formed their personal lives, and stolen their most precious possessions, was a psychological rape.

"Absolutely," Samuel says.

I ask, "Is it too late to call Tex and tell him to get the boy and the two monitor guys out of there? The outside guys could watch for—"

"That is the worst of two bad options, Son. I would rather deal with this within those walls. I am sure he has had people watching the place, our movements. He does not know who Bobby is but he would assume that he is someone important to us. He could easily have the boy and Tex followed, then attack them when they are most vulnerable. Other people could get hurt as well. No, I want to deal with this from a solid position. He might believe that there is strong psychological power in attacking all that is dear to me, but he fails to factor in the greater psychological power of defending one's turf."

His phone chirps. "I no longer like this thing," he says. "Mai, I have an incoming call. I will call you back." He clicks her off and retrieves the new one, which is still on speaker. The caller's tone is calm, his words measured; professional. Samuel listens, frowns. Two minutes later, he snaps his phone shut and white knuckles the steering wheel.

*

"What's the bad news," I ask.

"Just a second." He speed dials Mai.

"What now, Father?"

"Our store on *Pham Ngoc Thach* Road was hit about a half hour before Do`a was beaten. Our good friend Nguyen Duy Hai who lives in the back was also attacked, beaten."

"Bastards!" Mai shouts. "Is he okay?"

"He received a bad head injury, but the officer, who called me, said he will be fine."

"Are we going there?" I ask, wondering if there is time.

"No. Hai told the officer to tell me that the store was secure."

"This whole thing is... surreal," I say, as we careen onto a street that leads to the old soldiers' home. And insane.

"Other *canh sáts* have beat us here," Samuel says, indicating the flashing lights ahead. "As bad as it might be, we cannot stay. We will mourn Viet later."

"Yes, Father."

Samuel parks behind a police motorbike, gets out. Mai and the other police cars park behind us. I stand by my door for a moment to get a sense of what's going on, just as I have a thousand times on police calls. Cong, Phouc, Phat Ho, and Dung do the same by the van.

Two officers are standing on each side of a distraught looking white-haired man sitting on the steps, his forehead in his hands. Mai kneels next to the man, patting his knee. After exchanging a few words with the officers, Samuel, too, kneels next to him.

When the four old soldiers start to go up the steps, both officers stop them with raised palms, probably to keep them from contaminating the scene. The men nod and step back, and even from twenty feet away, I can see that the eyes in those grim faces want to rip the heads off those who killed their friend. They might be salty old war dogs, but it's been a lot of years since they've lost a buddy in battle.

From the porch, Samuel and Mai head into the house; Mai gestures for me to follow.

"That man is the doctor," she says, as we head across the sitting room where three days ago I met the troops. "He watched the men… kill Viet."

We follow Samuel down the narrow hall to the second room on the right. An officer stands by the door. He greets Samuel like they know each other and waves him into the room. Has a team dusted for prints and taken photos already? Incongruously, the policeman indicates that Mai and I should go no farther than the doorway.

LOREN W. CHRISTENSEN

Viet is lying at an angle across the bed, his purplish face hanging over the side, eyes staring sightlessly, his tongue protruding from the corner of his ever smiling, lipless mouth.

"Strangled?" I ask Samuel, recognizing the signs from about half a dozen hangings I've investigated, and from seeing Phat Ho's work tonight.

Samuel clenches his right hand and just as quickly relaxes it. "Yes," he says, his voice faint, tired.

Whispering, Mai says, "Officer Bay says they have checked through the house and out in the back. They found nothing. Also, the doctor says this happened about thirty minutes ago, maybe a little more."

"When we were at the store," Samuel says under his breath. I'm amazed he can hold it together. I'm not sure I could.

"Did the doctor say how it happened?" I ask.

Tears erupt from Mai's eyes. "Doctor say three men came in, one had a gun. They made the doctor sit in that chair in the corner, and they say they would shoot him if he tried to interfere. Then they held Viet's arms so he cannot fight. But the doctor said he give Viet..." She says something to Samuel.

"Sedative," he answers, his jaw trembling.

"Yes, sedative. I am sorry, Father. The doctor gave Viet a sedative before to help him sleep, so it was not necessary for the men to hold him down. Doctor said one man, biggest man, bald, crooked nose, put his fist on Viet's throat. He pushed down hard for a long time until Viet died."

This time Samuel doesn't relax his fists after clenching them.

"One of the men told the doctor that they would let him live so he could tell us what happened."

For the umpteenth time in the last ten hours, my adrenaline surges. Psychological warfare at its best. I can't imagine what Samuel, Mai, and the old soldiers are feeling.

Samuel speaks quietly with the officer before going over to Viet's body. He gently lifts Viet's head and muscles him around until Viet is lying lengthwise on the bed. He picks up a folded sheet from a chair, unfolds it, and gently covers him.

Out on the porch, Samuel again kneels to speak with the doctor, before coming over to us. "We got to get to the house," he says. "Mai, I want Phouc to stay here with Viet. The doctor is going to leave when the police leave, which won't be until after Viet's body is removed. One officer will stay here the rest of the night." He looks at me. "Bay, the officer guarding the bedroom door, is going to follow us over. He is a friend of the soldiers."

"Sounds good," I say. "And Harry is bringing more?"

"I hope," Samuel says.

*

Once again we're speeding through the streets, Samuel and me in the lead, Mai following in the van, and Bay following on his motorbike. This night has been insane and it's not over yet. I've had some nutso nights like this when I worked uniform. One hot summer night the Bloods and Crips were feuding and shooting each other about every thirty minutes somewhere in the city. Three or four police cars would form a caravan and rush to a scene, call ambulances, make arrests, console screaming mothers, then haul ass to another shooting scene where we would do it all over again. They sent forty officers from another precinct to help us but still we raced from one bloody incident to the next for eighteen long hours.

Samuel, chewing hard on his lower lip, isn't driving as fast as before since traffic has about doubled from forty-five minutes ago.

"I'm so sorry about Viet," I say, not sure if that's fueling his state of mind. When he doesn't say anything, I add, "He was a good soldier. He performed outstandingly in the warehouse."

Samuel's ten o'clock and two o'clock tightens on the steering wheel, then loosens a couple of seconds later. "Viet was the best. I will honor him when this is over."

The *Superman* theme. "Tex?" Samuel says into his cell. He listens for a moment.

"Please ask him about Bobby."

Samuel nods acknowledging me, and continues his conversation. Covering the mouthpiece, he tells me, "The boy is still in the tunnel. I told Tex to keep him in there. He says that the posts are all up to speed on what has happened. My neighbors do not get up until after sunrise so the street out front is still mostly free of traffic."

"Sounds good."

Samuel pins the cell between his raised shoulder and his ear as he continues to talk to Tex while driving the Volvo like Mario Andretti through the maze of streets. It's hard to tell what's going on in his head, though it seems that his exterior is starting to deteriorate. The evening hasn't broken him, but for sure it's chomping off pieces of the man's self-control.

His eyes suddenly widen and the cell slips from his shoulder. He grabs it. "What?" he shouts into it in English. The car slows. "When? Why are you telling me this just now?" Does he realize that he's speaking English?

"What is it?" I ask hesitantly.

Samuel returns to speaking Vietnamese, louder than before and faster. Tex's tinny voice is persistent, but Samuel keeps interrupting. It is a long thirty seconds before he snaps his phone closed and presses down on the throttle, hard.

"What? Is something happening at the house? Is Bobby—"

"Kim and Linh are there," he snaps.

"Where? At the house?"

He exhales hard and shakes his head in frustration. "Linh brought her back sometime after two this morning."

"Oh no… Does Mai know? She told me she spoke with Linh just before we got to Bien Hoa and that her mother wasn't doing well. She was weak and sleeping. I mean, is Kim alright?"

Samuel takes a deep breath. "Tex said Kim was insistent that she return to the house. When Linh tried to talk her out of it, she apparently became hysterical." He looks at me. "Mother *does not ever get hysterical*. So Linh called Tex and told him they were coming back."

"And Tex didn't tell you until now?"

"He adores Kim. She insisted that he not tell me, and though she badgered him, he would not tell her where we were tonight. Tex is loyal to both of us, you see, so he's caught in the middle. Kim knows nothing of what happened at Bien Hoa, the stores, or the soldiers' home. But she has powerful instincts." He taps in a number on his cell.

"Do you think she knows—"

"Linh" he says into the phone. What follows sounds like a father ripping into his daughter. After half a minute, he calms and talks normally.

He just told me how strong willed Kim is, so he knows that Linh had no choice but to follow her mother's dictates. I'm guessing the ripping part is Samuel dumping his frustration on his daughter. Now that he's got some much-needed venting out of his system, he's probably giving her an abridged version of what's going on.

A few seconds later, he snaps his phone shut and leans hard on the horn when a motorbike pulls abruptly into our lane as if we're not already occupying it. He keeps blasting it until the startled driver jumps the curb to find safety on the sidewalk. He shakes his fist as we pass.

Samuel focuses intently on his driving for a couple of minutes, then says, "It was as I suspected. Linh said that her mother was most insistent that she come back home. Said she was so adamant that when Linh first refused her, she walked out to the street to get a taxi. Apparently, her legs gave out and Linh caught her before she fell to the sidewalk. Even then, there was no convincing her that she should stay at Linh's house."

"Oh man," I say.

"Of course, Linh is not as strong and firm as Mai, so Kim has always been able to boss her more."

"But it sounds as if Kim wasn't going to be dissuaded anyway. What do you think is the matter? You didn't talk to her just now?"

Samuel shakes his head, and continues to shake it for several seconds as if he isn't aware that he's doing it.

"I must be honest with you, Son," he says, cranking the wheel hard to the left, pressing me into the door. I grab the dash in the event the hinges don't hold. "I am having a difficult time keeping myself under control. My adrenaline wants to consume me. But I cannot let that happen. I must stay in the moment."

His eyes are directed straight ahead, but he looks more like he's in a trance than watching the road.

"I must focus on the task of protecting and defending. I cannot let my anger control me." He honks at a three-wheel pedicab with two obese women in its seat and a very elderly man straining to pedal it. His trance-look intensifies. "My anger *will not* control me. My rage *will not* blind me to what needs to be done."

He moves his right hand from the wheel and touches the thumb-side edge to his chest, forming a one-handed, open-palm prayer. "*Nam mô* a-*di-dà Phật. Nam mô a-di-dà Phật. Nam mô a-di-dà Phật.*"

Sounds like a prayer—but now? When he's pushing the throttle to fifty on this narrow street? *Now* he's going to vent? I raise my index finger to make a point. "Uh, Samuel. I really think you need to keep both hands on the wheel."

*"Nam mô a-di-dà Phật. Nam mô a-di-dà Phật. Nam mô—"*

"Samuel?"

He snaps his head toward me, coming out of his trance. Frowns. "Oh, yes. Yes, of course," he says, resuming his ten and two grip and looking intently out the windshield. "Sorry, Son." He takes a deep breath and blows it out. "Went *diên cái đầu* there for a moment. Went crazy." He takes another deep breath and expels it. "I am back now. No sweat."

"Uh, no problem," I say, watching him to assure myself that he is, indeed, *back*. Guess he's human after all.

He taps in a number on his cell. "Mai? I just spoke with Linh and…"

I have a feeling she won't like the idea either.

"Son-of-a-bitch!" she shouts over the speaker phone. I was right.

"The only thing that will change is our approach." Samuel says, looking at me. "Mai you go straight to your mother's room. You stay there to protect Linh and your mother. The rest of us will deal with securing the house."

She hesitates but ultimately says, "Yes."

Samuel closes his phone. He and Mai must be thinking the same thing I am: Kim and Linh just added to our burden. They have become part of the problem.

Samuel shoots me a hard look. "We do what needs to be done, Son." He looks out the windshield and blinks hard as if trying to clear his eyes. "My wife made a choice. She has always made good ones all the years we have been together. Whatever her reason… she knew I would support her as I always have. She…"

I'm not sure what he means about Kim making a choice. The choice to come back to the house? Or is he talking about more than that? What did Mai say earlier? Something like, I am not optimistic about her health. She has grown so frail in the last few weeks. Does Kim's choice have something to do with her illness? I'm thinking, yes.

"We are close," he says softly. "I will check with Tex to see if we are clear to go in."

"And if not?"

He glances at me. "I feel comfortable making it up as we go along with you at my side, Son."

I feel a flutter in my chest. I smile and look down at my hands. "I feel the same, Father."

*Father.* Effortless. Feels right.

Samuel punches in a number on his cell. "Tex," he says, then speaks in Vietnamese while he hangs a right onto the street leading to the house. He pulls to the curb seventy-five yards from the gate; the van and police motorbike pull in behind us. In my side mirror, I see Cong and Phat Ho get out and take up positions facing outward a few yards behind the motorbike.

Up the street on the left side, a light post bathes the front gate in an eerie, yellowish glow. Sitting on the sidewalk on the right side of the street and about halfway between us and the gate is Samuel's man, the one who pretends to sell motorbike parts on a blanket. It's too early to set up shop so he's sitting against the wall smoking.

There is also a guy watching from a second story window on the right side farther down the street and a one-eyed guy pulling guard in the alley behind the house. Lai and Trai are supposed to be alternating foot patrol. I don't see anyone else on the street, so I'm assuming they are both inside watching the screens or guarding the backyard.

Samuel lowers the phone. "Tex says the posts report that everything looks peaceful. There have been only four motorbikes pass this street in the last forty-five minutes, two pedestrians and two pedicabs. All went by without even a glance at the gate and all exited at the far end of the block."

We sit silently for a moment, both of us looking out the window, both of us wondering what the next few hours, or few minutes will bring. Can it possibly be worse than the last few hours? I look over at Samuel. His body appears relaxed, a result of his decades of training, but his face is pinched, agonized.

"What was the name of that fishing village you and Kim are planning to retire to?"

Samuel's face softens a little. "*Châu Đốc*. It is a most wonderful place. Quiet." He takes a deep breath and releases it. I can tell he is gone to a shady place watching the sampans on the river. "So very quiet."

"Will you have an extra cot for a visitor?"

He looks at me. "For sure. And I will take you out on a fishing boat."

"Sounds great. Looking forward to it."

He nods, smiles with his eyes, and looks back toward the front of the house. The softness in his face disappears, replaced by the intensity of the mission. Samuel and I share the same blood, and though I'm sitting within arms reach of him, we're isolated by culture and language. Nonetheless, I know what is going on in his head. I've seen that same intensity in the faces of SWAT officers before they go through a door or make the fatal shot.

Officer Bay appears at his window and Samuel leans out to talk with him. A moment later, the bike officer zips around us and heads down the street.

I didn't understand their words, but I know Samuel sent the bike officer down to the other end of the block to be a set of eyes in the darkness. I know because that's what I would have done. I watch the motorbike crank a U turn. The lights go off, come back on, and go off again. He's in place.

Actually, sending the bike down there is about the only thing we've done tonight that is similar to how we would have done it on the police bureau. Everything else has been the opposite. It's been a night of new rules.

Samuel pokes in a number on his phone. Time to get the rest of the troops on board.

The troops. We're a peculiar group—my new family, and I would lay my life down for them and I may have to.

"Mai," Samuel says. "I am going to tell Tex we are coming in. Get Cong and Phat Ho back to the van and... Hold it," he says looking into his side mirror. "Wait for this to pass."

A pedicab, a pedal type, passes by us. With the canvas roof and support bars on its sides, I can just make out a man who glances our way and a woman on the other side of him.

"Tired night workers heading home," Samuel says. "We must wait until they pass the gate and then…" He tilts his head, his eyes still on the pedicab.

'What? What is it?"

He taps in a number.

"Look," I say. "I think he's stopping in front… yes, he's stopping in front of the gate."

"Come on, Tex. Answer."

Still ringing.

# CHAPTER
# TWENTY-THREE

The male passenger gets out of the pedicab and moves over to the gate, peers through it for a moment, waves.

"What's he doing?" I ask.

"He must know about the camera," Samuel says, waiting for Tex to answer his cell.

"Samuel?" Tex's tinny sounding voice.

Mai steps up to her father's window. "What is going on, Father?"

Samuel lifts his hand to silence her. He says something into the phone and Tex replies, his last word, Lu.

Samuel looks at me and then at Mai.

"Father, what is the pedicab doing—"

"Tex thinks the woman is Lu," he says.

I strain to see. "Lu? Why would he be—"

He holds up his index finger, frowning at whatever Tex is saying. "No, no," he says, finishing in Vietnamese.

Could this language barrier be any more frustrating? What the hell is going on? If Lu is in the pedicab—

"Okay," Samuel says into the phone. Then to us, "Tex says he zoomed in on the pedicab and he is sure it is Lu. Asleep, he thinks." He pauses to listen to Tex again, then mouths to me, "Blood," and points at the top of his head.

"On Lu?" Mai says, her face in the window, her voice barely constrained. "Blood on Lu?" She starts to head that way.

"Mai, stay here," Samuel snaps. "Stay here until I find out what is happening."

Before we hit the warehouse, Samuel said that Lu was worried because he thought Lai Van Tan's people were getting suspicious about all the questions he was asking. He said that someone had hit him. Maybe the boyfriend, or maybe someone else figured out that he was relaying info to us. Is that the boyfriend at the gate?

Samuel shakes his cell. "Tex? Tex? Lost my connection," he says irritably. He snaps his cell shut and reopens it. The *Superman* theme sounds before he can poke anything.

"Tex?"

Samuel frowns. The tinny voice isn't Tex. Samuel covers the mouth piece, and whispers, "Phong Tran."

Phong Tran? Oh, the guy sitting at Lai Van Tan's side in the board room. He's Samuel's contact person and the one I thought might be sympathetic to us.

In their conversation I think I hear the caller say "Lu."

"What is it, Father?"

Samuel waves Mai off and focuses on the caller. "*Cám ơn,*" he says.

"What, Father?" Mai asks impatiently when he closes his phone.

"Phong Tran says that Lu was beaten tonight and he thinks killed." Mai gasps, covering her mouth with her palm. "He also says that," he pokes a button on his cell, "that men are going to attack the house."

"When?" I ask.

"He said that…" Samuel looks at his phone. "Come on, Tex. Pick up." He looks at me. "Phong Tran said the attack is…" He frowns slightly as if having trouble translating Vietnamese to English. "… imminent."

"The gate," Mai says. "Opening. Who is opening—"

Samuels growls at the phone. "Tex. Pick up!"

"Look," I say, pointing through the windshield. "The motorbike policeman. He's turned on his headlight."

The sky is beginning to lighten, but it's still so dark on this tree-lined street that I can't make out the officer or the bike. Just the light.

"He must know something," Samuel says.

The motorbike's headlight is splashing the walls on the right side of the street, then the wall around Samuel's house on the left, then the right side of the street again.

Samuel floors the Volvo toward the pedicab where the driver is leaping off his seat.

The bike banks toward the gate and into the lights. What the hell?

"The bike!" I shout. "The cop. He's not on it!"

The riderless motorbike continues on it's projection, careening toward the pedicab, leaning farther and farther over as it does. Something on the bike's right side grinds into the pavement sending up a rooster tail of white sparks. An instant later, the entire bike lays down, sliding at least forty miles an hour and doubling the size of the fiery tail.

"It's going to hit the pedicab," I shout. "Slow down, Samuel. It might bounce this way."

The back wheel of the motorbike hits the pedicab's front right wheel hard enough to launch the remaining passenger face-first onto the pavement. I get just a glimpse, enough to see that it's a woman wearing an *áo dài*. Lu? The bike ricochets off the wheel and begins a fast, fiery slide directly toward us. Samuel swerves the car to the right but not soon enough. The motorbike collides with our front left side, instantaneously engulfing the hood and Samuel's side of the windshield in flames.

"Back up," I shout, twisting in my seat to look out the rear window. "Hit the brakes and back up as fast as you can. Watch out for the van, it's coming up on your left."

Samuel anchors the car and pops it into reverse. The Volvo bumps and scrapes over the motorbike, the metal on metal making a horrific screech. When the car breaks free, Samuel accelerates us backwards so fast that the passing van appears stopped. For an instant, I see Cong's face pressed against the window, his mouth open.

As I'd hoped, the gasoline that was burning on the hood and window, rolls off the front of the car to burn on the pavement.

"Get out," I shout. "There might be fire underneath."

I bail out, squat, and duck walk around the back of the car checking the undercarriage.

"No fire," I say, as Samuel looks under the car on his side.

Mai is running back to us, her gun in hand. "Are you okay? Father, Sam, are you okay?" Cong is running behind her.

Samuel raises his palms "We are fine, daughter. Please, go back. Hurry. The pedicab driver and the man went inside the gate."

Samuel turns his head toward the far side of the street where someone is moving quickly toward us. I think it's the guy who had been sitting against the wall. Samuel makes a we're-okay wave, and the man heads back to his post.

Flipping open his ringing cell, Samuel motions for me to follow him to the gate where Mai is kneeling by the person who was thrown from the pedicab.

"It *is* Lu," she shouts. "He is barely conscious."

Lu, wearing a blood-splattered, sky blue *áo dài*, is lying on his front, his face turned to the side. Blood trickles from his nose and left eye, and one side of his wig is matted with it. "Help me turn him over," Mai says.

"He will have to stay here," Samuel says, the phone still at his ear. "It might be safer than inside the gate."

"Grab the seat cushion from the pedicab, Sam," Mai says.

Lu stirs, clearly in pain. We slip the cushion under his head. Small comfort.

"Come on," Samuel says calmly. "Inside. Tex and the second-story post report that there are men coming over the south wall."

*

"Where's Tex?" I whisper rhetorically.

Mai and I are on one side of the stairs that lead into the house and Samuel is on the other, his cell pressed to his ear. Mai's right foot is one step up from her left, which tugs up her pant leg a little to expose the bottom couple of inches of her ankle holster. She had the gun out a few moments ago, but Samuel doesn't want any of us to use firearms unless there is absolutely no choice. She's tucked it into the small of her back.

In Bien Hoa, we were in a large warehouse area two or three miles from the city. We did our thing, we got out as quickly as possible, and we didn't see any police. But Saigon is an incredibly densely populated city and has a strict no-firearms policy. If we were to use a gun here, even in self-defense, the government bullies would be on us like white on rice.

"Not picking up" Samuel whispers. "He must have opened the gate from the monitor room, thinking the men were here to help Lu."

"I need to get to Mother's room," Mai whispers worriedly.

"Yes, you do," Samuel says, moving up the steps. "But we need to clear the living room first. Mai, you and Sam enter to the left and I will go right. From there, we will move to the archway." He turns and says something to Cong, Phat Ho, and Dung. "Phat Ho and Cong will go into the dining room to check on the backyard. Dung will stay here to secure this door. Son?"

"Agreed."

*Bam!*

Mai and I slam ourselves against the wall at the top of the steps, and Samuel takes cover behind the wall on his side of the door. Mai's retrieves her Glock.

"Came from inside, back of the house," Samuel says. "Heard a thump after the shot, maybe someone falling onto the floor."

"I heard it too" Mai says. "I am going in."

"You are staying here." Samuel's tone makes it clear that there is no discussion this time. "I will go."

With that he moves quickly through the foyer, his head turning left and right. Meeting no resistance, he dashes across the room and through the archway.

A long minute later, Mai lifts her vibrating cell to her ear. "Father, how is…" Mai's face relaxes. "Yes. Yes. Okay." She turns to Cong, Phat Ho, and Dung, and rattles something off. To me, "Father wants Dung, me, and you to go to the back of the house, and Phat Ho and Cong to secure the dining room."

"What happened? What was that shot?"

"Linh shoot man," she says, her face drained of color.

Linh, the timid one who needed protecting? "Where did she get the gun?"

"Hurry," she says, curling around the doorway. Dung lumbers behind me. We move across the living room, over the thick rug with the interwoven blue dragon, its mouth open and talons reaching, and stop before the archway. For a moment, my mind flashes back to the archway in the boy's house in Portland, the one that led to the stairwell, which led to the second landing, which led to—a flower. A white rose.

"We go," Mai says, moving around the archway. Dung and I follow.

"Your mother is fine," Samuel calls from the end of the hall where he is standing over a man lying face down, arms along his sides, legs together. "Holster your weapon, Mai. Dung, *lại đây.*"

Crying coming from somewhere, probably that room to Samuel's right. A bedroom?

Closer now, I can see that the man on the floor is the pedicab driver. Judging by the neat position of his arms and legs, he died instantly, falling face-first onto the stone floor with no kicking or thrashing about. Maybe Linh shot him through his medulla oblongata, the point under his nose, or through his ear hole, or just under the lobe. Any of those will kill the medulla oblongata part of the brain as well as the body before the recipient hits the floor. When I shot the tweaker in Portland right under his nose, it ended his life in an instant, which prevented him from shooting the shop owner.

Samuel speaks to Dung. Then to Mai, he says. "Your mother and sister are fine. Linh acted appropriately."

As Dung squats and jerks the dead man into a seated position, Mai squeezes around them and disappears into the room. Now all three women are talking; I think that's Linh I hear crying. Samuel shouts into the room.

"Yes, Father," Mai says. He probably told her to stay with them.

Dung pulls the man all the way up and drapes him over his shoulder. I see the driver's face for just an instant before it drops down along the big man's back. I was right, the bullet punched through just below his nose.

"Is that the gun?" I ask, watching Samuel shake live rounds out of the cylinder of a Smith and Wesson 357 revolver. He leaves the spent shell in.

"Yes, mine. When they heard the man coming down the hall, Mother told Linh where I keep it. Dung will put it in the man's hand when he lays him out front." He stuffs the weapon into Dung's front pocket. "The man, was armed, you see. There was a struggle in the driveway, his gun went off, and he was struck."

Now we're moving bodies to different locations and planting fake evidence. Could this night be any more loony tunes? Are the police here that inept or is Samuel relying on help from his friend, Captain Harry?

"A little of both," he says. "Okay, we need to see what is going on. Mai will be fine. She has her gun as a last resort."

While Dung creates the "scene of the shooting" outside, Samuel and I quick-peak around the archway. The living room remains clear.

I whisper. "We going to the dining room?"

"Slowly," he says.

When I start to move around the archway, Samuel's hand on my arm stops me. He takes the lead. My pop, always protecting me. When we reach the dining room archway, Samuel quick-peaks around the corner for a moment then motions for me to follow him.

Light from the living room and kitchen seeps into the darkened room. Phat Ho is pressed against the wall next to the sliding glass doors as Cong kneels next to a prone man who looks like the pedicab passenger. Cong is jamming his right arm straight up, the elbow joint locked in a standard police control hold. One I've taught for years. Each time the arm is simultaneously pushed toward the man's head and downward into his shoulder socket, a thousand pain receptors ignite in the joint, making the intruder kick his feet against the floor like a toddler having a tantrum.

"Did he have a weapon?" Samuel asks in English so I understand.

"Knife," Cong says, indicating with a jerk of his head a long curved blade in his own belt. "Khmer Rouge."

It's the same type of blade the man in the warehouse held over his head when he charged Cong and Mai. Nasty looking. So far these guys have shown themselves to be nothing more than scary looking dudes with piss poor tactics. Thankfully.

Samuel speaks to Phat Ho who shakes his head without looking away from the yard. "He does not see anything out there," Samuel says. He kneels down and says something to the prone man that doesn't sound like Vietnamese. The guy's reply sets off a twitch in the corner of Samuel's mouth. The intruder had better soften his words because Samuel's this close to—

The man screams at Samuel, sending spittle flying from his mouth onto the floor. Oh boy, don't need a translator to know he chose his words none too wisely.

Samuel snatches the man's upraised arm away from Cong and slams it so hard toward the man's head that the horrific sound of crunching bones and ripping tendons can probably be heard out in the yard.

Incredibly, not only does the man not cry out, he twists onto his right side, his dead arm underneath him, and kicks at

Samuel. The blow is easily blocked, but because he's kneeling on one knee, the force knocks Samuel off balance and onto his rear. Before the intruder can even think of a follow-up, Samuel grabs the man's ankle with one hand and his shirt front with his other. Then in one smooth, fast motion, Samuel draws his knee back to his chin in a tight chamber then thrusts his foot straight into the man's right side.

Silence. One thousand one, one thousand two…

The man screams, and it just might set off the Richter scale. I've been kicked in the liver a couple times and I've landed a few shots there on opponents. Most often, there is no reaction for a second or two, then that horrific pain and debilitation come calling.

His scream abruptly stops and his eyes glaze over.

"Is he…"

Samuel shakes his head. "No. He is going into shock." Dung lumbers into the dining room. "Dump him out onto the street, Dung." The big man looks at him, confused. "Oh," Samuel says, and repeats his order in Vietnamese. Guess crushing a man's liver makes a guy forget which language he's speaking.

"He is Khmer Rouge," Samuel says, as Dung hoists him up over his shoulder. "He was ordered to kill my family. All of us. The man in the hall was given the same order. That one will no longer have to think about it. This man will think about it when he goes into surgery for his crushed liver, and when his body struggles to fight infection, and when he is treated for gastrointestinal problems."

Geeze.

Phat Ho jerks his head toward something out in the yard. Samuel moves quickly over to the other side of the glass doors and peeks around the door facing. "There is someone lying over by the heavy bag," he says.

I move over next to Samuel and Cong steps behind Phat Ho. There's just enough illumination coming from one of the triplex's exterior lights to see a little of the yard.

"Two men," I say. "One down and another by that palm tree to the left."

"Lam," Samuel says, sliding open the door. "He is pointing his gun at the one who is down. But where is my friend?" He taps in a number, listens, and disconnects. "Tex is not answering"

I point toward the closest end of the triplex, and whisper, "Over there. Someone crouching in the shrubs, not moving. I think he's looking toward the monitor room."

Samuel nods. "You and I will move there together. I will watch the man and everything on the left side of the yard, beginning at that second palm tree. You follow and watch everything on the right side of that palm. Phat Ho, Cong, you go to the right and stay in the shadows along the south wall." They nod that they understand his English. "That wall is the only weak point."

The tree. The second day I was here that teenage burglar climbed it to get into the yard and was caught by Samuel's teacher, Shen Lang Rui. Mai had said it was going to be removed, but not for another two or three days.

He inches the door open and we slip out onto the porch in a low crouch and move down the steps. Phat Ho and Cong move off to the right.

The crouching man's back is to us, looking like he is waiting, or trying to decide what to do. The cobblestone walkway between the long shrub and the triplex is well lit, so maybe he's afraid to expose himself… Okay, I guess that isn't it because now he's duck walking out onto the cobblestones.

As the man starts to stand, a lone figure drops from the tiled roof onto his head and shoulders.

"Ah, there is Tex," Samuel whispers, relieved.

The intruder lands hard on his side and Tex lands lightly on his hands next to him. The man quickly sits up, shakes his head clear, and begins drawing his legs under him to stand. Tex has other plans. He slaps the guy's closest support arm out from under him, which drops him once again onto the concrete.

Tex springs onto the man's chest so fast that the intruder can't begin to sit up. I remember how surprisingly heavy the legless man is. The intruder throws a wild punch, which Tex shield blocks with one arm. Before he can get off a second one, Tex slaps his face with all the power he's developed from over thirty-five years of walking on his hands. The skull-jarring impact partially flips the man over, launching Tex onto the cobblestone where he lands gracefully on his hands again, his upper body swinging back and forth for a moment like a pendulum. He hand-steps over to the dazed man and shifts his weight to one arm.

"Tex," Samuel says calmly, just as his friend is about to slap him again.

The legless man looks up at us with eyes that are scary dark. "You want me kill man?"

"No. Just hold him."

Tex quickly scoots around so that he's behind the man's head. He cups the sides of the intruder's face, places his thumbs on the scrunched-closed eyes, and says, what I'm guessing is, "Don't move or I will press your eyes into you brain and move my thumbs in circles like a swizzle stick stirs a cocktail." I wonder how that control technique would go over in cop-hating Portland?

Samuel places the hard edge of his red Converse against the man's shin, and calmly speaks to him while at the same time grinding his weight into the tender, nerve-rich flesh. With Tex's thumbs ready to do mayhem in the man's eye sockets and Samuel's shoe slowly rubbing his pain receptors against his shinbone, the hapless man starts talking like a Chatty Kathy doll.

"Three came over the wall," Samuel translates. He asks the man another question. No response.

Samuel gestures to Tex, who leans forward onto his thumbs. Not a lot, but enough to make the man scream and buck. With his leg and head pinned, bucking his hips and thrashing his free leg is all he can do. He utters something through his trembling lips.

"He says there are more of them and they are coming. He does not know why they did not all come at once."

Probably part of Lai Van Tan's psychological warfare.

"Wait," I say. "Three came in? Lam has one out there by the bag."

"I fuck him up *boucoup* good," Tex says. "He breathe, but not go nowhere."

"One here," Samuel says. "That means one is unaccounted for."

We look through the bushes to check on Cong and Phat Ho. The morning gray light is beginning to dissolve the shadows so that we can just barely see the two old soldiers across the yard by the south wall.

"They haven't made contact with anyone," I say. So where could… "My room! Bobby!"

The door is ajar.

# CHAPTER
# TWENTY-FOUR

I've been standing here for four minutes and I just now notice that the door, only a dozen feet away, is partially open. Did Tex not shut it all the way after getting Bobby squared away in there to spend the night? Or did an intruder open it? Wouldn't they have seen that on the monitors? But Lam is out in the yard holding an intruder at gunpoint so that leaves only Trai watching six monitors, twelve half screens with something happening on nearly all of them. Could he have missed it?

I palm the door all the way open and bolt into the dark room. The bed has been pushed back and the trap door is lying next to the square opening in the floor. Oh man, an open trap-door would be an obvious place for an intruder to look for people hiding.

Please no. Don't let the boy be hurt. If anything happened…

"Bobby?" I yell loudly, scrambling down the wooden ladder.

"Sam!" His voice is far away, muffled. Alive. "Sa—"

Sounds of a struggle, grunts and bodies slamming together.

At the bottom of the hole, I scrunch myself as small as I can and peer through the twenty-five feet of tunnel to the carved-out room. The ceiling there is more than three feet above the top of the tunnel, so all I can see are two sets of legs, Bobby's and someone else's. Looks like that someone is jamming Bobby against the dirt wall.

"Peroneal nerve strike," I shout, hoping the man doesn't

understand and that Bobby remembers the strike I showed him. I squeeze into the tight tunnel, my shoulders and back crumbling dirt away from its sides. "Hit the outside of his front thigh with your knee."

He does, and I hear a grunt and see the struck leg sag to the right a little.

"Hit it again."

I'm inching along as fast as I can. The smell of dirt nauseating, like ancient swamp and rotten jungle, which it probably is. Don't know why it didn't bother me last time, but it does now. On top of that, dragging my body in the dirt is really inflaming the cement burns on my stomach and chest.

I cover the first ten feet without much of a physical hitch but now I'm slowing. Why? Because the walls are so close, that's why. So is the ceiling. Is the tunnel tapered? Why would the digger make it tapered? No, that can't be right. I don't remember that from last time I crawled through this thing. Got to be in my mind, but I swear the tunnel is getting sma…

*Uh oh.*

Uh oh is never a good thing to say to yourself when you're in a cramped tunnel. But my butt is stuck and my arms are pinned under me, like I'm at the bottom of a pushup, and I can't push up because there is a ton or more of hard-packed earth above me, and I can't push back or pull myself forward, either.

Bobby knees the man's outer leg. This time the guy grunts loudly and bends enough in the direction of the pain that I can see the top of his head for a moment.

Having trouble breathing now. Oh man. There's no room for my chest to expand, and my neck is cramping from holding my head up. No, the cramping can't be from that. Must be from the hit I got when Mai and I were jumped and from the fight with Khmer Rouge Man at the warehouse tonight. He really stretched my neck with that scissor move.

Hey, I'm wiggling my butt, which is more than I could do ten seconds ago, but I still can't push with my hands.

Sweating like crazy. Back of my neck is cramping bad now, right where it connects to my… I can't… hold it up any longer.

My face plops into the old swamp dirt. So foul. When I jerk my head up, I bang it painfully against the ceiling, showering dirt down on me. It's all over my sweaty face. Aagh, I just swallowed some.

Starting to lose it here folks. Why is this getting to me this time? I felt a little claustrophobia when Samuel and I crawled through here a few days ago, but this time… Maybe because I got some serious stress going on now. That's what my shrink would say. I just went through all that business at the warehouse, plus Samuel isn't here to joke with me like he did before.

Okay, nice psychoanalysis, but it doesn't help because now I'm feeling light headed. Nauseous. Nausea from dining on old jungle dirt with animal crap in it.

Got to stay calm. Got to stay calm. Force myself to relax. Relax. Come on body, reeeelax.

My butt disconnects with the ceiling. My hips are free. What the…? Guess I got confused in my little panic attack. Thought my hips were on the floor of the tunnel and my butt was jammed against the ceiling. Must have been pushing my rear up against it and I didn't know. Actually, I've got a couple inches to maneuver, but my jammed arms are still preventing me from going forward. My fisted hands are pinned at mid chest and my knuckles are gouging into my chest plate. I can't even uncurl my fingers. So hard to breathe.

Wait, now that I know I can make little up and down motions with my butt, I can move backwards an inch.

"Sam!" Bobby's face is at the end of the tunnel. "Sam, it worked. That leg nerve thing. He's down and hurtin'. That was freakin' awesome." He looks behind him at the room. "But I want to go now. It really sucks in here."

I spit out some dirt but more of it is caught in my throat. Panic rising again. The dirt is tickling my gag reflex. I snap my head to the side and bang my face into the wall. Oh my God! I'm going to choke to death down here.

Stay calm. Must stay calm. Staaaay calm.

The gob of dirt slowly moves down past my gag reflex.

"Bob-aah," dirt comes up from my throat into my mouth. I spit it out.

Bobby looks behind him again, then back at me. "I'm coming in, Sam," he says, oblivious to my plight. "I'm getting freaked in this room."

Freaked. That makes two of us. I hump a couple more times so that my hands are under my neck now so that I can uncurl my fingers. Small pleasures. Three more humps... My arms are free! I thrust them forward to release the cramps. Got dirt on my teeth, but I smile anyway, thinking how I must look like Superman flying through the tunnel.

"Sam," Bobby says crawling toward me with much greater ease than I'm exhibiting. "Move back."

I try to speak but my voice sounds like a growling Chihuahua. I spit up dirt again.

"You okay?"

Do I look okay? I nod and hit my head on the ceiling. Another dirt shower. But I can move now, just not as fast as Bobby. I draw my hands back toward me a few inches and push against the dirt floor with my palms. That gained me about four inches. Better than not moving at all, I always say whenever I'm stuck in a tunnel.

"Sam, I'm closing on you. Move faster," Bobby says, his face about a foot from mine. Teenagers. Never satisfied. "I'm not sure how long the dude is going to stay down. He's hurting but he might—"

His eyes widen a hair of a second before his face slams into the dirt. He begins sliding backwards, his fingers raking the soil.

"Sam!" he yells, his voice muffled by the dirt.

I grab his wrists but my leverage is poor.

"He's got my ankles!" He screams, spit and dirt spraying from his mouth. "Pull me, Sam. Harder."

I try, but my hands slip down over his sweat-slick wrists and my elbows hit the walls. We clasp hands for a few seconds before the man's strength advantage pulls them apart, so that now I'm holding only his middle finger on one hand and his thumb on the other.

"Ick m," I wheeze, hoping he understands.

"I… can't kick him. Can't… chamber my leg."

Bobby's thrashing is churning up a cloud of dust. I begin coughing, but somehow manage to maintain my grip on his fingers. A few seconds later, I hack a hard, sputtering cough that breaks my concentration and my grip on his thumb. Then his middle finger slips out of my hand and he's sucked backward out of the dirt tube.

"Saaaamm!"

Pushing with my feet and pulling on the dirt with my fingers. Got to get into the room, got to get into the room. Must be careful not to draw my arms too far back and get them jammed under me again.

Bobby is lying on the floor, but all I can see of the man are his arms and hands grabbing at the boy. Bobby kicks him, once, twice. All roundhouses. I can't see where his feet are landing, but I can hear them and they sound like solid hits. Must be body shots. Another roundhouse and the man grunts loudly.

I'm about five feet from the room, the equivalent, effort-wise, of crawling fifty yards uphill up on the surface. Found a nice little rhythm of pull, push, pull, push that's moving me forward at a steady pace and keeping my panic needle on the front edge of the red zone.

Now I can see the man up to his midsection. He's circling Bobby as the boy spins on his rear and kicks to keep the guy at bay. The man lashes out with a sloppy front kick and the boy sweeps it aside with his lower leg. Nice move. But the attacker's next kick lands hard on Bobby's ribs.

"Shin kick," I shout, my voice sounding almost normal, in spite of spitting out dirt.

Bobby looks into the tunnel, his face grimacing from the blow to his side. "Do what?"

"Look at *him*, not at me! Kick his shin hard and get up."

"Like," he chambers his knee, "this?" He rams the sole of his barefoot into the closest shin. The man grunts, lifts his leg, and covers the kicked spot with both hands.

"Exactly like that. Now get up and finish him. Hit his bladder like I showed you the other day."

Bobby's up and circling. I'm close enough to the room now that I can see the attacker's chest. He lunges at the boy, locking him into a tight clinch. They struggle.

"Knees, Bobby. Knee his bladder, then punch it."

The two slam into the back wall, shaking loose dirt and small stones. Bobby starts to drive in a knee, but the man spins him around three hundred and sixty degrees and right back into the wall. More dirt sifts down. The man who dug the tunnel and the room probably didn't factor in people ramming into it as if it were a football tackling sled. I'm about four push-pulls from the end of the tunnel now.

What is that? Something on the ground next to the table. Looks like… it is. A knife. Just the handle, though. My eyes travel up the wall. There. A blade, imbedded in the hard dirt. What the hell?

Bobby drives in a hard knee hit, but the man turns at the last second and the blow hits his hip instead of his bladder. He still feels it, though, because his torso dips low to that side. He recovers. Still in a clinch, the man spins the lighter boy around in a tight circle and flings him into the wall again. Bobby's head hits first this time, stunning him, dropping him to one knee.

"Bobby!" I shout, my head free of the tunnel. I start to pull myself all the way into the room when the man lunges across the small space and kicks at me. This time I voluntarily drop my face into the dirt, feeling his foot pass through my hair. It hits the top edge of the tunnel, giving me yet another dirt shower. I lift my head just enough to see him chamber his leg and fire off another. I snap my head hard to the right. The kick misses, but the side of my head hits the tunnel rim so hard that I see spots of light. Maybe, just maybe, sticking my head out of the tunnel isn't a good move.

Out of the corner of my dirt-filled eye, I see him chamber again. He's not a skilled kicker, but that doesn't mean that a hard boot to the face wouldn't hurt. Not waiting to see if the third time really is a charm, I scoot back into the tunnel, pushing with the heels of my hands and moving my pelvis like a two-hundred-pound inchworm.

His ugly face fills the tunnel exit, sweaty, in his forties, with a wispy goatee, a splattering of old pockmarks, and eyes that lack any semblance of humanity.

He dives at me, hands stretched in front of him, and splashes dirt into my face. Because I just did a push-back, he plops onto my extended arms, pinning them under his chest, palms down. His body seals off the majority of the light behind him, while mine is already sealing off most of the light from the bulb at the entryway behind me. What little illumination finds its way around my frame is reflected in his left eye.

Trying to extract my arms out from under him gets me nowhere; the angle is wrong—bad leverage and his weight is too much. I do my inchworm thing with my hips, but without the accompanying push of my pinned hands, I can't move back.

He smiles and dirt drops from his teeth like blood from a vampire's canines. He cups the sides of my face and cranks my head to my left. When I resist, he goes with the flow and twists it to the right. So I resist back to the left. I am, at this moment, extremely grateful that I've always included neck bridges in my workouts, but it's exhausted from the strain of holding my head up and hurting from two previous fights.

I try to chomp into his palm, but he's sees it coming and slides it up to push against my nose. The pressure is only on one side, so I can still breathe a little, but, I can feel the onset of panic.

Our faces are no more than a foot apart, our eyes locked, as he continues to push against my nose and twist my head while I strain not to let him. Maybe it's because my breathing is ragged or my panic is showing in my eyes, he moves his hand just enough to seal off the other side of my nose.

Noooo! I push my head against his hands but he still has the better leverage. The pressure on my nose is crushing and my eyes are tearing heavily. Something pops in my neck, a cord, a muscle, I don't know what. There's no pain, but that sound can't be a good thing.

He muscles my head against the wall. The good news is that my skull can't go any farther and the doubly good news is that his hand slipped off my nose. But now he's pushing the right side of my forehead, my right eye, and the right side of my mouth into the dirt, which is crumbling all around my face.

*Don't fight the push; move it in a different direction.*

My words. I've taught students that when someone pushes them against a wall with their hands, they shouldn't push back against the force because if the attacker is stronger, he wins. Since a person is only strong in one direction at a time, the key is to disrupt the course of their energy. If his energy is pushing straight in, they should abruptly force that energy up, down, or to the side.

I jerk my head down as hard as I can. It only moves about three inches before my chin smacks into the dirt, but it's enough that he loses his forward pressure a little. When he lifts his upper body a tad to adjust to the different position, I'm able to rotate my hands enough to turn them over so that now he's lying on my palms.

Just as he purchases another strong hand position on my head, probably to push my face into the loose dirt to smother me, I close both fists on his nipples, as Mai did on that jerk in the tea shop. That guy screamed and so does this one.

He releases my head and grabs at my upper arms to push me away, but he doesn't have sufficient room to affect my hold. So I squeeze harder and twist my hands right and left as if turning radio knobs to connect with my favorite radio station, a top forty, all screams all the time.

With no other option, he eats the pain and grabs at my head again. Okay, if he wants it so badly, he can have it. Using his nipples as handles, I pull myself about six inches into him and headbutt his nose. His screams take on a different pitch this time, one that hurts my ears. So I slam my forehead into his nose again. His pitch is even higher, and louder.

It dawns on me that I don't want to knock the man unconscious, since I don't have the leverage to push him out of the tunnel, and I don't know if the boy is in any condition to pull him.

So I bite him. I chomp into that fat part of the cheek that women rouge, sinking my teeth in deep and shaking my head like a dog with a chew toy. The good news is that his screams have reached a pitch only dogs can hear, but the bad news is that all his desperate thrashing is breaking dirt loose from the tunnel walls.

"Bobby!" I shout. "You okay?"

"I think so," he says weakly. The human plug is muffling his voice.

When I squeeze the man's nipples again, he doesn't react as intensely. Maybe I've destroyed his nerves. So I attack them differently by digging into them with my fingernails. This has a different affect on the man's pain receptors so that again he thrashes about, his shoulders banging both sides of the crumbling tunnel walls. A sprinkling of dirt falls from the ceiling this time.

All that thrashing frees my hands. Man, that feels good. I still can't punch him, but I can claw the bloody mess I've made out of his cheek.

"Bobby," I shout. Don't know if he can hear me over this guy's bellows. "Pull his legs. Pull him out."

"Okay… Saaaam!"

"Bobby? Bobby!"

"Sa… Sam!"

The man's hands are on my face again, pushing me.

"Sam! SAM!"

"Pull him," I shout through the man's fingers. I chomp on one of them. He yelps and yanks it away. I can taste blood.

"The wall, Sam!" The man's body jerks back about twelve inches. Yes, Bobby's pulling him.

"That's it," I shout. I push on the man's forehead. "Keep pulling. Pull him hard."

"Saaaam!"

What the hell? "Bobby?"

"The wall. It's… caving in on me."

*

"Pull him harder," I shout. "Pull him all the way out."

"Dirt," Bobby cries. "The wall—"

"Hit him in the groin, Son."

Bobby is freaking, but as long as I can hear his voice I know he's all right.

The man claws desperately at the dirt each time he slides back a few inches, but between me pushing his face, and the excruciating pain from his torn nipples, broken nose, bit cheek, and chomped finger, he has very little strength left to resist.

He suddenly cries out and shakes his head so hard and fast that it's nearly a blur. Kid must have punched him in the cookies.

He rolls onto his side a little, probably wanting to curl into the fetal position. There isn't enough room for that, but the move allows me to see Bobby's arms pulling on the man's legs.

"Come on, Bobby. He's half way out. Just a little more—"

A chunk of tunnel ceiling drops onto the man's head, a clump about the size of a basketball. One second it was there, the next it breaks away and drops six inches onto his skull and crumbles about his head. It blocks some of the light that was coming in from the tunnel.

He's not moving. I don't think that thump on the head was hard enough to hurt him; he's probably spent. We got to get him completely out so Bobby can get in.

"Push him, Sam," Bobby shouts. "I can't pull him anymore. I can't… reach him."

Can't reach him?

The man suddenly grabs my face again. I slap his hands aside, scoop up some freshly fallen dirt, and grind it into his crushed nose. Then, as he coughs and sputters, I hit that suffering nose with a palm-heel strike, a weak one, given my lousy position, but he screams nonetheless. He stops when another chunk of earth falls on his head. It's not as large as the first one, but anything falling from the ceiling is not a good thing since we're still six feet under and twenty-five feet away from my bedroom.

One last face push gets him out of the tunnel, taking with him much of the freshly fallen dirt. He shrinks into that fetal position he's been wanting.

"Bobby," I say, pulling myself forward until my head extends part way into the room. "Drag him off to the side and—Oh my…"

The right wall has given way and collapsed into the room filling the right half with nearly three feet of dirt. Bobby is standing in it mid-thigh deep, his face white as he watches transfixed the slow-moving avalanche spill more and more into the room.

"Hey, man."

He doesn't respond. "Bobby!"

His eyes find mine, his words come out measured and barely audible. "It's burying me. I can't move my legs. So heavy."

A chunk of the rim lands just in front of my face, and another piece from the ceiling inside the tunnel lands on the man's legs a couple of feet in front of me. My heart rate needle blips into the red. I'm thinking that as long as I'm occupying this part of the tunnel it can't collapse. Okay, that's not logical but I'm running with it. Counting on it.

"Take my hand," I say, extending mine. "I'll pull you out."

Bobby leans forward as far as he can against his locked knees. It's not enough; our hands are about a foot and a half apart. More dirt falls in front of me, some of it hitting my head. I can't leave the entrance. I look toward the wall straight across from me, the one with the knife blade sticking out of it. It's crumbling.

"That's how the first one started," Bobby says in monotone.

The man, who had been lying motionless for a few seconds, suddenly draws his knee back and thrusts his foot at me.

I check block his lower leg with my forearm and grab his foot with one hand. We do a tug-of-war for a moment while I squirm onto my side to free my other arm. Now I'm gripping his foot with both hands, one on the toe end, the other on his heel.

My mind leaps to a bad traffic accident I covered while in uniform, in which the passenger was killed and the driver was pinned in, his lower leg caught in a tangle of twisted metal under the dash. When we finally extracted it, his mangled foot spun two fast revolutions like a small propeller.

I know I can't twist his foot around twice, but I can crank it with all the strength I have left.

Man, this guy's screams are getting annoying.

I pull his broken ankle and the rest of him toward me. He's too weak and distracted to fight it, and there is nothing for him to grab hold of.

"Bobby," I say, pushing the man's leg toward him. I let go of his foot and grab his upper thigh so he doesn't retract his leg. "Grab his calf and use it to pull yourself out."

The dirt is still sliding toward the boy, faster now than it was a minute ago. It's nearing the top of his thigh.

Bobby grabs the leg easily and pulls on it. Nothing happens.

"I can't budge, Sam. The dirt is so heavy."

It's probably the side pressure of the moving earth that's pinning him.

"Listen to me. Hug his leg as hard as you can. Concentrate on just your right leg. Okay? Don't try to bend it because that pushes your knee against the dirt. Lean to your left and pull your leg straight up. Lift with your hip and push up with your toes. Put your mind into it and all those taekwondo trained hip muscles."

"Okay, Sam," he says, tears streaming over his cheeks.

The crack on the opposite wall has widened and dirt is beginning to pour through it like water through a broken pipe.

"What's with the weenie voice, man? You're a black belt. You're a warrior. If you go down in here, I'm going down with you. You got to save me and I got to save you." I look at the man writhing in pain from any one of his many injuries. "And we might as well save this dumb shit."

Bobby laughs, part of it a sob.

"In fact," I say. "Our friend here is going to help. You Ready?"

"Yeah."

"YOU READY?"

"YES!"

"Then PULL. That's it. Hold on tight to his leg and pull your leg up with all your heart, mind, and body."

I grab the man's crotch with all five fingers and crush what was wounded from Bobby's earlier punch. He squeals and, as I'd hoped, reflexively yanks his leg back. Coupled with Bobby's effort, that pulls the boy's leg out of the dirt, minus his sandal.

I extend my hand to him. "See if you can reach my…" We clasp hands. "Gotcha! Come on now, pull with both arms."

"Ow! Sam, don't pull me against my knee joint. Let me pull on you."

"Okay. I'm here. Pull."

The crack in the far wall splits open about a foot, dropping apple-sized dirt clods and stones into the room, then a fast stream of chunky earth.

"Pull, Bobby. Come on, pull."

The boy's body trembles with the exertion until finally his left leg is free. He lies face down on the dirt, his chest heaving.

The top half of the far wall collapses inward, spilling dirt and stones into the left half of the room and over the moaning man. He sits part way up, shakes the dirt from his face, and looks toward me and the tunnel.

"Bobby, focus. We got to get out of here, now."

The left wall, where it meets the back one, caves in, covering the man up to his waist. The light bulb that had been somehow attached to the wall is now protruding half way out of the mound of dirt, still casting its sickly yellow light. It won't be long until it's covered and we're in total darkness.

Dirt begins trickling down onto my head from the three-foot span of wall overhead. I can't chance crawling out of the tunnel, turning around, and going back in head first. If a mass of dirt were to fall and cover the tunnel entryway, we'd be stuck in the room.

I'll have to crawl through the tunnel backwards.

"Get in here, now," I say, fighting to control my voice, and my mind.

Bobby low crawls toward me as I back in, once again inch-worming my body and pushing with my hands. The last thing I see before his body blocks my view is the rest of the left wall caving in, the sudden weight of the dirt pushing the sitting man forward as if he were trying to touch his knees with his nose. Actually, he does.

"Tell him to follow us," I say, as Bobby ducks his head into the tunnel.

He leans back out and gets out a couple of words before dirt begins dropping down on his head from the wall above.

"Let's move," I say, scooting back as fast as I can, which isn't fast at all.

"Dirt's falling on my legs!" Bobby screams, his panicked face nearly touching mine, his eyes huge with terror. "Crawl faster, Sam. I don't want it to trap me."

"This is my max," I say, my stomach cramping from the strain on my core.

"My leg" Bobby snaps his head around to look back. "The guy is grabbing my leg. His hand—it's reaching out of the dirt!"

"Kick it with your other one."

He's grunts with each blow. "Okay, I'm free."

The only sound now is our ragged breathing and our bodies scooting on the earthen floor. The boy and I are nose to nose, our breath hot. He bangs his head into mine so hard that I see sparks in the dark.

"I can only go so fast," I say irritably. "Don't—"

*Whoooosh!*

Silence from the room.

"What was that?" Bobby says, turning his head to look behind him. His forehead hits the wall and dirt crumbles onto his hands. "It's all dark in there now."

Probably the last of the walls spilling into the room, filling it.

"Just keep crawling, Son. Focus on crawling. Focus."

That's what I've got to do too. Focus on inching my torso and pushing with my hands. Oh man, the cement burns on my chest and gut hurt. The too-small shirt I was given is bunched up around my armpits and the bandages Mai applied have long since been torn away. I'm guessing that this foul dirt doesn't have healing properties. Oh well, an infection is the least of my problems right now.

Suddenly, I can't get enough air.

Panic surges through my body, and I want to push myself up through six feet of hard-packed dirt and run around that beautiful yard screaming and sucking in air.

You got enough air, I tell myself. It's a lie, but I force the thought into my mind anyway.

"That man's dead, isn't he?" Bobby says in a small voice. We're nose to nose.

"Think how good that fresh air up top is going to taste, Bobby. Better than a chocolate shake, burger, fries, or anything you've ever had. Keep moving. We have only about six feet to go." I think it's farther but lying to him is the best option right now.

"I can do this," he says, more to himself than to me. "Okay. Yeah, okay. I can do this."

"If you can do it, I can. If I can do it, you can."

"That's kinda dumb, Sam."

"What did you expect, Shakespeare? We're underground in a friggin' hole."

Bobby suddenly lunges forward banging his head into my cheekbone.

"Aggh!" My eyes scrunch shut against the pain.

"Something's on my legs," he whispers.

I open them. "What do you mean—"

"Dirt. I think it's dirt. Why is there dirt falling on my… OhGodohGodohGod! Back up faster, Sam. I think the tunnel starting to…"

I can hear it now. It's coming from behind the boy. Like flour through a sifter. A gentle deadly whisper, following us.

Dull light from the tunnel's entrance finds it's way to barely illuminate Bobby's perspiring face and his terrified eyes. Snot curls over his top lip.

"The tunnel is caving in behind me," he manages.

My midsection is starting to cramp from doing the inch-worm thing, cramping bad. I try to push back without raising and lowering my hips, but my triceps are on fire and they're starting to cramp. I pause.

"What are you doing?" Bobby says desperately, his forehead against mine.

It's not the time or place to give him a talk about lactic acid build up. "I need five seconds to… just… Okay, I'm good."

I'm pushing and inching again. I try to look back to see how far we are from the opening, but I can't turn my head far enough.

"How far are we?" I ask. "Can you see?"

Bobby strains to look around my shoulder. "From your feet? Maybe five or six feet." He looks at me for a second, the wheels in his head turning. "How you going to get out? You can't turn around."

Good question. It was hard enough squishing myself small enough to get in head first, and I still scraped my back on the tunnel opening. But to climb out backwards?

Bobby's eyes widen. "Sam?"

I heard it. More sifting.

"It's falling on my butt," he says, his jaw quivering. "It's catching up to us."

I push back hard. There's more light now and I can see the panic on Bobby's face in full HD. I'm trying hard not to let it show on mine. Getting whiffs of fresh air now. It's wonderful, invigorating. I want more.

Dirt drops from the ceiling onto the boy's mid back.

His eyes lock on mine, trance-like. He pulls himself forward until his face is squished against my shoulder. Still, he keeps trying to move forward.

"Bobby."

Nothing.

"Bobby, look at me. Hey! Look—At—Me." He does. I push back to give him space. "Keep pulling." He follows. "That's it. Good. Excellent." I push back another couple inches. "Now do it again." He follows. "When is your birthday? When will you be eighteen?"

He looks at me as if I'd lost my mind, which I have a little. "My birthday?"

Cool air on my feet. "Yeah, birthday. Cake. Ice cream. A clown with a red nose. Eighteen."

I push back.

"I'll be seventeen this August, so I will be eighteen on August thirty-first of next year. Why?"

He follows.

"You'll be an adult then. If your parents haven't beaten you to death over this trip of yours, I'm inviting you to come up to Portland to visit me. Stay for a few weeks and I'll train you."

I push back.

His face brightens. "Really? That would be so—"

Dirt pours down on his upper back and shoulders.

Bobby screams. "Noooo!"

I can feel the bottom rung of the ladder with the toe of my shoe, which means my legs from my knees on down are out of the tunnel. I try to come up on my knees but my butt hits the ceiling. Dirt drops onto me. The boy's forehead is pressing into mine again. Dirt rains over his terrified face and bounces into my mouth. Behind him, blackness. The tunnel is gone except for the space we're occupying—and it's filling fast.

"Stay with me, Son," I say against his cheek. "We're getting out of this. My feet are on the first rung... now the second rung. Stay close to me. There will be lots of good air in a few seconds."

My lower body is off the ground now and my feet are on the third or forth rung from the bottom. Already trashed from the hard pushing, my triceps are spasming. My stomach is cramping again and a knot is forming in my lower back.

Can't think of those things now. Got to focus on the motion of walking up the ladder backwards and supporting my weight on my quivering arms. Tex would be great at this.

Dirt pours down on Bobby's head. His legs are completely submerged and he hasn't moved his arms in about ten seconds. Hopefully, it's just a bit of loose soil that's covering him and not the full weight of the earth above. He shakes his head as if surfacing in a swimming pool.

Supporting most of my weight on my quivering right arm, I push my left hand into the dirt to find his. Got it. "Grip my hand. Yes, like that. Now pull on it and dig with your toes. You've got to move forward. Good, good. You're moving now. Fight for it, Son. Fight!"

The strain on my core is almost more than I can bear. Bobby's extra weight, and the weight of the dirt piling up on him is too much. My legs and body are at a forty-five degree angle now, my head almost out of the tunnel. My gut, legs, and arms are spasming. I'm not sure which is going to give out first.

No no no. That's not going to happen. I *will* ascend. Keep climbing with my feet. Keep hand walking backwards. Keep pulling the boy. Keep on, keepin' on.

Bobby's head clears the tunnel, but the rest of him is under dirt. And it's still falling on him. Still sifting. Sifting. *Siiiiift.*

*Like sand through an hourglass, so are the days of our lives.*

A voice-over would say that at the beginning of a soap opera my mother used to watch. Can't remember the name of it.

Will the vertical hole collapse? It shouldn't but I don't know.

"I'm stuck, Sam," Bobby says, unable to raise his head any higher than my trembling arms that are supporting nearly all my weight. "There's so much dirt on me."

I slip one foot over what has to be the highest rung then my other foot. Blood floods into my head fast and furious, my ears roaring like I'm in a subway station.

"Grab my other wrist, Bobby," I say. My voice sounds like I'm underwater. I press my palms into the ground to stabilize my arms. "Yes, that's good. Now pull as hard as you can and wiggle your body like a snake."

He jerks so hard on my left arm that my left foot slips off the rung. For a second, I think my right might slip off, but somehow it maintains its purchase. I can't reconnect my left to the rung because I'm hanging too far to the right. Fortunately, I'm still supporting most of my weight on my hands. Got to stay strong. If my arms give out—and it's getting close to that—I'll crumple into a pile on top of the boy.

How long can a person hang upside down before they pass out? Anyone ever ask an opossum? My left arm is shaking bad, real bad. I can't... Oh man! I can't... my right foot is slipping off...

A hand grips my loose, left ankle. Another grips my right one. I twist my body to look up and while I can't turn enough to see him, I know it's got to be Dung. Who else? Dung! He likes me. He really, really likes me.

I grip Bobby's wrists as hard as I can. "Hold on, Son. Hold on with all that you've got. You're getting out."

Dung's grip on my ankles is crushing, but I don't care. Bobby finally breaks free of the dirt and hangs from my wrist as big Dung pulls us out of what was about to be our grave.

"Mai friend me," the big man grumbles, as I float upward. "Not friend you."

# CHAPTER TWENTY-FIVE

"It was collapsing, Samuel. The dirt, was caving in. It wanted to bury Bobby and me down there. *It*, the tunnel, the dirt. It got the man, then it wanted us. It pursued us… It wanted to keep us… down there."

Bobby and I are sitting on the floor shaking and coughing up our last pieces of dirt. Are my eyes as wild looking as his? He's probably feeling the same way I am: physically drained and ultra high, like we've been eating uppers for a week without sleeping.

Samuel, kneeling on one knee between us, smiles and lightly touches our arms. "Please, both of you," he says, his voice soft, monotone. There's just the three of us in my room. I don't know where Dung went. "Lie all the way down on your backs."

I'm so fatigued I'll do anything Samuel says, and Bobby is still out of it and compliant as an infant. We stretch out, side by side, two strides away from the hole. "Good," Samuel says. "Now rest your arms on the floor."

Don't know if Bobby went down on his knees first when we got to the surface, or me. I just know that my legs wouldn't support me. Even now, ten minutes later, I couldn't stand on them if I were ordered to at gunpoint. So… tired. So very tired.

Samuel places his fingertips just below our navels. Weird, but I don't care right now. I'm just happy to be looking up at a ceiling that is solid and seven feet above me.

"Close your eyes." His words are spaced, not quite a whisper. "Do not speak… Just breathe slowly and deeply… Draw your breath all the way down to where you feel my fingers."

Bobby is breathing like an old work horse… So am I, now that I take a moment to notice. Samuel is trying to calm us, though I'd rather burn off my anxiety by… doing what? I can't even stand.

Strange warmth now where Samuel's fingers are touching me. A sort of… vibrating warmth. And it's spreading, I think. Yes, now I feel it in my abdomen. Is this what he did to himself in Portland?

He and Mai sat side by side in my kitchen, breathing in unison as she touched his wound with her fingertips. If that wasn't strange enough, each time they exhaled, they—whistled. Not a ditty, more like a release valve. Just when I thought things couldn't get any stranger, his bleeding stopped. Fifteen minutes earlier, he had been bleeding all over Mai, the chair, and the floor. To add to my amazement, he stood and rotated his arm a few times as if it were stiff from sleeping on it. Later, I asked Mai if he could do that to other people and she said not yet, but he was working on it.

Working on it. He said the same thing when he told me about his efforts to master the Fourth Level of speed as well as his telepathic ability. Looks like all his "working on it" is paying off. The energy, or whatever it is, is spreading more now, down to my legs and up through my stomach.

When I start to open my eyes, Samuel gently says, "Keep your eyes closed. I want both of you to breath in through your nose and draw your breath to your center, your *dāntián,* the spot I am touching."

His voice is soft, melodic. "If your nose is clogged with dirt, breathe in through your mouth. *See* the air coming in as white light traveling down your chest and into your *dāntián*. See the spot grow increasingly brighter and feel it grow even warmer than it is now. Think of it as a ball of white energy. Now, slowly release the air back out your mouth, taking with it fatigue, pain, anxiety from your body."

He increases the pressure of his touch just a little, which sends a slight jolt of electricity up and down my body. It isn't an unpleasant feeling. Actually… Oh man. I can feel my legs growing stronger and the muscles in my arms and chest regaining their strength.

"Good," he says. "That is one breath. Now breathe in again, drawing the white light of energy down your chest and into your *dāntián. Feel* that ball of energy spreading through your body. *Feel* how wonderful it is. *Feel* how energizing it is as the new energy reaches every part of you. Now release the air out of your mouth, letting go of all your fatigue and pain and anxiety. That is two breaths."

Five minutes later, we finish our forty-eighth breath and I feel amazing, like I just had a luxurious nap. The breathing and visualizing helped, but I'm convinced it's Samuel's touch that is mostly responsible for this incredible regeneration. He even did that whistling thing for about ten breaths.

After guiding us through two more breath exchanges, he tells us to breathe normally for a moment and experience the energy surging through our bodies.

"Feel the energy," his voice whispers into our brains. "*Feeeel* it and bring it with you now as you… open your eyes." He removes his fingers.

Bobby sits up quickly and looks around, his mind just realizing he's no longer underground. How wonderful I feel, so good that I could go back in that tunnel.… What am I saying? I look at Samuel's smiling face as I raise up onto my elbows.

"What did you do?" I ask.

He shakes his head, shrugs. "I am so sorry about the tunnel, Sam. I did not know you were down there until a few minutes ago. I started to follow you to the door, but Trai called from the monitor room and said Bay, the motorbike policeman, was leaning against the front gate. I did not think about the tunnel. I just thought you were checking the room. So Tex and Dung stayed with the man Tex knocked down while I went out front to see if Bay was badly hurt. When I came back, I hurried to the monitor room where I thought you would have gone after checking your room. They said they had not seen you. That is when it dawned on me that you must have gone down in the tunnel. I am so sorry." He shakes his head at the thought. "I should have been able to read you. But I... You could have been—"

I sit all the way up and take hold of his upper arm. "You chose right. There was no more room in that tunnel for anyone else anyway." He shakes his head and I know he hasn't let go of the unwarranted guilt. "What happened to the policeman?" I ask, to distract him.

Out of the corner of my eye I see Bobby stir a little. When I put my hand on the boy's shoulder, he slowly turns his head toward me, his eyes still holding onto that dazed look. He has yet to say a word.

"He will be okay in a few minutes," Samuel says. "Bay was kicked off his motorbike."

"Kicked?"

"He said he saw the pedicab pull up to the gate and was going to ride down to check it out. He had just started rolling when he saw something come at him out of the corner of his eye from the shadows behind the south wall. It was a man leaping into the air. He could not see him clearly, except for his red shirt and bald head. The man kicked him in his side, hard enough to launch him off his motorbike. Bay was so stunned that he did not know the bike continued to go on until he looked down the street and saw it hit the pedicab, and us."

"Damn. Kicked off his motorbike. You said he was bald? The man who hurt Do`a was bald. And the man who killed Viet."

Samuel's nod is barely perceptible.

"You think the kicker went over the wall?"

"No. Lam said he did not come in. If there is another wave, he will probably be in that group." He looks at Bobby, a worried father's concern written all over his face.

"He fought well," I say. "He is a real warrior. It was awful down there. Hell. But he kept his head when most would have panicked. In fact, I came real close to panicking a couple of times."

"Sam?" Bobby says, sounding like he's coming out of a deep sleep.

"How you feeling, troop?"

He twists his head right and left, popping his neck. "I uh… I guess I feel… awesome. Head's still fuzzy, but it's like I could run a mile."

Samuel feigns innocence.

I smile. "Yeah, same here. You want to go out and run a mile?"

"No." He glances toward the hole. "That man. He's still down there."

I lightly squeeze his shoulder muscles. "You handled yourself well, Taekwondo Man. No adult could have done a better job."

The boy nods a little, his eyes focused on the hole. "I was sleeping down there. I heard shouting coming through the tunnel. I thought it was you... like you were back and something was going on. So I crawled through real fast and started climbing the ladder when that man... he was standing above me and looking down. He had a knife." Bobby's words are coming faster and faster. "He said something like, 'Good, they won't have to dig a grave for you.' I dropped down and went back into the tunnel. He chased after me... all the way into that room. He tried to stab me, but I ducked and his knife stuck in the wall and the handle broke and—"

"Can you two stand?" Samuel asks, his hand on the back of the boy's neck.

"Come on," I say, rocking forward onto my knees and taking the boy's arm. "Let's get up. You help me up and I'll help you."

Incredibly, my legs support me. I think I could even do a couple of kicking rounds on the heavy bag.

Bobby tentatively tests his weight on his. He looks at Samuel, his eyes large. "Wow," he says, shaking his head. "Mystical. I feel so strong and my head doesn't hurt anymore." He looks toward the hole, shivers, and looks away quickly.

"What happened while we were gone," I ask Samuel.

"Outside," he says, moving toward the door.

I peer into the hole as we pass. It hasn't completely collapsed, though dirt has spilled from the walls of the tunnel entrance across the bottom of the hole.

That awful sifting sound...

\*

The onset of a new day has turned the sky into a grayish blue. Samuel, Bobby, and I are standing where Tex jumped on the intruder about forty-five minutes ago. Seems a whole lot longer than that. I guess fighting for your life in a collapsing dirt tunnel has a way of stretching out time.

Peering through the hedge, I see Tex posted behind a big palm near the *koi* pond. He senses us, turns, and shoots a salute our way. Across the yard, Phat Ho and Cong kneel flush with the south wall so that an intruder won't see them until they've committed themselves over the top.

I know that works because a rookie partner of mine scooted over a solid wood fence and was promptly shot in the jaw by a hold-up man pressed flat against the other side. He survived and everyone learned to never go over a wall until you know for sure the other side is clear.

"Dung carried the injured men out the gate and dumped them on the sidewalk next to the others. He is there with Bay watching the front."

"How hurt is the officer?" I ask.

"He will be fine. He was not going fast when it happened, and he fortunately landed mostly on his arm and shoulder. His head hit just a little. It could have been worse." Samuel shakes his head, probably feeling some responsibility for his friend's injuries. "I talked with Harry on the phone and brought him up to speed. He is very angry about all this. He has gathered some trusted officers and they are on their way."

"About damn time. Is Mai okay? Kim, Linh?"

Something passes across Samuel's eyes. "I talked to Mai a moment ago. Mother is asleep." He pauses, maybe thinking about her return. "I just hope all this did not take too much out of her."

"She will be okay," I say, not knowing if it's true. "I'm sure the strain just tired her."

He nods and looks around the yard. After a long moment, he says, "During the war, we were attacked many times at morning's early light just like this. It is still dark enough not to see well and the troops would be groggy with sleep." He scans the yard, his eyes missing nothing while his brain remembers. "In prison, my cell mate, an Air Force pilot, would sometimes cry when seeing the morning's arrival."

"Cry?"

He looks at me for a moment and then resumes scanning the yard. "It made him sad, you see. Sad that he did not die in the night."

I don't know if it's the gray light or the long night, or both, but Samuel looks to have aged ten years. His eyes are alert, though, just as I imagine they were in the jungle so many years ago and in that prison.

He nods at whatever is in his mind, shrugs a what-are-you-going-to-do, and glances at me without turning his head. "Name was Captain William Blakely. It took him twelve months but he finally got his wish."

Tex says something just louder than a whisper.

Samuel tenses. "He says that the usual street noise on the south side, people going to work and such, has stopped."

"Why?" I ask.

"I think because someone is stopping it." He lifts his cell but it rings before he can tap in a number. "Yes?"

"What is happening?" Bobby asks me, his voice shaky.

"Don't know."

"Okay," Samuel says into the phone. He points with it toward the monitor room.

"Is something going to happen, Sam?" Bobby asks, walking so close to me that our hips are touching.

"I'm not sure. But you'll be fine. The monitor room is like a safe room."

"Oh," he says, tentatively as we near the room. "There's no dirt tunnel, right?"

Trai opens the door.

"Samuel," Lam says, looking intently at the monitor screen farthest from the door. "I think bad news."

*

The image shows the entire side street and the big tree that the first three scaled to get over the wall. Like the back alley, it's a dirt road with empty potholes, the rain water that filled them during the storm now evaporated into the increasing heat. Harsh morning sunlight finding its way through low tree limbs and around the edge of a tall building, splash the road and the side of the wall. One long sun streak disappears on the right side of the monitor.

"One man there," Lam says, tapping the top of the screen, indicating a tall bald man wearing a red overshirt and shorts. He's turned sideways, looking toward the street that passes in front of the house and the dirt side street.

"The man who kicked the policeman off his motorbike," Samuel says.

And beat Do`a and choked Viet to death.

Trai, three monitors over and leaning in close to the screen, says something.

Samuel, Bobby, and I step up behind him. The screen shows five men on the backside of the house. Two of them have pulled Samuel's man out of his car and are kicking him on the ground.

"Samuel, we've got to help—"

"Men go," Trai says, pointing at the quintet sprinting away from the motionless man and disappearing at the side of the monitor.

Lam points at his screen. "Look. Assholes here."

His screen, the right side now partially distorted by sunlight that's splashed on the camera, shows the men running down the dirt road toward the tree.

"They come wall," Lam says.

Behind me, Samuel talks rapidly into his cell, probably warning Cong and Tex.

The biggest of the group leaps up and grabs a low hanging branch, finds a foot hold and pulls himself up and into the tree. A second man jumps for the limb, but his fingers fail to take hold and he drops to the ground. His buddies boost him up and his hands find purchase on the limb.

Samuel is back on his phone. "What is he saying, Bobby," I ask.

"It's the ambulance people. He's telling them to enter the back alley from the north. He's getting help for the man who got kicked back there."

Now the sun is washing out about a third of the monitor and sending streaks and starburst into the other two thirds. We can still make out the men, but the bald one wearing the red shirt at the end of the road is somewhere behind the washout. A third man moves under the limb… but he abruptly turns and looks across the dirt road. We can't see what he's looking at because it's off the monitor's scope. Now the other two men are looking.

"What are they looking at?" I ask. "What's over there?"

"A small passageway between two buildings," Samuel says. "It leads all the way to the main street."

The whiteout on the monitor hasn't increased, though the light streaking into the unaffected area is intense, like laser beams with starbursts along their length. Through it, we can make out the three men moving toward the small passage.

"Which monitor shows the south wall from inside?" I ask.

"This one, I think." Bobby says, bending toward a monitor between Lam and Trai.

Trai scoots his chair over to it and zooms the shot toward the top of the wall. He scans left to right, stopping where the infamous tree extends above it. The top half of a face appears over the wall's edge, a hand on each side of it. Like a 'Kilroy was here.' Now we can see his entire face, shoulders, and his arms as he scoots himself over.

Samuel, still looking at the dirt road monitor, taps the top of the screen. "Zoom," he commands. Before Lam does, I can see that the remaining men have yet to move, all three still looking toward what appears to be a pair of legs at the top of the screen. Now the guy in the red shirt and shorts joins them. Lam zooms in on the legs: gray slacks, blue shoes.

"Blue Converse," Samuel says. "Sifu."

"Whoa," Bobby says, still looking at the yard monitor. "That guy just jumped up and grabbed that dude's arm who was coming over the wall and pulled him off. Man, he hit the ground hard."

I look just as Phat Ho wraps a scarf around the seated man's neck, catches the weighted end in his mouth, and pulls the garrote tight. Cong whips a knife from his belt and sticks it under the man's eye.

"Check it out," Bobby says. "Guy has one arm. What's he doing? And look at the size of that blade the other dude has. This is some serious caca."

"Samuel, they aren't going to…"

"Do not worry, Son," Samuel says, without moving his eyes away from the other monitor. "They will not kill him unless he tries to get a weapon. But I do not think he will try."

Judging by the man's bulging face and Cong's knife point just under his eye, I think Samuel's absolutely right.

Trai backs the image out until we can see the second man's face and arms coming over the wall. His eyes widen almost comically when he sees his buddy down on the ground. He quickly disappears back into the tree.

"If you back out the camera," I say to Lam, "I think one more man will be joining the group." Lam does and sure enough, the man who changed his mind drops down to the ground. "What do you think Sifu is saying to them."

Samuel shakes his head. "I do not know. But whatever it is, it has their full attention and it is stopping them from going over the wall. Trai, show me the yard. I want to check on Tex."

Trai broadens the shot of the third monitor. Tex is still hunkered down, his head moving back and forth as he watches the yard.

"He is good," Samuel says.

"We need to get out there," I say, "to help Sifu. Cong and Phat Ho have the intruder secured inside so I think—"

"It would be too late," Samuel says. On the monitor, the legs move toward the men, revealing hands, arms, blue overshirt, and long gray hair. It's Sifu, alright, and he looks as casual as he did when watching the *koi* in the pond.

"I don't understand, Samuel. We can run around the block or, I don't know, someone can lift me over the wall, or—"

"Son," Samuel says calmly. "It will be too late—for all those men."

# CHAPTER TWENTY-SIX

The right side of the screen is still washed by harsh sunlight on the camera lens. The diagonal light streaking across the left side appears to be diminishing, though it still affects the clarity of the image. Shen Lang Rui stands motionless, his hands at his sides as the five men form a semicircle around him, like a scene in an old Hong Kong chop-socky movie.

I ask Samuel, "Why don't they just ignore him and go over the wall?"

He shrugs. "It is possible one of them knows him. Or maybe they sense the power of his presence, his *chi*, and they feel they must deal with him before they proceed."

"I don't understand why we aren't helping him," Bobby says worriedly, his shoulder touching mine. "He's an old man."

There are four light streaks on the monitor now, down from five, and the one closest to Sifu is creating small sparkles of light. One is on the master's chest, whiting out some of his torso. Red Shirt points at one of the men across from him and jabs his finger toward Sifu. The man, whose back is to the video camera, quickly lifts the back of his shirt and extracts a gun from his waistband.

I think Sifu is moving toward the man, though I can't be sure because the light streaks have started bouncing about. One of them partially covers the gunman's upper body for just an instant, washing him out… Okay, we got clarity now…

My God!

The gunman's head, his eyes bugged, his lips pulled back in an ugly grimace, has been twisted all the way around, one hundred and eighty degrees, so that he's facing the camera, while his torso still faces Sifu, who stands with his arms along his sides. The man crumples into the dirt, the gun still in his hand. Shen Lang Rui steps back away from him and looks at the other men.

"Sam?" Bobby whispers. "What just happened? I couldn't see the old man do anything."

I don't have an answer. I mean, I saw the end result but I... The boy wouldn't understand; I'm not sure I do.

The sun streaks start dancing on the screen again and through them, I can make out one of the men picking up the dropped weapon. Sifu is suddenly—and I mean suddenly—on him and... hits him? I think he hit him. The master's body just sort of jerked. It's like watching an old movie film that had been pieced together with a few frames missing. I didn't actually see... I don't think I saw... I don't think I saw his arms move.

The man who picked up the weapon is still standing, his body shaking as if he were standing on some kind of a vibrating surface. He collapses straight down to the dirt.

"*Choi oi*!" Lam says, shaking his head. He zooms in on the man's face.

"His face," I say, staring with disbelief at what looks like his jaw. It's been twisted or something so that his chin... It's protruding just short of his ear.

Samuel's voice is low, sad, I think. "Sifu's punch broke the man's jaw bone away from his skull, but the skin kept it from flying loose."

I'm speechless. The other day I saw Shen Lang Rui punch a chunk of palm tree off and send it flying several feet. A palm's bark is much stronger than human skin so he must have controlled the impact of his punch when he hit the man. Still, I didn't see it.

Lam backs the shot out, just in time to see three of the men take off in a panicked dash toward the street that passes in front of the house. Lam draws the camera back far enough that we can see them round the corner, the last man looking back at Red Shirt who is gesturing for them to come back.

Samuel is bent and watching the monitor carefully. "This man is a fool," he says. "He kicked the policeman off his motorbike, but his skill is no match for Sifu. Is he blind to what happened to the other two?"

"Sifu?" Bobby says. "I know you said he was a sifu but—whoa!"

Samuel suddenly straightens, his eyes focused on the far wall above the closed mini blinds. The only light in here is coming from the monitors, but I swear I see his face blanch. He looks at me, his eyes… seeing something? His head swivels back to face the wall.

"Samuel? What is it?"

He backs away from the monitor. "You uh… you and Bobby stay here." He looks down at the screen. "I must go out there."

"I'll go with you."

"Stay here," he says, his voice just above a whisper, his eyes on the far wall, his chest heaving like he just ran a sprint. "Stay here, watch the boy, take care of things."

"Samuel, what is…"

He's out the door.

I look at Trai, who looks as confused as I must. "Can you follow him on the monitors?"

"I can do," he says.

On Lam's monitor, Red Shirt leaps into the air in what looks like a stupid attempt to scissor Sifu's head.

*Vovinam*, I wonder, the same martial art my opponent fought with in the warehouse. Dumb move, hoss. A real dumb move against Shen Lang Rui.

The old man steps back, avoiding the technique, and sweeps the man's feet out from under him as he lands. The bald man hits the dirt hard.

"Awesome," Bobby says. "But why doesn't he destroy him like he did the other two?"

"Maybe because the man has not shown a weapon. He has only shown how ignorant he is by leaping into the air."

Red Shirt scrambles to his feet and throws a high round-house kick at Sifu, who ducks it and, with extraordinary speed, jabs his fingers into the man's crotch.

"Oooo that's gotta hurt," Bobby laughs, when Red Shirt snaps forward and clutches his groin. He spews his breakfast into the dirt. "And that's just gross," the boy adds.

"Trying to break his fighting spirit," I say.

"His nuts too," Bobby notes. "Made the dude toss chunks."

The man whose head was turned around remains motionless, his rear end in a pothole. The other with his jaw out of joint—literally out of joint—has not stopped rolling from side to side and clutching his face. I can't begin to imagine what it must feel like to have a major piece of my skull ripped away.

Shen Lang Rui stands calmly waiting for Red Shirt to straighten. When he finally does, shakily, and with a lot of grimacing, Sifu points his finger down the road.

The big man nods, then looks over at his two men lying on the ground. He looks back toward the street, takes a couple of steps in that direction, stops. He looks at Sifu and shakes his head. Meaning what?

Red Shirt cross steps fast, launching a sidekick at Sifu that would kill an elephant. But the master is no longer where he was. Now he's beside the stupid man, his hands a blur on Red Shirt's chest, abdomen, and arms. The moves are too fast to decipher what he's doing. In a blink, I see the man's shirt shredded as if he were being attacked by a jungle cat. I watch the shreds whip around with a life of their own and what they reveal of his skin looks bloody.

The bald man thuds into the dirt, nearly landing on his buddy, the one who will be forced to have liquid meals for a couple of years.

A high-ranking opponent of Jigoro Kano, founder of judo, once said that fighting the master "was like trying to fight an empty jacket." I think we just saw what that means. One instant Sifu was standing at the end of Red Shirt's incoming foot, and in the next he's standing next to his torso raining a storm of blows all over the man's upper body.

"No no no!" Lam says loudly to his monitor. "Asshole fall by gun."

His screen shows a different angle, one with Red Shirt on his side, his back toward Sifu, and the gun lying next to his thigh. There is no way the master can see it.

"Where is Samuel, Trai?"

"He here," he says, pointing at the far right screen that shows Samuel running down the sidewalk toward the south wall junction. Tex is behind him, his hands slapping the sidewalk impossibly fast. Now Mai bursts through the open gate, running hard in the same direction.

"Asshole! Asshole!" Lam shouts at his monitor.

Red Shirt has picked up the gun, holding it close to his abdomen and out of Sifu's sight. The master looks at him as if he knows something is up.

In the academy, we were trained that when there is no cover and you're close to an armed threat lying on the ground, you should move toward the head, which makes for an awkward shot for the bad guy and buys you a second or two longer to do your thing. But Sifu is just standing there looking… confused? Yes, confused. Why?

Sifu moves his right foot back a step. No, wait, that wasn't a step. It was more like a stumble. Is he swaying now? He grasps his left arm near his shoulder as he takes a stumbling step forward.

In the background, Samuel rounds the corner fast, his head down, arms pumping.

Red Shirt rolls over onto his back and grimaces in pain from whatever Sifu did to him. His arm is draped across his abdomen now, the gun still partially hidden.

Mai rips around the far corner and Tex follows a moment later, his hands slapping the ground like pistons.

Samuel, about ten strides away from Sifu, appears to be shouting. He can't possible see the gun so what is he—

Sifu's body sags for a moment, his head down, and his arms limp at his sides.

Red Shirt arcs the gun across his body.

Sifu crumples straight down into the dirt, legs folded under him, his head downcast as if sitting in meditation. Except his hands aren't clasped in his lap. They're laying in the dirt on each side of him, palms facing upward, fingers limp.

Samuel must see the gun now because he cuts in front of his teacher, protecting him from the bullet.

Fire spits out the end of Red Shirt's weapon. A geyser of dirt erupts back where the dirt road meets the street.

At a full-on run, Samuel kicks Red Shirt in the face, snapping his head back with tremendous force and sending his body rolling. When Red Shirt stops, he doesn't move. Samuel picks up the gun, pops out the clip, jacks a round into the dirt, and hands the butt end to Mai. He looks toward Tex who has stopped next to Sifu, his hand on the master's shoulder, his head dipped to see the older man's face.

Tex looks over at his friend.

Samuel hesitates and stands motionless, as if he can't move or doesn't want to. Then he rushes to Sifu. Kneeling in the dirt, he wraps his arm around the master's shoulders and lays him gently onto his back. Mai waits, her arms hanging limply, her right hand holding the gun with two fingers.

Tex places the heel of one hand on the center of Sifu's chest and his other hand on top of his first one. He begins compressions, but he needs to go faster, a hundred or more a minute they taught us at in-service. With his fingertips, Samuel touches his teacher's chest, just over his heart. It looks like he's doing that breathing thing he did with Bobby and me, his eyes closed, or maybe he's looking down at his great teacher.

Mai kneels next to her father, without haste.

*

A couple minutes after I joined the others, and a few minutes before the ambulance arrived, Sifu's eyes fluttered open and looked up into Samuel's. Tex stopped the compressions, but Samuel continued to touch his teacher's forehead, making that strange whistle each time he exhaled. When the master's lips moved, Samuel quickly lowered his ear to his mouth. A moment later, Sifu's eyes closed, his face softened, and he stilled.

One of the crew pronounced him dead at eight forty, twenty minutes after trying to revive him.

Mai and I are on each side of Samuel now, not touching him but in position should we have to. Tex is next to Mai, his arm holding onto her leg. We watch the ambulance move slowly to the end of the dirt road, make a left onto the street, and disappear. No siren.

Behind us, another ambulance crew is working on Red Shirt and the man with the broken-off chin. Earlier, they placed what looked like a heart monitor on the one whose head had been twisted about. They disconnected it after a few minutes and focused on the other two. Several officers look on, one pointing a pistol at Red Shirt as the medics work.

Before I ran out of the monitor room, I saw another ambulance on one of the screens pull up next to the injured man in the back alley. I think he will be okay because he was standing and leaning on his car.

"Is Harry here?" Samuel asks, his voice frail.

"When I left the house, Harry hadn't arrived yet," I say. "The officer at the gate said he was a few minutes away. He told me I had to stay there, but I took off before he could stop me."

"Don't worry about it," Mai says. "Harry will fix everything. Father, we should go back to the house. Do you want me to ask a policeman to drive you there?"

He doesn't answer for so long that I wonder if he might not have heard her. Finally, he says, "I want to walk."

I can hear Tex sniff as we move ever so slowly down the dirt road. We turn right onto the sidewalk and head toward the front gate where at least half a dozen police cars are parked every which way.

Samuel stops, his face puzzled, his voice just above a whisper. "One of the ambulance people said that his identification noted his age as seventy-three. All these years I thought my teacher was my age, or a year or two older. I do not remember how I came to that conclusion." He doesn't say anything for several seconds, then, "Sifu used Level Four on the man who died. I told you about that, right, Son?"

"Yes," I say.

We've actually talked about Level Four several times but Samuel isn't thinking clearly right now. That explains why I couldn't see what Sifu did. The sunlight was distorting the screen, but it wouldn't have mattered if the image had been high def because there would have been nothing to see anyway. Except for the results.

"You said that it is dangerous and that you didn't know for sure how it worked. You thought it transcended the physical, that it was willed. You said you couldn't control it but Sifu could."

Samuel nods slowly, his eyes downcast. After a moment, he says, "The time I achieved Level Four, I nearly collapsed after. I remember my heart beat so rapidly I thought it might burst from my chest, and I was so weak I had to lie down for a long while." He pauses for several seconds. "Seventy-three is only eight years older than sixty-five, but that is a significant number of years at that age." Mai has interlaced her arm into his, and Tex is once again holding onto Mai's leg.

"I think," Samuel says, pausing for a moment, "I think Level Four was too much for his heart. I know he had not been feeling well and he had seen a doctor, but I do not know what for."

"Father," Mai says gently. "Sifu died helping us. Fighting to keep us safe."

Samuel nods.

Down at the gate, Harry's rotund figure lumbers out of a police car. He waves and begins walking toward us.

"'Even death is not to be feared by one who has lived wisely,'" Samuel says.

The three of us look at him.

"That is what Sifu said into my ear. Buddha's words." He nods his head for a long moment, his eyes on the sidewalk. "Even in the end, he was teaching me. My sifu."

# EPILOGUE

Sifu Shen Lang Rui was buried three days ago. Father—I've been calling him that for several days now—said that his teacher was mostly a Buddhist, though he enjoyed going to Catholic churches from time to time. Since he was a Chinese man living in Vietnam, Father blended the two cultures into the funeral.

Following the Vietnamese Buddhist custom, he cleaned and dressed his teacher, placed him in a coffin, and set it up in the living room with lots of incense. White and pale-colored flowers were sent by friends and placed beautifully around the room, to which Mai and I added three dozen white lotus. Mai said our flowers represented complete purification. Father found an eight by ten photograph of Sifu sitting at their dinner table in their condo and placed it on the coffin.

To honor Sifu's Chinese heritage and customs, he was dressed in black slacks, white shirt, and his blue Converse, all acceptable colors for the burial. Following custom, Father broke Sifu's comb in half and kept one part for himself and placed the other in the coffin. Mai, Kim, Linh, Anh, and Ly were told not to wear jewelry, and no one was to wear red because it denotes happiness in Chinese.

Father ensured that Sifu wore nothing that was red, which Chinese custom believes would turn him into a ghost. However, red paper was draped over some of the figurines, all of which had to be positioned far away from the coffin. Before Father sealed it for the last time, all of us were told to face away because the Chinese believe that witnessing the process is unlucky.

Sifu was buried in a cemetery where he and Father had trained many times over the years. Father bribed the officials there to bury him in the shade of a grove of trees, a favorite place for their workouts. He said that burying his teacher in the same place where he as a student had so profoundly changed as a martial artist and as a human being, would lock in all that he had learned from his great teacher.

Harry the police captain micromanaged the investigation of the attack. A similar one in the United States that caused three deaths, multiple injuries, and a tunnel cave in, would be news for a week with players interviewed on *The Today Show* and *CNN*. That didn't happen here because Harry instructed his hand-picked officers on how to 'handle' different aspects of the case. If he hadn't, my father and I would have been put through the ringer. Never mind that the fight in the tunnel was self-defense and Father was fighting to protect his home and family. I haven't asked how Harry managed it all and how much was paid to specific officials, but for now it looks real good for us. I guess their way of handling situations can come in handy even when you're the good guys.

A work crew dug out the underground room and recovered the body of the man Bobby and I fought. I know that horrible incident and the death bothers the boy; it certainly does me. I'm not feeling guilt that the man died down there, it's the idea that he was buried alive that's so awful on the psyche.

Harry told my father that our family hadn't been linked to the release of the girls held captive in the warehouse in Bien Hoa and the subsequent killing of several people, all of whom had been traced to Lai Van Tan. Harry said the Bien Hoa police would have done their own manipulating to keep Lai Van Tan out of the picture, but a watchdog group called the

International Human Rights of Exploited Children got wind of the rescue. Father thinks his friends at the orphanage might have made that happen. Apparently, Lai Van Tan is learning that his power and money is meaningless to the pit bull human rights group. Actually, his power is pretty well shot anyway, and the same with his organization. But guys like him have a way of coming back. Hopefully, the human rights group will make that most difficult for him.

Father stayed with Kim for a day and a half after Sifu's heart attack, never once leaving the room. Mai said it wasn't until the next night, sometime after three a.m. that she heard a noise out in the garden. When she looked out her window, she saw our father weeping by the *koi* pond. He joined us for breakfast the next morning, looking like he hadn't slept for a while, which I'm sure he hadn't.

Bobby's parents called from the *Tan Son Nhat* Airport while the police were still at the house. They had a return flight to the United States in ninety minutes and asked if I could bring the boy to the airport. We showered the tunnel off and changed into clean clothes in twenty minutes flat. Mai wanted to take us, but I encouraged her to stay because I thought Samuel needed her more. She told the taxi driver where to take us and to wait and bring me back to the house. She gave Bobby a big hug, and the boy and Tex shared a quiet talk before Bobby gave Tex an awkward hug that nearly knocked the legless man over.

Bobby didn't speak during the ride. I know the boy and I are going to have nightmares of that terrible tunnel attack, watching the deadly alley fight on the monitors, and witnessing poor Shen Lang Rui's fatal heart attack. Bobby is mature, but he's still a kid who has been exposed to terrible violence and death.

I hated to just send him off without us having a long talk, a debriefing of sorts, but there wasn't time. I made sure he had my phone number, Mai's number, my email, and hers. I encouraged him to sleep on the plane and get a couple nights of good rest at home before we talk about what all happened here. I found that process to work well with witnesses of violence.

Since there wouldn't be enough time at the airport to talk to his parents about what had happened, I told him that I would be glad to call them after they got home. Bobby said he would tell them about it first and then brief me as to what parts he skimmed over or didn't mention at all.

His parents, both in their fifties and barely five feet tall, were more happy than angry to see their son. I'm betting the anger will show itself when things settle. They thanked me profusely for doing such a good job keeping him safe. Bobby and I looked at each other and almost laughed.

It was sad seeing him go. Sometimes I think people are put into our lives for a reason, other times I'm not so sure. Bobby came along so that I could help a young man who was reaping the repercussions of making a bad decision. I guess it could be argued that his contact with me nearly cost him his life, but my contact with him nearly cost me mine as well. Maybe we were simply destined to share such a horrific experience so that we both grew a little from it. Maybe we have more to share. Well, whatever the reason, I request from the Big Overseer one thing: Could you make these lessons a little easier, a little less traumatic? How about one that doesn't give Bobby and me nightmares and claustrophobia forever?

On the other hand, it's often said the hard lessons are the most profound. Maybe this was one to show me that I'm still a protector. I failed terribly at that in Portland, but I was able to succeed with Bobby. So what was Bobby's lesson?

Maybe that all other challenges in his life will seem like a leisurely stroll in the park compared to this one.

I was already missing him so much that I barely noticed the traffic madness on the way back to the house. Maybe I'm getting used to it. Maybe I'm getting comfortable here. Maybe after all that's happened, thinking I'm getting comfortable is a pretty dumb thing to think. Lots of maybes.

Lu received a head concussion, broken jaw, and torn neck tendons. Apparently his boyfriend, one of Lai Van Tan's goons, got suspicious and confronted Lu about all his questions. When Lu got frightened and tried to leave, the boyfriend beat him severely. Then Lai Van Tan ordered him killed. The plan was to have Lu stabbed by the front gate on camera, part of the Lai Van Tan's psychological warfare. That didn't happen, probably because the pedicab driver and the male passenger, the boyfriend, saw the Volvo and van when they passed by us. Or maybe it was the phantom police motorbike that put a crimp in their plans. Lu will be okay, eventually.

I met Anh, Mai's other sister, a warm and big-hearted woman. She wasn't blessed with her sisters' good looks, but she had a wonderful sense of humor. One time at breakfast she told me that she had just gone to the doctor and he said that her chronic bad back was a result of getting older. When she told him that she wanted a second opinion, he said, "Okay, you're homely too." Her goofy jokes were much needed.

Mai and I have shared some wonderful moments. We've had long talks, long walks, and periods when we didn't need to speak at all. We've been to the eighth floor of the building under construction twice. The first time we just sat on the window ledge, sipped wine, and watched the sun go down and the stars come up. Last night we went up again and this time we made love. We didn't spar as foreplay like we did the first time, though we did dance again to the music in our hearts.

She whispered that she loved me and I told her I liked her butt. When she started to do that nipple twist thing on me, I quickly confessed that I was crazy in love with her. She got that look on her face when she doesn't understand my English, and asked if crazy in love was good. I assured it was. We were both scared by our feelings because we didn't know what the future held for us.

Mark, my friend and boss in Detectives, called a day after Shen Lang Rui died. He asked how I was doing and feeling. At first, I didn't tell him anything about what had happened since I'd been in Saigon, though I did tell him that it was hot, the food was fantastic, and the traffic was nutso.

He said that the front office, in an effort to save money on upper echelon salaries, had offered him an early retirement and that he was thinking about taking it. He could leave in six weeks and his long-time boyfriend, David, a dentist, could retire anytime he wants. We chatted for several minutes about who was doing what to whom on the job then, after a long pregnant pause, Mark got to the main reason he was calling.

"I've been thinking a lot about what happened, about what I know," he said.

When he came to my house that night a few days before I came over here, he said that he had figured it out, which I interpreted as meaning he knew I was somehow implicated in the extraordinary violence that happened at Portland State University. He didn't say what all he knew, but judging by how angry he was at me in my living room, I can assume he figured out a lot of it.

"Okay," I said to him on the phone, then I let it hang there to see where he was going with it.

He took a deep breath and exhaled before he spoke. "You and I have been friends a long time," he said. "I realized early on that you are an ethical and moral man. I saw that you lived and worked by strict principles of doing what you think is right, treating people with respect, even when those people had committed the most atrocious crimes. Maybe you were born that way, maybe your mother and grandfather raised you that way, or maybe it was your martial arts training."

"All three," I said.

"Whatever the reason, I have to trust that you know what you're doing. That you have the right reasons for concealing—"

"Mark," I interrupted. "Pour yourself a cup of coffee. I'm going to tell you everything."

For the next half hour, I told him about Lai Van Tan and how he pursued Father to Portland and how that led to the violence at Portland State University. I told him about the sex-trade business here and the battle we had freeing the girls. When I finished telling him of the fight in the tunnel, Mark was quiet for a long moment. Then, "Thank you, Sam. How awful this has been for you. But I feel even better now about my decision. It's a big weight off my chest."

"Mine too, boss. I apologize for leaving you out of it. Please know that I don't take any of this lightly."

He took a deep breath, exhaled. "Remember in the academy when there were no grays, when everything was black and white?"

"Were we ever that young?"

"When you coming home?" he asked. "You still got a job here."

I sighed. "Oh man... I don't know. Maybe another week or so. I want to help in whatever way I can to get things situated here with my family."

Last night Father and I talked into the wee hours. He told me that he didn't think Kim would live much longer. The doctors had always been uncertain, but he had always been positive that she would survive. That is, until of late when she began deteriorating. He said she no longer responds to the medication, and his limited healing abilities have had no effect. He thinks she knows what is going on with her, which is the reason she insisted on coming back to the house.

When I asked if Mai knew, he said he thought so. He said she is incredibly close to her mother and he just hadn't gathered his courage to sit down with her and talk it out.

We were sitting on the bench by the *koi* pond, the night sounds soothing, a lone cricket chirped over where the south wall met the east one, a slight wind rustled the palm tree fronds but did nothing to reduce the terrible humidity. Thunder was grumbling somewhere in the northern sky, reminding me of what Mai said about the nightly rumble of distant artillery during the war. I wondered if Father was remembering that. My guess is that it's never far from his mind.

He scooted off the bench and squatted by the edge of the pond. The white *koi* swam over to him and nibbled at the finger that gently stirred the water.

He turned around to face me, dropping one knee to the ground. "I have thought a lot about taking a journey to the Mekong Delta. It is south of Saigon, a very large area that supplies much rice to the world. About three years ago, a friend told me that during the war some people, no more than three or four, saw two towering statues there, hidden somewhere on a plantation or along one of the many rivers. Who knows, they might be gone now or covered by overgrowth. Both were supposedly fifty feet high, carved by a man known as the "coconut monk." Father smiled at that for a moment. "Coconut monk. I like that."

"What are the statues, Father?"

"One is of Jesus and one is of Buddha. They are embracing, you see."

"Wow. That would be incredible to see. What a journey."

Father nodded but didn't say anything for a while as he poked at the dirt with a twig. Behind him, the white *koi* hadn't moved, its eyes watching. After a while, Father looked up at me, his eyes wet. "I am not old, but I am getting there." He shrugged. "For a while, a little voice has been telling me to go look for those statues."

"Then you should listen to it," I said. "Listening to that voice has done well for you all these years."

"You are correct, sir." He smiled. "Ed McMahon used to say that on the *Tonight Show* with his bud Johnny Carson. They are both gone now."

I didn't say anything.

"My instincts have been talking to me about you, Son."

"Oh? Do I even want to know?"

He took a breath, let it out. "They are just my instincts; they are not written in stone."

"But…"

"You being here has been incredible. And I wish that somehow you could stay."

"But…"

"My instincts are telling me that your journey is back in Portland."

# Acknowledgements

Many thanks to my family, friends and helpers who made this book possible: David Ripianzi for taking a chance and for sharing his wisdom about the book business, Leslie Takao for her sharp editing and insight into the characters, Kevin Faulk for his help editing, Dr. Matt Hing for sharing his knowledge of burn victims, retired SWAT officer Mark Butler for his guidance with the assault on the warehouse, Chief Steve Holley for his advice on surviving in a burning car, A'lyse Place for her help with Bobby's voice, and to Doug Greene and Tom Nguyen for expanding my knowledge about the Vietnamese culture and the myriad details of Ho Chi Minh City, or Saigon, which has changed dramatically since I was there during the war. Special thanks to Dr. Dan Christensen, Carrie Christensen, and Amy and Jace Widmer for their encouragement.

And as always to Lisa Place, my love and best friend for her encouragement and for her willingness to hear me read my day's writing even when she was exhausted from her job.

# ABOUT THE AUTHOR

Loren W. Christensen is a Vietnam veteran and retired police officer with 29 years of law enforcement experience. As a martial arts student and teacher since 1965, he has earned a total of 11 black belts in three arts and was inducted into the Masters Hall of Fame in 2011. As a writer, Loren has penned 45 nonfiction books, including over two dozen books on the martial arts, and dozens of magazine articles on a variety of subjects. He has starred in seven instructional martial arts DVDs. *Dukkha Reverb is* his second fiction in the Dukkha series. He can be contacted through his website at www.lwcbooks.com.

www.ingramcontent.com/pod-product-compliance
Lightning Source LLC
Chambersburg PA
CBHW050100120726
47904CB00004B/1154